Mary's
Place

A Novel

CHARLOTTE HINGER

University of Nebraska Press   Lincoln

The University of Nebraska Press is part of a land-grant institution
with campuses and programs on the past, present, and future
homelands of the Pawnee, Ponca, Otoe-Missouria, Omaha, Dakota,
Lakota, Kaw, Cheyenne, and Arapaho Peoples, as well as those
of the relocated Ho-Chunk, Sac and Fox, and Iowa Peoples.

Library of Congress Cataloging-in-Publication Data
Names: Hinger, Charlotte, 1940– author.
Title: Mary's place: a novel / Charlotte Hinger.
Description: Lincoln: University of Nebraska Press, 2024.
Identifiers: LCCN 2023036717
ISBN 9781496238054 (paperback)
ISBN 9781496239884 (epub)
ISBN 9781496239891 (pdf)
Subjects: LCSH: Agriculture—Economic aspects—
United States—History—20th century—Fiction. |
BISAC: FICTION / Small Town & Rural | FICTION / Women |
LCGFT: Historical fiction. | Domestic fiction. | Novels.
Classification: LCC PS3558.I534 M37 2024 |
DDC 813/.54—dc23/eng/20230814
LC record available at https://lccn.loc.gov/2023036717

Designed and set in Fanwood Text by L. Welch.

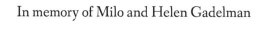
In memory of Milo and Helen Gadelman

I could not love thee, Dear, so much,
Loved I not honour more.

RICHARD LOVELACE

MARY'S PLACE

Prologue

His heart leaped as the clock struck the first of the twelve strokes of midnight. Jay Clinton Espy willed his hands to stop trembling. His blood pulsed with each chime. He forced himself to lay the papers on his desk. What he was about to do could wait until the noise stopped.

For the first time in his long and honorable life, he was about to put his hand to something that would not stand up to sunlight and questions. He had not come to this decision easily.

The cold expanse of the empty bank amplified the sound. The tones resonated from a massive grandfather clock he had retained through three redecorating projects over fifty years. His great-grandfather's clock. John Foster Espy's clock.

Folks still told the story of how in 1887 John Foster Espy came riding into the county in a fine black buggy pulled by a high-stepping black trotter. They did not like him. Not his highfalutin horse nor his highfalutin ways. They could not imagine what had possessed him to come in the first place. Where he didn't fit in and wasn't wanted.

John Foster found a carpenter and built a ten-by-ten building with a false front and a wood landing and wrote "First Bank of Gateway" over the entrance. He sat in this structure every day from eight to six. Stubborn, folks noted. A stayer. They understood stubbornness and staying. And if there was no hope at all for success, if he was just plumb thrilled with the impossibility of the situation, wouldn't give it up for anything, he clearly belonged in Western Kansas after all.

He was a cold bastard. But he was *their* cold bastard.

Come sundown John Foster would take his great black satchel and head back to his room at the hotel. His bank had its first customer after he nabbed a drover who tried to take his bag one night. He marched the foul-smelling cowboy off to the sheriff. Well, the townsfolk reasoned, what counted in a banker was competence, not personality. He was clearly qualified to guard their money.

One year later he went to Denver and bought the clock to place in his new twenty-by-twenty-four building. For show. Just to let folks know their banker could spend if he had a mind to. Not that it was anyone's business, by god, what a man was worth.

The clock struck five, breaking J.C.'s reverie. He swallowed against a surge of bitterness. So it had come to this.

He waited for the chiming to stop. A distraction. All his life he had understood the edge that came from clear-eyed vigilance. Victory belonged not to the swiftest or the strongest, but to those who could pay attention the longest. He did not miss two-foot putts. He had never conceded a bridge hand.

He needed all his wits about him now. There would be no turning back. The clock struck ten and Jay Clinton ran his clammy hand through his remaining wisps of hair. It was a habitual gesture, left from the time his hair had been thick with wiry brown waves. Espy hair—proud and tight—shared by several generations of men who had guided the bank through wars and depressions.

It was during the thirties that the whispering about the Espys began.

Porter Cleveland Espy started buying up land during the Dust Bowl days—a field here and a section there—to keep it from outsiders and to save the ground for the sake of the community. But the Espys had grown rich, and it didn't sit well with folks who lost their farms.

Jay Clinton looked up at his ancestors' portraits as the clock struck eleven. Three stern men who had preceded him. He was uneasy when he looked at his ancestors. He felt their eyes watching him, finding him wanting. His picture should already be hanging there. Because by now he should have passed down the bank to his and Madeline's only child, Forrest Alexander Espy. Madeline—gone twenty years now—had doted on the boy.

When this crisis passed he would have to deal squarely with the problem of Forrest. It was time to face the confusion and the pain.

His stomach lurched at the final chime. Midnight. It was time. He reached for the files lying in front of him. He resolutely whacked the edges of the folders against the desk and bent to his work.

He extracted five checks from bank statements that would be returned to customers. All of them had women's signatures. He pulled five identical documents from the file before him. All were universal commercial code statements, public notices of what had been pledged as collateral when some of the bank's biggest customers had bought their land.

Taking them from the courthouse had been easy enough. So easy he had decided next time he would campaign against the flighty woman who was register of deeds. He had simply sorted through the papers while she had her back turned, then extracted the ones he wanted. The five unsigned ucc statements. These five pieces of paper could get him into a bunch of trouble. The oversight had occurred in less troubled times, before 1985, when no one thought such details would matter.

With two of the signatures, it had been a matter of "tell the little woman to drop by when she has time." Back then, if paperwork reached the courthouse without the wife's name, it wasn't worth fussing over.

Of the five, one man had bought land before he was married, and nothing had been transferred into joint ownership. One signature, he was sure, had simply been overlooked in the vast amount of paperwork that flowed through the bank every day.

He was counting on the fact that few people remembered exactly what they signed in a bank. They were so glad when a banker agreed to loan them money that a covenant with the devil could be slipped past them.

He flicked on the Xerox machine and copied all five checks onto a sheet of clean white paper. He put the checks back into their separate statements then returned them to the bookkeeping department.

He returned to the copier and opened the lid. He carefully laid the blank line of each of the ucc statements over the corresponding signature on the paper. He signed four and then stopped.

He had saved forging Mary Barrett's signature for last. Iron Barrett's wife. He laid down the pen and closed his eyes against a tide of despair.

Iron was his best friend, despite their difference in age. Tall, grave, Lincolnesque, and slow to speak, Barrett was a throwback to a period when a man's word was his bond. A forty-seven-year-old anomaly.

Their friendship had spanned thirty years. They both understood honor. Iron, more than anyone, would understand what it cost Jay Clinton to do this. And if one woman would have absolute contempt for his perfidy, it would be Mary Barrett. He stared at the piece of paper.

He blinked back sudden tears. It was stupid to stop here. Idiotic. He had already gone too far to back out. This was the farm that could bring him down. This was the family who could destroy the whole community. The Barretts could destroy his bank.

He broke out in a cold sweat. He was overlooking something. He didn't know what. But his instincts had saved him more than once in his lifetime in this bank. When a sense was that strong, he didn't need to know why. The why would come later.

He willed his fingers to hold steady before he forged Mary Barrett's signature on the fifth document. He walked back to his desk and neatly laid the five slips of paper in the folder. He was certain that tomorrow he could sneak them back into the courthouse as easily as he had removed them.

He reached for his heavy glass ashtray and flicked on his lighter. Carefully, he set fire to the paper containing the copied signatures. It flickered and curled.

When there was nothing left but ashes, he flushed the contents down the stool. Then he rinsed the ashtray, dried it with a paper towel, and sprayed the room with a smoker's deodorizer. He put the folder with the five agreements back in his briefcase.

He looked around one last time, bitter at how much had changed. Checks microfilmed by computers. Mountains of paperwork in duplicates and triplicates.

Bank examiners swarming like gnats, raising questions. Hell, he knew who was good for their money and who wasn't, and it didn't have much to do with their balance sheets.

It hit him the next day, after the documents were back in the courthouse. Microfilm. What if the courthouse now microfilmed all of their records just like the banks?

If they did, he had provided evidence that he was a forger. The microfilm would show no women's signatures on the original documents. He had tied the knot in his own noose. The damned microfilm.

Plus, Mary made Iron bring home a copy of everything he signed. All the paperwork was placed in a safe at their house. They didn't have a safety deposit box at the bank. Now the note at the courthouse bore Mary's signature and the copy in the Barretts' personal safe did not.

For the first time in fifty years, he locked the door to his office in the middle of the day. His mind raced as he clasped his hands across his roiling stomach. Even as his gut had been telling him last night that he was overlooking something crucial, he had gone right ahead and forged her name.

Sickened, he tried to tell himself that there would never be a reason to check microfilm. Then he coldly clamped down on wishful thinking. Wishing didn't keep banks afloat; cold hard logic did. The government surely had something in mind when it began photographing zillions of records.

If he could think of a way to void or rewrite the old notes the ucc statements pertained to and apply the listed collateral to new ones, he could legally destroy the original ucc statements with their altered signatures.

He rose and paced the floor.

A will, he thought suddenly. Perhaps he could persuade Iron to make a will. That would force them to reshuffle everything and get Mary's signature on all the necessary papers. Hell, half his customers needed to make a will. Doing so would tidy up the problem of listing collateral and would straighten out the stray unsigned papers. However, a banker couldn't insist that customers spend money for estate planning, he thought grimly.

Then he thought of Forrest.

Perhaps he could tie it into Forrest's mania for having all the bank's business on computers. It made perfect sense. What he couldn't do with a club, he could do with a wink.

"Time to work my son into the business," he would say. Sounded innocuous enough. In fact, it sounded damn good.

It would take a quick meeting or two to explain it to his three loan officers. Patrick Wein never questioned anything. His only concern would be understanding the procedure. Gene Ramouth had been after him to check out computers for the past year.

Only Otto Jones, the senior vice president, knew what was going on at any given time. Quickly J.C. anticipated Otto's questions. Sure, strong answers came to his mind at once. Answers that would sit well with Otto. It was a fine plan. Simple.

And it was not crooked.

1

Mary Barrett flashed a smile at Earnest Hayworth, who had been delivering their mail for the past fifteen years.

"What now?" he asked, grinning at the leather carpentry apron over her slim-cut Levis. She wore a faded chambray shirt, her bright red hair streaming down her back under a bandanna. "Nothing, just general repairs," she said. They were old friends, and she had been amused by his lively interest in her projects through the years.

Hayworth drove on, leaving Mary with an armload of mail. She glanced at the letter on top of the pile. "To Iron from J.C. Espy," marked personal and urgent. She laughed. J.C. knew of Iron's ritual for handling his mail. He sorted it into three stacks: bills, junk mail, and "others."

Iron was rigidly prompt in paying bills, but junk mail and the "others" were strictly a spare time activity. Knowing this, J.C. had charged her years ago with seeing to it that Iron paid attention to letters from the bank. Mary glanced at the sun. It was going on noon, but she decided to take J.C.'s letter directly to Iron rather than waiting until he came in at mealtime. He was in the back machine shed inspecting equipment for needed repairs before they began the spring work.

She stopped in front of a sign on the fence post that marked the beginning of their property: A 4-H Family Lives Here. She drew a rag from her apron and polished it, as she did every day on her way back from the half mile to the mailbox.

Walking briskly, she admired their farmstead, the order they had managed to impose. They had built many of the smaller sheds themselves.

Enshrined on a low platform of concrete blocks was a rusted and weathered walking plow, brought to Western Kansas in 1880 by Iron's great-great-grandfather, Jonas Barrett, when he homesteaded the one hundred sixty acres that were at the core of their property. Iron wanted the plow left out in the open for the family to ponder when they thought times were hard. The plow, used by Jonas Barrett to break out a mere three acres that first year, was a rebuke to their whining.

In a large pasture back of the main barn were one hundred fifty head of the finest breeding cows in the tri-state area. Iron had spent years building his Hereford stock. A huge main barn, painted the muted classic red with white trim that marked all of their buildings, dominated the farmyard. Three smaller buildings to the north of the barn housed machinery and equipment.

No weeds marred the Barrett homestead. Mary whisked around on their garden tractor from early spring until fall, whacking back anything that threatened tidiness.

Across from the barn, next to an unused hog pen, stood an old windmill. And far, far up, clear at the top, was a blue Christmas light. Just one.

It was a stupid, private, loving thing, and they had never told anyone why it was there. When pressed, they just grinned, declining to explain the whimsical single blue light.

Childhood sweethearts, they had been so young and so in love that first year of marriage. Eager to apply accumulated 4-h lessons to their own land and their own property, they couldn't work hard enough and fast enough. But there were grave differences between them, in looks as well as temperament.

Iron was deliberate, lean and hard, full of integrity, like the good sheriff in an old Western. His clear gray eyes studied everything before he spoke. Mary flew at trouble head-on, like a banty hen, even when the fiery flapping worked against her.

Iron Barrett's code was based on the Golden Rule, and to the best of his ability he treated everyone else as he wished to be treated. He read the Bible occasionally. Warily. He pored over the scriptures soberly, gingerly considering the wisdom therein, as if the words were snakes that would bite him on the ankle and poison his sure, steady sense of right and wrong. Nevertheless, when he was troubled, he turned to the Good Book and hunted until he found a passage he thought the Good Lord *should* be applying to a situation. He made it fit.

Although he was not a dedicated churchgoer, he went with Mary from time to time. Ever since he was a small child, he had known it was not a good idea to rile God up. He served the Lord by caring for his land.

Iron Barrett didn't hold much with squandering or foolishness or make work.

Mary loved beautiful things. Hungered for them. It was not a matter of prestige or show. It was akin to a feeling that crawled over her when pictures were hung in the wrong place, or when the colors in quilts weren't in harmony.

That first Christmas, she had asked him to string lights around the farmstead as their neighbors up the road had done.

Iron had refused.

"I've got real work to do, Mary. I don't have time for that kind of stuff. There's fences to mend while there's a lull in the fieldwork."

So she did it herself, one morning early in December. She climbed high, high up the windmill, in the bitterly cold morning air, clipping on her precious string of lights as she went. When she finished, panting, shaking with exertion but proud as punch, she waited for Iron to come in for the noon meal.

"I've got something to show you," she said, looking at him defiantly. This man simply had to understand something about her, if their marriage was to be any good at all. He surely knew by now she was not a meek little thing. She wasn't very sweet either. She would not let a man rule her. "I want you to see something."

Despite her resolve, her stomach turned, anticipating his disapproval. She led him to the windmill, pointed at the brave trail of lights, and waited.

He did not speak, just stood there, a wave of emotions passing over his face. Mary winced at the first quick flash of anger. But the look that finally settled was one of infinite tenderness. He reached for her. "They look right pretty," he said carefully. "Why don't you plug them in?"

And so she did. To her dismay, only one bulb worked. One blue bulb at the very top. She had spent the entire morning for the sake of one blue bulb.

Shocked, she turned, and he hugged her fiercely.

"You're supposed to test them first," he said simply.

She started to laugh and cry all at the same time.

"Mary," Iron said, in his somber way, "after we eat, I'll redo them for you. I did a lot of thinking while I was fixing fences this morning. You're entitled to stuff you've set your heart on. Just like me. We're partners in this place, you know. Just don't try to make me understand things I can't."

He shoved his hands into the back pockets of his jeans and stabbed a ridge into the ground with the toe of his boot, then looked at her squarely.

"You don't have to," she said, amazed. "The one blue light is enough. You don't have to restring the whole thing."

She pressed herself against him and they swayed back and forth, her heart throbbing like a bass drum. She loved, adored, and idolized this strong, infinitely thoughtful, steady man.

"One dumb little blue light is enough."

So she hadn't gone back up to take it down when Christmas was over. The light had stayed there for twenty-seven years with the end of the cord capped, to be uncovered and plugged into an extension in the hog barn for ten minutes on Christmas Day. Used sparingly, it had never burned out.

"One blue light is enough," they would say to one another through the years, when decisions kept them awake at night and they didn't agree. "There doesn't have to be a whole string."

However, there was an agreement between them that when one of them balked at pressing ahead—on buying more land or a piano they couldn't really afford—the other had to have the courage to go it alone. Without attempting to persuade the other against his will.

Stringing a blue light was a solo feat.

As she walked toward the shed with the letter from the bank, her blood pulsed with anticipation. The land would soon start greening up.

The interior of the shed was shadowy and heavy with the familiar pungent scent of oil and grease. She blinked, trying to adjust to the dimness. "Iron," she called. "I have a letter for you from J.C."

He crawled out from under a combine, gave her a quick kiss, and took the letter. He opened it and scanned its contents. She watched, amused at the emotions flickering across his face, then moved closer to peer over his shoulder.

"The old codger wants us to make a will."

"He what?" She reached for the letter. Although the words were smooth as silk, there was an unmistakable demand couched in the phrasing.

Iron spun around, and a small muscle in his jaw throbbed. "I'm not going to die and I'm not ready to make a will. And when I do, can't see where it's J.C.'s business."

"Says here the letter is going to all his clients bound together in family farms. It might be a good idea, Iron, in case something happens to you."

He said nothing.

"Lisette?" Mary asked gently, diving right into the heart of the problem with a deftness bordering on telepathic. Knowing that communicating with their son's wife about the farm would be more than he could bear.

A muscle jumped in his jaw. "If J.C. is really set on this, you're going to have to be the one to talk to her."

"Okay," she said. "You go to the bank and find out what's going on, and I'll work on the kids."

"I'll talk to Dennis," Iron said quickly. "Leave him to me."

Her face flamed at the implied rebuke. She whirled around and walked back toward the house.

2

Dennis, their firstborn, had caused the first rift between her and Iron. When she offered her breast, the child suckled a short while then stiffened and arched his back. It happened over and over.

"Nothing wrong with the bottle," Mary said, tears streaming down her face.

Iron urged her to keep at it. "I want my son to have the best. Get off to a good start."

Finally, in despair, Mary applied ointment to her caked and bleeding nipples and stopped trying. It worried Iron. She could feel his disappointment. She could not find the words to tell him that their baby boy fed like a little piranha.

Iron doted on his baby boy, and she was shut out as her husband played patty cake, read the child books, fed him Pablum, carried him around the farmyard, and gave him his bottle. She was frightened by her awkwardness when she held her son. Frightened by her inability to talk to Iron. Frightened by the sense of loss she felt when Dennis and Iron were together.

When Mary and Iron fought, they usually squared off like two pit bulls, fierce and honest. It was only when Dennis was involved that there were dark undertones. It hadn't changed since he was a baby.

Slugging out a will would just be one more incident where dissension over Dennis would plague them.

Her thoughts raced as she walked across the farmyard. After she was gone, someone else would live in her house, till this soil, be favored by the healing fire of her Western Kansas sunsets. And now J.C. was demanding they decide who.

Disconcerted by the thought of anyone else running her household, she stopped and gazed at her wonderful sprawling three-story house gleaming in the noonday sun. Everyone called it Mary's Place. Broad-railed, roofed porches surrounded the main structure, which was topped by a gabled attic with windowed eaves. On the east side of the second story was a screened-in sleeping porch. The sparkling white-lapped wood siding boasted intricate gingerbread scallops and curlicues. It had cupolas and weathervanes and alcoves and enough scary hidey-holes to keep children entertained for a whole summer.

There were five bedrooms upstairs—one for each child when they had all still been living at home—in addition to a guest room, and a lovely bedroom–sitting room for Iron and Mary.

The main fireplace in the living room also opened to their bedroom. As the kids grew older and the very walls of the house seemed to pulse with the noise of their children, their friends and, later, their grandchildren, some nights Iron and Mary retreated very early to the peace of this sanctuary. The room was dominated by a four-poster bed, where they slept tangled up like rag dolls.

She started as the inner screen door on the back porch slammed and Dennis came down the steps carrying her Microsoft manual.

"Hi, Mom," he said easily. "I'm having a little trouble editing a batch command."

She bristled. He had been in her desk drawer again. How many times had she asked him to stay out of their personal belongings? Yet when she had first mentioned it to Iron, he had taken Dennis's side at once, saying he couldn't see a bit of difference between that and the girls ambling in borrowing cake pans and utensils.

Dennis looked at her guilelessly, holding up the book and daring her to challenge him. At once, she felt the familiar surge of guilt over being uneasy around her firstborn child. She sighed, knowing she would back down. She always did where he was concerned.

"Ask next time," she said crossly.

"Will do," he said easily. "I didn't think you'd mind."

She nodded stiffly and watched as he walked down their lane with the proud grace of an Irish prince. He was tall and broad-shouldered, like Iron, but he had her wonderful thick auburn hair. Only God knew which ancestors had contributed the genes responsible for his easy charm.

His grandmother, Alma, worshipped the ground he walked on. From the time he could toddle, Dennis had brought her wildflowers or asked Alma to bake cookies or show him where to find blackberries. He had gone from being a chubby, charming toddler—his grandmother's delight—to a young, motivated computerized agribusinessman—his grandmother's confidant and adviser.

But Iron could not tolerate dishonesty. Wrong was wrong. So Mary watched her husband's growing disappointment when as a boy Dennis cheated on his 4-H records, then cheated in sports as a teenager, then cheated on taxes when he was grown. But when Mary nattered at Iron about Dennis, saying as the boy's father he should do something, for some perverse reason, Iron immediately defended his son.

It was after Dennis was born that she had begun to acquire her home.

She first saw the old Cunningham place one day when she had fled their trailer, blinded by tears, after Iron had reprimanded her for letting Dennis cry.

She had been bouncing along the back roads in their old pickup for miles when she came upon the ramshackle old farmhouse. Long-abandoned and vandalized as it was, it beckoned to her. She parked the pickup and walked up onto the porch, stood a moment before the sagging door. It wasn't locked, and when she opened it, she was engulfed by an aura, a sense of warmth and rightness.

It salved a grief she couldn't explain. The house wanted her, needed her. Not one to dwell on what she couldn't understand, she entered and lost her heart. The pull of the place mounted as she wandered through, somehow knowing which spot cried out for a piano, which for an oak table.

Outside again, she found a sign, overgrown with weeds, plopped down at the side of a pine tree in front: "House will be razed July 31. Contact Security Builders to salvage materials."

She drove back home, tires smoking, wild with plans. She and Iron were still living in a singlewide trailer on their property. She burst through the door, her unruly red hair puffing out from underneath her kerchief, their quarrel forgotten.

"Oh honey, I've found my house. The one I want to live in the rest of my life. Oh please, come see. Come look. Honey, I'll just die if we can't get it. It's going for nothing. It can be moved. Moved right here." She pulled him to his feet.

"We can't afford to do anything, Mary. We haven't even paid off our hospital bills for the baby."

"There isn't any money involved. Don't *think*. Please don't think. Just this once. Look first. You're not going to understand until you see it. Bundle up Dennis and come see. Please, Iron." Her voice trembled with pain. Tears welled up in her eyes. "Don't make me beg. I've never asked you for much."

Bewildered, he stared at her, reached for Dennis, and followed her out to the pickup.

Mary drove quickly, taut with misery, willing him to see her vision. But once there, she knew by the look on his face he saw only sagging porches, peeling paint, flimsy windowpanes, small, boxy rooms, an antiquated kitchen, and curling linoleum.

He stood frozen and miserable, looked at her, then rolled a stick with the toe of his boot, his hands shoved into the back pockets of his jeans.

"It can't be the money," she said. "They're giving the place away."

"It's not the initial cash outlay, Mary. It's the work. Neither one of us has time for this kind of labor."

"Please? Iron, I know what I'm getting into. I was State 4-H woodworking champion. A junior leader in electricity. I got blues on all my plumbing. I was county champion in the home decorating project. I *know* how to do this kind of work."

"You think this place won't take money? It'll nickel and dime us to death for the rest of our lives. We'd be better off waiting until we can afford to build. And do you have any *idea* what it costs to move a house?"

"I can get the money to move it, some way. Iron, please? I want this house. I can't just blue light this one. J.C. would never lend me the money by myself. Not for a house. You've got to be in it with me."

"It's not a question of 'I won't,' honey. The point is, you can't. It would all be too much for you."

She knew he regretted the words the moment they were out of his mouth. Even as he spoke, he glanced at her with his clear gray eyes then had the sense to look away.

"Can't?" she said mockingly, her head cocked to one side. "Can't?"

He sighed deeply and flexed his fingers, stared at the palms of his hands as though there were answers written there.

She waited.

"Okay, Mary. If you can figure out how to get the money to move this abomination, I'll go to the bank with you, and we'll borrow enough to pay closing costs and taxes and get you a couple thousand for starter money."

"Whoopee." She leaped into the air then threw her arms around Iron.

A week later, when Iron came in for the noon meal, Mary had little bottles and packets scattered all over the kitchen. She looked up from the brochures and pamphlets she was reading and waved airily toward the kettle simmering on the back burner.

"Just stew today, honey. Sorry. Been busy."

Warily, he ladled up the steaming mixture, sat down, and began to eat.

"Iron Barrett, sir, kiddo," she said, plopping down across from him with an order book in her hand. "I'm your new Avon representative, and I want to know how many bottles of cologne you intend to order."

"None. I like the way I smell just fine, thank you."

"I'm ordering you two bottles of Chaps," she said sweetly.

"I won't wear it."

"That's all right, you'll have it on hand if you change your mind."

Three weeks later, they went to the bank and closed the deal to buy the old Cunningham house. The loan included enough money for moving costs.

Iron smoked steadily all the way home. She chattered nonstop. He stopped her just as she opened the door and started to step out of the pickup. "We need to have an understanding." He rested his arms around the curve of the steering wheel. "Don't try to finagle me into helping you with that house. I'm bone tired at the end of the day—*if* I ever get to the end of a day. I hate carpentry work, and I'm not going to do it and I mean it. It would suit me just fine to live in a singlewide trailer the rest of my life."

"I know that. I won't burden you with any of this, Iron."

"Something else too. You know how I feel about folks who duck bills. I'd rather starve than not pay someone money I owe them. So don't charge *anything* connected with this little project. Have the money in hand before you do a thing."

"Deal," she had said quickly. "Just don't go in it—don't even peek—until I'm ready for you."

Mary's Place. Stunned, she looked at the gleaming white house. A will. When she died, whose would it be?

She could not imagine leaving her house to anyone but their younger daughter, Connie, who was like a splendid little pony. Sturdy, efficient, and infinitely patient. Mary's Place would be in good hands. But how could they even things up? Dennis and Elizabeth should get something of comparable value. But what? She and Iron had nothing apart from this house and their land.

The Barrett land, of course, would go to all three children as co-heirs. Or something. She wasn't too clear on how these things were done, but certainly no one child would get the land.

It worried her that all three children put together couldn't match Iron's abilities as a farmer. He had an uncanny sense of timing and an Indian's reverence for the earth as a living, breathing, creative, powerful mother-god.

Many was the morning when he rose at three driven by some mysterious compulsion to finish planting a field or harvesting a crop. When the rains or the wind came later in the day, Mary marveled at how he could possibly know these things.

Mary squared her shoulders and took a breath. Making the will, pacifying J.C., might be doable if she could keep Iron settled down long enough to work with Dennis's wife.

3

"Maybe this will thing won't amount to much," Iron said as he sat down to the noon meal. He took ample helpings of roast beef, mashed potatoes and gravy, and green beans before he spoke again. "Maybe this estate planning bullshit is some newfangled scheme Forrest has dreamed up. I'll find out first thing in the morning. In the meantime, don't say anything to the kids."

"Too late! I called Lisette just before you came in," Mary said. "I told her we needed to get everyone together to talk over some family business."

"You didn't mention a will?" asked Iron sharply.

"No. I just said business."

"Good. And?"

"She said we could go right ahead and decide whatever we needed to without her. Same as we do with everything else."

"Figures." A vein throbbed in Iron's temple, and the cords on his neck tightened. Helplessly he stared at his calloused hands.

"Her words, not mine, honey. I'm just quoting."

Sadly, Mary studied her husband's face as he drank his coffee.

"No need to trouble Lisette with any will business," Iron said abruptly, "if it comes to that and maybe it won't. Or Elizabeth's and Connie's husbands either. Let's just talk to our offspring and leave their spouses out of it. Keep it simple."

"We can't do that. We're a family business. All tangled up together."

Looking at Iron's stony face, Mary remembered when Dennis brought Lisette home. It had been over semester break during his sophomore year in college. She had nearly worked herself to death cleaning and cooking. Getting ready for her. Dennis had never brought a girl to meet them before.

Mary knew they would just love her.

Elizabeth and Connie were at a 4-H judging contest that Friday when Dennis and his girlfriend arrived. Later, Mary thought it was just as well the girls weren't around that first evening.

Iron and Mary had waited on the porch, swinging, watching, listening. By the time the Pontiac turned the corner and came up the lane they were worn down from anticipation.

Dennis pulled up in front of the house. Jumping from the car, he rushed across the yard to hug Mary and give his father an affectionate slap on the shoulder.

When she pushed Dennis away at arm's length so she could inspect him fully, Mary saw an amused flicker in his eyes. He walked back to the car, opened the door on the passenger's side, and beckoned to a petite woman with long black hair, parted in the middle and secured with a beaded headband.

Mary froze. She looked at Iron and saw the telltale leap of the muscle in his jaw.

The woman smiled and scooted to one side then eased out of the car as though her muscles were cramped, or she were disengaging herself from a burden. She wore frayed, hip-hugging bell-bottomed jeans. Her bronze gauze shirt was loosely tucked into a wide leather belt. Tie-dyed accents of tan and rust splotched her tattered canvas vest. A heavily beaded and fringed shoulder purse slipped off her shoulder, and when she knelt to retrieve it she used words that made Mary want to reach for a bar of soap. The woman rose and flipped a cigarette out of her mouth.

Tattoos, Mary noticed with despair. *And dirty nails.* She would bet Dennis had not met this woman in a college classroom.

"Mom. Dad." Dennis proudly put his arm around the woman's shoulder. "I want you to meet my wife. Lisette."

All the color drained from Iron's face. Mary's throat constricted.

Suddenly there was a movement from inside the car, and a little girl's head popped up in the window.

"Mommy," she called sleepily.

Dennis opened the door again, and the child leaped from the seat, threw her arms around his neck, and wrapped her legs around his waist.

"And this is Sabrina. I'm adopting her, so I guess that makes her your first grandchild," he said, grinning.

Mary swallowed as she stared into the child's dark, dark eyes. Rage welled up inside her. How dare Dennis put them in this position? How could he do this to them? Or, for that matter, to this woman. Or this poor little girl. It wasn't fair to them either.

"Lisette, we weren't told about this marriage in advance. Forgive me if it takes a bit for me to get used to the idea. Please go on inside the house so we can talk to Dennis," Mary said carefully, her eyes fixed on her son's face.

Startled, Lisette turned and stared at Dennis. Her face tightened with dismay. She flashed a look of sympathy at Mary, who approved of Lisette's quick clamping of her lips. She saw this stranger woman, this Lisette, swallow her pride. It was not one of her own virtues, Mary knew, but she appreciated this quality in others.

"Go right on inside," Mary said gently. "There's a bathroom down the hall. Just make yourself at home."

Mary heard the crunch of soft footsteps on the gravel as Lisette and the child walked off.

"What in the hell do you think you're doing, Dennis?" Her voice was low and savage. "How could you possibly have done this? To her, to us, to that poor little girl. There is absolutely no excuse for this lack of preparation or charity. No excuse for not laying a little groundwork first."

Iron was white-faced and continued to look steadily, wordlessly at Dennis, then he walked to the car to help him unload. Mary went inside the house.

Lisette sat on the sofa in the combination kitchen and family room, holding Sabrina on her lap.

"You must be starved," Mary said. "And I think I see a little cookie monster."

Lisette smiled tersely at Sabrina's shy nod. The child slid off her mother's lap and delicately accepted a chocolate chip cookie from the plate Mary held.

Mary tried to think of the Right Words. "Look, I'm really sorry. The only way I know how to explain things is finding out that he . . . you two . . .

were already married left us feeling cheated or something. Cheated out of a wedding and the chance to get used to things gradually."

"He fucked up, that's all," Lisette said kindly. "It happens to the best of us."

Mary's heart plummeted. *God help us.* Her fingers fluttered against the soft hollow in her throat. *God help us all.*

"I've never seen a kitchen like this," Lisette said with wonder. "It must have cost a fortune."

The room, with its soaring cathedral ceiling and its massive stone fireplace, was the most important room in the house. The kitchen was Mary's pride and joy. Her turf. The appliances had veneers of the same golden oak she had chosen for the cabinets. There were triple greenhouse windows, and a mammoth island with a CB radio. On the east wall was a line of floor-to-ceiling storage cabinets with a long built-in desk at the end. Mary's computer was centered there along with an assortment of stylish black mess accessories.

Flanking the fireplace, behind the massive oak table, were bookcases holding row after row of scrapbooks.

"Are those all family pictures?" Lisette asked.

"Family and 4-H." Mary reached for one of the books. "We have pictures of all our 4-H animals and projects." She sat down beside Lisette. "Let's see, this book is for '69, so that calf was Henrietta, Connie's heifer. She took state that year."

"You remember all their *names*?"

"Of course. Each and every one."

Looking back, Mary wished she had gone right on talking about the kitchen and 4-H that first night, and nothing else. Iron and Dennis hadn't been back in the room together for five minutes before all hell broke loose.

They were seated around the table, just starting to eat supper. "I've always wanted to live on a farm," Lisette said happily. "Now that I'm getting a chance, I can't believe it's such a fancy one."

Mary looked at her blankly.

Dennis looked down at his plate. "I was going to tell you later," he mumbled. "I'm quitting school. I'm coming back home to farm with you,

Dad." He smiled charmingly, but Iron jumped to his feet, tipping over his chair. The little girl began to cry when it crashed.

Seeing the fright on the child's face, Iron checked his words. Leaning forward, he braced his arms on the table. "You've never wanted to farm, Dennis. It was one of the hardest things I've ever had to face up to. But you'll never be a farmer. And you're not dropping out of school. That's final."

"Too late," Dennis said. "It's a done deal. I've quit. And I do want to farm. You're wrong."

Iron didn't sleep at all that night. "There's something fishy going on," he said the next morning. "I'm calling Manhattan." His voice quavered when he got off the phone. "Dennis didn't go to school last semester. Not at all. He flunked out his freshman year."

He stared at Mary, sank onto the couch. "He's just been taking my money. Taking my money for the last five months. Partying. God only knows where it all went."

"He couldn't have!"

But he had. Without a trace of remorse. With an apology as weak as café coffee.

Out of pity for Lisette and the little girl, they decided to let Dennis live with them for a week, which stretched into a month, then two. Finally, seeing Dennis's willingness to put his shoulder to the wheel—he didn't miss a trick; there was no job too dirty, too small—Iron made a place for him on the farm.

But what Iron was once eager to give, he now doled out to his son grudgingly. He blamed this city girl—not a 4-Her and never had been—for leading their son astray. Off the beaten track. Needing a father for her illegitimate child.

After he had been back home a year, Dennis chafed under Iron's thumb. He asked his grandmother to act as an intermediary.

"Either kick the boy out or treat him right, Iron," demanded Alma Barrett.

"I'm plenty fair enough," Iron said.

"It's not a matter of fair. You're always fair. But you're carrying too big a grudge. Watching him too close. Waiting for him to mess up."

"He's got honest work, a roof over his head."

"Sure. And the life of an indentured servant. He deserves better."

"I still don't understand how the kid could change his mind about farming just like that," Iron said finally.

"He's been away!" Mary said. "He's seen more. Now he knows how good he's always had it. How can he *not* want to come back to the farm? That's the only part of this that makes sense to me. *That* I can understand."

Finally, Dennis and Lisette and Sabrina—who had fallen in love with all the animals—moved into a small stucco house a mile down the road from Mary's Place.

Then their son, who could talk a cat out of a dairy, asked for some autonomy in making farm management decisions and Iron consented. Dennis earnestly began to discuss the merits of different strands of hybrid wheat, fertilizers, planting and harvesting cycles. The other young farmers in the area who were his friends "were goers," he informed his father archly, "willing to try a thing or two."

More often than not, Iron would roll his eyes and walk off in the middle of a discussion, but he had to concede that putting farm records on a computer was cutting bookwork in half. However, when Dennis pushed hard for authority to buy new equipment, Iron balked. Furious, Dennis pointed out the time they would save.

"You're living in the Stone Age with that old tractor, that old combine. My god, Dad, you don't even have a clue as to what the new stuff will do. Everyone is upgrading, and we should too."

"It don't pencil," Iron said calmly. "No way this place will generate enough money to pay for equipment costing that much. It won't work, and I won't do it. You're not going to either. A man owes his Maker and his community and family a decent day's work. At least eight hours, maybe ten, six days a week. What would I do with that extra time? Spend it at the coffee shop? Playing golf?"

"Other men your age are easing up a bit, letting their sons take over. It wouldn't hurt you to relax your hold on the reins, Dad. It's a new era in farming. My friends are on the cutting edge of agriculture. They know it's just plain stupid for a man to work himself into a state of exhaustion."

"Your friends are also buying condominiums and taking flying lessons and going on vacations that the CEO of General Motors would envy, and god knows what all else. As long as I'm in charge of this farm, I'll decide how the money will be spent. And it's not going for froufrous."

This time when Alma Barrett came around to intervene on her grandson's behalf, Iron was intractable.

"Have you read the story of the Prodigal Son, Iron? You've always had a forgiving heart," pleaded Alma. "The boy needs some say-so in the finances."

"Then he can go get some of his own money and quit telling me how to spend mine. This has nothing to do with forgiveness. This has to do with common sense."

Alma scoffed and co-signed a note at the bank with her grandson to start a repair shop right next to his house. Always mechanically inclined, Dennis was soon booked solid with work. The brisk traffic in and out of the machine shop was indisputable evidence his son was a good mechanic, if not a natural farmer. Slowly, Dennis won Iron over.

Two years later, Lisette gave birth to Benjamin, who was a pint-sized copy of Iron and dogged his grandfather like a little shadow.

They melded into a new family. Bigger and better than before. Only Lisette remained an outsider. She just would not or could not fit in, and her unhappiness erupted in attacks on Iron, never Mary. Now, nine years after that first meeting, Mary still felt edgy when her husband and her daughter-in-law were in the same room together.

Abruptly, she rose from the table. She walked over to the counter and cut Iron a piece of cherry pie, topped it with a generous helping of ice cream.

"I hope the thought of working with her won't stop you from going along with J.C."

"It won't," he snapped.

Mary winced. After all these years Iron still hadn't warmed to his daughter-in-law.

4

J.C. rose and extended his hand when Iron walked into his office.

"You wouldn't be part owner of a law office, would you, J.C.? What's going on?"

J.C. slouched in his chair and laced his fingers over his paunchy little belly. "No expense involved with what I want signed. Forrest had a little document drawn up that went out to our largest farmers. Have a seat and I'll go over it with you. It's no big deal, Iron."

J.C.'s mouth was dry. He needed a mint, something, so saliva would kick in. He pressed the intercom button. "Cynthia," he hollered. "Bring Iron some coffee. Water too."

Iron sat stiffly opposite his desk.

"It's kind of a temporary will until you get around to doing the real thing." J.C. sighed, knowing his friend's steely-eyed look all too well. "Let me give you some of the background. A lot of the rules are changing for farm loans. You weren't singled out for that letter. Didn't you notice all the other men waiting in the lobby?"

Iron nodded. "Thought it was funny to see so many here on a sale day."

"The feds are tightening up on agriculture banks. They don't like things done with a smile and a handshake anymore. Makes 'em nervous. So you and some of our other larger farmers need to cooperate with us and write up how you plan to handle your loans at the bank if you should happen to die."

"I've always been a reasonable man, J.C."

The banker grinned.

"You can't tell me a banker has a right to tell a man he's got to make a will."

"No, of course we can't. We don't have the right to do that. And I'm not saying you have to. But the time isn't too far away when you're going to be slowing down just a little."

"I've just turned forty-seven, not eighty." The muscles in Iron's shoulders tightened. "I plan to put in a decent day's work for a good thirty plus years yet."

"Things happen," said J.C. "Accidents, disasters."

Iron looked at him. "There's always been a chance of that. I want to know, why now?"

J.C. drew a deep breath. *Steady, steady.* It was no time to lose his temper. But how many times had he listened to farmers as strong as Iron Barrett who would not, could not, tolerate the thought of dying or retiring? Then they died in an accident or of a heart attack right in their prime, leaving behind estates that a battery of CPAs working full time couldn't straighten out. Although he had never seen a finer specimen of physical health than the man sitting right there before him.

Iron was flat-bellied and hard, with the kind of solid muscles men raised on a farm develop through pitching bales of hay and hauling water and shoveling dirt. He was as solid as his nickname. "Iron" had replaced "Franklin" from the time he was four years old and Alma watched him try to bang a wheel back onto his toy tractor.

"Why now? Because land prices have dropped nearly overnight. Word has come down that we're not to loan money on what a farmer's land is worth."

Iron scoffed. "What else?"

"We'll have to loan on the income a man's acreage can produce. Cash flow is the new watchword. No one gives a damn what the farmer thinks he could sell the land for in the sweet by and by. How much *money* is that land making?"

Cynthia came in with a tray. She was clearly annoyed at the unusual interruption and glanced curiously at Iron. She nodded at J.C., who thanked her curtly, ignored the coffee, and reached for the pitcher of water.

"No one's land *can* make as much money as mine," Iron said after Cynthia left. "When I get to plant. You're the one who wanted me to sign up for all the government programs that take God's good earth out of production."

"Didn't you hear what I said?" J.C. slapped his palm down on his desk. "I said *is* making. Not *can* make. *Is.* You've got to get that through your head. We don't care if it *could* make eighty bushels of wheat. *Is* it? Are you generating a good cash flow?"

"Enough to keep my loan payments current," snapped Iron. "That's the only thing you have a right to care about, J.C."

"No need to get het up. Listen! I'm trying to tell you something. Agricultural banks are in trouble. That's why we're dotting all the i's and crossing the t's right now. Because that's the way the government wants it. And your family has the biggest operation in the county. That's why now." J.C.'s voice rose, and veins stood out in his temples. "And bank examiners want to know *why* we've loaned one person so much money. That's why now."

"Have you tried pointing out to those examiners that I've never once missed a payment of your precious interest or any of the principal due?" Iron sat bolt upright on the edge of his chair. "Have you pointed out to those cold-blooded loan sharks that I've paid back more money than any other single person in this bank's history down through the years?"

"They don't look at it that way," said J.C. unhappily. "Hell, I know you'd dig ditches if you had to, to work off a debt. Same as Mary would scrub floors, if push came to shove. But from their point of view, we've loaned you an awful lot of money, and with the drop in the price of land, there's not enough collateral in back of your loans."

"You thought it was enough when you lent the money to me."

"All I'm asking you to do is sign a few forms Forrest drew up. It's kind of a little temporary will. No big deal, and it will be at the bank's expense."

"That'll be a first." Iron snorted.

"Later on, when you want to go to the bother of something more detailed, you can have it revised." For a moment J.C. was tempted to tell Iron that his family's papers weren't in order. But it didn't take much to make a farmer turn on a banker. Just the wrong word could make a farmer suspicious. Rile up their deep inherited distrust of the moneylender. For now, he wanted this man to use the bank's form.

The last thing he wanted was for Iron Barrett to consult a lawyer on his own. Funny things happened when lawyers got in the way. A good lawyer might wonder what Mary had actually signed. A good lawyer might point out that if Mary hadn't signed all of the security agreements there was a natural out. A good lawyer might think to check the microfilm. Sweat dotted J.C.'s forehead. He had to get this done without provoking Iron any further.

In case of any real trouble, if man and wife weren't jointly responsible for debts, the little woman could just put half their holdings in her name, if she hadn't signed anything to begin with. Checkmate a bank by cutting their collateral in half. Stay a banker's hand from repossessing land.

J.C. knew Iron was right. The Barretts had paid back more money, serviced more debt in thirty years than twenty bank examiners would personally pay back in a lifetime. But there were now agencies wanting everything up to *their* standards.

None of the friendships between banker and farmer went so deep that a homestead heir wouldn't fight like a wounded bear to protect the family land. Jay Clinton Espy would just as soon not arouse this instinct in Iron.

"I'm not talking about your ability to service debt if you live," said J.C., trying a gentler approach. "I'm talking about what would happen if you got killed. Banks are often the ones holding the sack if the kids don't get along. I don't have to tell you that."

"They're my kids," Iron said. "I raised them right. You think they're going to go around cheating people?"

"No. That's not it. But how about the in-laws causing trouble?"

Iron flinched and J.C. knew he had hit a sore spot. He pressed it at once.

"Their husbands and wives," J.C. prodded. "What about them?"

Iron reached in his breast pocket for a cigarette, lit it, and inhaled deeply, his eyes troubled.

"Damn it, Iron, I need your help. I'm asking you. You owe me. You owe me money, and you owe me a certain amount of consideration. We've got a lot of folks looking over our shoulders nowadays. The feds don't like gentlemen's agreements. They like things down in writing."

"Have I ever. Ever once. Defaulted on a note, or dealt with the bank in any way that was *not* one hundred percent honorable?"

"No, but that's not the point . . ."

"Then how can you carry on like you were personally doing me a favor all these years. A bank is supposed to lend money, isn't it? That's what you're here for."

J.C. sighed, recognizing an impasse. There would be no point in pushing. Iron wouldn't budge until he had mulled it over, a process that had been known to take months. And he needed to obtain Mary's signature legitimately and get more collateral listed on their notes before the examiners came around again. The Barretts' account had already been flagged.

"Make no mistake about it, Iron. It is not business as usual around here. Just keep that in mind. *It is not business as usual.*" J.C. rose, cutting off the discussion.

He watched Iron depart. His stomach roiled. He could not for the life of him understand why it was so hard to persuade a farmer to make a will.

Men in other occupations did so, without giving it another thought. Professional men, tradesmen, laborers, doctors, lawyers, merchants, and even oil field workers didn't hesitate to have a plan on file. But farmers put it off forever. It was as though they couldn't stand the thought of passing down the farm.

He stared gloomily at the row of family portraits lining the west wall of the bank. His should be hanging there. Forrest should be running things by now. He was too old and tired to be fighting with farmers all the time.

He sighed, worried that Iron was holding back because Forrest was involved. As soon as the crisis passed, he had to do something about his son.

5

Iron paused long enough to light a Camel when he stopped outside the bank. Glancing up, he saw Clifton Hathaway across the street. Hathaway was a small man with sharp, sly eyes and a citified look. Like he was a professor, not a farmer. He wore chinos, instead of jeans, and a straw Stetson, rather than a baseball cap advertising the name of a seed company.

Hathaway was his neighbor to the north, and Iron had hated him since high school.

Iron and Mary had eloped at the end of their junior year, and the school board could not decide what to do about the "Barrett problem." If a girl turned up pregnant, married or unmarried, she was expected to complete her studies at home. But Mary wasn't pregnant, so the board decided that the young couple could graduate with the rest of the class.

Urged by their parents after graduation, they both enrolled at Kansas State University. His degree in agriculture economics was interrupted by the unexpected death of his father, and Mary settled for an associate's degree in accounting at the local community college.

Hathaway disappeared into the barber shop, and Iron mused on their high school years. The man had insisted that Mary be denied the valedictorianship. Outraged, Iron had torpedoed Hathaway's application for Star Farmer awarded by the Future Farmers of America, pointing out that most of the "skills and competencies" listed were bald-faced lies.

Hathaway still hovered over Iron's life like an old fart. He was one of the three elected men on the county Agricultural Stabilization and Conservation Service Committee. No one could do anything about the Secretary of Agriculture, short of assassination, but the county ASCS committee was composed of men of their own choosing.

With Hathaway, as when Nixon was elected, Iron had never personally known a soul who voted for him. Yet there he was, year after year, deciding who was complying with government programs and who wasn't. Who got deficiency payments and who didn't. The government made the policies, but the ASCS committee saw to it that they were carried out.

Iron hadn't had any dealings with the ASCS until five years ago, when J.C. Espy pointed out the merits of enrolling in farm programs.

"Not trying to tell you what to do," J.C. had said. "Just think you ought to study about it some."

But Iron knew the steel behind the suggestion, and it was more than attractive at the time. His father-in-law, Albert Ewing, had even written from Florida urging him to sign up.

Fortunately, he enrolled in the feed-grain area of the program before the bottom dropped out of the grain prices. Just in time to develop a corn base for the Payment in Kind program. Although he appreciated the PIK checks, he had never lost the uneasiness he'd felt when Hathaway came on the committee a year later.

Iron walked to the filling station, where he had left his pickup, and called Mary. "Come with me to the sale today. If you aren't up to your axles in something." He scooped up the extra quarters he had laid on the stainless-steel ledge inside the phone booth.

"I can't. Connie and Lisette are coming over this afternoon to bake pies for Parents' Night."

"So? They don't need you for that."

"You mean they shouldn't."

He pressed his fingers against his ear to muffle the sharp clang of a crowbar beating against a tire rim.

"You know how much I like to tag along on sale day. I'll see what I can do. How did your talk with J.C. go?"

"Not real well. J.C. is fidgeting around like a horse before a thunderstorm. I have a feeling all this will thing amounts to is that Forrest is bedeviling him with some hare-brained plan again and he's taking it out on anyone within spitting distance."

"If Forrest were my son, I'd be mad enough to spit too."

He glanced at his watch. "You sure you can't go? J.C. did spook me a bit. You can hold my hand or something."

"Or something." She laughed. "Give me a half hour to get the girls started. We can eat at the sale."

As Iron turned up their lane, he blinked at the white brightness of Mary's Place gleaming in the sun. There were three stories by the time she had finished, counting the windowed attic. Not that she ever *had* actually finished. The house had progressed in fits and starts of carefully planned additions. Through the years, many carpenters, electricians, and tradesmen had worked on various segments of the house, although Mary still did much of the work herself. Three of the rooms had been annexed from other abandoned houses she had come across.

He would never forget the day, a year after they had the wreck of the old Cunningham place moved onto their land. He had gone along with her request not to look before she was ready. Finally she had announced that there was a combination kitchen–family room, a bathroom, and two bedrooms in livable condition.

"Ready?" Mary asked, when she led him over to the house and opened the front door.

On the east side of the house, there were three windows set at an angled bay above a padded seat. The windows had beveled borders and, when Mary opened the door, the sun prismed off these edges and sent rainbows shimmering across the room.

Sunbeams ricocheted off the shining oak floors she had sanded and varnished, then they glinted off the nickel of an antique stove. Mary had set bread to baking, and a beef stew simmered on the back burner of the stove.

Slyly wooed with sunshine and yeast, his heart fell into Mary's loving trap. He stood motionless, disoriented. He couldn't locate the source of the warmth that flowed toward him. It was as though she had sealed the sun into the golden oak woodwork. After losing his father, Iron had periods when he was swept by a sadness akin to homesickness. As he looked around the room, dazzled by Mary's rainbows, he knew that when he was in this room he would never be afflicted by that deep, senseless pining again.

"Welcome home, honey," she said. In her eyes was a joy so deep he laughed and brushed away a tear and looked at his wife with wonder. For once, his reaction had been everything she desired.

Yet sometimes he worried that they were tempting the jealousy of the gods with the pleasure they took in their home, their farm. A goose had walked over his grave, his mother would say.

A pothole jerked Iron out of his reverie. He parked the pickup in front of their house and honked the horn.

Mary came slamming out the front door with her lips set in the thin line that meant trouble with the girls again. Connie and Lisette had developed a cautious friendship, but they could spiral anything up into a fight.

There was something infinitely touching to him about Mary mad. Storming around in her faded Levis and old T-shirts and cowboy boots, red hair crackling beneath her kerchief.

"I can't go after all, Iron," she said. "Looks like I have nursery duty again."

"What happened?"

"I don't know. They were fine when they got here. Making plans for 4-H Days. I was upstairs getting ready to go, and the phone rang just before you pulled up. One of them answered, and when I came downstairs everything had changed. Neither one would look at me."

"Tell them to grow up."

"Yeah, fat chance. You'd better hurry or you'll be late. See you at supper." She waved goodbye as he pulled around the circle drive.

Connie stood at the island, furiously rolling out pie crusts. Lisette read and re-read the recipe, not meeting Mary's eyes.

"Okay, just what is going on?"

The very air in the room seemed charged. Neither of the women spoke.

"What?" asked Mary, truly alarmed now. "*Is* something really the matter?"

Connie's cheeks reddened. She deftly crimped the crust around the edges of the pan.

"Who was that on the phone?"

"It was Elizabeth, Mom," Connie said, after a quick glance at Lisette. "She's getting a divorce. She wanted one of us to tell you."

Stunned, Mary did not reply. Moving in slow motion, she shrugged off her jeans jacket, walked out to the porch, and hung it on a peg. She came back in and pulled an apron over her head.

"I guess we've all seen it coming. They never did seem right for each other."

"He's an arrogant little shit," said Lisette flatly. "She's well rid of him."

Mary shot her a look. Lisette pursed her lips.

"I wish Elizabeth had listened to us to begin with," Mary said unhappily. "We tried to tell her."

"Did you and Iron listen to your parents?" Lisette jabbed.

Mary flushed, recalling their elopement. "No," she said, "we didn't. But the idea of a divorce is going to take some getting used to."

"There's more," Connie said. "She's coming back to Kansas. She'll be home in a week."

"Here? This town?"

"Right!"

Mary sank like a stone into the nearest chair. "What in the world does she plan to do? There's no room for another lawyer in this town."

Mary lowered her head and splayed her fingers across her brow. *Well, welcome to hell.*

It always took Connie and Lisette a good two weeks to settle down after a short visit from Elizabeth. She could just imagine what they would be like if Elizabeth were around full time.

During Elizabeth's visits, Connie would flaunt her staggering capacity for work. She would study her work-worn hands and complain bitterly that she and Mike never did anything fun and she would like, just once, to have some decent clothes before she died.

Lisette, riddled with envy, would refer in tragic tones to the life she had left behind and hint at what she could have become had she not married a farmer. Then she would bedevil not Dennis, but her father-in-law. Mary could count on Lisette starting a fight with Iron.

One thing they all shared was that they came to Mary for the fixing.

"Elizabeth is crazy," blurted Lisette. "Grade-A, certifiable. She had it made. She's pure D nuts."

"I thought you just said Bob is not a good person," Connie mocked. "That she would be better off without him."

"Without *him*, not San Francisco," Lisette said. "She has a fancy townhouse. Plays, museums, culture. She gets to be around people who read a book or two now and then."

"It's easy to *think* the grass is greener," Mary said sharply.

"I *know* the grass is greener," Lisette said. "Here, for the rest of my life, forever and ever as long as I live, it will be the farm, the farm. Always the farm."

"Well, *yes*," Mary said. "Yes, of course that's the way it is."

Connie hooted, and Lisette rolled her eyes.

Mary was disgusted with them both, and angry with Elizabeth for dissolving a marriage just like that. "You two keep right on with the pies. There's no point in *not* making them. I haven't taken care of Grandma yet today. A little fresh air will do me some good, and I need some time to think."

Mary walked briskly toward her mother-in-law's place. Alma Barrett was a diabetic. Mary went there daily to give her a shot and take care of chores. Head swirling, she thought about the financial implications of a divorce in the family.

All of their finances were tied to land passed down to Alma from her husband, Herman Barrett. That inheritance—passed down over a century—had begun with the original 160 acres claimed by Jonas Barrett through the Homestead Act of 1862. He was no fool and took advantage of the Timber Culture Act, which stated that if a settler was twenty-one and planted trees on another 40 acres he could claim another 160. In 1909 Congress acknowledged, through the Enlarged Homestead Act, that farming on the Great Plains was so risky that any man foolish enough to try it deserved another 320 acres. By buying a little farm here, a little farm there, the Barretts' holdings grew to 3000 acres.

Connie's husband, Mike Hewlett, leased 240 acres from an aging farmer too stubborn to sell out. Together, Mike and Iron also leased 360 acres of the Lewis Boyd land. Mary's Place stood on the 500 acres of grassland that supported their cattle and that she and Iron owned outright. At least Iron's sisters, Anna and Clarissa, trusted Iron's judgment. They both lived in Florida and were simply happy to get checks every December.

Last year, Dennis had talked Iron into buying the Smethers Place—another 1000—and upgrading their tractor. The extra indebtedness worried Iron.

Dennis constantly pushed Iron to buy more land and equipment, but Iron balked after the Smethers purchase. "It would be different if Dennis liked to do field work," he told Mary, "but he expects me and Mike to keep up all this land while he tinkers around in his shop and flits back and forth to fancy meetings."

"You hate all those meetings and someone in this household has to understand what the government is up to. But, if he's that set on adding more land, he should think about buying some on his own—like Connie and Mike."

Mary kept the books for all the combinations of Barrett farms. By hand, at first. Then, when the community college offered the first outreach class in computers, she switched to the new technology with a zeal.

By the time she reached her mother-in-law's place, she had decided telling Alma about Bob and Elizabeth was Iron's responsibility. She was grateful there were no children involved. If Dennis and Lisette ever divorced, it would devastate Sabrina. The high-strung child was now thirteen, and for nine years Mary had lovingly nurtured her. Sabrina's trust still wobbled like the legs of a colt. Her brother, Benjamin, however, was as stable as his grandfather.

There had been two surprises with Dennis and Lisette's marriage. The first was that it had lasted at all. The second was that Alma Barrett had taken to Lisette like she was the reincarnation of Joan of Arc.

Mary breezed into Alma's house like it was any other plain vanilla day.

"Thank goodness you're here. I've been having the most god-awful time."

"What's the matter?"

"The washer went off level again during the spin load and jiggled the drain hose out of the pipe. I tried to mop it all up, honey, but these old hands just couldn't wring hard enough. I'm sorry."

"I'll take care of it right now," Mary said. "You sit down and I'll see what I can do."

Alma was a thin, frail woman with parchment skin and a sweet, resigned expression. Her pale, rabbity face disguised a stubborn streak. She always wore a neatly ironed apron over a calico house dress topped with one of her many cardigans, acquired from garage sales.

Alma Barrett was ashamed when she caused trouble for her daughter-in-law, and Mary often found consoling her to be more work than fixing the problem. She went into the laundry room and gathered up the soggy clothes, put the hose back in, then squeezed the excess water into cement tubs. She found a dry stack of newspapers and paper towels and wiped up the floor.

She dropped onto her stomach and peered under the washer. The leveling foot on the right front side was bent. She called the Sears store and ordered a replacement part. "No need to send out a repairman, Tom" she said. "Connie and I can fix it easy enough. It's just a matter of screwing the new leg back in."

Alma shrank like a whipped pup as she waited for her daughter-in-law to draw her insulin. "I'm sorry," she said sincerely. "I don't mean to be a bother."

"Nonsense. Don't fret yourself." Mary plunged in the syringe, capped it, and threw it into the wastebasket. Then, curious, she bent and dug out a pamphlet Alma had thrown there.

"What's this?"

"Seeds," Alma said. "A brochure from a seed company. Dennis wants to try sunflower seeds this year. I told him to go ahead."

"He *what*? Where?"

"On the corn ground."

"But he can't grow sunflowers, Mom. What could Dennis have been thinking?"

"The boy should get to try something different if he's a mind to."

"Right," Mary said grimly. "We all should. But we can't anymore. That land is in the PIK program, and we can't get it out unless we forfeit a chunk of money. How could he have forgotten that since he talked us into the program to begin with?"

Working Alma behind our backs again, she thought furiously. Dennis had nearly lowered their corn base. Was he crazy? Never mind that he wanted to plant a crop he knew nothing about—he had nearly lowered their corn base. She shook her head with a bitter laugh. The government paid them not to grow corn.

The amount of money paid through the Payment in Kind program depended on the percentage of land they held out of production. To reduce the national grain surplus, the government issued certificates redeemable for grain they would have grown. These farm programs were underwritten by a maze of financial institutions, too often dealing in junk bonds sold to savings and loans.

"I hate those programs. All of them," Mary said. She crumbled up the brochure and hurled it back into the wastebasket. "I wish Iron had held his ground with Dennis. How can we *trust* a government that pays farmers not to grow grain."

The old woman sniffed.

"Dennis just can't make these kinds of decisions on his own, Alma. As far as the government and the bank are concerned, all of our family's businesses are tied together."

"You do all the book work," Alma said sullenly, picking a ball of fuzz off the sleeve of her cardigan. "Isn't like they were going to keep it a secret. There's no laws *making* a farmer sign up for any of the programs," Alma said. "No one twisted your arm."

"We were one of the last holdouts, and you and Dennis applied plenty of pressure. We've put ourselves at the mercy of bureaucrats who don't know a pig from a cow."

"Phooey. Wasn't just me and Dennis who talked you into it. It was J.C. Espy. Just try to get a bank to loan you money if you don't want anything to do with government programs."

"Well maybe J.C. would like to start deciphering all these booklets and bulletins for us. But never mind." She patted Alma's veined hand. "I need your tax information. I'll try to get your return done this week."

Alma went to the desk and pulled out a collection of envelopes. Mary flipped through them.

She paused, frowned. The interest statement listing moneys earned on certificates of deposit at the First Bank of Gateway was greatly understated. Alma had probably transferred the CDs to another bank. It wouldn't be the first time. All it took was the offer of a toaster or a mixer.

"See you tomorrow," she said tersely, clutching the statements as she walked out the door.

And Elizabeth is coming home, she thought grimly. *To top it all off, Elizabeth is coming home.*

6

Iron walked through the holding pens at the sale barn and looked over some fine yearlings with a practiced eye. Mary had run all the figures and what ifs on the computer, and he knew how far he could push his finances. If the price was right on these calves today, he would go for it.

He gave them a final inspection then stopped cold. Each of these calves had the Cummings brand on its hip, and they were not listed on the hand-bill. He had talked to Jack just last week, and the man hadn't mentioned wanting to sell any cattle.

He bought a cup of coffee and went inside. He saw Darrel Weaver and Mike Marenthal, waved, and scrambled up the tiered seats that banked steeply to the floor of the oval sale ring.

"What's going on with Jack Cummings?" he asked after greeting the two men. "Doesn't even make sense that he would sell those calves instead of feeding them out."

"He's losing his farm," Darrel said. "His loans were at the Carlton County bank, and it went under."

"What would the bank going under have to do with anything? Jack has the finest farm in the tri-county area."

"Don't know. Just know they're selling him out. Makes me want to throw up. There's strange things going on in this country."

"Even so, he should have said something to me. Given us all a heads up. Ain't natural to not be here today," Marenthal said.

Dumbstruck with sorrow for his friend, Iron fell silent. He reached for his cigarettes. His lighter failed, and Darrell passed him a pack of matches. The odor of sulfur assaulted him just as black clouds darkened the light coming through a nearby window. Suddenly chilled, he pulled on his jeans jacket and turned his attention back to the sale and geared up for the bidding.

Fifty bawling critters shot from a door at one side and lurched around the ring. The rapid-fire chant of the auctioneer rose above the clamor. A poker-faced buyer gave a subtle hand signal. Then the cattle were prodded out of the arena, and a new bunch surged in.

The heavy odor of ammonia wafted on top of smoke and sweat. Fluorescent lights glowed dimly above the sawdust on the floor. The air itself was visible, filtrated with musty and manure-laden particles of dust.

In about an hour, the cattle Iron wanted came through. His stomach tightened. He swiftly assessed the feeders once more. He could not see a single flaw. He lifted a finger at the .75 a hundred sought by the auctioneer. There was only one other bidder, and he quickly fell out at .79. It was the best buy Iron had made on cattle in years.

He made his way over to the sales clerk and quickly wrote out a check for $59,250. He glanced at his watch. It was just three o'clock.

A bull hauler from a livestock truck line waited, bird-dogging the buyers, buying them coffee and sipping whiskey in hopes they would hire his trucks. Iron quickly arranged to have his cattle delivered to a local feedlot whose business it would be to feed them out. He went to a pay phone and called the bank to arrange for the loan to cover his check as he always did.

"J.C., please, Cynthia. I'm calling from the sale barn. I know it's after hours. Just tell him I'll come by tomorrow morning to fix up the papers for some cattle I've bought."

"Please hold, Iron."

"Okay." He glanced at his watch. His business here was finished. No need to stay any longer. He wanted to head for the house.

"J.C. wants you to come in, Iron," Cynthia said a moment later. "We'll watch for you and unlock the back door."

"All right," Iron said, bewildered by the banker's request.

J.C. looked at him sharply when he walked into his office.

"Cynthia said you've bought some cattle and need to see me about the paperwork," J.C. said curtly.

"Bought a pen of feeders. At a great price. $59,250. Best deal I've made in years."

The banker eyed him coldly. "Didn't you hear a word I said earlier? Thought I made it clear this morning. It's no longer business as usual around here. I meant it then, and I mean it now."

"I don't understand."

"Why can't you understand? I'm using plain English. Couldn't make it any clearer. We've got to have more collateral in back of our notes. The gravy train has stopped."

"What does that have to do with me buying cattle? Collateral? Feeder calves are their own collateral."

"Not anymore. The cattle market is too risky. The bank can't afford to take any chances. What I don't need is you running around buying pens of cattle without so much as a phone call to this bank, just assuming that we're going to loan you the money."

"But J.C., we've always done it this way. It's always just been understood. A man can't just go calling his banker in the middle of the night or whenever. When I run across a bargain—be it livestock or equipment—I've got to strike while the iron is hot. You've always trusted my judgment."

"It's over, Iron," he said wearily. "A thing of the past. Not my trust in you. I know your word is your bond. But it's not business as usual, because regulations are changing. I said it plain and simple. You just weren't in the mind to hear."

"You mean to tell me," Iron said, his hands suddenly clammy and very still, "you mean to tell me that you *aren't* going to loan me the money for these cattle."

"That's right."

"My God, man. I've already written the check. Just what do you expect me to do?"

"Believe it or not, Iron Barrett, what you do about a $59,250 hot check isn't my problem." Espy's withered skin lost even more color.

Iron sat on the edge of his chair, trying to control his temper, his fists clenching and unclenching. There was nothing to be gained by telling off his banker. Not just his banker, he corrected himself solemnly. His friend. In thirty years of banking here, he had never been denied a loan. Not once. Getting a formal note drawn after a purchase was done all the time and for quite a few farmers. Not just him.

"J.C., you can't do this. I've never written a hot check in my life."

"Iron, you've got no call to make me feel bad over this. I did everything but draw you a picture this morning. A lot of people are looking over my shoulder right now. And I can't help that. I begged you to cooperate."

Iron sat very still, alarmed by the fury in J.C.'s voice.

The banker's hands trembled as he toyed with his pen. "I'll hold your check and try to find someone who will lend you the money by closing tomorrow. You're lucky deposits are processed first."

"You mean to tell me you honestly can't give me the money. Not just that you won't—to teach me a lesson?"

"Yes. That's what I've been trying to tell you."

Espy made a quick phone call.

"I've got a man here who wants a loan," he said. "One of my best customers. I would be pleased if you would treat him right. Yes, yes, I understand. No, it's not that at all. It's just that we've got to watch what our bank has loaned to any one individual right now." There was a short pause. "That's all right. I understand."

He clicked down the phone. "No good," J.C. said. "They're being squeezed too." He glanced at his watch. "It's late back East. Bad time to try to squeeze money out of people. Come back tomorrow around three. I'll have something put together for you by then."

J.C. started calling around in earnest the moment Iron left but soon saw it was no good. No bank was going to loan a man who wasn't even their customer nearly $60,000 in twenty-four hours to buy a pen of cattle they hadn't even seen.

Gloomily, he thought of the jumbo CDs Forrest had wanted the bank to invest in. He hadn't gone along. Now he wished he had. They were being offered by loan brokers involved with foreign investors, and he had stayed away on principle.

Maybe it was time to try some of his son's ideas. They had to acquire new investors, new capital. It would be too late to help Iron, but in time for some of his other customers. Maybe.

There was only one man in this county he knew of that could get that kind of money overnight.

Himself.

The First Bank of Gateway never loaned money to him or Forrest or any of their officers. That had been the policy of the Espy family ever since the bank was founded. A policy that made Forrest livid.

"If you're good for the money, another bank will back you," J.C. always replied calmly to Forrest's tirades. "If you're not good for it, you have no business borrowing it from this bank either."

J.C. paced the floor restlessly. There was a clear way to cover Iron's check.. But it was a bad business move. He decided to sleep on the problem, hoping an alternative would come to mind overnight.

Sleepless and uninspired, he came into the bank the next morning and picked up the phone. He called his friend Charlie Accor, the president of a medium-sized bank in Upstate New York, and took out a personal loan for $60,000. The money would be deposited into his account electronically that same day.

J.C. went to the files, pulled out a blank form, and calmly drew up a personal note loaning $60,000 to Franklin C. Barrett.

This isn't the bank that's doing this, Barrett, he thought bleakly. *This is my own money that's at risk this time.*

When he had finished, he grunted in disgust and pushed the paper aside with one finger as though it were contaminated. It looked just like everything else Iron had signed in this bank. Gloomily, he doubted the man would even notice the difference.

Iron came in around three, and bitterly J.C. watched him sign the note without giving it a second glance. Just as he'd predicted, it hadn't registered with the dumb bastard that he didn't own the cattle. His banker did.

"I'm sorry," Iron said. "For some reason, I just didn't understand the seriousness of the situation here. I had no idea this bank was in trouble."

"Just don't take these little loans for granted from now on. I'm not the one who's making these rules. Please cooperate with me until the pressure is off."

"Well, I *will*, J.C. I just didn't understand."

"Your operation affects a lot of people. You and Mary, all your kids, your mother, your sisters. This bank. This community."

"There's a lot of little farmers who are going to be hurt bad if someone is putting the squeeze on this bank," Iron said, shaking his head in disbelief. "I hate to see that. I truly do."

J.C. ran his hand through his hair in exasperation. *The little farmers. Not him.* Iron still hadn't gotten the picture. "Would you *please* go along with me and get your papers in order? Make your will?"

Iron stood and extended his hand. "You bet. I appreciate all you've done for me. Damn right I'm going to help you. I'll put your little will thing together right away."

J.C. sank back into his chair and brooded. Why didn't the fool have any money? Why didn't *any* of them have any cash? He would never understand why a farmer always wanted to buy more land when he got his hands on an extra dollar.

He sat there long after Iron left. Stayed, taking solace in his familiar surroundings of marble and brass and vinyl and coins.

Drawing strength for the task ahead.

Two hours after sundown, Elizabeth Barrett McAlister turned up the lane, feeling cheated that she hadn't gotten to approach Mary's Place in the daylight. It never failed to thrill her.

There was a light shining in Mary's kitchen. Her wonderful, fabulous kitchen. It was her mother's pride and joy and had been Elizabeth's first inkling that her folks were worth a lot of money.

In 1976, when farmers were breaking financial records with five dollar a bushel wheat, Iron had separated 40 acres from the 500 he and Mary owned jointly and deeded it to Mary as sole owner. The house and farmstead stood on this parcel.

"This is your house, honey," he insisted, over her protests that it belonged to both of them. "This piece of paper is simply a tribute to your hard work and imagination."

Later that year, Mary decided they could afford to add on the knock 'em dead kitchen she had yearned for all her life. While Mary was building on the kitchen was the only time Elizabeth could remember town kids looking up to farm kids. Like they were all rich.

Elizabeth was flooded by memories of 1976, when the government let America smother the world in grain. The great food-producing beast the country had kept chained was loosed, and the farmers went crazy. Despite previous government programs to control production, they had always known it was a sin not to grow grain.

Dry land, irrigated land, the prairies, mountainsides, hills, valleys, it would all grow wheat, given the right moisture. Rumor had it that wheat would sprout in the crack of an old barn door given the right mix of fertilizer. The wheat was so thick that year that Elizabeth had skimmed a Frisbee across it, skipping it like a rock over a pond. It continued to sway when it stopped, suspended by stalks of molten gold.

The mood in farm communities was intoxicating. Land speculators were once again coming to Kansas. Even nonirrigated land was selling for a small fortune. Bankers happily lent money to wheat tycoons.

But the old folks, who had seen wheat tycoons come and go, warned about the north winds that were sure to come.

The north wind blew in from Russia with breath-stopping suddenness. The wheat-buying friends of the American farmer invaded Afghanistan in late December of 1979, freezing them all. President Carter responded by slapping on a grain embargo. The next onslaught came in the form of exorbitant interest rates, as high as 19 percent in some communities.

Bludgeoned into submission, the great beast of agriculture bowed its bloody head and stumbled back into the barn. Chained once again. Ashamed now of its sinful grain-growing excesses.

Bankers in Western Kansas knew the coldest wind of all had come blowing in the spring of 1981. In an unprecedented fluke of nature, early May had brought a devastating cold front freezing the wheat, just after it headed out.

It seemed odd to Elizabeth, as she turned into their drive, that she would think of that heartbreaking year of '81, right on the heels of her favorite year: '76. But they were the two years of her strongest emotions about the farm. She would never forget the look on her father's face that morning when he came in the house and told them the wheat had frozen.

"Wheat doesn't freeze, Iron," Mary said.

"Did this year." His face was the color of ashes.

The crop was wiped out overnight. There was a sick gray-black tinge pocking the whole field. It was not insured. They had hail insurance and fire insurance. But who had ever heard of insuring wheat against freezing?

Elizabeth switched off the engine and started to climb out of the car, but Mary was there before she could get her feet on the ground.

"Oh, *there* you are. We were starting to worry."

She looked at her mother's anxious face and her father's sad, compassionate eyes then burst into tears, a little girl once again. Needing her parents.

7

Elizabeth woke to the sound of Mary's garden tractor. She peered out the window and watched her mother's steady progress as the earth churned beneath the steel tines of the tiller. Her husband had scoffed when he learned Iron's Christmas gift had cost $10,000.

"That money should have been invested."

"It was. In satisfaction. Mom loves having a big garden."

"That's why God created grocery stores, Elizabeth, so people don't have to do that kind of work."

"It's not work to her. She *likes* doing it."

Bob just rolled his eyes.

Suddenly they were in a fight again—stumbling onto a down escalator. She envied her parents' marriage, although Mary protected Iron in subtle ways.

"Your father always does the right thing," Mary had said admiringly ever since Elizabeth could remember. "He never compromises his principles." Elizabeth smiled. Mary saw to it that he never had to. She kept him pure.

Elizabeth showered then threw on her jeans and a sweatshirt and went downstairs into the kitchen. Bewildered, she looked at the array of breads and desserts already cooling on the island. Mary's anxiety could be measured by the amount of food she fixed. She poured a cup of coffee from a thin, dented aluminum pot. Glitzy replacements offered by their children had ended up on shelves.

She took her cup outside and sat on the porch steps. Mary shut off the tractor at once and jumped down.

"Good morning. I hoped you'd sleep in. You must be exhausted after that long drive."

"It's not the drive. It's all I've been through lately."

"Iron wants to have all the family over tonight. Is it too soon? Do you mind?"

"So that's what all the cooking is for! No, of course I don't mind."

"Good. He's set on getting a few little papers together for J.C. while you're home."

"What kind of little papers?"

"It's sort of a little will."

"Mom! You need a comprehensive estate plan—not sort of a little will. Whose bright idea is this?"

"Well J.C.'s. Forrest's actually," mumbled Mary. "I'm sure Iron wouldn't mind your taking a peek beforehand."

Elizabeth read through the document her father had handed her. It was clearly designed to protect the bank. Iron just needed to insert Mary's name into some blanks.

"They certainly didn't knock themselves out putting this together," she said wryly. "Let me get on Mom's computer and I'll write something a little more detailed. It won't take more than an hour or two, and I promise you I'll keep the bank happy."

"Good," said Iron. His eyes were guarded as he reached for another cigarette.

"Okay, so what's bugging you, Daddy?"

He looked at her quickly and laughed. "Still my little mind reader, aren't you, Sis?"

She waited.

"I've been studying about what's fair and right. This family is the same as mine was." He stared at his calloused hands. "I mean I'm the oldest son and I have two sisters. Dad left the money and the land to Mom, but I'm the executor of his estate. I have the power to make all the decisions. In our family, Dennis is the oldest son, and he has two sisters. It seems like the right thing to do would be to leave the money and the land to Mary and make Dennis the executor."

She stared at him mutely, then found her tongue. "But there's something holding you back."

Iron nodded and looked at her quickly then averted his eyes as though he were ashamed of his thoughts. "It would be Dennis's job to see to it that all of you will get the income you're entitled to, same as I see to it that Anna and Clarissa get their fair share of the money every year."

But you're Iron Barrett! Like Lincoln, you'd spend your life paying back a penny. Elizabeth held her breath a moment to keep from blurting out the words. *Dennis is Dennis.*

"Running a farm is so much easier when one person has the authority to go ahead with decisions," Iron said.

"If it's the right person," Elizabeth cautioned.

"We all know for a fact that Mary will probably outlive us all," Iron said. "I would hate to think that when she's an old lady she will still be hell-bent on doing things her own way. She'll go to her grave with a broom in one hand and a floppy disk in another. Probably come back from the dead long enough to arrange her own funeral."

"I don't know what you're getting at, Daddy. You've always praised Mom's business sense. Her willingness to call a spade, a spade."

"To be honest, Elizabeth, your mother is a little funny where Dennis is concerned. She's always looking for the worst in the boy."

Elizabeth glanced away. Friction over Dennis had always been present between Iron and Mary. It wasn't a secret.

And you're always looking for the best where Dennis is concerned, she thought. *And not finding it. And it's breaking your heart. That's what's really holding you back from making Dennis the executor.* Iron could not tolerate dishonesty. He couldn't admit, either consciously or unconsciously, that it was present in his own son.

Elizabeth knew how quickly and unreasonably Iron could spring to Dennis's defense, so she tiptoed through the words that came to her mind, gave Iron a hard look, and spoke carefully.

"Our situation is unique, Daddy. It's not the same as when grandpa left you in charge, because we have more than one sibling living on this land. Anna and Clarissa are clear off in another state. I think you should make a will that speaks your mind, right now. You'll be better off in the long run."

"A real will?"

"Yes, a real one," she said with a smile.

"Okay. I don't ever want to go through this ordeal again."

"I can have it finished by this evening. Does Dennis know you've given some thought to putting him in sole control?"

"No. But I'm sure he expects it. And then there's Mike."

"I thought you liked Mike."

"I do. But doggone it, honey, the man doesn't have the sense God gave a green goose. He's always talking about the environment and sustainable agriculture."

"Connie has enough common sense for both."

"Connie can't stand to hurt people's feelings." The lines on Iron's face deepened. "Never has. That goes double where her husband is concerned."

"Have you heard of a revocable trust? I think it would be just perfect in your situation."

"A trust! I don't want a bunch of bankers and lawyers telling my kids what to do. Or selling us out."

"Not that kind. Your own family will be trustees and make all the decisions. That way no one person can sell the land, and there won't be any questions about division of income. And the tax benefits are enormous."

Bingo, she thought, seeing the leap of interest. He brightened when she went over the tax savings.

"And remember this can be revoked. Changed at any time. Canceled out."

"Sounds good. Do it," Iron said.

Elizabeth whisked upstairs and rummaged through her briefcase for the disk containing standard forms. She loaded the file for revocable trusts and printed out multiple copies when she finished the document.

～～～～～

Connie and Mike arrived first. Elizabeth hugged her sister then turned to their pig-tailed eight-year-old daughter, Susan, who was wearing a bright green 4-H windbreaker. "Well look at you. You're old enough to join now," she said with delight as she wrapped her niece in a warm hug. "Food projects to begin with, I'm guessing."

Susan beamed. "Yes, and knitting, too. Grandma is helping me. I brought it to show you."

"Let me see how much these two have grown first," she said, turning to the four-year-old twins, Andy and Andrea.

"Oh Connie! They're adorable." Elizabeth reached for her plump, round-cheeked niece and nephew. They wore jeans and identical red plaid shirts with blue suspenders. Their hair—a lighter, brighter shade than Connie's red—was highlighted by the flames blazing in the fireplace.

"I remember her." Andrea turned to her twin. "Don't you?"

Andy nodded.

Elizabeth hugged them fiercely. "Well, I should hope!"

"You brought us puzzles last time."

She laughed at the crafty expression on the boy's face. "I didn't have time to shop before I came, honey, but we can run into town tomorrow and I'll let you pick something out all by yourself. If that's all right with your mother."

Mike Hewlett came through the back door carrying a wicker basket containing more food to add to the already excessive amount Mary had cooked up. They exchanged brief hugs before he ambled off to join Iron in the family room.

Connie's husband was a ruddy-faced man who had enough fat overlying his strong muscles to hint at a weight problem in middle age. He was the only young farmer she knew who insisted on wearing bib overalls—as though they were a badge of honor.

A few minutes later, Iron helped Alma into the house, and Elizabeth went over to embrace her frail little grandmother.

Shortly afterward, Dennis and Lisette arrived with Sabrina and Benjamin.

"Sabrina! You've grown up on me!"

Pleased, her beautiful black-haired niece gave her a small hug. Then she shyly looked away. Her eyes were as dark as the center of a sunflower.

Benjamin's thatch of black hair clearly marked him as Lisette's son, but the nine-year-old's square jaw and the set of his shoulders came from Dennis. His clear gray eyes were the same shade as Iron's, and the boy's unwavering gaze was as serious as his grandfather's. Elizabeth laughed softly at his embarrassed toleration of her hug.

"Supper's ready," Mary called. She jumped up and down throughout the meal, waiting on everyone, refilling dishes, beaming at them all.

"This old table is as good a place as any for our meeting," Iron said after they cleared the dishes.

Connie asked Susan to take the twins and join Sabrina and Benjamin in the living room. Then they all settled into their seats and looked at Iron.

8

"I know you all are wondering why I called this meeting," Iron said. "It's about my will. Elizabeth helped me prepare it."

Dennis looked at Elizabeth suspiciously.

"It's time to talk about passing down the farm. My banker wants to know what's going to become of this place when I die. Bank examiners want to see things on paper nowadays. But first I want to argue out a few things in person."

He looked up at a faint click. Elizabeth laid a tape recorder in front of him.

Mary stared.

"Don't worry," Elizabeth said. "This is just for our family's use. Sometimes it's hard to remember what's been said later, and this will serve to jog everyone's memory. I'll be glad to erase it as soon as we get all the pertinent details in black and white."

"Well, I don't like it," Dennis said.

"I do." Connie scowled. Her arms were folded across her chest, her freckles stark on her pale skin. "I would like this meeting recorded. That way we won't have to worry about things being twisted around afterwards."

Dennis's eyes flashed but, before he could speak, Elizabeth quickly held up her hand.

"Let's compromise. I'm no slouch at shorthand. I'll just jot down all the main points."

"Fine. That's fair enough. Now then." Iron looked at his children and cleared his throat. "I don't know any way to do this but to jump in feet first. The problem with a farm is that it *is* a farm and an ongoing operation. So Elizabeth has drawn up a revocable trust for us."

Dennis's eyes narrowed. He gripped the arms of his chair; the skin across his knuckles whitened.

"It's time for plain talk," Iron said. "Here's the way this revocable trust is going to work. When I die, you're all going to be trustees and make decisions as a team. That way no one can sell the land. There will be a fair and equal division of income."

As she scrutinized her brother's shrewd face, Elizabeth knew at once why Dennis had come back to the farm. He thought he was going to be the sole executor when Iron died. She had always questioned his sudden affection for the Barretts' land.

Dennis exploded to his feet. Alma stared at her grandson and blinked hard as though she doubted her own senses.

Pay attention to all of this, Grandma, Elizabeth coached silently. *This is what your pride and joy is really like.*

"Fixing it so no one can sell the land, ever, is just plain stupid. And as to an equal division of income! My slice of the pie should reflect the blood and sweat I've put into this place. I'm the only son. I work my tail end off year after year just to keep this place from slipping back into the Stone Age."

Elizabeth's eyes widened at the slap at Iron's slowness to adopt new ways. Then Dennis turned on her.

"I've not been off earning fancy salaries like some of you. I damn sure could have been."

Stunned, Elizabeth put her palms on the table and started to rise. Fancy salary indeed! She would like to show him sometime what her job worked out to by the hour. It had been his choice to drop out of school and come back to the farm. No one had forced him.

Before she could get to her feet, Connie took Dennis on. "I assume by your 'Stone Age' crack you're referring to Mike's interest in sustainable agriculture."

Surprised by the swiftness of her little sister's response, Elizabeth sat back down in her chair and listened.

"We *care* about the land, Dennis. This farm is more than just a cash cow to some of us. Mike and I are the ones who've worked like dogs. He's the one who does the dirty work and takes the heat around here, while you're tinkering with some piece of machinery. You've treated him like a mule, a hired man, all these years . . . for a pittance. He's been exploited and dumped on, and it's not right. You all act like he's a dunce."

Everyone was deathly still. All of her senses heightened, Elizabeth watched the faces of her family like she would scrutinize a jury.

"We feel used," Connie persisted. "Mike has had to farm your land, Dad, and put his own ideas aside for your outdated . . . methods." She swallowed hard at a warning glance from Mary. "It's wrong. There are other ways of doing things. We lease a paltry 240 acres from an old man that will probably never sell it to us. We don't ever get to try things our own way. So maybe we ought to think about moving. Unless we can actually buy some of your land, Grandma."

Everyone stared at Mike and Connie. Iron stood corner-post rigid while all the color drained from his face.

"Don't even *think* about it." Alma's voice shook. "Don't even let the thought cross your mind that one single acre of this place will ever be up for sale to you two as individuals. Move if you please. But my land will always be owned by *all* the Barrett family. Not just *some* of the Barrett family."

Tears streamed down Connie's cheeks.

"Connie, I don't know what to say," Iron stammered. "I had no idea you felt that way."

Mike rose and placed his arm around her shoulders. "We don't want to ruffle any feathers here, Iron, Grandma. It's just that I have my own ideas on how to do things, and I don't want to wait until you die to use them. We've been grateful for the start you've given us, but we're just itching to be on our own."

Iron braced his elbows on the table for support. "I don't understand, Mike. We farm the Lewis Boyd place together. I've given you plenty of leeway there."

"You asked for plain talk, Iron," Mike said. "No, we farm the Boyd place your way. I can't make a single decision without getting approval first. That applies to any financial decisions too."

"Which wouldn't be the case if we weren't enrolled in all these farm programs," Mary said.

Dennis flushed.

"We want to separate our business from this family. We want to buy our own land. Strike out on our own," Mike said. "And I agree with you on farm programs, Mary. I don't like them either."

"There's another problem," Connie said. "A problem that no one seems to be willing to talk about. There's not enough money coming in from this place to support all our families. We're always strapped for cash. Every cent goes back into this operation. We might as well be serfs. I can't buy a pair of shoes without the purchase being scrutinized."

"My point exactly," Lisette said, speaking for the first time.

"You have no room to talk, Lisette," Connie said. "I have never figured out where you two get your money."

"Dennis has a skill." Alma looked fondly at Dennis as though her grandson's words of a few moments ago had never been uttered. "He's another Henry Ford. A genius. And he has a bit of pride about him, Connie. He doesn't carry on like he's a pauper. He puts a good face on things so those that cherish him won't feel reprimanded."

Mike hastily pressed the flat of his hand against Connie's back, stopping her from saying more.

Connie fumbled in the pocket of her cardigan and, finding a crumpled tissue, dabbed at her tears before she spoke again. "Don't you see? Any of you? Mike and I just aren't getting anything out of this—financially or emotionally. It's not worth it to us anymore."

Elizabeth studied her mother. Mary looked like a coiled spring ready to fly apart. Then she saw her catch Iron's eye and mouth some words. Iron gave a slight nod. As she watched the shifting emotions play in Mary's eyes, Elizabeth smiled at the nearly telepathic communication between her parents.

Mary stood.

"I have my own announcement to make." She reached for her younger daughter's hands and held them gently. "You're getting the house, Connie. You're going to inherit Mary's Place someday."

Connie's eyes grew wide. "Mom, I didn't know," she stammered.

"Elizabeth, Lisette," Mary said anxiously, turning to look at the other women, "I don't want to leave you two out. But obviously, a house can't be left to more than one family. I'm not sure just how I'm going to make it up to you. But I will. I'm sure it's plain to everyone that Connie needs to know, right here and now, that she will be getting the house."

With a lawyer's alertness to undercurrents, Elizabeth's eyes swept across each face—registering their reactions.

She glanced at Dennis's face while Mary spoke. Then she couldn't take her eyes off him. He flushed with rage. He clenched his jaw tightly to stop the trembling. His reaction to not being given sole control of the farm had been pallid compared to the wrath she saw there now. He looked crazy and Elizabeth was frightened.

"You can't do that," Dennis said. The tendons in his neck tightened. "You can't do that."

Elizabeth sprang like a tiger. "She most certainly can, Dennis. The house belongs to Mom. She can leave it to whomever she likes. Besides, Connie is the only one of us who *can* keep the place up. It would kill me and Lisette off."

"Oh, we all know I'm the fly in the ointment," Lisette said. "They don't want me living here. Your parents have never liked me, Dennis. Pure and simple." She rose and started to walk out of the room.

"Lisette," Mary called.

"Let her go." Iron's voice rose.

"No," Elizabeth said furiously. "Come back and sit down, Lisette." Reluctantly the woman turned and walked back to her chair. "This family has got to make some decisions. Can't you see that? Any of you?"

"Not now, Elizabeth." Mary's voice was thick with despair. "Later, after we've calmed down."

"Mom, don't! Don't stop this process. We may not like it, but it won't kill us. There's not going to be a better time than now. Can't any of you see how important this is?"

"We left the dishes," Mary said. "The food is drying on them. Let it go until later, honey. When we're not so het up."

"Forget the dishes for once in your life. Do you know what you do, Mom? What you've always done when you can't personally fix a problem?" Even as she spoke, Elizabeth knew her words were ill-chosen, ill-advised, a mistake, but it was as though she couldn't stop herself. "You pick up a hammer or a saw and go off and build something. Something you can see. Something you can touch. Something you can do."

"Elizabeth!"

Her heart contracted at the rage in her father's voice.

"Don't you ever speak to your mother in that tone of voice again."

"I'm sorry, Daddy." She bit her lip in dismay. "I apologize if I've hurt your feelings, Mom."

"I'll remind you that this whole fiasco was partly your fault, Elizabeth. If we had stuck to the little agreement the bank wanted to sign in the first place, we'd have been better off."

"Oh that's not true. The bank would have been better off."

"Don't contradict your father, Elizabeth," Mary said curtly.

Elizabeth touched her splayed fingers to her forehead. *It's no use*, she thought bitterly. *It's like trying to reason with the Mad Hatter and the dormouse.* Check and checkmate—just like that. Then she looked at Dennis and, seeing the malicious triumph in his eyes, her blood chilled. She had seen the same eyes in far too many courtrooms.

In that instant, she decided not to tell them that she had been considering an offer to practice law in Gateway City. It would never, ever work. She might have known that moving back would be a disaster.

"And I apologize to you too, Daddy. All of you. I didn't intend for things to go this way."

"Lots of things have been said here that are better left unsaid. But you're right about one thing, Elizabeth. Making a will calls for a few decisions." Iron's voice shook with anger. "And I've just now made one."

Elizabeth looked at her father and took a deep breath. The lines around his mouth seemed chiseled to a new depth. He looked like a wounded old stag besieged by a pack of dogs. Turned for the last stand.

Slowly Iron rose and walked around the table, gathering up each copy of the trust. When he had collected them all, he carried them to the front of the room. There was not a sound. Everyone's eyes followed him.

He tore the papers in half with one deft movement of his powerful hands. "There. Done."

Then he curled his fists and looked at his children, his arms hanging heavily at his sides.

"Now, listen to me. Here's the way it's going to be. All of my land and your grandmother's land will be left to the grandchildren. Sabrina too. Born or yet unborn," he added, looking at Elizabeth. "Mary's Place is going to Connie. That's your mother's decision to make, and she's made it. I'm bypassing my own children. This is the last word on this particular subject."

Confused by the implications, Connie reached for Mike's hand. Dennis's face contorted with hatred as he stared at Elizabeth.

"No."

Turning, all eyes fixed on Alma.

"No. It's not the last word. *I* have the last word. And I say if *you* can leave it to the grandchildren, I can too. I can bypass you, Franklin." She used her son's given name only when she was furious. "I can bypass you and leave it all to your children. *My* grandchildren: Elizabeth, Connie, and Dennis. Or just one," she said softly. "Just one of them."

Elizabeth groaned inwardly. Everyone knew who the "just one" would be. Her eyes darted to Dennis, who did not bother to conceal his glee.

"Grandma," Connie protested, but Mike hushed her before she could say another word.

"Never mind," Alma said. "I don't see no reason for changing the arrangement my husband made. Now let's go back to the way everything was before this meeting started and forget everything that's been said here."

Elizabeth swallowed hard. Nothing would ever be the same. They couldn't go back. She could feel Dennis's mind racing, racing.

"And fixing things so nobody can sell any of the land is a dandy idea." Alma glared at Dennis. "I'm going to study on it."

You're no match for him, Grandma, Elizabeth thought. *You never have been.* But it would take Dennis a while.

"Come on, Mary." Iron's shoulders sagged. "It's been a long day. Let's go to bed." He looked at Alma before he turned away. His voice was bleak with misery.

"You're dead right about one thing, Mom. This was all a piss-poor idea. I'm not signing anything leaving anything to anyone. That includes the form the bank sent. J.C. Espy can go square to hell as far as I'm concerned."

9

Mary Barrett whirled through her morning routine but without the usual pleasure she took in restoring order.

She still smarted from Elizabeth's words. Unable to understand them. "You always pick up a hammer," her daughter had said, "and build something you can see."

Well, what is wrong with that? It was better than lying around brooding. Mary sprayed homemade window solution on the mirror in the master bathroom then paused and stared at the woman in the mirror. Hair tucked under a red bandanna, as usual. Standard five-button Levis, faded but not torn. Blue chambray shirt worn unbuttoned over a navy-blue tank top. Reed-thin. Lightly she touched her face, shyly pleased at the youthfulness of the skin tone.

But her hands seemed to mock her vanity. She examined the prominent veins, the callouses, the short nails. They always betrayed her, these hands, which she studied again as though she had never seen them before. With Elizabeth's words still ringing in her ears, she wondered what it would feel like not to work. Slowly she walked to the hall closet and put away her portable container of rags and spray bottles.

Elizabeth had announced she would be leaving for Manhattan, Kansas, at the end of the week to join an agency that helped farmers in crisis. Mary had hoped she would stay home long enough to heal the wounds that had split the family since the "Will Fight," as they now called it. However, Elizabeth walked over to Connie and Mike's twice a day as though she couldn't tolerate her own parents, so Mary knew there was no point in urging her to stick around.

Downstairs, she poured a cup of coffee and sat in the large wing chair in the family room. She looked out the bay window past the oak tree, and the white rail fence that bordered the farmyard, to the sweep of pasture in the distance.

A muscle in her jaw tensed when a jackrabbit streaked toward the base of the cedar windbreak. Jackrabbits and cottontails nearly drove her crazy. They ate everything—vegetables, roses, flowers, trees, shrubs—including the prickly barberry.

There had been deadly warfare between her and the rabbits for twenty years. In the beginning, she had surrounded each and every landscape plant and garden space with ugly chicken wire. Horrible. So she put up white rails marking off smaller areas for the vegetable gardens and flowers and stapled the chicken wire to the lowest rail.

By planting enough Blaze roses to climb the length of the fence, she managed to draw a person's eye away from the metal netting. It kept the rabbits out. But she hated the work all the fencing involved: bracing the chicken wire and keeping the rails painted and the roses pruned and fertilized.

All at once she was in despair at the time she spent fighting rabbits and mending fences. On the farm and within the family. Little benign-looking furry things, which multiplied like cancer cells and threatened to overrun them all.

She sat very still, thinking hard. There was a ritual she had followed through the years. When there were problems, she worked out in her mind and in her soul what she really wanted. Best-case scenario. Next she decided on her bottom line. Then she rolled up her sleeves and went to work for the spread—the difference between what she really wanted and what she would never stand for in a million years. The spread was everything.

She couldn't make her children all love one another, which was what she really wanted right now. However, she could narrow the gap between that and this terrible tension, which she absolutely could not stand.

"We need to talk to the kids," she said, when Iron came in that evening. "I want to put a stop to this nonsense. Acting like we're all rank strangers. I refuse to spend one more minute second guessing how my own children are going to take every word I say."

"It's wearing me to the bone," Iron admitted. He looked at the two plates set on the table. "Isn't Elizabeth going to eat supper with us?"

"No, she called to say she'll eat with Connie and Mike. She's been over there all afternoon."

"What have we done to deserve this?"

"Nothing. But we're not going to live like this either. Life is too short. I'm going to talk to Lisette and find out what it will take to make her happy."

Iron scowled. "Nothing we can do will make Lisette happy. Fast as that woman changes moods, it's a wonder her kids aren't half crazy."

"It can't be easy to plan on a major in art history and end up living on a farm."

"That's not our fault," Iron said. "No call for her to take it out on us. Besides, she was just at K-State for three semesters. It's not like she was on some great career path. But go ahead and talk to her if you think it will do some good. I'll talk to Connie and Mike."

"I've been thinking about some of the things Connie said." Mary looked at Iron warily, hoping he wouldn't take offense.

"She brought me up short," Iron said. "It's Mike who developed some of our best marketing strategies. It was Mike who talked me into cutting down on some pesticides and trying new varieties of grain. I've been thinking too. We do take them for granted. We do make fun of Mike's ways too much of the time."

Mary touched her forehead and breathed a quick prayer of relief. "That leaves Elizabeth. She's still hopping mad because you tore up that trust she put together. You two have never quarreled before."

"Been thinking about her too." Iron sighed and fumbled for his cigarettes. "I'll wait up for her tonight and won't let her go up to bed until we've finished slugging everything out. And that might be what it takes, but I'll bet we clear the air."

The morning after Iron made peace with Elizabeth, Mary went to Dennis and Lisette's.

"Come in, come in," Lisette said warmly. A wide smile split her face.

Dumbfounded, Mary walked into the kitchen. "Lisette, I'm here to try to make amends for some things that have been said. Iron and I want to know if there's anything we can do to make you a little happier."

"You did. A lot happier." Her voice quivered. "You know, Mary, I've never really felt like I was a part of this family. It wasn't until the other night when Iron said he was leaving the farm to the grandchildren—including Sabrina—that I realized the kids and I had a place here. It was without a doubt the happiest moment of my life."

Mary stared at her, scarcely able to believe what she was hearing. Weak with relief, she started to laugh.

"Even though the whole will deal is off, Iron *intended* to leave the money to all the grandchildren," Lisette said. "Including my Sabrina. There's going to be some changes in this household now. A lot of changes."

Mary started to warn her if the changes involved Dennis, to be very, very careful. But she held her tongue, ashamed that such thoughts had popped into her head.

Dennis nursed his fourth beer and brooded over the mistakes he had made during the Will Fight. His stomach tightened as he recalled his loss of control, the look in Alma's eyes when he'd said fixing it so no one could sell the land was stupid. She may have praised him as a mechanical genius in the next breath, but he knew in his gut the old woman was mulling everything over.

He walked to the fridge to get another Bud just as Lisette came through the back door carrying groceries. She set the bags on the kitchen counter and began putting them away. "We need to talk," she said.

Wordlessly, he went back to his chair and groped for the remote, which had slipped down into the side of the recliner. He tuned in to the Royals pregame. Lisette walked over to the set and turned it off.

He smoldered as she stood facing him, her arms folded across her chest. She'd been strutting around like she was Queen of the Universe ever since the Will Fight.

"Dennis, I don't want to ask you for grocery money anymore," she said, putting fists on her hips. "I want you to put my signature on a checking account."

"No need for that. Don't I give you all the money you need?"

"I want to be able to buy something whenever I feel like it. Like Mary and Connie and Elizabeth." Despite her defiant posture, there was a little quiver in her voice.

"You don't know that much about money, Lisette."

"I've never had a chance to learn."

"It's not a woman's place to take on money worries. I'm just trying to spare you." He took another swig of beer.

Lisette gave a little huff of disbelief. "And there's something I've just come to realize. I'm the mother of your son. I've been a little slow catching on to the importance of that to this family." She brushed her long black hair back from her cheek.

He said nothing.

"I know you don't love me, but you're stuck with me." Her voice softened with misery. "You can't get rid of me without risking me taking you for every last penny in a divorce settlement. I understood that after the fight over the will. I could split this family operation, couldn't I? A divorce wouldn't sit right with Grandma Alma. Hard telling what her reaction would be."

"No one's too freaked out over Bob and Elizabeth."

"They had a prenuptial agreement. Besides, they don't have kids."

"Don't press your luck," Dennis said, crushing the beer can with one hand, "or I'll bounce your ass out this door so fast it will make your head spin. You won't see these kids again before you die."

"That's always worked before," she said coldly. "Because I knew which one of us a judge would believe. God knows how charming you can be. I've been scared to death that if I divorced you, I would lose my kids. I knew you would accuse me of every sin under the sun despite being under oath and everyone would believe you, not me."

She closed her eyes and winked back tears. "Benjy is like Iron's shadow. And Sabrina adores Mary. It would be like cutting their hearts out to move them away from their grandparents. I would never do it. But, fair warning, access to a checking account is just the first of many changes we're going to make in this household."

Dennis eyed her coldly. He gripped the arms of the recliner. She eyed his white knuckles and laughed. "Don't even *think* about it, Dennis. Don't even *think* about touching me. I'd see you in jail before sundown."

"I have never hit you, Lisette."

"Only because you don't dare, Dennis. Not because you love me." Her voice quivered again. "Your repu-*ta*-shun. Your precious repu-*ta*-shun. A trip to the emergency room would blow it all to hell, Dennis. Then where would you be with your precious family? Your doting grandmother?"

The twins came racing down the walk and met Iron at the gate.

"Grandpa!" He stooped and reached for them both at once and carried them onto the porch. Smiling anxiously, Connie opened the door and let him inside. Mike got up at once and switched off the TV.

Iron swallowed. They were good people, Connie and Mike. Before the Will Fight he had always felt as comfortable in the Hewletts' house as he did in his own.

Suddenly all the words he had planned left him. "I can't stand for us to be on the outs," he said. He bounced a twin on each knee and talked around their bobbing heads.

"We can't either," Connie said, flustered to the point of tears. "But Dad, we're scared to death. You know Dennis is going to start working Grandma. She turns to Silly Putty the minute he goes near her. It was like a light bulb went off in his head when Grandma Alma said what she did about passing down the farm to her grandchildren instead of you and Mom."

"Look, it didn't sit right with my mother when Dennis jumped on Elizabeth for trying to fix it so none of you could sell any land. Don't underestimate your Grandma Alma's common sense. Or mine."

"Don't you underestimate Dennis's way with her," Connie countered.

"I didn't come here to talk about Dennis and Grandma," Iron said. "I've come here to talk about you two and your future on this place. I've thought over what you said, Mike. You're right. There's got to be something more in this for you two than what you're getting right now. Not just after I die. What do you have in mind, exactly?"

Mike hooked his thumbs in the straps of his overalls. "Would you consider selling us the five hundred acres you and Mary own together? You know Grandma won't sell any of the original Barrett land. No other farms around here are for sale. If you won't sell, we have to look in other counties. It's not that we really want to move."

Iron began to jiggle the twins rapidly to hide his despair. Mary would never go along. She was still trying to think of the best way to compensate Dennis and Lisette for leaving Connie the house when she died. Selling them their land, too, wouldn't fit in with her sense of fair play. She would get on her high horse and raise seven kinds of hell if she thought he was favoring one of their kids over another. Besides, it didn't seem natural to think about selling land. Even to his own children.

Don't go, he thought. *Please don't go.* He hid his feelings behind a sickly smile. Connie had more than a little of Mary's stubborn streak.

"Problem is, I don't think there's any way in hell for you to get financing," he said. "Not now, with farm loans drying up. And even if you could, with the price of wheat down, how do you think you can make payments on the ground?"

"We would diversify," Mike said enthusiastically. He went to the roll-top desk and took out a sheaf of papers. "We want to convert some of our wheat ground to oats. Oats are selling like hotcakes since the oat bran thing kicked in. 'Right Thing to Do,' and all that."

"But how long will that last? Until the next expert ruins the whole thing and the market plunges? Remember the red meat fiasco? When the energy crisis started driving up the prices in grocery stores? The next thing we knew, the women's magazines told housewives to stop buying meat to save money. When that didn't work, they told them beef was killing them. We've never recovered from it."

"That may be true. But you have to go with a product as long as it's working, then switch."

"Well, the problem is, it takes a long time to learn how to grow something," Iron said. "You know that. It took us ten years to learn how to grow corn out in this part of the state. Then another ten years to figure out that it wasn't a very good idea after all. By the time you learn what you're doing with oats, the market will change."

"There's faster ways than trial and error."

Iron smiled as he looked at the pile of agricultural journals stacked on Mike's desk.

"We have the down payment saved up," Connie said.

"The hell! That's great, Connie. I don't know how you did it. I'm proud of you both." Iron beamed his approval, then his grin faded when he realized they actually *could* move away.

"I can't carry any of the financing if I sell to you. I would if I could, but I can't. And I need some time to think this through." He swallowed the lump in his throat, choking back the threat of tears. "But I'll go to bat for you."

He was rewarded by a brilliant smile from his daughter.

"I'd hug you, but all your spots are taken," she said, eyeing the twins.

"And I have a request." He eased the twins onto the floor and stood. "I'm going to talk this over with J.C. Don't say anything to anyone until I'm sure everything will go through."

"Not even Mom?"

"Nope. We might not be able to pull it off and if we can't, I don't want to rile your mother up again. If everything goes south, I won't mention it to her. I want this family to settle down."

"Won't Mom have to sign all the papers?"

"Sure, if it ever gets that far."

"Mike," he said, turning back from the doorway. "One thing about it. It will be your land. Your chance to make your own mistakes. I guess you're entitled. Same as me."

On the way home, Iron fretted about not talking things over with Mary right from the start, but he knew what her response would be. Even if she agreed with his thinking, God knew Mary couldn't keep a secret off her face and out of her eyes, and there was no point in telling Dennis and Elizabeth just yet either. It would just cause trouble.

By the time he swung into their driveway, he had come to a decision. He would just, by God, do it. Sell Connie and Mike part of the farm and tell Mary at the very last minute. He walked onto the back porch feeling gloomy, because despite their long history of marching off and stringing blue lights on their own, he and Mary always argued everything out first.

Not hearing her pros and cons from the very beginning made him uneasy.

10

It had been a week since Forrest had been to work, and J.C. Espy found himself covering for his son to the staff like an alcoholic's spouse. He reached for his Rolaids and tried to remember the last time he and Forrest had had a peaceful talk about financial matters. His hands shook as he reviewed a stack of loan applications.

After reading the first one, he tossed it aside in disgust. Not only was he rejecting it; he would love to have that farmer know that even if he planted from fencerow to fencerow, he stacked the cattle two deep, and all his cows had twins, there was no way in hell he could get out of debt.

His mood didn't improve any as he scrutinized the next application, which was from Sidney Porter, an implement dealer who was trying to hang on until things got better. Well, J.C. had news for him. Things would never get better as long as the government kept meddling.

The Payment in Kind program had just about done in the local businesses. It was one of the many reasons his bank was in so much trouble right now. The direct ag loans were burdensome enough, but the default rate on secondary ag notes was picking up momentum like a rolling snowball.

The fertilizer and chemical and implement dealers and the thousands of networks undergirding agriculture had had a bomb dropped on them with the inception of PIK. As business after business folded, with owners stealing away like thieves in the night, the tax base had eroded, leaving skeletal towns.

Sidney Porter, the implement dealer, like the First Bank of Gateway, had extended too much credit to all the right people at the wrong time. J.C. sighed. He simply could not afford to lend the man any more money.

But he mentally counted all the people employed by the implement business. There had to be another way, he decided. That business was too important to the community.

He dialed quickly.

"Sidney. Morning. This is J.C. Please stop by the bank this afternoon. We need to talk about your loan. Let's see if we can work something out."

J.C. gently laid the phone back down in its cradle. Damn right he was going to work something out for Sidney Porter. For the good of the community.

His melancholy reverie was broken by the intercom. "John Day here to see you."

"Send him in."

After listening to the man's yearly request for operating money, J.C. drew a deep breath.

"No."

"Huh?" John Day paled.

J.C. knew it had never occurred to John that he wouldn't get the money. As always. Like his father before him. His grandfather before that. Year in, year out, season after season.

"What am I supposed to do?" Day asked, disbelieving. "Just where am I supposed to go?"

That's not my problem, thought J.C. *You think someone's going to bail my bank out when I need money?* But he didn't need enemies, and he would surely have a bunch in the months ahead. "Try the Production Credit office. They are supposed to have some money available."

"I don't want to do business with those folks. There's too much paperwork at the pcc. Hell, J.C., I don't have time for all those forms."

J.C. masked his quick anger then started at the buzz from the intercom. He pressed the button, relieved at an excuse to send Day on his way.

"Yes, Cynthia."

"Iron Barrett just got here and wants to know if you have a minute."

"Sure. Send him right in." He rose and extended his hand. "Best of luck, John."

Despite the knot in his guts, he managed a tight smile for his largest debtor.

"What's on your mind, Iron?"

When Barrett told him that Connie and Mike wanted to buy his and Mary's land, J.C.'s hand lurched like he had palsy before he brought his body back under control. Slowly he expelled all of his breath, and his mind reeled as he tried to think of the ramifications.

Delaying his reply, he pulled open his desk drawer and reached for a breath mint, thinking, thinking, thinking, as he slowly tore away the paper with his arthritic hands.

His initial reaction was a quick leap of hope. Hope, because this meant loans made directly to the Barretts' operation would be paid down. Then hope was replaced by a surge of nausea. Connie and Mike Hewlett were directly involved in that enterprise. There was no way his bank could loan them the money. The examiners would swarm like killer bees.

On the other hand, another bank would loan the young couple the money in a heartbeat. *The signatures, the signatures! Damn my shortsightedness.* If they marched off to another bank, the forgery would be exposed at some point during the examination of the paperwork. He couldn't let that happen.

"What does Mary think about all this?"

"I haven't talked it over with her yet. Wanted to see what you thought first."

With lightning alertness, J.C. saw a way out and probed for more information.

"Thought you two talked everything over."

"We do." Then, reluctantly, Iron told him how much it would upset Mary to sell their land to Connie and Mike without dealing in the other two kids.

"So don't tell her."

Iron looked at him suspiciously. "I'm just putting it off a bit, not trying to hide it from her. Besides, there'll be papers for her to sign."

"That's not necessary," J.C. said quickly. "Not necessary at all in this case. Kind of embarrassing, but we forgot to have her sign your note here at the bank. It's no wonder, as much paperwork as we deal with. Tell you what, Iron. Let me see what I can do. Just don't go anyplace else shopping for money, and don't say anything to anyone, including Mary, for a while yet."

Until I have your will, thought J.C. *Until Mary's signature is on every-thing it's supposed to be, and I pull those* UCC *statements out of the court-house.*

Iron looked doubtful.

"It's no big deal," J.C. said. "We may have some new investors coming in, and I don't want to have to redo a bunch of forms. As I've told you before, when it comes to your family and this bank, there's a few complications."

"There's another family complication you might want to know about, J.C." Iron pulled his chair closer to the banker's desk. "Elizabeth and Bob are getting a divorce."

"I'm sorry to hear that."

"I'm not," Iron said. "I never liked him."

J.C. smiled. "He never was really good enough for our girl, was he?" Elizabeth had filled in at the bank several summers while the regular tellers rotated vacations. J.C. had followed her accomplishments through the years as proudly as though she were his own daughter.

"Is she going to be all right?" J.C. asked.

"Sure. You know Elizabeth. She's as tough as her mother. She's home now, going to work in Manhattan starting next week."

"Good. She isn't crazy enough to be happy in California. She belongs right here in Kansas."

Iron chuckled and reached for his hat. "Well, I guess I've given you plenty to think about for one day."

"You have at that."

Iron rose to leave and extended his hand. The banker stood and shook it then squeezed his old friend's shoulder in a rare display of affection.

"We've seen some times, we two, haven't we, Iron? Check with me again next week."

"Will do. You know how much I appreciate it."

"Another thing, if you would pass the word along to other farmers that you're not giving us a hard time over the will, it would help us out.".

Iron whirled around. "It's all off. Forget it. It will be a cold day in hell before I sign any papers leaving one cent to anyone until I'm good and ready. Which is probably never."

J.C.'s bones turned to water. He'd thought Iron understood the urgency. "And may I ask why, you proud bastard?"

"No," Iron said coldly, "you may not. It's none of your goddamn business."

~~~~~~~~~~

J.C. buzzed Cynthia and asked her to hold all calls. He buried his face in his hands.

How did I manage to get myself into such a grade A mess? How could Iron have reneged on making a will? He knew the man all too well to hope he would change his mind.

Exhausted, he started to look at alternatives. If he could get Connie and Mike financed separately, paying down Iron's land note, that would sit very well indeed with the bank examiners even if it wouldn't reduce the Barretts' operating loan.

But it couldn't be through this bank. Worse, he couldn't let them go to another bank and risk having someone else look over all the signed papers.

He slammed his fist into his palm. Damn his stupidity! The ucc statement at the courthouse was now forged with Mary's signature, but the copy at the bank and in the Barretts' personal safe was unsigned. If he had left both documents untouched, he would be home free.

That night, he slept fitfully, jerking awake, his pajamas soaked with sweat, hoping a simple solution would occur to him. By dawn he knew sleeping on his problem a hundred nights wouldn't help. There wasn't any good way out of this. With a deepening sense of gloom, he knew there was only one alternative left.

~~~~~~~~~~

The next morning, J.C. drummed his pencil on the desk and looked at the row of ancestors hanging on the wall. His stomach roiled. But he called his broker and gave him an order to sell his holdings of gold.

"I know the market is down. Just do it." He knew when he was making a dumb move without some smart ass on Wall Street pointing it out to him. His investments in gold were the only assets he owned besides stock in the bank. He asked that the proceeds be sent to his account at a New York bank. Then he called Charlie Accor and asked him to draw up certain papers. His own personal money once again was backing a Barrett bailout.

Two days later, J.C. phoned Connie and asked her and Mike to come to his office with Iron the following Monday.

Elizabeth was sitting in Connie's kitchen when the call came.

Connie clapped her hands together and gave a little spin the moment she hung up the phone. Her eyes sparkled.

"What on earth?" Elizabeth asked, smiling at Connie. "Did you win the Publishers Clearing House Sweepstakes? Can we look forward to a visit from Ed McMahon?"

"Better than that," Connie said, "oh much, much better than that."

"Well, what then?"

"I'm not supposed to tell anyone. Not even Mom. But that was J.C. Espy. Dad is selling us his and Mom's five hundred acres. Everything went through. We're closing the deal next week."

"Honey, he can't do that," Elizabeth said gently. "Not tell, I mean. Mom has to know. There's things to sign. Stuff like that."

"No there's not." Connie's cheeks flamed. "J.C. said so, and Dad said so. In this case it's not necessary. Mom's name isn't on the main land note."

"How do you suppose that happened?"

"I don't know."

"It sounds incredible," Elizabeth said, "but I don't doubt it for a minute. I remember how haphazard some of the processes were the summers I worked there."

Not wanting to deny her little sister this moment of pure joy, she decided to call J.C. and see what was going on before she said another negative word. "I've never known Dad not to tell Mom everything."

"He says he just can't this time. Mom would tell Dennis. You know she would. She'd feel like she *should*, and we just can't risk it right now. You know how Dennis is. He'd think of some way to blow the deal."

"So that's it. The light is beginning to dawn on our father after all."

"Please don't say anything to Mom. Please. It's a matter of timing. We just want to delay it a while. With all the funny things going on with

Grandma right now, it's hard telling what Dennis would do to block the sale."

"He would certainly do *something*," Elizabeth said thoughtfully. "I'm surprised Dad is this cagey. It's not his usual way of operating."

"Well, our precious brother's little outburst over the will was an eye-opener to Dad in more ways than one. Mom's always seen Dennis as he really is, but she thinks it's her fault. Dad knows deep inside that Dennis is a rotter but sticks up for him anyway."

"You've convinced me," Elizabeth said. "And you *are* right. All of you." There was no need for her to call J.C. Not only could she follow these arguments, she agreed with the decision.

Normally she was all too aware of the complications of family secrets. However, she had to give her father credit that if ever secrets were called for now was the time. Her thoughts traveled right around the same circle her father's had followed.

Connie and Mike would move away if Iron didn't sell them the land, Mary would insist on total openness if she knew about the sale. All hell would break loose when the news reached Dennis, and he would think of some way to stop the sale—probably by involving Grandma Alma.

"You can count on me, honey." She rose and quickly moved over to Connie and hugged her. "And I'm just happy you're getting something that means so much to you both. Even if I don't understand why anyone would want to live on a farm."

11

Why was his bank in trouble? Why did he keep waking from a dead sleep drenched in sweat and with an ache in his guts, doubled with pain? Why did he stare out the window, night after night, at a cold, bloodless moon filled with a sense of dread so heavy that it turned his skin to gray clay?

Because people weren't paying back their sons-a-bitching loans. That's why.

J.C. pressed the intercom button to his son's office. Angrily, he buzzed over and over again. Hard telling where Forrest was today.

Little prairie fires kept springing up. Just when he had one set of notes under control—after he had coaxed, pleaded, threatened, and bullied some whining farmer into shoring up his notes to keep the FDIC happy, giving him a cash flow, listing some more collateral, or selling off some assets and reducing his indebtedness—then another hot little pile of notes caught fire. Another farmer in trouble. There were only so many hours in the day. So many people he could advise and coax.

At first he had sent Forrest out to personally inspect some of the collateral listed on the note. "See if the cattle are there, son. Walk around. Count 'em. Make sure they're worth what they're listed for on the note."

It quickly became apparent that discerning whether a critter was dead or alive was the extent of Forrest's abilities. He wasn't much better with machinery.

All Forrest had to do was get the collateral *listed* on the note so the FDIC would know the loan was well secured. But could Forrest do such a simple little thing? No, by God. His son could not. By the time Forrest Alexander Espy finished antagonizing the farmer, J.C. was lucky if the family was still a depositor.

The intercom buzzed.

"Forrest is on his way back, J.C."

His son approached with the grace of a fencer. It was one of God's great mysteries to J.C. how such an ugly man as himself, and Madeline—who had been no prize in the looks department either—had produced this handsome son.

Forrest had light blue eyes and the wonderfully thick Espy hair. His heavy black brows gave him a brooding, mysterious look. The pleated trousers he wore today were made from a nubby silk blend fabric. His leather aviator's jacket had come from a men's specialty shop in Dallas.

J.C. knew that Forrest Alexander Espy, the son who would be taking his place someday, would rather spend his time determining which briefcase had the highest status than figuring out how to afford the briefcase.

He lay awake at night worrying about Forrest, who was now thirty-seven years old. Old enough to start putting in a decent day's work.

"Morning, Dad."

"Where've you been, son?"

"Down in Texas. Checking out a deal everyone is cleaning up on in that state."

J.C. nodded, sensing that once again Forrest was about to present him with some fabulous opportunity. In oil. In real estate. If there was some squirrelly venture that needed financing, Forrest was the man to see.

"It's just right for Kansas. I recommend we be the first bank out here to invest in private prison systems."

"Folks out here don't want prison systems. Or nuclear waste dumps. Or missiles."

"It doesn't matter what they want," Forrest said. "Little towns are dying. We've got to take on a few problems of society out here. It's our duty."

J.C. snorted his contempt, recognizing canned altruism. Duty indeed! When did Forrest ever care about duty?

"It won't work. Folks here don't like smart-ass outsiders who want to change small towns. They like living in small towns because they *are* small towns."

"Well, you can't just freeze a place like a modern-day Brigadoon." Forrest's eyes swept over the portraits of Espys lining the walls.

"I know that. God, don't I know."

Forrest occasionally showed flashes of common sense that gladdened J.C.'s heart. Made him hope he was judging the boy too severely. Trying to put too old a head on his son's body.

"So why not try to make them see how a prison could help the town grow?" Forrest persisted. "It would furnish jobs. Everything from construction to custodial work. We could talk to groups, women's clubs, the Lions. Start with letters to the editor. That kind of thing."

"Because the good citizens of this town, especially the women, don't want it." J.C.'s voice rose. "And most important of all, *I* don't want a prison out here. I don't want dealers and addicts hanging around this town. Or prostitutes or criminals or welfare cases, corrupting our youth and making people afraid to leave their doors unlocked."

Forrest scowled.

"And I don't want to argue." J.C.'s voice softened. "I want to talk about those fancy investors you've been boosting. I've decided it's high time this bank branched out a little."

"High time is an understatement." His son beamed.

J.C. allowed himself a small smile. Last year, Forrest had found people—not farmers—who wanted to invest money in his bank. New capital. New blood. Not just new depositors. Honest-to-god investors. Before he sold his gold, J.C. had always refused them. He didn't want outsiders owning stock in the bank. Other than shares owned by bank employees through the years, mainly his loan officers, the stock had always been kept in the family.

In the past there had been many chances to bring in new money. First Bank of Gateway had always been one of the best agricultural banks in the state. Now, however, just when he needed them badly, investors were edgy about banks tied to one industry.

It was also time to start cutting his son a little slack. Time to diversify. "You've checked everything out, Forrest? Everything? Like I've taught you? These guys are sound? Honest? They won't want to tell us how to run things, will they? I don't want some fancy city slicker in here telling me what to do."

Forrest laughed. "The B. F. Laden company represents a group of small investors who want to buy into the First Bank of Gateway. They're as good as gold, and they have no desire to meddle. It will be a new infusion of capital, without complications."

"Take care of it then. Make all the arrangements," J.C. said. "I've taught you how. Just do it." He was profoundly relieved that new money would be coming into the bank. A load had been lifted from him and shifted onto his son.

J.C. Espy locked the door to the bank. His hands shook as he put the ring of keys in his pocket. The money Forrest had brought in had not been enough to compensate for a number of notes becoming substandard. A pen of cattle sold at a loss. A bin of wheat dumped on the market at the wrong time.

Next year.

He was refinancing the remaining balance on far too many notes—including the interest—until next year.

J.C. gazed at all the people his bank employed as he walked toward the conference room. Tellers and bookkeepers and loan officers and secretaries and a receptionist and maintenance people. So many jobs depended on his judgment. So many families. He thought of all the customers he served.

The three other men besides himself and Forrest who had the power to make loans—Otto Jones, Patrick Wein, and Gene Ramouth—were already seated. He took his place at the head of the table and checked his watch. Forrest was late as usual.

Sober-faced bank examiners were clustered around the conference table. It was a full examination this time. They had come blowing in like a ground blizzard, unannounced, as was their custom. Having worked their way through his pile of loans, they were ready to begin the exit review. They were here for the second time this year, which meant the First Bank of Gateway had attracted a lot of unhealthy attention.

He knew the "watch list" was increasing. These were loans the examiners had marked as being substandard or doubtful because they were worried about the customers' cash flow. Obvious bad loans that did not list enough collateral or loans that were delinquent or nonperforming would be charged against the bank's capital as bad debts.

Lawrence Collier, the examiner in charge, cleared his throat. He was a beefy, dark-haired man whose clothes were too tight. His suit coat strained across his arms, and his tie constricted his breath. "We're reclassifying some of your notes from substandard to doubtful, Mr. Espy. Starting with Franklin Barrett."

"He can buy and sell us both out and never miss the cash," J.C. protested hotly. "If he's not good for the money, I don't know what this country is coming to."

"We don't *care* what he's worth," Collier said. "We don't want you loaning the man a hundred dollars to buy a bird dog if you can't see—on paper—how he's going to pay back his loan. Cash flow in black and white."

"His position has improved since the last time you were here. He's sold off some of his land," said J.C., sweating now, not bothering to mention that the sale was to Barrett's own son-in-law. "Sold off a bunch, in fact, and the money was applied against his land note."

It had never occurred to J.C. that the sale wouldn't be enough to keep the bank examiners from poking around in Iron's business. He'd thought he had solved that problem.

"Great," Collier said. "But we still don't want any new loans made to this man. Maybe we can take him off the watch list the next time around, but not now."

Heads swiveled toward the door when Forrest walked in. He greeted each man present with a firm, confident handshake, and a clap on the shoulder when he knew a man's name. Ones who had been there before.

Forrest looked capable of presiding over a board meeting at Chase Manhattan. He saw the flicker of approval in the examiners' eyes as they took in the impeccably tailored sharkskin suit, the thick Espy hair, the firm, full jaw. He looked like a man on his way up.

"Gentlemen, my son has found new investors," J.C. announced proudly. Plus, his son was making big new loans to farmers outside the county. Bringing fresh blood into the bank.

"Well, that's just great," Collier said. "Your bank could use a little good news. Not that you don't need to do something about this." He raised his eyebrows at the stack of notes they had flagged.

"As to your loans, Forrest. We're glad to see the bank loaning to someone besides farmers, but we have a few questions about a couple of loans to corporations."

J.C.'s insides turned sodden, and he fought the gorge rising from his stomach. For an instant the room whirled, and he couldn't hear Collier's words.

Forrest had brought in new investors, but J.C. wasn't aware of any loans the bank had made to corporations.

"This company you've loaned $80,000 to—Alternate Energy, Inc.—where's the paperwork on them? Their cash flows? Income statements? Balance sheets? We couldn't find their papers."

"No problem," said Forrest easily. "It's on the way. I had to mail the note back for additional signatures."

J.C. looked across the table at Forrest but kept his face still. An $80,000 loan that he didn't know about? How could that be possible? But he recognized the name. Alternate Energy, Inc. was one of their new investors. His heart beat heavily like an old engine toiling to haul a load it could no longer carry.

Forrest deftly defended all of his notes just as he had been taught. All of J.C.'s officers had been instructed years ago to speak up at these meetings. "Show a little spirit, by God. Examiners have been known to change their minds and upgrade some notes, if there's good, sound reasons in back of the lending."

At the end of the meeting, some of the agricultural notes were charged off as bad debts despite his arguments. And now there was a new stack of doubtful notes accompanied by dire warnings that if "something isn't *done* about these by the next time we come around, they, too, will be charged off."

"Something done" meant he had to find a way to bully a farmer into paying back some money.

The examiners completed the exit review, and J.C. confronted his son. "Forrest, do you have something to tell me?"

His words roared through the bank, bouncing off the marble and brass and vinyl and iron and coins. Like a wounded, skinny, mangy, hairless old lion rallying strength for the last hunt, he paced back and forth. "What have you done, Forrest? Done to us all?"

"Nothing, Dad. Nothing that can hurt us. I swear it. The papers will be here in a couple of days. We'll talk then. Now's not the time." He started to leave.

J.C. shook with fury.

"We'll talk now, goddamn it. Right now. Are there any other loans you've made that I don't know about?"

Forrest hesitated for an instant then kept on walking right out the front door.

J.C. started his own review of the notes. His hands trembled as he picked each paper off the pile and studied it. Damn the computers. He couldn't tell a thing that was going on anymore. Not a thing. But he was going to find out. Fast. Whether Forrest was his only begotten son or not, he had to know what was going on.

His jaw tightened as he fumbled through his private address book. He quickly located a company in Denver specializing in forensic financial investigations. A bank examination was not an audit. They were entirely different processes. He engaged the firm to audit his own bank.

He tried to calm down. Until the investigators completed their work, he had to tend to business. Protect his customers. Protect his stockholders.

Sullenly J.C. recalled the scolding by the bank examiners—he had heard it a thousand times—about how his bank needed to make loans to people other than farmers. Well, by God, he didn't much like anyone who wasn't a farmer. He just didn't trust them.

Collateral doesn't mean near as much as character, he thought savagely. He had tried to tell the bank examiners that. There were notes he knew the debtors would move heaven and earth to pay off. They would do anything. Dig ditches, scrub floors. Whatever it took to honor their word.

"No more loans to Barrett," Collier had said. "Not a dime."

Stupid son-of-a-bitch. If any man was good for the money, it was Iron Barrett. He had talked until he was blue in the face, and it hadn't done one bit of good. The feds meant it. Only now, this time around, it was his own personal money in back of Iron. Not just the bank's assets.

When he had sold his gold six months ago to bail Barrett out, he had assumed there wouldn't be any problem with the family paying him back. Now he had just been given orders not to loan another cent to the man.

That included operating money. J.C. knew all too well what could happen when he was forced to cut off a farmer's credit line.

Suddenly chilled, he knew he had to make Iron understand the importance of getting along with the bank examiners. Barrett had to follow all the rules. Be nice. Toady up a bit.

J.C. set his mouth in a grim line, steeling himself for the job ahead. Remembering the stubborn bastard's refusal to cooperate in making a simple little will, which was precious little to ask of a man. It was nothing, nothing in comparison to things Iron would be asked to do in the future.

He would get a hold of Iron first thing in the morning and let him know he had been cut off.

12

Mary pulled up to the front door of Dennis's farmstead. "I hope Lisette is ready," she said, glancing at Connie.

It was a bright Saturday in April, and they were going to county 4-H Days. The twins were wedged in the back seat among boxes of cooking supplies.

Susan would be giving her first demonstration today. The child's mouth moved silently, rehearsing her talk. Her pigtails were anchored with plaid ribbons matching the bright tartan dress. She had polished her brown oxfords until they gleamed.

Sabrina waved from the doorway, and Benjamin's face appeared in an upstairs window. Lisette stepped out on the porch. She wore a bulky grape-colored sweater over a tweed A-line skirt and textured tights with granny shoes. Her long black braid was secured with a leather fastener. Lisette had carved out a niche as one of the best photography and crafts leaders the county had ever had. At least one of her students won a blue ribbon every year at the state fair.

Mary felt a surge of thanksgiving as she helped Sabrina and Benjamin load supplies. Her prayers had been answered. Everyone was speaking again. Lisette had never been happier. Connie was exuberant, which Mary attributed to Iron's giving Mike more recognition for his ideas. Elizabeth's new job in Manhattan appeared to be going well. She phoned home as regularly now as she had before the Will Fight.

J.C. Espy had not mentioned the will again after Iron had told him how it was going to be. The whole grim business of the bank meddling in their affairs was behind them.

Iron would come later with the horse trailer loaded with Benjamin's steer. The boy was going to give a demonstration on "The Best and the

Brightest; Grooming an Animal for Show." He was also scheduled for a vocal solo. A neighbor would bring Alma Barrett to hear Susan's talk.

Iron and Mary were the community leaders of the Gateway Go-Getters, one of eight 4-H clubs in the county. They were responsible for organizing and overseeing the vast network of projects, events, and records their club would undertake. As Mary turned onto the highway, she recalled past 4-H Days, when she'd hovered over her kids. Now she was anxious for her grandchildren.

In the rearview mirror Mary saw the twins making faces and smiled. In three more years they would start choosing projects, and she and Iron would probably still be leading the club, as they had for the past six years.

The Barretts pulled up to the high school and began to carry their boxes and equipment into the Gateway Go-Getters' home room. Mary was bombarded with questions at once. There were small groups striving to harmonize on songs, and children from seven to nineteen years of age rehearsed their talks.

Nervous parents and children milled around like cattle, and even battle-hardened junior leaders, charged with calming everyone down, were affected by the younger children's nerves.

"Mrs. Barrett." Mary turned to the harried county extension agent, who had entered their room. "Is Iron here yet? There's a call for him."

"Not yet," she said. She glanced at her watch. "He should be here in another half hour though." Puzzled, she frowned as the man walked off, then she turned back to the children.

"Do you have everything, Susan?"

Susan nodded. She had checked her supplies. She would give a senior demonstration, do a project talk, play a piano solo, and give a dramatic recitation. She was also secretary of the Gateway Go-Getters and would have the minutes to construct after the model meeting.

Mary checked the schedules and located each room, quickly taking note of children needing extra help and encouragement. At ten o'clock, the Barretts filed into the room designated for junior demonstrations. Mike and Dennis were already there. Susan went to her father at once. Her lips quivered and her freckles were stark on her white face. Mike knelt beside her and whispered in her ear.

Iron walked in and Susan's face lit up.

Connie tied a snow-white bibbed apron over her daughter's dress. Susan carried her box of equipment to the front of the room and placed her posters on the easel. When the judges gave her the nod, she began.

"I'm Susan Hewlett," she said, smiling nervously, "from the Gateway Go-Getters. And I will show you how to . . . Crack it Like an Eggspert." She pointed to a poster of a chick peeking out of a shell as she spoke.

Mary tensed as she repeated all the words in her mind. The next seven minutes would culminate six weeks of hard work. Susan had stenciled all her posters herself and made them listen endlessly to her polished talk. Susan beamed at the array of relatives cheering her on.

"Do you know how important it is to separate an egg correctly?" she asked, picking up the egg.

She whacked the center of the shell firmly, too firmly, against the rim of the bowl, breaking the yolk. A tinge of yellow began to drip down the side. Susan's eyes widened with despair.

"Recover," Mary coached silently. "Pull yourself together, honey."

For a moment, Susan stood still, then her pigtails seemed to crackle with electricity and she looked squarely at the judges. "You're not supposed to crack it this hard," she said calmly. "I've broken the yolk. Let me show you the next steps anyway. You insert your thumbs in the cracks and then rock the yolk back and forth from shell to shell, letting the whites slip into the bowl."

When she finished, she laid the shell aside on a paper towel, wiped her hands on the moist washcloth she had brought in a plastic bag, picked up her pointer, and turned once again to the posters to give her summary.

"Are there any questions?" she asked, looking brightly around the room.

The first judge splayed her fingers across her twitching mouth to suppress a smile and looked up at the girl. "What do you do with the old yolks?"

"They're good in sponge cakes, and also some custard recipes call for yolks only."

"If there are no further questions, this concludes my demonstration," Susan said quickly. The whole Barrett family as well as the judges applauded vigorously.

She gathered up her equipment and put it inside the box, and all the Barretts filed out of the room. When they were out in the hallway, they all clustered around Susan, who burst into tears.

Mary immediately comforted her. "You did a *good* job, honey. The most important thing—*always*—is to go on. Recover! And that's what you did." Susan's face brightened as the family volunteered examples of their own work gone wrong.

"I remember what Mom used to tell us," Connie said to her daughter. "It's not the purple ribbons that make you a winner. It's the attitude you allow yourself to take toward the whites."

Susan gasped. Connie bit her lip.

"I don't mean that you're going to get a white, honey," she said, giving her daughter's shoulder a quick squeeze. "I just mean don't let your mistakes get you down."

"I cannot believe that it's a good idea to judge little kids," Lisette said darkly. "I think it's barbaric."

"We'd better get back to our home room," Mary said. "Several of the kids skipped breakfast today, and the Staples kids' posters are a mess. Did you bring the shoeshine kit and the magic markers?"

Iron nodded.

"Fine. Why don't you run to Safeway before Benjy's talk and buy some milk. We need to get some protein down them before they start on the doughnuts, or they won't last the day."

"Okay." Iron started a list. "I'll call Kentucky Fried Chicken right away and order several buckets for lunch."

Mary nodded. There were always children short of money. It was a tradition for her and Iron to pay for the chicken so no one would be put on the spot.

"Get plenty of potato salad to go with it."

"Iron, got a minute?"

They both turned at once and looked at J.C. Espy, whose face was as gray as the paper on Mary's clipboard.

"Sorry to disturb your day, Mary," he said, "but I need Iron to come down to the bank for about an hour."

She looked at J.C. incredulously. The hair prickled on the back of her neck, and she saw the quick alarm in Iron's eyes.

"Sorry," the banker said. "I know this is a big event for your family."

Her face twisted with apprehension as she watched Iron follow J.C. out the door. Then she hurried after Sabrina.

Sabrina would be playing the *Deuxieme Arabesque* by Debussy. Mary worried that the fragile technicality of the piece might be over the judges' heads and the top ribbon would go to the one playing the most dramatic selection. She was always on edge when Sabrina was involved. Lisette was tough. A street fighter. But Sabrina was as fragile as a butterfly.

Distracted, she listened to Sabrina's flawless rendition of the piece. She couldn't imagine what would be so important that J.C. would want to interrupt Iron during 4-h Days. When her granddaughter finished, Mary clapped mechanically and glanced at her watch.

When they returned to the home room, it was eleven o'clock and Iron still wasn't back. When noon came, she handed Connie the keys to the station wagon and asked her to pick up the chicken.

After lunch, all thirty members assembled in their home room and staged little trial runs of different aspects of the model meeting. Mary paced the floor. Iron wasn't back. It had been three hours since he left, not the one hour J.C. had promised.

The model meeting—a prototype of a perfect monthly 4-h meeting— was enough to make most community leaders tear their hair out. It took considerable bullying of both the members and their parents to pull it off.

What was keeping Iron? He absolutely had to be back in time for the model meeting. Perfect attendance would give them extra points. She checked the group's grooming. Then they all trooped into the gymnasium for the competition.

"The Gateway Go-Getters," announced the junior leader.

The members pretended to be chatting in little groups, then Betty McMann, who was president of the club, whacked her gavel, calling the meeting to order. Mary was glad Betty didn't rattle easily as Iron had not made it back. She took her chair and the officers filed up to the table at the front of the room.

Suddenly the doors in the back flew open, and Iron came in, his face taut and drawn.

"Please excuse the interruption, Madam President," he said, standing formally for a moment, before he sat down in the remaining vacant chair across the aisle from Mary.

"The model meeting of the Gateway Go-Getters will now come to order," Betty McMann said happily, after nodding to Iron. "Please rise and say the flag salute and the 4-H pledge."

Shocked at the look in Iron's eyes, Mary could not focus on the meeting.

"Roll call will be answered by giving a fact about Kansas," announced Sabrina.

"Kansas had the third highest literacy rate in the nation before the 1900s," Iron said, standing when his granddaughter called his name.

"Mrs. Barrett. Mrs. Barrett?"

Mary rose to her feet. She couldn't take her eyes off Iron's face. It was colorless under the hot fluorescent lights.

"Our state bird is the meadowlark," she said then realized she'd used little Herbie Mayhew's fact. Flustered, she turned to Herbie, who sulled up at once.

Aside from that snafu, the program went flawlessly. Mary knew there was not another club that came close to their model meetings. The Gateway Go-Getters would get to take this presentation to the regional competition in another month. Exhausted, she looked around at the thirty kids she needed to round up again. Most of whom would have forgotten their lines.

They left the room, and she quickly went to Iron, mechanically praising the children as she pushed through the group. "What's wrong?" she asked. "What happened? You look terrible."

He walked down to the end of the hall, where they would have privacy. "J.C. said the bank can't loan me any more money. They are cutting off my whole line of credit. Including operating money."

Stunned, she reached for his arm. "What in God's green earth has gone wrong?"

"I don't know, Mary. He couldn't say. Or wouldn't say. I've never seen J.C. this bad. Jumpy. Wouldn't talk. If he won't talk to me, you can bet he's not talking to anyone."

"What are we going to do?"

"Something is going on that I don't understand. When you stop to think of the business we've given that bank for twenty-five years and never *once* missed a payment. Not once. I can't imagine what has come over him."

"It could be worse," she said quickly. "We've already borrowed what we need for this year, haven't we?"

" Not nearly enough. If I'd have known he was going to shut me off I'd have gotten all the money I needed in January. But how was I to know? There's no use borrowing money until you need it."

"You don't suppose the bank is in trouble?"

"Don't see how it could be. Old J.C. has the first nickel he ever inherited."

"Well, something has to be wrong, Iron. He wouldn't just stop loaning money to people like us without some reason."

"I know we've had our differences, but J.C. and I have always been just like that." He held up two fingers side by side. Iron's voice thickened. Hurt to the core.

"There's other banks," Mary said.

"And I'm going to start shopping for one. The First Bank of Gateway isn't the only place in the world to get a loan."

"I still can't believe it."

"It's not just the money, Mary. It's the principle of the thing. J.C. has always been my friend, not just my banker, and we've always had an understanding."

Lisette poked her head around the corner. "Results are in."

They followed her into the auditorium.

Susan received a blue ribbon from the kindly judges. They had noted her excellent handling of her mistake on the evaluation sheet as well as her immaculate posters. Sabrina took the reserve grand champion ribbon in the piano division. And the Gateway Go-Getters received the purple grand champion ribbon for the model meeting and would go on to the district competition next month. The other ribbons blurred in Mary's mind.

On the way home, as the family pored over the evaluation sheets, Mary read the comments on the model meeting.

"The community leaders were much too tense," one judge had written. "4-Hers should be having *fun*, and community leaders should be setting the tone for these meetings."

Mary splayed her fingers across her face and laughed bitterly.

Iron was moody throughout the weekend. Sunday evening he came into the kitchen while she was doing dishes. "We need to talk when you have a minute."

She wiped her hands and sat down at the table. "Now's as good a time as any."

"Mary, I've decided not to find another bank. The only thing that can be worse than one banker would be two of the bastards."

"Can we get along without borrowing more?"

"Yes. It won't be easy, but I've done some figuring. There's enough stuff I can sell around this place to pay off the operating loan. That isn't due until December. As long as we keep up our payments on the interest and principal, there's no way in the world this bank can get me in trouble."

"Can we pay back this year's operating money and clear enough to handle next year's expenses too? That's what you're really wanting to do, isn't it?"

He was silent for a moment before he replied.

"With luck. It's going to take a lot of luck, and it'll mean having to screw down our expenses pretty tight until we get over the hump."

"I don't mind. You think I'll mind? Lord, it'll be like old times again. They were *fun*, Iron. In their own way."

"I remember. Yes, they were fun and it'll be like old times."

"Remember when we were first married and paid cash for everything? You know what I'd like the most?" Mary said. "Never having to think about the bank or bankers ever again."

13

"Forrest. Do you have any idea what you've done to us all? This bank? This community? All the people who work here?" J.C.'s voice was thick with grief.

Forrest's eyes were inscrutable as J.C. flipped through the auditor's report. "I can explain, Dad."

"No need. No need. It's all there in black and white, Forrest. All of our new investors, every single one of them, every penny, every blessed penny they're putting into this bank has come from you kiting their loans. If they asked to borrow $70,000, you asked them to take $100,000 and then invest the extra $30,000 in our bank. What in the goddamned gold-plated hell did you see as the end to all this?"

"It would have worked out, I'm telling you. In time. These men are in real estate construction. They would have been able to pay the money back and the extra they borrowed from the money they received from . . ."

"Shut up, Forrest. Do you think I'm a fool? Jesus H. Christ, what have you brought on us all?"

"Given time . . ."

"Time? We need capital, not time. Well, I found a new investor." He inspected Forrest's face, wanting to see something there besides greed. Wanting to see something besides pure self-interest.

"And it's a done deal, Forrest. There's not a damn thing you can do about it." J.C. glanced at the stern portraits of his ancestors. Their rock-hard chins. Their steely eyes. "I called my lawyers last week and had them break the Espy trust. Your two-million-dollar inheritance was pumped back into the bank at closing time yesterday. You are now the major stockholder in the First Bank of Gateway."

"You can't do that." A muscle in Forrest's jaw leaped. His voice rose. "You can't do that."

Once money was put into a bank's capital accounts, the government made it nearly impossible to get it back out without inviting the kind of investigation neither of them wanted.

"The hell I can't," J.C. said. "I could and I did. Shows what you think of this place deep down inside, doesn't it? Think you'll ever see the money again, Forrest? What's your gut feeling? Are you going to come out of this a pauper or a rich man?"

"You had no right, no right to take my money. To rob my trust."

"Wrong. It's my trust. Until I die, I'm the sole and only trustee of the Espy trust. And in my impeccable business judgment, this bank is a sound and wonderful place to put your money." He oiled his words, wanting them to cling. "Of course, I could be wrong. I'm taking *your* word for that. You're the one who keeps carrying on about the soundness of the new investors. My own gut feeling is that we're on pretty shaky ground, Forrest. In *my* judgment, there's going to be hell to pay when the examiners come around."

"God damn you. You vicious old man."

His son. His son.

His bank. His bank.

Hearing Forrest's curse, J.C.'s soul turtled up into his old banker's shell, laid down layer upon layer by generations of Espys. Proud and honorable men who had sired proud and honorable sons.

"And in *my* judgment, Forrest, this bank needed a new infusion of capital. For real this time. Only that's not just my opinion. That's a fact. I have an audit here to prove it. We just got that new infusion of capital. Now get out of my sight. You sicken me."

He turned away and walked slowly back to his office.

He never spoke to his son again.

J.C. Espy was looking out the window that Thursday, August 15, 1985, when the shiny black cars rolled into Gateway City. His mind numbed up and blanked out the metallic gleam. For an instant, he refused to see them again.

He closed his eyes and splayed his fingers across his face. Something in him split as though lightning grounded him to his chair. His fear smelled and tasted of sulfur. For a moment he was wild to find some other explanation for the shiny black cars. A funeral perhaps. But he knew, he knew what they were at once. The shiny black cars were coming for him.

They always came after a bank on a Thursday.

Then the air was filled with the sound of sirens, and there were flashing red lights.

His son. His son.

His bank. His bank.

Only in cases of suspected fraud did they come this suddenly. Normally the bank's owner knew several days in advance. He closed his eyes again.

J.C. was not a crook, and he should have had the customary courtesy warning. He should have had time to urge depositors with accounts over $100,000 to move the uninsured excess to another bank. He should have had time for a number of things. Would have had, if it weren't for Forrest.

"Dear God," he prayed as he laid his pen carefully on his desk and rose unsteadily to his feet. "Dear God, I've never asked you for much. This time, please, if you've got it in you to help a tired old man, please let me face these people with dignity."

The bank closing team came in from a number of surrounding counties, where they had spent the night. Over the past couple of years, the FDIC personnel had learned not to have all their people cluster in one town or one motel the night before. It was too easy for someone to guess their purpose and spread the word. Early warnings brought the risk of having a run on the bank or, where fraud was involved, gave bankers time to sweep the dirt under the rug.

Thirty people stormed the bank with portable computers. Bright young men with three-piece suits and young women with silk ties gathered into prim roses against the collars of their starched white blouses.

It was fifteen minutes until noon.

The team from the FDIC was accompanied by the sheriff, two highway patrolmen, and a locksmith, who immediately headed for the vault to change the combination.

Jay Clinton Espy walked forward to meet the chief liquidation officer. He paused, shuddered, winked back tears as his eyes swept down the heavy gold-framed portraits of his ancestors hanging on the wall. It was coming to an end. He did not need to worry about an heir after all.

"Mr. Espy."

The old man nodded.

"I'm Stanley Morrison, and it is my duty to inform you that, by order of the state bank commissioner, Eugene T. Winthrop Jr., this bank ceases to exist and your charter has been revoked. The Federal Deposit Insurance Corporation has been named as receiver. The First Bank of Gateway has been purchased by Abner Wise. It will reopen Monday morning, under a new charter, as the Agland State Bank."

J.C. felt a rush of blood to his face. His throat tightened.. He could not bring himself to look at his employees. Customers froze in confusion. Awareness came slowly. Hastily depositors pocketed the money they had planned to place in their accounts and stood in unhappy clusters, eyeing the door.

"We are sealing the deposit boxes at once and ask that all the staff turn over their keys."

Espy's hands shook as he unfastened the ring he wore at his waist. He sorted off all the keys involving bank functions. The remainder dangled lightly at his side.

Quickly a young woman walked from one employee to another, collecting keys, which she turned over to Morrison.

"Go change the combination of the post office box," Morrison said to her curtly.

"Some of the staff receive personal mail here," J.C. said.

"They can pick it up Monday, after we've sorted through it," said Morrison. "Until we can inspect the contents, we'll assume everything coming into this bank is the property of the FDIC."

J.C. looked away in despair. He and his bank had been knocked flat like wheat after hail. But if someone had bought the bank then some of the farmers would be protected. Not all, but some.

The bright young men and women whirled like dust devils, touching down long enough to slap stickers on every safety deposit box, all the furniture, everything within the bank. "Property of the FDIC."

During the weekend, the team would work furiously to sort out those depositors who also owed money to the bank.

A phone rang and Cynthia Benton reached for it, but before she could pick up the receiver, Morrison stopped her.

"Let it ring," he said quickly.

"But we're still supposed to be open for business," she stammered stupidly. "I have to answer it."

"Let it ring for now. By the time they call back, you'll have instructions. We need your help and cooperation," Morrison said. "Any of you who wish to stay on through the afternoon, to help us find papers and documents and give general clerical assistance, will be paid an hourly wage by the FDIC."

He turned to Cynthia. "If you want to answer the phone, we'll pay you for it and we'll tell you what you must say."

"I can't think," she said, pressing her palms over her ears. "Of *course* someone has to answer the phone. Of *course* I'll do it."

Morrison handed her a three-by-five card. She read the words, and her face paled. She walked back to her desk. The phone rang again and, in her confusion, she accidentally punched the speaker function, broadcasting the conversation throughout the bank.

"This is the FDIC," she read slowly from the card. "The First Bank of Gateway no longer exists. The bank will open Monday morning, under new ownership, as the Agland State Bank."

"Cynthia? I know that's you. What in the hell is going on? Honey? Cynthia?"

Tears streamed down J.C.'s secretary's face.

"Cynthia?" The voice became more urgent as the woman repeated her name. "Something's wrong, isn't it? Is there a robbery going on?"

Everyone listened in stunned silence, standing like statues.

"Hang up, honey," the caller whispered hoarsely. "I'm going to call the police."

Cynthia slowly replaced the receiver, stood, and fumbled for her purse. She ran across the lobby then stopped at the locked door. Morrison crossed the lobby and opened it. He smiled sadly at the customers, who quickly followed the receptionist.

They've closed the bank. Word would sweep through the community. *They've closed our bank.*

J.C. solemnly looked from one employee's face to the other. *Previous employees*, he thought bitterly. *Previously employed.* He saw their fear turn to anger, as though he had betrayed them. As though he could have given them warning.

Otto Jones did not come out of his office. J.C. could see him through the window. Otto sat unmoving except for the shudder of his shoulders as he sobbed into cupped hands. Every cent the vice president owned was invested in bank stock, which he had planned to sell when he retired. No other savings.

Otto was sixty-one, and the chances of him finding work elsewhere were slim. He could assess the value of an agricultural loan more accurately than any man J.C. knew, but the stigma of being a loan officer in a failed bank would haunt him wherever he applied for work.

Then all the employees began to cluster around J.C. where he stood, in the north corner of the lobby.

"What are we supposed to do?" asked Helen Warsaw. "Are we supposed to come to work Monday morning? I want to know who in the hell decides all this. How can a bank be just fine one day and closed the next?"

"I don't know," mumbled J.C., gobbling for air like a guppy in a bowl gone foul. "I don't *know* what you're supposed to do."

"Why are they treating us like we're thieves, J.C.?" asked Patrick Wein. "Did you do something wrong we don't know about?"

"What am I supposed to do?" Helen persisted, planting herself in front of J.C., legs akimbo, her fists digging into her waist. "I've got kids to feed, and you *know* what the chances are of finding a job in this town. Or any other town in Western Kansas for that matter."

"I'm pregnant," said Lydia Spencer, the newest teller. "What about my health insurance?"

J.C. flinched as he looked at the pretty blond woman.

"I'm still insured for having the baby, aren't I? Isn't there a law about health insurance? I mean they can't just let all of us go. Who will work for the new owners?"

J.C. had no answers. Not for any of their questions.

The FDIC team went to work. They counted money then turned to auditing books. The bank would reopen Monday morning under a new name, under new management, with new people and new ways.

Stanley Morrison came up, cleared his throat, and stood expectantly by the front door, jingling the new keys in his hand.

"Those of you who wish to stay and help us will be paid an hourly wage," he said. "Those of you who plan to leave should go now."

Every single employee filed out, one by one, until J.C. stood alone, looking at the invaders. He raised his eyes to Morrison and gave a slight defeated nod. Then he walked back into his office, put on his hat and his overcoat, and slowly walked toward the front door.

He turned for one last look at his birthright, cobbled together by generations of Espys.

Then the doors to the First Bank of Gateway closed behind him forever.

14

That Saturday the town hall was packed for the FDIC borrowers' meeting. The meeting was open to anyone who wanted to attend and ask questions. In previous closings, folks had often been too dispirited or too mad to show up. This was not the case in Gateway City.

Stanley Morrison rose and addressed the audience. Nervously, he checked the placement of the two policemen, close to the door, whose eyes darted back and forth, looking for troublemakers. Sometimes borrowers' meetings ended in bloodshed. But more often there was just fear-laden craziness. Shouted obscenities, sudden tears.

Seated on the platform beside the FDIC personnel were the new owners. Morrison grimaced as he turned to the lawyer sitting next to him. "Ugly crowd. Better be on your toes."

"Right," Jim Portal said. He was dressed in jeans and a striped T-shirt on the advice of a farm advocacy spokesman, who had cautioned, "Ditch the three-piece suits. Look more like one of the boys."

Morrison's reaction to the clothing suggestion had been realistic. "No one will like the FDIC team no matter what we wear."

Each time the door to the auditorium opened, those assembled swung around to see who had entered. Who else was trapped.

When Iron and Mary Barrett walked through the door, an electrical alertness hummed through the crowd.

"God, I can't believe old Iron is caught in a crack."

"Not hardly," said Owen Worcester, who managed the local co-op. "But I've never known of anything that's ever mattered to this town when Iron Barrett wasn't there putting his two cents in."

Iron wore a leather blazer over his jeans. He didn't remove his Stetson when he came into the room. His dark hair was set off by his white shirt and the turquoise in his bolo tie. Mary wore a lightweight cinnamon-colored linen suit, with an autumn-toned paisley blouse. "Their funeral clothes," a woman whispered to the lady next to her.

Iron nodded stiffly at his friends and neighbors as he and Mary made their way down the row to available seats. His mouth was set in a rigid line, and he stared straight ahead. There were dark smudges under Mary's eyes.

About two minutes before the meeting was due to start, the door opened and in walked Jay Clinton Espy. Majestic in his loneliness, the withered old lion of a man did not look anyone in the eye. His steps faltered briefly before he made his way to a lone seat in a side aisle.

His color was more ghastly than usual, and he looked as though he hadn't slept for a week. He had debated over whether to come, but in the end he could not stay away. He could not let one hundred years of a family bank be wiped out without seeing and hearing and knowing everything about its passage into extinction. It was like viewing a corpse to make the death real.

He was flooded with memories as he surveyed the room.

The old curtains in the auditorium were worn. Funny, he hadn't noticed before. Seemed like just yesterday he had made the loan to the community theater for their purchase. They had promised to pay it back in three seasons, but it hadn't worked out. It had stretched to ten, with apologies all around every year. He had extended it, of course.

He saw family after family he knew far too much about. Much more than any one person had a right to know. It wasn't true that a minister was the first to know about trouble. It was the banker every time. When most of the records were still being kept by hand and he was in the habit of scrutinizing checks, he could tell instantly when a family was heading toward danger.

He knew when a man was having an affair. The pattern of spending changed so conspicuously it was a wonder more wives didn't spot it. He knew by the checks to the liquor store which families were struggling with alcohol. He knew what the wives spent on clothes. He knew about their marital problems by the checks to counseling services. He knew every last detail of their medical expenses. He even knew when the kids and grandkids had been home by the sudden rise in checks to the grocery store.

Most of all, he knew when they were lying about these things when they applied for a loan.

Yonder sat Jim and Louise Carter, their slow-witted son between them. They owed the bank over $10,000 by now, he thought bitterly. He had lent foolishly, out of soft-heartedness, unable to resist Louise's pleading. His fault, that loan. No collateral, of course. A pattern had started years ago, which had crept up about $500 a year from the time Leroy was born. He was twenty-two now.

J.C.'s hands trembled as he thought of all the medical loans he'd had no business making, when times had begun to change and health-care costs had risen out of sight. No health insurance for a number of these families.

When they were young, they thought they'd never get sick. When they were older, companies wouldn't touch them, or they couldn't possibly afford the premiums.

Then when it was too late, they turned to their banker. Bleeding, showing him their wounds, haunting his dreams.

"Hell J.C., you wouldn't turn down a sick man, would you? An old friend?" And he hadn't.

He was tired. So tired he felt as though he could sleep for a year. The FDIC wouldn't give a damn about their health. He shouldn't have.

Suddenly his fatigue turned to rage. *Where were you, any of you, when I was the one in need?* Wrath, hot and molten, coursed through him. *Where were you when I asked for a signature? When I asked you to list your collateral? When I asked you, begged you, pleaded with you to sell down just a little so I could save our bank?*

Piss on you. You can all go right straight to hell and fry throughout eternity.

Stanley Morrison blew air into the mike and tapped it lightly. J.C. held onto his fury and listened.

"Good afternoon," Morrison said pleasantly, "I would like to welcome all the residents of Gateway City on behalf of the FDIC. The purpose of this meeting is to answer any questions you might have about the bank closing and to introduce you to the new owners."

The purpose of this wretched meeting, J.C. thought, *is to try to convince you it's business as usual, and it's not, my friends. Believe me, it's not.*

"First of all, I want you to know how fortunate you are that we were able to find a buyer for your bank. There is a great deal of difference between permanently closing a bank in a community and merely transferring the ownership."

Not so much difference for some of us, thought J.C. *What's the difference between being stabbed or shot? When you're dead, you're dead.*

"On my right is Abner Wise, who has assumed a great deal of risk. He has used $70,000 of personal capital out of his pocket to buy this bank."

J.C.'s tongue was like a wad of cotton in his mouth. For old stockholders to keep a bank, the government would make them come up with enough money to restore *all* the required capital. No mere $70,000 investment would be allowed for them.

I've put in over two million, J.C. thought bleakly. *Trying to save it. I've put everything my family ever owned or earned into this bank, trying to get it back on its feet. I'm as broke as everyone here will be. Most of them. I sold my gold, even mortgaged my house for the sake of a man who wouldn't even do me the courtesy of making out a simple will. I stripped my trust, you uncooperative stupid, sullen motherfuckers.*

Abner Wise started to rise and then, seeing that no one was clapping, he sat back down.

"And to his left is his wife, Rachel," Morrison continued, "who will be taking an active part in the bank."

Unnerved by the coldness with which her husband had been received, she responded with a curt nod. An aging cross between Joan Crawford and Zha Zha Gabor, she wore large jet and rhinestone earrings, and her arms sparkled with bracelets. Her black broadcloth suit, with oversized shoulder pads, sported glittering embellishment on the bodice.

"If you have any questions," Morrison said, "we'd be pleased to take them."

Old Mr. Stillwell rose and removed his seed cap.

"I don't understand what this all means," he said slowly. "Closing a bank."

"To the majority of the people who do business at the bank, it won't mean a thing," Morrison said. "Things will go on just like they were before.

Nothing at all will change for depositors. Social security checks deposited directly will be handled the same way. You can still use your same checkbooks. The interest will remain the same on your CDs."

"I want to know if you've been messing around with my safety deposit box?" a man called out, without bothering to stand.

"Of course not," Morrison said quickly. "You've probably heard that we brought a locksmith, and that's true, but it was just to change the combination to the main vault. We do that everywhere we go. Certainly it does not imply any wrongdoing here in this bank."

"Just what does change then?"

"The new owners will decide which loans they want to keep. We've already made a list of loans at risk before this bank was declared insolvent. Mr. and Mrs. Wise will evaluate all of these loans and notify you if Agland State Bank won't continue to finance you. For some of you, whose loans are undersecured, it will simply mean adding more collateral to your note and proceeding as usual. Nevertheless, Mr. Wise has the right to turn over to us loans they don't want to assume."

Oh God, that I would have had the chance to just pick over the loans and choose the good ones, thought J.C. *Just hand the old loans, the bad loans, the nonperforming loans over to the FDIC.*

"Will the FDIC loan me money for spring planting?"

"I'm afraid not. We are not a lending institution. We are basically an insurance company. Our job is to see that depositors' funds are safe."

"Where are we supposed to go for money if Wise doesn't like the looks of our loans?"

"There are a number of farm advocacy groups who will work with you, help you prepare financial statements," Morrison said smoothly.

But J.C. noticed a twitch in the liquidator's eye. The hard questions were beginning.

"I asked who would loan us money for spring crops," the speaker repeated.

"That's not our problem," Morrison said. "Those of you who have notes the new owners decline will get a notice shortly. If you are in this number, you have two years to get new financing. For those of you who don't get a letter, it means the new bank will keep right on servicing your loan."

"Then those of us who have plenty of land in back of our notes don't have to worry? Those of us who have enough collateral?"

"Actually, no," Morrison replied. "No one should assume anything. It's all up to the new owners."

J.C.'s stomach roiled at the farmer's complacency. He had tried to tell customer after customer that loans were not being made anymore on the value of the land. They were being made on the amount of money that piece of land was going to produce. Cash flow. Pure and simple. That man's note would be thrown out, sure as hell.

1981—the year of the big freeze—was when the slide really began. Deprived of the major source of their income, which had always been wheat in Western Kansas, borrower after borrower had come trickling into the bank, not able to pay off that year's operating loan, let alone the interest—and now needing the money for next year's crop.

So he had rolled the loans over, with the balance of interest and principal due tacked onto the new note. He had no choice. What was he going to do? Sell them out?

Then interest rates went through the roof nationwide. Banks had to pay higher interest on their customers' certificates of deposit, or they would leave. However, when J.C. charged more interest for loans, most farm operations couldn't sustain the increase. Small family farms disappeared and were replaced by highly efficient family corporations.

Penn Central Railroad went under, and farm banks had to pay for it in the form of increased insurance rates paid to the FDIC. This insurance premium rose steadily as bank after bank went belly up, even before the savings and loan debacle.

"What if we can't get new financing?"

J.C. swiveled to look at the speaker. No "if" about it for that man. He couldn't. *At first you'll start selling down*, the banker thought darkly, *that's what you'll do. It'll work for a little while.*

When the interest rates went through the ceiling, farmers started selling their land to reduce the amount of their notes, as it clearly wasn't going to produce enough income to stay on top of their debts. Then there was too much land on the market for the first time in fifty years, and land value went down.

That's when bank examiners first came wheeling in, saying land backing a note wasn't enough collateral. Then farmers had to pay capital gains tax on the money realized on the land they sold to pay back the loan. J.C. remembered it well. Then they had to sell some machinery to pay the capital gains tax on the land they had sold. Then they had to sell something else to pay the tax on money realized from selling the machinery.

Then bankers weren't seen as a stabilizing and heroic part of the community. Bankers were viewed as bad guys out to get farmers. Folks started mumbling at local diners. There were rumors, innuendos of this person or that person in trouble.

And mantras were invoked to ward off danger: "It's their own fault they're losing the farm," people whispered darkly. "If they had managed better. Not lived so high on the hog. Putting on airs."

Self-righteousness became a chant as though it provided protection. "If the damn fool hadn't bought a Japanese car instead of a Ford or that combine or sent their kids out of state to school instead of Kansas State or bought Reeboks instead of Sears on sale or a red velvet chair or the Reader's Digest Christmas album offer or Rhode Island Reds instead of White Plymouth chickens or a new cultivator."

"No wonder. No wonder they lost the farm."

The chanting grew weaker as farm after farm came under the auctioneer's gavel. Farms that were models of efficiency. Farmers who were without blemish.

"Are there more questions?" Morrison asked. "If not, the doors will be open as usual for business Monday morning as the Agland State Bank. Some of you will be notified by the FDIC that they are retaining your loan. Now we have a representative from the Interfaith Rural Life Committee who would like to make an announcement."

"There will be a borrowers' meeting at the grade school next Tuesday," said the young man, "to help you in your dealings with the FDIC. There will be legal counsel available, and we'll go over some steps for negotiating effectively with the new owners."

J.C. smiled grimly. He could count on two hands the number who would actually take advantage of the help offered.

Farmers and alcoholics. Alcoholics and farmers. Neither had any problems. They could handle it all by themselves, thank you very much.

"Now," said Rachel Wise, "we invite you all to come into the lunchroom. We have a little reception set up. We want to meet you. Get to know you better. We have a few souvenirs on hand that you are all welcome to."

J.C. rose slowly, determined to do The Right Thing. He headed for the little meet and greet to set an example for others in the community. He would drink a little cup of coffee and eat a little doughnut and give a little handshake to the new owners, knowing that their chances for success would be enhanced if he implied that all was not so very grim after all. It was all just a formality, this closing of a hundred-year-old bank.

Iron and Mary waited for him at the back of the auditorium. There were bright unshed tears in Mary's eyes. Iron stepped forward and extended his hand and started to speak, but the words died in his throat as J.C. looked at him coldly for a few seconds then walked on past.

People looked away as the old banker walked steadily toward the bright light flooding from the lunchroom. His guts were ready to fall out of his body, but he was determined to put on one last show on behalf of his bank.

Not so hard to put one foot in front of the other. Not so difficult for a proud and honorable man with a long history of doing hard things.

He paused in the doorway, and they were waiting for him. Abner and Rachel Wise and all the cheery staff from the FDIC. Lined up. Waiting to shake his hand. There was a bizarre collection of bank memorabilia accumulated through the years spread out on the table. Mostly leftover favors from old Christmas parties. Balloons and mug cups and trays and pencils and magnetic clips. Anything the new owners wanted to get rid of.

He started through the door, then the blood drained from his face. Propped up against the table were his portraits of John Foster Espy, Frank Leander Espy, and Porter Cleveland Espy.

"Those pictures," he said weakly when he could regain control of his tongue. "They're mine. My ancestors. Those are personal possessions." His stomach roiled with pain.

"We didn't know," said Rachel Wise, "or we would have sent them to you at once. Naturally, I want to have the place redecorated immediately. Anything else of sentimental value?"

"There's an old clock," he said wistfully. "Very old."

"Ah, ah, ah," she chided brightly, shaking her finger in his face. "You sly old dog, you. Sorry. Nice try, but I *do* know an antique when I see one. The clock stays. We get to retain any of the furnishings we care to keep, you know. The clock really is quite wonderful."

He nodded and looked away to stay his tears.

"We'll help put the pictures in your car. Good thing you told me before I stripped them. I would give my eyeteeth for those frames. There's quite a market for frames nowadays, and those are very valuable."

J.C. gave her a terrible look she did not have the sense to notice.

"Anything else? Anything at all? Would you like one of the balloons?"

15

Mary glanced up from the stove. She wished she hadn't pushed on to canning this third batch of tomatoes. Despite the air conditioning, the kitchen was hot from steaming kettles of water. But she'd blanched another sinkful and had to follow through.

Iron came through the back door carrying the mail.

"Sorry, hon. I'm running behind. Dinner's going to be late."

"No problem." He went to the desk at the end of the island and quickly sorted all the junk mail into one pile. Then he pulled his checkbook out of the drawer and began paying bills.

Mary glanced at his taut face, judging his mood. Working rapidly, she plopped each bright red globe into a jar and added boiling water. She eased a sterilized lid over the mouth and then screwed on the metal band with a deft twist of her strong hands.

By the time her tomatoes were sealed in the pressure cooker, she sensed that Iron was finally in the mood to talk, and she leaned back against the sink. "You okay?"

"Yup." He swiveled to face her. "Just can't get J.C. out of my mind. I never thought I'd see the day when he wouldn't speak to me. I still don't understand it. I didn't play any part in bringing him down."

"He's mad at everyone," said Mary. "He didn't speak to anyone else either."

"Do you realize how many little farmers are going to be hurt by this? Been thinking. I want to help everyone in any way we can. I'm not going to lie for anyone, or help them cheat or go against the law, but if *any* of our neighbors come to us in need, at any time, and we can help them out, I'll do it." He tapped a Camel out of the pack.

"About J.C., do you suppose going along with the will thing would have made a difference?"

"I don't think anything we did or didn't do would have made a difference. If he wants to take his troubles out on his friends and carry on like me and a few other farmers making a will or listing collateral or doing any of the damn fool things he dreamed up would have saved his bank, that's his choice." Thoughtfully, he blew a smoke ring.

Mary carried the tomato skins over to the trash can then washed her hands. "Maybe if you went and talked to J.C. and told him about the Will Fight. Maybe if he understood how much *trouble* it was causing in our family."

"No," Iron said. "That's final. Let him come here and talk to me. I don't owe him any explanations. He overstepped. He had no right to ask us to make a will to begin with."

"Lisette still has the flu," Mary said, deciding to switch to a neutral subject. "I told her I'd take Sabrina to Hays to the judging clinic Saturday. I'll grocery shop tomorrow. Anything you want?"

He shook his head. Bills paid, he held a certified letter from the United States government up to the light. He carefully slit the edges of the envelope with his pocketknife.

Mary turned from the sink, stepped over to the cooktop, and gave the gravy one last quick stir.

Iron exploded to his feet and hurled his glass ashtray against the fireplace wall, shattering it into a hundred crystal shards.

Mary froze and stared dumbly at the gravy. Iron's swearing filled the kitchen. His face flushed with fury.

"What? What's happened?" Her fingers touched the throbbing soft part of her throat as though to protect it from attack.

"The new owner of the bank, Abner Wise, has turned all of my loans over to the FDIC."

Her blood pounded against her temples hearing words Iron never used around her. "Don't do things like that. Don't talk like that." She gestured helplessly at the ashtray. "You're scaring me. This has to be a mistake. We're as well off as anyone in this county."

She was frightened by more than his words, by more than the violence of shattered crystal. It was the sick, quick look of fright on his face that made her clamp down hard on herself before her own terror made things worse.

"A mistake," she whispered. "That's all it is, honey. A stupid mistake."

He calmed like a racehorse being gentled by a knowing trainer.

"If that's so, you'd think the incompetent fools would check things out before they go around scaring folks half to death."

"What are you going to do? What are we supposed to do next?"

"Nothing."

"What do you mean, nothing? Mistakes have to be straightened out, no matter who makes them." She brushed her hands across her apron, snatched the letter from him, and scanned the contents. "It says here that we are to go see the chief liquidation officer as soon as possible."

"Don't care what it says. I've got real work to do. I haven't got time to go kowtowing to some bureaucrat who doesn't know a stalk of wheat from an ear of corn."

"Iron! Let's check this out."

"Enough, Mary. I've got more important things to do than play games with a money-grubbing banker." His mouth hardened. "It's time for me to drill wheat, and that's what I'm going to do. If they give me too much flak, there are plenty of other banks around who will just jump at the chance to loan us money."

"Oh, I know," she said. "I *know* that. Still, it's such a shock, Iron. Like we've done something wrong."

"Well, we haven't, and I won't have you feeling like we have."

She read the letter again, slowly this time.

"It says here we *must* go talk to these people, Iron."

"I don't want you to start ding-donging at me either," he snapped. "I've got enough real problems of my own around here without trying to educate some stupid banker. Abner Wise is as dumb as a rock. You could tell that just by looking at him, sitting up there on that stage."

"But he *is* the new owner," she stammered.

"Sending out these high-sounding letters is just his way of throwing his weight around. Letting us know there's a new kid on the block. If we got a letter, you can bet everyone else did too."

"Honey," Mary protested. Then, seeing that he looked like a tiger ready to spring at the nearest slab of meat, she softened her voice before she tried another approach. "There was a notice in the paper that the Interfaith Rural Life Committee is sponsoring a borrowers' meeting to tell people how to handle problems with the FDIC. It's next Thursday in the grade school. Do you want to go?"

"Hell no. And I don't want you showing up there by yourself either."

Furiously, she turned away and finished dishing up. "What would it hurt? I might learn something."

"I mean it, Mary. Just stay away from all those do-gooders, poking around."

"Iron! The meeting is supposed to help us learn how to work out a cash flow and talk to the folks at the FDIC."

"I already know how to talk to people, and my cash flow is nobody's business."

"They'll show how to cope with all the forms."

"I'm telling you there's not going to be any forms to cope with for us. You were right. This is all a big mistake. Besides, if there *are* forms, I'm an American. I can read. Don't need no self-righteous fools telling me what something means."

"Better sit down," she said tersely, "before this all gets cold."

They ate in silence.

"It's kind of funny when you stop to think about it," Iron said after he finished. "There's going to be a lot of red faces in that bank when they realize they accidentally culled out our notes right off the bat."

Mary's brow furrowed. "I thought we could put the bank out of our minds after we decided to cut back and not borrow any more operating money this year, but here we are again."

"I'll go talk to them, Mary. As soon as I have time. Right after I get my wheat in. Sorry. Didn't mean to take it out on you."

Iron and Mike drove their International trucks into town to pick up seed wheat. The time, the date, the day, the texture of the air, the exact angle of the malevolent sun, hot as judgment, was soon to be burned on Iron's mind forever after.

Dennis followed his father and his brother-in-law in the pickup. They were running low on salt blocks for the cattle, and he planned to pick them up and a roll of chicken wire at Hendricks Feed Store.

The sun shimmered like molten copper that still summer morning. Iron always aimed toward planting wheat the last week in August rather than stretching it to the first week in September. Normally a week's extra heat didn't fret him nearly as much as risking a change in the unpredictable Kansas weather, but this day promised to be a scorcher.

He groaned when he pulled into the yard of the elevator and saw that there were three trucks ahead of him. He glanced at Mike in the rearview mirror. His son-in-law laughed and waved the morning paper, signaling that he intended to read while they waited their turn to weigh the empty trucks. The trucks would be weighed again after they were loaded with seed wheat and the dealers paid on the loaded weight confirmed by the elevator.

Iron shrugged and turned up the radio. Dennis drove past with a grin and jabbed his finger in the direction of the local café, indicating he would meet them there later.

The brick scale house was located beside an old railroad track and was kept tidy up to a fifty-yard radius. Beyond that was scattered junk partially overgrown with weeds.

The last truck ahead of him pulled off the slab of suspended concrete, and Iron in turn drove his empty truck onto the scaling area. He took the stamped, dated ticket from the woman who did the weighing and tucked it into his sun visor then waited for Mike to repeat the process.

They drove two miles out in the country, where his friends were waiting to load his seed wheat. The grain would be augured onto the trucks. It would take about thirty minutes to load each one, and he looked forward to visiting with Sonny Newark and Tim Piker.

Collectively, the Barretts had three thousand acres of wheat ground, fifteen hundred of which were planted every year. The other acres were summer-fallowed—set aside and not farmed at all—to give the land a rest. If the rainfall was normal, this ground was simply tilled several times during the growing season to keep down the weeds.

Iron paid five dollars a bushel for certified seed. He bought a hybrid every other year from Newark and Piker, who trucked new seed back from Texas A&M. Iron had never given anyone else his business.

On the off year, he reseeded from wheat he'd set aside from his own crops. However, he disliked stretching the holdover to a third year, because he didn't want to take a chance on weakening the disease resistant properties of the robust strain.

Newark, with his slightly hooked nose, looked like a young suntanned owl wearing overalls. He beckoned the truck into position beside the steel grain bin. Piker was dark-skinned and lanky. Grave as a Roman senator, he listened more than he talked. When he did finally speak, folks paid attention. Iron put a lot of stock into the opinions of these two men.

"Did you go to the bank meeting?" asked Sonny as soon as they had positioned the equipment.

"Sure did," Iron said. "It's a sorry state of affairs when an Espy doesn't own the First Bank of Gateway."

"Well, Old Man Espy's never been one of my favorites," Sonny said. "It was an Espy that sold out my granddad in the Depression. Doesn't bother me a bit to see him get a taste of his own medicine."

"A lot of people are going to be hurt," Iron said. "I hate to see that."

"I don't," Sonny said. "Most of them who are going to get into trouble are lazy slackers anyway. It'll serve about half of them right and get them off the government gravy train."

Iron thought about the letter from the bank. Sonny and Tim must have gotten one, too, but he decided not to bring it up in front of Mike, who was listening intently to every word.

"What do you mean hurt?" Mike said. "I hear a lot of folks are coming out of this smelling like a rose. They're cutting deals with the FDIC. Getting their notes written down."

Piker spoke up at once. "Ain't right. Why should I have to work like a dog and drive an old pickup? Pay every last blessed cent I owe and watch someone else have their debts forgiven just like they won the lottery?"

"Sounds good to me," Mike mumbled.

Iron and Tim and Sonny looked at the ground and kept a delicate silence, passively reproving Mike for his blunder.

After the seed wheat was augered, Iron and Mike drove back to the elevator to weigh both vehicles again.

Clifton Hathaway pulled alongside Iron's truck before he could drive onto the scales.

"Hear you have a little problem at the bank, Barrett," he hollered out his pickup window. His eyes glittered meanly, and Iron jerked stiffly alert, too stunned to reply.

"You wouldn't be trying to pull a quicky on the boys who sold you this grain, would you?"

"Speak plain, Hathaway. What in the hell are you talking about?"

"Hear the check your wife wrote Friday to the grocery store bounced. Don't suppose you've gotten word yet. 'Spect you will when you pick up your mail this morning."

Iron's blood froze in his veins. He made a fist and slammed it against the steering wheel then rubbed his bruised knuckles. The grocer, Henry Green, always tacked up hot checks on a bulletin board back of the checkout stand.

"Iron? What's going on?" asked Mike, as he started to open his door.

"Nothing. Just stay right there."

"Seems like the right thing for me to do would be to call the men who sold you this seed before you drive off," Hathaway said. "Seeing as how I'm their friend."

"Don't go near a phone, Hathaway. You think I'm trying to cheat Tim and Sonny out of their grain money? There's been a mistake. I've never written a hot check in my life."

"That's not the way I hear it." Then, wary of the look on Iron's face, Hathaway drove out of the yard.

"Mike, park that truck off to the side and go find Dennis. I need the pickup."

Mike left for the café on foot and returned with Dennis and the pickup in a scant ten minutes.

"Dad, what's wrong?"

"You two stay here. In the trucks. Don't move, and don't weigh yet. There's something I've got to see for myself, right now."

The gravel sprayed away from his tires and the pickup lurched as he jammed into gear and drove to the grocery store. He shut off the key, leaped out, and paused for an instant before he pushed through the door. His mouth filled with bitter saliva.

They always had money in their household checking account. He had never in his whole entire life had a check bounce. If one of his checks was tacked up there for all the world to see, he would sue Abner Wise until the new owner begged for mercy. If the Agland State Bank even *thought* about not honoring his checks, he would ruin Wise.

But before he sent heads rolling, he wanted to be sure of his facts.

He had to see it for himself.

16

There were only a couple of customers around when Iron walked in. He walked over to the main checkout line and peered at the display behind the counter. Instead of the usual smattering, Henry's corkboard was full of bad checks.

Centered was the check Mary had written Friday, stamped "payment refused." Not the "insufficient funds" he'd expected to see.

Rage pulsated inside him. His hands shook. If he hadn't seen it for himself, he wouldn't have believed it.

The bandy-legged, bearded little grocer, Henry Green, came over and took his place behind the counter. Green's eyes were hooded and heavy, his face flushed. He planted himself firmly, like a little billy goat, ready to take on all comers.

Iron crossed his arms over his chest and towered like a straight pine over the owner of the grocery store.

"Give me that check, Henry." Iron's voice was crow harsh. "You short-sighted idiot. We've bought our groceries here for twenty-five years and you have the gall to stick that up where everyone can see it like I'm a deadbeat and a cheat trying to screw you out of your money. You know me, and you know my family."

"Ain't going to do it," Henry said. "It's my only protection, by God. The only insurance I have I'll ever get my money." He turned and waved at the corkboard. "See those? You think you're the only one? This will ruin me. All these years you thought it was just fine when I put other people's checks up there. Like it was justice. Shoe's on the other foot now."

Knowing Iron Barrett would never buy so much as a loaf of bread in his store again and he had nothing to lose, Henry warmed to his subject. "And 'nother thing. I'm sick of all you high and mighty farmers coming in acting like you own the whole county just because you've always made so much money. How does it feel to worry, Iron?"

Iron doubled his fists. "Give me that check, Henry."

The grocer shook his head. "You think the government's going to bail me out when times get hard? You think anyone gave a damn about little old Henry Green when folks started going to Walmart buying their paper towels and their Saran Wrap just because it was three cents cheaper? You think anyone's going to come up with a disaster program for grocery store owners?"

"Give me that check."

Henry trembled like a sassy child fearful of being struck, but he didn't back down. "No. If you want it you can get it back the same way everyone else does. Bring me the cash, and I'll give you the check."

Cold reason iced over Iron's rising heat. With a glance at two women, who were clearly spellbound at the whole exchange, as were the clerks and stock boys, Iron rubbed his knuckles against the sides of his jeans, nodded curtly, and walked out, not trusting himself to say another word.

He drove back to the elevator.

Dennis and Mike looked at him quizzically.

"You men got any cash on you?"

"About five dollars," Mike said.

"Ten here," Dennis said.

"That's not enough. We've got a big problem with the new bankers. Park these trucks where they're out of the way. You don't have to sit here in this heat. Go to the café or anywhere that suits you. I'm going to talk to Abner Wise."

"Want us to come along?" Mike asked.

"Nope. This is something I need to handle by myself."

Spinning around, he half-ran back to the pickup and was out of the elevator yard before Mike and Dennis could lob another question.

Iron stormed into the bank and headed for the reception desk. He glanced at the desk where Cynthia Benton had always worked. The woman sitting there wore a maroon blazer over a starched white blouse and a little maroon bola tie, as did the teller standing next to her and all the women straight down the line.

He saw a man standing in the office directly across the lobby and he, too, was attired in a maroon blazer—over black slacks, which corresponded with the women's straight black skirts.

The new receptionist was all bones and angles. Her crisp dark hair was restrained by layers of spray. She moved in little puppet-like jerks that set Iron's teeth on edge. She straightened a small sign, facing outward, with the name Eleanor Gladstone printed in gold letters on a black background.

"May I help you?" she asked.

"I want to see Abner Wise at once."

"I'm sorry, sir. He's out for the day."

"What do you mean out? Why would he be out?" J.C. Espy had never missed a day's work in his life. Iron's rage gave way to confusion. He felt as though he had stepped into a foreign country. A muscle in his jaw twitched as he looked around the bank.

"Sir, perhaps I should begin by informing you that this bank has been put into receivership by the FDIC and that there are new owners. Did you go to the community meeting?" She rattled off the words as rapidly as a woodpecker, as though she were repeating them for the fiftieth time that day.

Disoriented, he nodded. There was a hole in this bank with Old Man Espy not being in the back room where he had always been.

"What would you like to see us about this morning?"

Iron looked at her sharply, and a muscle twisted in his jaw. It never had been and never would be a receptionist's place to ask about the purpose of his trip to the bank.

"I guess I need to talk to the FDIC fellow. I'm not sure what his name is."

"You have a loan that's being retained by the FDIC?"

"I need to see that man," Iron said again, refusing to give Miss Gladstone any more information.

"That man is our chief liquidation officer, Clyde Peterson." Her eyes scanned her appointment book. "The first time I can get you in is tomorrow at 2:00. Unless you want to wait around today. There's always a chance someone won't turn up. In the meantime, perhaps you would like to start reading some of our literature." She whirled in her chair and plucked a pamphlet from her immaculate files.

"Hell no, I don't want to wait. I can't come in again tomorrow. I'm a working man."

"Your options are an appointment tomorrow afternoon or waiting with the rest of the men, sir," she said with an indifference that was not at all faked. Her smile didn't touch her eyes as she swiveled back to her files.

Turning, Iron saw that there wasn't an empty chair in the bank. They were all taken by friends of his. Seed-capped and humiliated. Not bothering with small talk, the majority were self-conscious and restless. Chain-smoking, working their hands, pretending to read the back issues of *Successful Farming* and *Farm Journal* that were spread out on the coffee table. But mostly mad, at having to squander a perfectly good work day sitting in a bank.

"Look here. I've got to see that Peterson fellow right now."

He could not bring himself to tell this maroon-jacketed robot that he actually needed money to eat on. The stupid new owner had made a terrible, terrible mistake and wouldn't let him write checks.

He decided he was not going to take his place with that row of frightened, gaunt-eyed men. As though he were in some kind of trouble. Like some red-necked grubber of a farmer who didn't have sense enough to keep his head above water. With the word spreading, like a prairie fire, around town that he was in trouble. And it would. It would be up and down the street before he made it back home.

In fact, he didn't want to be seen going in the chief liquidation officer's door.

Shocked, he took off his hat and ran his hand through his hair. It was just last Christmas season he drank scotch with old J.C. and shot the bull. Joked, swore. Had been the bank's fair-haired boy.

He could not be seen going through Peterson's door. It would be bad for the bank, bad for the town, to let word get out that he was in any kind of trouble. But there was the check posted in Henry Green's store.

"Get me in now. Just give the man my name. It's in the bank's best interests as well as mine not to make me wait. Is he in J.C.'s old office?"

"He's in the room just off the rear entrance, sir. I don't have the slightest idea who used to have that office." She walked down the hallway. A moment later, she told Iron to go on back.

Chief liquidation officer Clyde Peterson rose halfway from his chair and gestured for Iron to sit down. Peterson was a tall, slump-shouldered man with starkly arched black brows. A sparse little mustache hovered above his petulant lips. He wore a poorly cut brown suit made from polyester fabric that would last another thirty years.

"Mr. Barrett. I've been hoping you would come in. You're one of the first people we wanted to see because of the size of your loans. In fact, I've been going over your file this morning." Peterson gestured toward the folder lying on his desk.

"I want to know what the hell is going on," Iron blurted.

"I'm sure I don't have the slightest idea what you're talking about," Peterson said.

"You have no right to refuse payment on my checks like I was some kind of tramp passing through town."

"There are a couple of things we need to get straight from the very beginning, Mr. Barrett. We have every right in the world to freeze your assets. In fact, it's high time you realized you don't have any assets. What you have is a bunch of debts. And I do mean a whole bunch."

Iron exploded. "Why you ignorant fool. I own more land than anyone in this county."

"You owe *on* more land than anyone in this county. And if you think we can't take a cussing out around here, you've got another think coming. I've been sworn at by men who know a lot more words than you."

Iron came up out of his chair and braced his arms on Peterson's desk. "You had no right to bounce my check."

"Oh, but we did. I'm here to get the most money possible back for the FDIC. That's my job. If farmers are willing to cooperate, we'll listen to their plans for keeping things afloat. In some cases we even write down their loans."

"Write down?"

"For some folks, we'll lower the amount due. For instance if a man owes the old bank $100,000, we'll forgive part of it and just make him pay back $70,000. If he appears to be a good risk. It makes more sense for us to lose $30,000 than put a no-count place up for auction that will just bring $20,000, for a total loss of $80,000."

Iron's blood heated like a river of fire. It was the kind of deal Tim had scoffed at this morning.

"You may be used to dealing with low-life, no-honor, cheating city slickers where you come from, Peterson, but I pay my debts. In full. If I borrow a dollar, I pay back a dollar. Even if you offered to cut my debt in half, I wouldn't take it. It's wrong, and I'm not going to do it. I'm not asking for any favors. I just want the use of what's rightfully mine. I want it now. Take the hold off my checking. And I want to know why you didn't have the courtesy to tell me about this first."

"Ah, but we did. According to our records you were sent a certified letter just last week saying you had to come in and talk to us."

Suddenly wary, Iron quelled his anger.

"You can't tell me you didn't get that letter, Barrett. The postman had to get your signature, or your wife's signature."

"Well, yes," Iron said slowly, "I did get it."

"Why didn't you call to make an appointment?"

Iron swallowed. "I didn't think it meant immediately. I was going to come in after I got my wheat planted."

"Well, you know now that it meant immediately."

Suddenly Iron felt as though he had always known this person. Mean-spirited, petty, the Clyde Petersons had always been around.

"Look, all this hassling is a waste of time," Iron said. "Let me talk to the new president. For the sake of saving time when I should be out in the field, I'll just go ahead and do business with the new owners. It will be simpler for everyone if I keep right on banking here."

Peterson stared at him as though he were the eighth wonder of the world. "My God, what does it take to get through to you people?" he said. "You're the third one today who can't seem to get it through your head that you simply can't bank here anymore. You have to go someplace else to borrow money."

"Damn right I'm going someplace else to borrow money."

"Not until we take inventory."

"What?"

"Inventory. We'll be out to make sure we have a complete list of everything we own."

"You step on my property, and I'll whip your ass."

"That's just it," Peterson said. "It's not your property. It's ours. And we'll come on it whenever we damn well please."

Iron rose, no longer suppressing his anger, but knowing he should leave before he lost all self-control. Had to get out. Had to. He left by the back door.

Peterson had learned in other closings that if he could make an example of just the right farmer, it had a demoralizing effect on the rest of the seed-capped bumpkins. It didn't take long before everyone got cooperative as lambs.

He buzzed Miss Gladstone and asked her to send in the two men who were in charge of taking inventory.

Iron drove off, gravel spraying behind the wheels of his pickup. His jaw tightened when he realized he still didn't have any money. The check was still hanging in Henry Green's store. He drove to the ATM on the other side of town. He had never drawn cash against his Visa before, so it took several bumbled attempts before he had gotten through all the bleeping sequences and had his eighty dollars in hand.

Silently he redeemed his check from the hostile little grocer. Then he went to the café and walked over to the booth where Mike and Dennis sat drinking coffee. Dennis was doodling on a napkin.

"I have a problem with the bank," Iron said curtly. "A big problem."

Dennis's head shot up. He stiffened and snapped the pencil between his clenched fists. "What kind of a problem? People like us don't have problems with banks." He looked at his father coldly.

"Tell you all about it later," Iron said, shutting Dennis off with a look. "I'm going out to Tim and Sonny's again, and I'll meet you at the elevator in about an hour. Go back and sit in the trucks, but don't start home until I tell you to. Don't move a wheel."

He whirled around and left. He walked to the pay phone on the corner, called Mary, and told her not to wait supper. He managed to get off the line without saying much else.

He drove out to Newark and Pikers. He had always paid for his grain within a week. Always. Despite the heat, he shivered, remembering the two men's contempt this morning for farmers in just his position.

Shame slunk across his body like an old rat, silent and loathsome. When he turned into their driveway, he swallowed against the bile rising in his throat then gulped for air.

He didn't bother to pretty it up. "I want you two men to hear it straight from me, that I have a problem with the new bankers," he began. "Didn't learn about it till this morning."

He looked away, remembering the letter he should have taken seriously. "Anyway, you're going to get paid a little later than usual, but it won't be much longer. Guess I can count on you to carry me," he added with a weak, sick grin.

"Sure thing, Iron." They spoke together, eager to show their faith in him.

"I want you to know the trucks are parked right now at the elevator. Dennis and Mike are ready to bring the seed right back if you want me to."

"Hell, no need for that," Sonny said quickly. "We know you're good for it."

"God sakes, Iron," Tim said. "I'm surprised you'd even suggest it. If we can't count on you, the whole damn world is going to hell."

"'Preciate it." Iron shuddered with relief.

Tim smiled and winked and gave an airy little wave.

But what was seared on Iron's brain, as indelibly as a number tattooed in a concentration camp, was the split second of stunned silence, the primitive wariness that had immobilized the two men's faces before they could recover.

On the way back to town, his foot slipped off the accelerator when he realized nothing had been done about his frozen checking account. Not one thing. What would they do? Not just in the long run, but right now?

Then he remembered the satisfaction he had felt in drawing cash against his Visa without having to ask one self-righteous soul for approval. There had to be plenty of ways to get them over the hump until he found a new bank.

They would soon see—the bankers, the FDIC, the Henry Greens of the world—just who they had decided to mess with. Giddy with determination, his will slipped into gear as reliably as an old John Deere tractor waiting to be fired up.

17

"Sabrina," Connie called. "Your mom's looking for you."

Connie stepped inside Old Barn. It housed the Barrett children's livestock projects. Early afternoon shadows dappled the floor. Dust motes danced in the heavy air filtering through the cracks and knotholes splintering the seasoned wood walls. She paused in the doorway and breathed in the familiar earthy odor of old hay, manure, and bits of fermenting feed that had fallen into cracks.

She peered around, but even the slumbering comfort provided by the restful gray and tan monotones of Old Barn could not dispel the uneasiness that had been prickling her since early morning.

The men should have rolled in with the seed wheat hours ago. Mary had called around noon to let her know the men wouldn't be back in time for supper. There was something, something in her mother's voice.

When Mary called again late afternoon asking Connie if she wanted to drive to the creek with her and Lisette and pick more wild plums, she accepted at once, welcoming the chance for the twins to run off extra energy.

"Is there anything wrong, Mom?" she asked.

"I don't know," Mary had said. "Iron sounded funny, but there's no sense stewing around twiddling our thumbs when we could be working."

A sharp yelp caught Connie's attention and she turned. Andy and Andrea were quarreling over the old tire swing dangling from the massive oak in the backyard.

"Share!" she commanded, yelling across the farmyard.

"Aunt Connie?" Sabrina slipped through the door in the rear.

"Oh hi, hon. I was beginning to think you weren't around."

"I came over to walk Molly."

"Good," Connie said. "A lot of kids mess up by slacking off before State."

Molly, Sabrina's heifer, was county champion in the breeding division and, in just a month, they would be transporting her to the Kansas State Fair at Hutchinson.

"I'm done," Sabrina said. "I'm going to put her up."

She slipped back outside and returned, leading a splendid mahogany red, white-faced Hereford calf. The county show had been held one month before, so Molly still bore the immaculate exaggerated grooming of a champion.

The calf had been washed, scrubbed with a riceroot brush, and close clipped in front of the halter line. Then her tailhead had been judiciously trimmed to enhance the long back line. The hair on her front legs had been brushed down for a more feminine appearance as opposed to combing the hair up on steers for a rugged effect.

Connie smiled.

"What's so funny?" asked Sabrina.

"Nothing. I was remembering how your mother carried on when she first saw us getting a steer ready for show."

Only it hadn't been that funny at the time. Lisette had come into Old Barn to watch.

Mary had been back combing the switch—the end of the tail. After it was ratted, she plastered it with spray then tied and shaped the hair into a perfect ball. A light coat of oil would be sprayed on and combed into the calf's coat before it entered the ring.

"Well, Judas Priest," Lisette burst out after sullenly watching Mary and Iron and Connie fuss over the animal. "I simply cannot believe this. And there hasn't been a spare nickel for me to have my hair done once since I've come here."

"That's because you wouldn't bring as much at a sale as this heifer," Iron quipped with a perfectly straight face.

Lisette ran from the barn, tears streaming down her face.

"I was only funning," Iron mumbled.

"Never mind," Mary said with a quirk of a smile, despite her dismay. "I'll talk to her a little later."

Connie sighed, remembering all the work it had taken to settle Lisette down again. Mary talked to her, and talked to her, and talked to her. For nine solid years, it seemed that someone was always talking to Lisette. Then it changed in a twinkling after the Will Fight. Now the woman was prancing around like she was a rodeo queen.

Connie eyed the calf's strong back and clear eyes and the hooves that still shone with lacquer. She smiled at the bright pleasure on her niece's face. Mary had wisely suggested that Sabrina enroll in the beef-breeding project rather than the beef-marketing project as she knew her granddaughter was too tenderhearted to raise calves for slaughter. The purpose of the breeding project was to build a herd. Molly would produce top quality calves for twelve years and die of old age. So would her fertile offspring.

"Molly looks wonderful. You've done the best job, Sabrina."

She laughed. "People don't have much to do with making good calves, Aunt Connie. That's God's territory."

"Not one hundred percent, kid. You've never missed choring or taking care of your animals. Luck counts for a lot, but it won't offset neglect. Are you keeping up with your records? Writing down everything? Fees? Trucking? Insurance? Vet bills?" Connie had been State records champion three years running back in high school.

"Yes," Sabrina said.

"Just don't get behind. That's the main thing. Don't put anything off." She looked up when the shadows shifted.

"Here's Mom now," she said. Mary came through the doorway.

"Watch this," Sabrina said, as she picked up her showstick. She stroked Molly's underline and gently lifted her head to display the perfect placement of her feet.

The two women clapped.

"If you two are convinced that Molly is the finest calf in seven states, I'll get on with my chores," Sabrina said with a quick bow. "Before she dies of starvation."

"Do you want to go pick plums with us, honey?" asked Mary, watching her granddaughter trying to lift a bucket that was too heavy for her. "Your mom and I can help you finish up later."

"Not a chance, Grandma. I've got to practice piano when I get home."

"Okay, but don't try to lift so much by yourself. Break the feed down into smaller amounts and make more trips," Mary said. "Iron should be back before long. If you feel too tired to ride your bike home, make your grandfather take you when he gets here."

Mary and Connie laughed at the disdain on Sabrina's face at the suggestion the little two-mile trek would be too much.

Sabrina put down her feed bucket, stopped, and arched her back. In three more weeks, she would be starting her first year of high school. She was terrified at the thought of trying to keep up and confused by the multitude of changes in her body. Her need for extra sleep put her further and further behind.

Her etymology project—chasing down the blasted bugs this summer—had nearly done her in. She hadn't realized what it would cost her until it was too late to drop the project without it counting against her. Her and the club.

Don't drop. There were days when the words beat like a drum in her brain. Don't drop piano. Don't drop a project. Don't drop athletics.

She didn't look up when she heard a vehicle coming down the lane. It never occurred to her it could be anyone but her grandfather and uncles until her dog started barking frantically.

She set down her buckets and peered through the barn door. Two men jumped out of a pickup, one with a fancy camera sporting an enormous zoom lens. A Polaroid in bright blue casing dangled from a separate strap. The other man had a video camera.

The one with the 35mm crossed the barnyard and immediately began taking pictures of the line of equipment out in the yard. He scanned the row containing the planters, plows, cultivators, tractors, drills—photographing anything that Iron had not put into the storage shed.

Then he opened the doors on the main barn and started shooting all the equipment within.

Sabrina called out when they started toward Old Barn. "Hey there, what's going on?"

"Just taking inventory, sis."

"Inventory of what?"

They continued to click away.

"Your assets."

Confused, she stood in the doorway. "You can't come in here," she said, trying to shut the double doors. They exchanged looks and the tallest man took her hands and pulled them away from the handles. "Yes, we can. Now stand to one side, miss. It's our job. We need to see if you have livestock hidden away."

"The only livestock in there is Molly, and she's mine. What's going on? Nothing's hidden."

He shoved her aside and began clicking away while the man with the camcorder began sweeping the lens down the stalls.

"That's my calf. My 4-H calf." She hurled herself at the man, knocking the Nikon out of his hands, dislodging the expensive zoom lens. He whirled around.

"I ought to . . . better not have ruined my camera."

The swarthy man put down the camcorder and picked up the Nikon's zoom. "We'd better call a halt to all this, Pete, and talk to the boss. Go take some Polaroids of everything we've shot so far, just in case she messed up your Nikon."

"Get out. Just get out," Sabrina sobbed. "Wait until I tell my grandpa."

He ignored her and took several shots of Molly, laying the rapidly developing pictures on top of the rail of the manger as they whirred out.

"Don't do that," cried Sabrina again, shoving him in the small of the back. He steadied himself, turned and stared, then scooped up all the dry pictures, leaving a wet one behind.

"We'll be back. Count on it."

"Something's wrong. Sabrina's bike is still here," Connie said, when she and Mary pulled into the drive. "She should have finished choring long before now. And Iron isn't back yet."

The women looked at each other. Lisette jumped out of the pickup and ran toward the barn.

Sabrina sat on a bale of hay next to her calf, her shoulders shaking with trembling sobs. She pressed the Polaroid against her chest.

"Some men want Molly. My calf. Grandma, what's going on?" The words jerked from her in hysterical spasms.

"Who was here, Sabrina? Did . . . did they touch you?"

"No." Her eyelids were swollen and her face was blotched. "But I tried to stop them and then they pushed me away from the door and just started taking pictures."

"Oh my God," Mary said, her knees giving way. She reached for the left-behind, now fully developed photo.

"A picture of Molly?" Lisette asked incredulously.

Mary pieced together the story Sabrina was telling in fits and starts.

Connie threw a horse blanket around Sabrina's shoulders and tried to guide her toward the house, but she pulled away.

"No," screamed Sabrina. Frantically, she clung to the calf's neck. "They said they'd be back. They'll take Molly. I've got to stay."

"Don't worry, honey. You can bet we won't let anything like this happen around here again. Of course you were scared," Connie said soothingly. "You had every right to be scared."

"I promise you, Sabrina. No one will touch your calf," Mary assured her. "Take her up to our bedroom, Lisette. I want her to lie down for a while. There will be hell to pay for this when Iron finds out."

"Who were they, Mom?"

"I don't know, but I'm assuming they're linked to Iron's phone call this morning. And I'm going to town myself—right now—to find him and see what's going on." She shook with fury.

"No need," Lisette said. "They're just pulling up the lane."

Mary and Lisette ran for the trucks and reached them before the men could cut the engines. Connie stayed behind, her arm still protectively around Sabrina's shoulders.

"Some men were here. What's going on, Iron?" Mary gave a stumbling account of the invasion and handed him the picture. "They told her they were taking inventory."

A nerve jerked in Iron's jaw as he studied it. "A camcorder? And a Polaroid? They had to be from the FDIC."

"The bank? The new banker did this?"

"No doubt. But I warned Peterson to stay off my property. What kind of pseudo Nazis would scare a little kid?"

"The bank, Iron? Why would the bank want to inventory our farm?"

"I've run into some complications with the new owner. But it's not going to take me long to get it all worked out." Iron turned to Mike and Dennis. "We're going back to town right now. There's going to be a reckoning with a certain chief liquidation officer. Just wait until I get my hands on Peterson."

Iron had told them about the family's assets being frozen on the drive back from town, but he couldn't bring himself to talk about the check tacked on the corkboard at the grocery store. He would tell Mary after he dealt with Peterson.

"I think I should stay here," Dennis said. "Someone needs to be here with the women just in case something else comes up." He turned for a moment to keep his father from seeing the contempt in his eyes. He could just see Iron charging into the bank making everything worse.

"You might be right," Iron said. "I'd hate for those goons to come back without any of us men around."

"Maybe it would be a good idea to wait until tomorrow before you see Peterson. When you've had a chance to cool off."

"Dennis! Don't even think about it," Lisette said angrily. "We're never going to 'cool off' over this. We should sue the bastards."

"I'm staying here," Dennis said. "My place is by the side of our little girl."

He saw at once he had hit the right tone, but there was no way for him to stop his father from going back to the bank. Later, maybe he could find a way to let the chief liquidation officer know he was different from the rest of the family. He could be reasoned with. He was intelligent. Living in the twentieth century. He didn't carry on over a piece of land like it was holy ground, and he knew the worth of a dollar.

It was nearly five o'clock, but most of the bank staff was still there. Iron pounded at the back door. "Open up. I need to see Peterson." The receptionist stared then went back to Peterson's office, returned, and unlocked the door. They rushed down the hall. Peterson shrank before the two angry men.

"Your men frightened my little granddaughter half out of her wits," Iron said. "You can't get away with that."

"I did hear the boys had a little run-in out at your place."

"Not just a little run-in. You were trespassing."

"I told you earlier we would be out to take inventory."

"And I told you if you set one foot on my place, I'd whip your ass. Maybe I should have said sue your ass instead. Get ready for it."

Peterson blanched. He didn't need any lawsuits. His job was to settle everything as economically as possible. "You haven't got a prayer," he sneered.

"No?" asked Mike, who had been watching the man's face. "You don't think there's a bit of pain and suffering involved in threatening to take a little girl's 4-H calf? Ever heard of punitive damages, mister? Awards tend to be pretty generous in this county."

"No person can tell one cow from another. If that cow was the kid's 4-H calf. Which I doubt. No jury would expect us to sort it out just like that."

"Think again, Peterson," Mike said. "Think real hard now about what you're saying. You really think this is what an ordinary calf looks like?" He waved the Polaroid. "You really think that most heifers have teased and sprayed tails and satiny hooves and blocked and clipped coats. My, my, son. Is a jury ever going to be impressed with you! I can hardly wait."

A shadow of apprehension flitted across Peterson's face before he could recover. "Give me that picture," he said.

Mike slowly shook his head.

"Get out. Both of you," shouted Peterson.

"You bet we will. It's our pleasure. But we'll be back," Mike said. "We will, or our lawyer will, or who knows? Maybe even the sheriff."

When they were back in the pickup, Iron let out a gleeful whoop. They repeated every word of the conversation on the way home and later went over it verbatim for the women.

"And you should have seen the spineless wonder's face when Mike showed him that picture. It put the fear of God in him, I tell you." Iron beamed at his son-in-law and laughed as he recalled Peterson's expression.

"It's not really very funny," Connie said, moving to comfort Sabrina, who was still overcome with intermittent fits of weeping.

Dennis smiled and made it a point to laugh at all the right times, but he was very glad that he had not been a party to Mike and Iron's little victory.

Alma Barrett had been fetched to share the triumphant evening. Lisette sat beside her, listening and doing counted cross-stitch. There was a peculiar affinity between Lisette and Alma. They both had the same quirky knack for packing a dead-on assessment of any situation into one caustic line.

"I'm not surprised," Alma said darkly when Iron told her about the mandatory inventory. "Bankers are mean as snakes."

Iron grinned and nodded. "Snakes can be defanged, Mom."

Alma quietly crocheted and listened to them tell and retell the story. "Not a good idea to tangle with bankers," she said finally.

18

Mary called Elizabeth the next morning and gleefully told her about Iron and Mike's encounter with Clyde Peterson. "Your father was wonderful! Peterson was the first to blink. He lost his cool when Iron mentioned a lawsuit."

"Are you crazy?" Elizabeth asked. "You both have to be out of your minds to antagonize the chief liquidation officer. I need to talk to Daddy right now. I advise farmers every week. He's got to understand what he's up against. Put him on the phone."

She watched Iron's face as he listened to his daughter. Elizabeth was clearly doing most of the talking, while Iron responded in grunts.

"I don't have any money in any other bank. Never needed to before. Just banked with J.C." He stabbed at his shirt pocket for his pack of Camels. "I can't let you do that. It's not that I don't appreciate it." His jaw tightened. "Guess we have no choice then,"

His face was ashen when he finally placed the receiver back on the hook.

With a quick glance at Mary, he lit another cigarette before he answered the silent question in her eyes.

"Elizabeth pointed out that we don't have access to any money. She says she has some put by to see us through. And she wants us to hang on to that picture. So keep it in a safe place. Never thought I'd see the day when I would be bumming off my own kids."

"What are we going to do?"

"I'm going to plant wheat," Iron said. "Plant wheat and think. That's what I'm going to do."

The whole family was driving Iron crazy. Mary called Elizabeth daily. If it wasn't "Elizabeth says," it was "Mike says" or "Dennis says." They swarmed at him like gnats.

Elizabeth, who had not yet transferred her savings from her bank in San Francisco, was buying their bare necessities. All the family's savings and checking accounts were tied up tighter than a rodeo calf. Including little dabs of the grandkids' 4-H money.

The exception of course was Alma, who had a zany patchwork of accounts scattered hither and yon for the sake of a free toaster or a plaid blanket.

Everyone in the family was becoming a crazy star-spangled activist, thought Iron. Everyone had a plan, a strategy for proceeding.

He opened the back door and saw Benjy hosing down the tractor. Though he was touched by the boy's desire to make him feel better, Iron was irritated by other folks' solicitousness toward him, implying that he needed handling. Ashamed of his pettiness, he found himself closing the screen door softly so Benjy wouldn't hear him leave. He couldn't bear the sympathy on his grandson's face.

He needed time to think, but they wouldn't let him. It was like being nibbled to death by ducks. He was working on a plan to get them out of trouble. A big one. But he didn't like to talk about ideas while he was mulling them over. Too much yapping muddied the waters.

Besides, what was needed right now was doing, not thinking. His main concern was planting wheat. Not dealing with the FDIC. He had the grain. The field was ready. He did not intend to do one blessed thing about the United States government until his wheat was in the ground.

When Mary came to collect Sabrina's 4-H enrollment cards, she found her granddaughter lolling in front of the TV.

"Are you all signed up, honey?" Mary asked with false cheerfulness.

"It's on the counter," Sabrina said, not taking her eyes from the screen.

Mary scanned the form. The only thing marked was a solitary cooking project.

"Sabrina! For heaven's sake. You've dropped practically everything. You've got to keep on with your breeding stock project or you'll lose everything you've worked for."

"I can still take care of Molly without signing up for a 4-H project. Then we won't have to come up with the money to take her to the state fair. You know how much it costs to go to Hutchinson and buy food and stay in a motel, Grandma."

"Oh sweetie, we don't have to cut back that far. You kids don't have to give up anything. Nothing will change for any of you. This is a problem for the adults. And your clothing project. What about that? This was the year you were going to make your suit."

"Good wool costs. So why not skip my tailoring project this year? And my home improvement project. This was my year to add a new dresser, but how can we?"

"I will not tolerate that kind of negative attitude, Sabrina. There is always a way. Always." Mary's hands trembled as she laid Sabrina's card down on the counter. "Now, I've never done this before, but I'm simply overruling you and checking the projects I know you would be taking if you were thinking straight. You'll thank me for it later."

"What brought all this on?" Mary asked, when she found Lisette outside in the garden.

"She's worried about losing her temper when those men came over. She thinks the FDIC will do something terrible to Iron because of her."

"That's nonsense. Not one speck of this is any of her problem."

"I'm thinking about getting some counseling for her," Lisette said. "Sabrina was looking forward to school, her projects, everything. But not anymore."

"There's no need for such a drastic step," Mary said. "She just needs to keep busy. She'll be fine when she has something new to think about."

"My daughter is hurting. She's no dummy, you know."

"Well, no wonder she's scared stiff! You and Dennis are both carrying on like we're on the way to the poor farm."

"What I'm bringing to this situation is a little dose of reality," Lisette said. "I don't have my head buried in the sand like the rest of you."

"You've got to stop scaring these kids."

"*We've* got to stop scaring these kids, all of us," Lisette said.

Iron stared at the magazines in the wall rack of Lloyd Kurtz's law office. By the time he had finished planting wheat, he had mulled over Elizabeth's advice and was looking forward to nailing the FDIC's hide to the wall. He rose when the young man entered the room. Seated again, he laid out his case and handed Kurtz the photo of Sabrina's calf.

"Mr. Barrett, these people didn't do a thing to your granddaughter." Kurtz glanced at the picture then handed it back.

Stunned, Iron stared at the attorney. Kurtz was young and plump with chipmunkish cheeks and a boyish fringe of hair, but he was as close as the county came to a killer lawyer. Iron wanted a fighter.

"They trespassed on my property, scared a little girl half out of her wits, and you say they didn't do anything?" He half rose out of his chair.

"All they did, sir, was take a picture of some cattle."

"Do you mean to tell me those people have a right to come onto my property anytime they want?"

"This is where things get a bit delicate. From their point of view, they were on their own property, not yours. As far as the FDIC is concerned, they own it, not you. It's their calf they took a picture of, not yours."

"It's my granddaughter's calf. Not theirs and not mine."

"Maybe."

Because Kurtz didn't comment on the special grooming evident in the picture, Iron decided it wouldn't be worth the trouble to educate him. He rose. "Send me the bill."

"I would be happy to help you apply for a FMHA loan," Kurtz said, following him to the door.

Iron stopped, turned, and skewered the young man with a withering look. The Farmer's Home Administration loaned to borrowers of last resort. Farmers no banks would touch. Farmers with a high default rate.

Kurtz looked away from the scorn in Iron's eyes.

"That won't be necessary. I'll find another bank."

"Then you need to start thinking in terms of bankruptcy."

"Never. Never as long as I live, not as long as I'm capable of drawing a breath, would I do such a thing or allow any of my children to make such a move. I'm an honest man and the son of an honest man. We pay our debts. We don't declare bankruptcy."

He slammed out the door before Kurtz could reply.

Iron stood quietly for a moment in the kitchen doorway, one palm braced against the doorjamb. Watching Mary work calmed him. She had moved from canning tomatoes to canning peaches. Her cycles for putting food by were as predictable as the flights of birds.

A faint odor of coffee was always present in her kitchen. A steaming pan of light Karo syrup and sugar boiled up and speckled a hot burner before Mary could adjust the heat.

She sensed his presence before he made a sound. "Don't just stand there. How did it go? I've been on pins and needles."

"He says we're in a bunch of trouble." Quickly he told her how Kurtz had dismissed the invasion of their farm as trivial. Not worth getting upset over.

Mary's eyes flashed.

"I know what your reaction was to that. Did you show him the Polaroid of Sabrina's calf?"

Iron nodded.

"He didn't notice anything unusual about a calf with its switch teased into a ball?"

"Nope. He's not the noticing kind, so I didn't point it out. He's a sorry excuse for a lawyer. We're lucky to have found that out right off the bat. It'll save us a lot of grief down the road."

The timer went off, and Mary looked blankly at the sink, trying to remember where she was with the peaches.

"I've made an important decision, honey." He studied Mary's face, loath to go on. "I've been thinking about it a long time, but my visit to the lawyer made me see that there's just no other way out."

She was frightened by his solemnity and immediately sat down in the nearest chair. She waited, her hands still, cupped carefully on her lap.

"I'm selling all our cattle, Mary."

"You can't mean that. It's out of the question!"

He watched her gather a volley of words, stopped her before she could get even one of them out.

"I'm going to, Mary. I've decided. I'm blue lighting this one."

She cringed at his words. The blue light. A unilateral decision. No discussion entertained. She ignored his clear signal to back off. "It can't be the right thing to do. I can't believe you mean to go through with it."

"That herd will get us off the hook, Mary. They're worth a lot of money. We have no other choice."

The herd had taken twenty years to build. By selling, he could pay off enough of his note to acquire financing from any other bank in the region. He could barely quell the numbing heartsickness that rose inside him, but the idea was sound. Beneath the fury and the despair was the exhilaration of gaining control again.

"Iron, you can't be serious. Honey, honey, don't do it." Mary's fingers twisted a piece of her apron into a little ball, and she stayed tight as a coiled spring in her chair, willing herself to guard her tongue. To persuade, not inflame her husband.

"Have you really thought this through? Surely there's another way!"

"I've thought of nothing else. We have no choice, honey."

She shook her head in disbelief, waylaid by her husband's resolve. She began to cry. He reached for a Kleenex then went to her, lifted her chin, and clumsily dried her tears.

"Enough, Mary. I mean it. We've never let our kids carry on over hard choices. I'm not going to let you fall into that trap either. Self-pity won't get us anywhere."

She looked for some trace of softness on his face, but it was stern and hard.

"Remember what you've always told the kids," he reminded her sharply. "It's not the purple ribbons that make you a winner. It's the attitude you allow yourself to take toward the whites."

"That's a dumb, cruel thing to say. Having to sell our cattle is hardly like getting a poor ribbon in a contest."

"You're wrong, It's the same. It's just that it feels a lot worse when you're a grown-up."

She went to the bathroom and wiped her face with a cold cloth. When she had composed herself, she went back to the kitchen and laid her head against her husband's chest. She trembled as his arms enfolded her, and they swayed back and forth.

"Can we go out to the pasture tonight, one more time, just the two of us, and look at our cattle together? Before we tell the kids?"

"Date," he agreed, his eyes softening. "One last look. Then no more tears. This will give us total control again. Snatch our lives back from strangers."

"But let me cry now. It's breaking my heart. I would give anything, anything, to have things the way they were before this nightmare started. And if selling our herd will give us our lives back, then let's do it. But until our last look, don't scold me for crying."

"I'm glad you're coming around, Mary. My God, Kurtz even said for us to start thinking about bankruptcy. I wasn't going to tell you that."

"He what? He couldn't have! Doesn't he know we're not that kind of people?"

"He does now. I told him off good and proper. But it just goes to show the kind of folks we're getting tangled up with. No 'count, no honor low-lifes who would weasel out of debts and cheat their friends. I feel like I'm choking, Mary. Like I can't breathe. I want out of this. Right now."

"Of course you do." She grasped his hands and kissed his huge, calloused palms.

"Such good hands," she murmured. "You're a good man, Iron. This should not be happening to you. Or me either."

There was a full moon that night. They bounced across the pasture in the old pickup. The earth was bathed in soft light. The silvery leaves of scattered cottonwood trees rippled in the breeze. The magnificent herd of white-faced Hereford cows and heifers milled, confused and restless at the intrusion. The steers had been sold for feeder cattle earlier in the year.

Iron cut the ignition, and they got out, sat on the tailgate, and looked at the herd. He reached for his wife and cradled her head against his broad chest, and she began to sob. He held her in silence until her tears were spent.

"Best you get it all out now," he said. "So we can put on a good face for the kids. We have to tell them right away."

"People will talk," she said, suddenly stricken. "You know they will. Since we're selling the herd practically overnight."

"We can't have the FDIC people nosing around. Telling us what to do. Scaring the grandkids to death. Believe me, it's worth it."

He gazed at his cattle and steeled himself for the work ahead. He had to gain control again.

Control of his life for the sake of his family.

19

Iron did not falter when he told Mike and Dennis he was going to sell his cattle. "It has to be done," he said.

Mike tensed, too stunned to speak.

"Are you sure that's the right thing to do?" Dennis asked.

"It's the only thing that will get us out of a whale of a lot of trouble."

"Can't wait to drop this on Sabrina and Benjy," Dennis said sullenly.

"No need to bother the women or the kids with all the financial details," Iron protested. "Just tell them I've decided to sell the cattle."

"They need to know more than that. The women, the kids—what we're up against. Where we stand," Mike said.

"He's right, Dad." Dennis added another spoonful of sugar to his coffee. "Benjy's been so scared he hasn't been eating or sleeping well. The other day he asked me if you were dying. It took him two weeks to work up the nerve to ask that question. It's the only reason he could think of for Mom bawling half the time and everyone walking around with long faces."

Iron ran his fingers through his hair. His face tightened with despair. "My grandkids don't need to know everything. Why put old folks' worries off on them?"

"They need to know in a general way," Mike persisted. "We've got to tell them something."

"All right." Iron rose suddenly, sending his cup of coffee skidding across the island. "Tell them this then: Tell them their grandfather was inept financially. He borrowed too much money at too high an interest rate for land we didn't need."

"It wasn't your fault, Iron, that the government changed the rules overnight," Mike said.

"Tell them that I believed every lying government sleazebag coming down the turnpike, saying prices were going up and we should plant fence-row to fencerow and feed the world and get rich."

"Iron," Mike protested, seeing a look on Iron's face he'd never seen before: bewilderment.

"Tell them their grandfather is about to lose homestead land that has been in this family for a hundred years. Explain to the little children how a man can manage to lose land that came down to him free and clear. Tell them how I managed to screw up in six months' time everything all the men in this family have done right for the last century."

His voice rose in intensity. His huge hands dangled helplessly at his sides.

"Tell them that I'm now forced to sell the finest cow herd in North America. Tell them that we're $100,000 short of being able to get a loan from another bank. Tell them the word is out and people who have known me all my life won't look me in the eye—and cross the street to keep from having to talk to me."

Dennis looked daggers at his father. As though he agreed with him.

"Tell them that I'm one of those poor managers the newspapers keep carrying on about. Tell them that I have managed to ruin the lives of four generations."

Iron slammed out of the room.

Sickened, Mike swallowed hard and looked down at the table.

"Well, just tell me anything he's said that isn't true," Dennis said. "I'm sick and tired of this family carrying on like he's a hero in some Greek tragedy that just fell on us out of a clear blue sky. He's brought it all on himself. He's clung to old ways and old thinking until it's done him in. It's as simple as that. He just ain't got it anymore. And if we're not careful, he'll take us all down with him."

"That's not true, Dennis. It's happening all around us. All these farmers can't be wrong."

"It's old men clinging to control that's brought these farms to such a state." Dennis reached for his cap and headed for the door. A way to redeem himself with the family had just occurred to him. A modern, high-tech way. One that would show Iron what forward thinking could do. "I'm going to see Grandma. She's living proof that you don't have to become senile when you get old."

<hr />

Two days later Dennis came to the machine shed where Iron was working on his old Farmall tractor.

"Iron, we should sell the cattle at a video auction," Dennis said. "There's advantages to going that route instead of parading them around in a ring."

"Can't imagine what they would be."

"It's a lot easier on the cattle, not to have to haul them to an auction barn. Just have them taped in their own pasture. They'll have less stress, and we won't have to worry about them picking up a parasite or disease."

The gossip, the camaraderie of the sale ring was in Iron's blood. He didn't cotton to the idea of cattle buyers being able to participate in an auction via satellite, bidding over the phone from their own living rooms. It seemed sterile and bloodless to bypass the charged, intoxicating energy of the sale `ring.

"You'll have nationwide participation," Dennis added.

"No way I'll consider doing that." Iron laid down his wrench and wiped his hands on a grease rag. "Like we're doing something to be ashamed of. Hiding stuff from our neighbors. I'd rather go out the old-fashioned way. In the sale ring."

He shoved his hands in the back pockets of his jeans.

"You can't count on a good attendance at a sale. It's too chancy," Dennis persisted. This was his chance to show his grandmother and his family how to do things right and make a buck or two.

He relished the effect his handling of this sale would have on Alma. Clearly she would be better off leaving her land to a forward-thinking grandson, instead of a petrified son who lacked imagination.

"Nope. Sorry," Iron said. "At least we'll have the satisfaction of setting a good example for other people. Show 'em how to hold up their heads."

"You owe this family something more than setting a good example. You stand to make a lot more money selling by video. I wish you'd start thinking about something besides your own pride."

Shaken, Iron watched Dennis storm off.

Later that evening Alma called. "Dennis told me about wanting to go video," she said. "I think you should do it."

Iron realized how feeble his objections sounded. Maybe Alma and Dennis were right. Perhaps it was time to listen to younger ideas. Right or not, they were wearing him down.

The next day he called his son and told him to make all the arrangements.

"Check everything out. I've been looking at the brochure. I want my cattle offered in a special breeding stock auction," Iron said. "Not a sale mixed with fats and feeders."

Elated, Dennis assured Iron there was no way it could go wrong. "You can count on me to do it right."

When the crew from the Superior Livestock Auction Company came for the taping, Iron watched in gloomy silence, tersely answering questions for the description in the brochure. The company charged two dollars a head for the service, and he had the option of turning down the sale if the price was too low.

Mike came up with the $300 for the taping, explaining that he had cashed in a two-thousand-dollar government bond his grandparents had bought for him when he was born. "I've been saving it for a rainy day," he said. "Guess this qualifies."

"Would you like a shot of your family in front of the herd?" the man holding the camera asked.

Iron shook his head and, with a small sad smile, turned and walked toward the house.

The cattle were offered the following week.

"Might as well make a party of this," Mary said. "I'm going to invite Alma and all the kids over." Cheerfully, she gave Iron a little pat on the cheek as she hurried past.

The sale was on a Saturday afternoon. Mary rotated their satellite dish to Galaxy 6 and tuned in to channel 23. The family grouped around the TV, passing bowls of popcorn and the auction catalog back and forth.

"They did a good job with all the information," Iron observed. Once again, he studied the insert describing his herd. It contained the weight, breed type, delivery date, and weighing conditions, and the assurance that his cattle had been on a full health program.

Then seeing the directions to Mary's Place in print caused his grief to well up afresh.

"There they are," shouted Benjy as their herd flashed past with a rapid-fire description during the preview.

"Folks say this is some of the finest breeding stock in the state," said the auctioneer. "Cattle bearing the Mary's Place brand have taken more than their share of show money for over ten years."

Iron's hopes soared when the preview ended and the auction began. The bidding had been active and high that day, without a single seller passing out—rejecting the bid.

The camera cut rapidly from shots of numbered lots of cattle to the impassive faces of the auctioneers chanting bids in a relentless staccato. Rows of young women manned the phones, receiving calls from all over the country.

"What's to keep some ornery kid from calling in and bidding just for the hell of it?" Lisette asked.

"Honey, President Reagan couldn't bid on these cattle without getting registered and preapproved," Dennis said. "Buyers are given a number and phone authorization code. Believe me, approval isn't easy to come by."

"Lot number 2956," barked the auctioneer.

"It's us," screamed Benjy, jumping from one foot to the other. The camera zoomed in on a heifer with a single white stocking foot before it moved back for a long shot. "And there's Michael Jackson!"

"You can't call a girl cow by a boy's name," jeered Susan.

"Can if I want to," Benjy retorted.

"Hush, we can't hear." Lisette laughed. "All of you kids, settle down."

Mary closed her eyes for an instant and squeezed Iron's hand until the veins stood out in her arm. "I can't stand this," she murmured. He trembled beneath her touch.

"One hundred fifty head of registered Hereford cows and calves. Fancy, fancy," said the auctioneer. "Offered by Iron Barrett. If you know cattle and have been around show rings, then we need say no more. This is the chance of a lifetime for all you Hereford men out there."

In a heartbeat, he tongued into the rapid vibration of the auctioneer's rhythm.

Mary gave a little yelp at the abruptness and touched her fingers to the base of her throat.

At the top of the screen, imposed on the colorful tape of their perfect cattle, the flashing bid kept moving upward. A muscle in Iron's jaw leaped as he closed his eyes for a second. When he opened them, the bid was higher, then higher yet. Far more than they would have gotten at a county sale.

Finally the number stabilized at $89 per hundred weight.

The family exploded with joy. Iron spun Mary around and around, and Mike whooped and gave Connie a hug.

Lisette beamed at Dennis and turned to Sabrina, who was ecstatic. "See! There will be plenty of money for all your 4-H projects."

"Our prayers are answered," Mary said.

Alma nodded with approval at her grandson.

Iron blinked his eyes at the final bid, reached for a pencil, and did some quick figuring. "We're going to make enough money to pay off all but ten thousand dollars of our loan," he shouted. "And that's chickenfeed. We can earn that much digging ditches."

Connie and Lisette left with the children, who were bright with delight. Not understanding everything that had happened but knowing their world was right again. Alma said her goodbyes with an adoring glance at Dennis.

Iron got the call at suppertime.

"What?" Mary asked, as he softly laid the receiver back into the cradle. He looked as though he had learned of a death in the family.

"That was the Superior Livestock Auction Company. The sale didn't go through."

"Why? What happened?"

"They just got a call from Clyde Peterson. He told them our cattle belong to the FDIC and they hadn't authorized putting them up for sale."

"But we were going to apply the money toward our bank note," Mary stammered. "Surely Peterson knows that."

"The bastard told Superior we were trying to take our money and run. Seems we're on some kind of a list that's been circulated to everyone. Everyone. The elevators, livestock markets. Everyone. Anyplace where we might try to sell our assets. The FDIC didn't get the information to the video companies. They didn't think about them. Dennis, didn't I tell you to check everything out? Didn't you tell me you knew what you were doing?"

Dennis's face was ash gray. "I didn't know. How was I supposed to know?"

A vein throbbed in Iron's temple. "You told me you had checked everything out."

"This isn't my fault," Dennis said hotly. "It would have been the same if you had sold them at a county sale. The FDIC wouldn't have let you do it."

"But I would have known that in advance," Iron said. "I never would have let things get this far."

"Like hell. You're the one who dissed the FDIC to begin with. Do you think Peterson would have just signed off on this sale if you had been in charge? I'm sick and tired of being dumped on when things go wrong."

Mary jumped when her son rushed outside and left in a spray of gravel.

Iron was dazed. "The Superior people sounded like I was trying to pull a fast one. Said if I'd talked to the liquidation officer, I'd have known I couldn't do this."

"Dennis was supposed to cover all the bases, Iron, not you," Mike said with a compassionate glance. "This was supposed to be Dennis's show. He promised us he'd checked everything out."

Iron ground his fist into the palm of his hand and then massaged his white knuckles. "According to the man at Superior, we can't buy or sell anything without the FDIC's approval, and all checks have to be made out to the FDIC."

"We can't wait for the FDIC's approval before we sell something," Mary said. "By the time the government completes the paperwork to sell anything, the bird will have flown. The cattle market changes in a heartbeat.

Besides, what does Clyde Peterson know about buying and selling? Cattle or anything else."

"They don't care," Iron said bitterly. "They just don't care how long it took me to build up that cow herd. They're plenty willing to settle for forty cents on the dollar or whatever."

She laid her hand on his arm.

"I have enough left from cashing my bond to pay a few bills and get the kids started to school," Mike said. "But we've got to have money to feed the cattle and operate on. And I don't know where in the hell we're going to get it. No other bank will touch us until we get some of this mess straightened out."

"That's the kind of thing they were going to tell us at that meeting I wanted to go to," Mary said unhappily.

"I don't want you going around advertising our misery," Iron said.

Stung, she bit her lip and looked away.

"What meeting?" Mike asked.

"A borrowers' meeting," Mary said. "It was sponsored by a church group. They were supposed to tell folks what they need to know to deal with the FDIC."

"Find out who was in charge, and I'll give them a ring," Mike said curtly.

"Won't do any good," Iron said. "What would they know about farming?"

"Let some of the rest of us take over for a while," Mike said. "It's all of our problem."

"I let my son take over. And you can see where that got me."

Mary located the number of the Rural Life Worker, and Mike called at once. "The next step is to go to the FDIC and formally apply for a small operating loan to tide us over until we can negotiate a final settlement," he said after he hung up the phone.

Iron's jaw tightened into a rigid mass of bone.

"I want to be the one to do it, Iron. Sorry, but the man said it should be the most diplomatic one among us, and that ain't you."

"Agreed. There's no way I can bring myself to toady up to those bastards."

"Well, I can," Mike said. "It will be no small chore, but I'll do it. We made Peterson madder than hell over that picture. I'll tell him we were all upset. Not thinking straight that day."

"You're going to apologize to Clyde Peterson?" Iron asked.

"If I have to," Mike said calmly. "If that's what it takes. Mary, I need you to get some information together. I'll go in bright and early tomorrow morning."

20

The next morning, carrying a briefcase of financial information, Mike Hewlett walked into the bank and told the receptionist he wanted to see the chief liquidation officer. He wore khaki slacks and a Madras sports coat over a button-down oxford shirt just in case the FDIC staff associated jeans and seed caps with folks who hated their guts.

"Mr. Peterson is out of town today," she said, "but other people can help you."

Mike frowned. He wanted to deal directly with Peterson but quickly decided that working with a junior officer might be to his advantage. "All right."

"Just take a seat, please. Miss Winston will be with you in a moment. She'll need a bit of time to review your file."

Upon hearing the "Miss" he was glad he had taken care with his clothes. He had always gotten on well with women. Though he was not flirtatious or a ladies' man, he had an amiable big-brotherly quality that women found reassuring.

"Mr. Hewlett, Miss Winston will see you now."

He followed the receptionist down the hall and blinked in surprise when he saw the tiny woman sitting behind the desk. According to her nameplate Miss Winston was a liquidation specialist.

Petite and dark-skinned, she had the overly serious manner of a young woman just out of college holding her very first real job. Wary now, Mike shook her extended hand, noting the career-minded correctness of the hard squeeze.

"What can I do for you today, Mr. Hewlett?"

"I'm negotiating for my father-in-law, Iron Barrett. I believe you've looked at our file."

"Yes, and I'm delighted you came in. I see we had a serious misunderstanding about the video auction."

"Yes, we did. I can assure you that we acted out of ignorance, Miss Winston. However, it's in connection with that auction that I'm here today. I'm sure you can understand that since we weren't allowed to sell our cattle, we now need an operating loan."

She blinked. "Why would you need an operating loan?"

Dumbfounded, Mike tried to keep his words even and his voice level. "We need money to feed our cattle, Miss Winston."

"Can't they just eat grass?"

Mike drew a deep breath. Careful, careful, he coached himself. His ability to control his temper was why he was sitting here right now, instead of Iron. "We pasture them during summer of course. Although they need supplements even then. During the winter they need feed."

Miss Winston flushed, and she looked sternly at the paper. "I see," she said solemnly.

But Mike sensed she didn't see at all. She didn't know a thing about feeding cattle or any other kind of livestock or farming in general.

She frowned again and tapped her pencil rapidly. She straightened in her chair. "I suggest that you slaughter the cattle, Mr. Hewlett."

"Slaughter?" he asked incredulously.

"Cattle are meant to be eaten or to give milk, aren't they?"

Mike had been prepared for dealing with Peterson's condescending manner. He had come prepared to deal with bumbling bureaucrats and all manner of ineptness, but nothing had prepared him for dealing with this level of ignorance.

"This is a cow/calf herd, miss. Breeding stock. Registered cattle." He could see that nothing he was saying rang a bell.

"I believe you must slaughter them anyway, and I'm denying your request for a loan."

"No good," Mike told Iron later. "I couldn't get the money. There's only one thing to do, and that's to auction all the cattle again. Let the FDIC arrange it with the check cut in their name."

The lines on Iron's face deepened.

"Sorry." Mike waited. He had not told Iron about Miss Winston's stupidity or the fear that had gripped him about an hour after he left the bank. They had to get out from under these people as soon as possible. It was like a combine moving toward them, reaping everything in its path—the wheat with the chaff.

"Maybe we could just sell off some of the equipment," mused Iron, "and keep the cattle. I'm thinking maybe selling them wasn't such a good idea after all."

"What will we do for money for feed?" Mike asked.

"We'll buy it with the money from any machinery we sell."

"They won't let us, Iron. That's the point. According to them it's not ours to sell. If we sell a tractor, they won't let us buy feed. They'll make us apply the money to the main note."

Iron snapped open his lighter, lit his Camel, and paced the floor.

"I'm not selling the cattle. I've changed my mind."

"You've got to," Mike stammered. "There's no other way. They've got us cornered."

"I'll find a way."

"We don't have much feed left. We're running out of time."

"There's a way."

Mike looked at him then, seeing the naked pain, the tremor in Iron's hands as he brought the cigarette to his lips. He waited him out.

Slowly Iron blew out a ring of smoke. "Never, never thought I could bring myself to do this. But I'm going to ask my mother to cash in the CDS she's got set aside to pay for long-term care. Most of them are in other banks."

Mike's heart sank. He closed his eyes, too stunned to speak.

"Can't do that, son," Alma said. "Would if I could."

Iron looked at her, trying to understand. "Mom, I wouldn't ask this of you if I thought there was the slightest chance I couldn't make it good."

"Oh, I know that. You're my boy. You think I don't know that? I mean I can't. They're gone."

"Gone?"

"To Dennis. Dennis needed them to tide him over in his shop. He needed supplies, new equipment. I thought you knew."

So that's why he seems to be such a good manager, with money to spare, Iron thought. *He's been fleecing his grandmother.*

"Don't worry about it, Mom. It was just a thought." Iron rose and squeezed her shoulder. "We're going to get by just fine. Your CDs would have made it a little easier. That's all."

"Wish I could have helped," Alma said. "Can't help you both."

Iron left quickly, unable to quell his anger.

"So that's why the interest statement from the bank didn't jive with my tax information last spring," Mary said. "The CDs weren't there anymore."

Iron looked out the window with a fixed, unseeing gaze. Breaking out of his trance, he turned to Mary. A muscle in his jaw jerked. "I don't want to talk to Dennis. I don't want to look at him. I don't want him around. I don't want him included in financial planning, or family holidays. I'd stop him from going to my own funeral if I could. I can do everything but disinherit him, because he's taken everything from me I could ever leave him."

My farm, my farm.

My son, my son.

Unbidden, J.C.'s face at the bank closing came to mind.

Mike passed Mary as she was walking back from giving Alma her insulin shot. "Want a ride?" he called as he stopped his pickup, spraying gravel. "I was heading toward your place anyway."

"Sure." She opened the door and stepped inside. "What's on your mind?"

"The farm."

"No kidding."

"Mary, we've got to come up with a decent plan."

"Iron will . . ."

"Iron is so mad at Dennis that he's like talking to a rock right now." Mike's ruddy face trickled with sweat.

Sighing, she answered, "You're right. I know you're right."

"We need a cohesive approach to all this, Mary. Something thought out that makes sense. Lisette means well, and she knows Dennis is in the wrong, but she wants to outwit people like a little street fighter. Alma thinks she can set things right by cutting back. Did you know she's started reusing her old coffee grounds? Like a little penny pinching is going to do the trick."

"No, I didn't know, but it sounds just like her."

"The point is, we need a plan. Everyone is doing stuff willy-nilly and isolated. The family should stick together."

"We've never been through anything like this before. How can we know what to do?"

"We've got to start. Get some information together, Mary. Find out what we own and what we owe and what it will take us to live on and then we'll go from there. If Iron won't do this, you'll have to. Then we'll find a decent lawyer and see what we could and should be doing, before we get ourselves into worse trouble than we already are."

"Oh, I hate to do that," she said, blinking back tears. "Just step into Iron's place like I don't trust him to do things. It won't sit right with him."

"You must," Mike said. "For all our sakes."

"He's not going to like it."

Iron's anger frightened Mary. A silent stranger, he rushed out of the house each morning, jaw set, and worked with the indifferent efficiency of a Bradley tank. He slept in fits and starts, with shallow breaths interspersed with sighs and groans. Some nights he lay wide awake on his back with his arms locked behind his head, blinking sightlessly into the dark from 3:00 AM until the alarm went off.

"We can't just do nothing," she whispered desperately one night, sensing he had been awake for hours. "We have to do something."

He did not reply. Furiously she turned onto her side and buried her face in the pillow.

Mike was right. Iron was far too angry to make any intelligent moves toward dealing with the FDIC. Eventually he would probably do the right thing, the smart thing, but it might be too late. She fretted over aggravating him further; she was about to invade his territory. He had always made any large financial decisions regarding farm operations.

That noon he sat brooding in the wing chair, staring out the window at the pasture as though he expected a miracle to appear there.

"Iron," she said hesitantly.

He turned with the stony look on his face she was starting to know all too well.

"I want to talk to you about everything that's happening to us."

He rose abruptly. "It'll have to wait until supper. I've got work to do."

At supper that night, he filled his plate and carried it to the recliner in front of the TV and sat with his eyes not wavering from the set. Even during commercials.

He's faking it, thought Mary furiously. *He's never watched* Wheel of Fortune *in his life. He just doesn't want to talk to me.*

She gathered up the dishes and carried them to the sink. Then, bracing herself, she walked over to the TV and turned it off with a decisive click.

"I need to talk to you about the farm and the FDIC," she said. "Right now. Mike says we've got to get a bunch of information together and figure out how to buy feed."

Iron exploded. "I'm sick and tired of all of you hounding me. Asking for answers I don't have. Hell, my own family is worse than the FDIC."

She drew back from his anger and sank into the recliner opposite him. "Iron, please."

"Shut up. Just shut up about it, Mary. I'm sick of your nagging. All of you. Mike's the worst of all. I need a little time to think and a little support to get on top of things. We can't afford to make any more wrong moves around here."

She plopped down into the nearest chair, frozen with despair, her hands clenched tightly on her lap. Never, never before had he ever told her to shut up.

"You don't have time, Iron. That's what we've been trying to tell you." Then her heart thundered with resentment and she blew sky high. "You don't have any right to criticize your poor son-in-law, who is just trying to do his best. He's one of the few people who's actually contributed any money to this household. He cashed a savings bond he had hung onto forever."

"I said ease up. I'm tired of you telling me what to do and how to think."

"Don't talk to me like that!" Her voice quavered. "You've never talked that way to me before, Iron. Never. No matter what else we've been through."

He stood, staring stonily out the window, his hands thrust in the back pockets of his jeans. He turned, unable to say he was sorry, but his features softened and he looked at his hands, rubbing his gnarled work-scarred knuckles over and over. Then he held out his arms with a guilty expression on his face, moving to embrace her.

Mary looked at him hard, incredulous that he thought that was all it would take, then she whirled around and walked off.

She woke up before Iron the next morning, poured a cup of coffee, and took it outside to the rose arbor. Gloomily she looked at all the neglected canes—long overdue for pruning, loaded with dead roses. She was falling terribly behind on all her work. If she didn't get on top of it soon, she would never get caught up. The morning was gray and miserable, and she needed her jacket, but not badly enough to go after it and risk encountering Iron.

Having been married for twenty-seven years, she was used to his silences until he worked through problems. After stewing for weeks he would discuss everything in a rush. But this blind refusal to confide in her at all was breaking her heart.

Far up in the sky a flock of geese formed a wobbly V as they winged steadily toward the south. She watched them until they were out of sight. She envied their sure sense of where they were supposed to go, what they were supposed to do.

Springtime, harvest, Christmas, Easter, county 4-h Days, fair time. That hadn't changed. The cycles were there. But she was no longer certain what her response was supposed to be. She felt off kilter, like a planet shoved subtly out of orbit.

Her head shot up when a rabbit entered the rose arbor. It had eaten a hole in the plastic bird barrier fence she had put up in spring. "Get out," she cried, tears staining her cheeks. "Go on, get." She sprang to her feet and rushed at it, clapping her hands. It bounded away, slipping easily back through the hole.

Then she squared her shoulders. So. It was going to be up to her to get things done.

All right, she thought, seething inside, I'm going to play like I'm a widow, instead of a wife. I'll play like everything is entirely up to me. Which it is! She decided to start gathering information.

She changed into new jeans and a fresh plaid shirt and tank top and drove to the courthouse. Hoping she wouldn't meet anyone she knew, she crossed the marble-floored lobby and studied the collection of free pamphlets displayed outside the extension office. She gathered up a bunch of government bulletins, including every single flyer on Ag Law and coping with financial crises.

Furtively, she hurried out. When she reached the car, she was suddenly ashamed of her secretiveness. The county newspaper had had an article the week before about financial planning software available through the ASCS office.

We are in trouble, she thought bitterly. *I'm sick and tired of playing like everything is just rosy.* She drove to the ASCS office and asked for the software. Her cheeks rusted up like red plums at the knowing glances, the silence in the room, but she kept her hands still and her chin raised.

It would be all over the county by nightfall that she had asked for this information. Of course rumors had been flying about after the bank closing, but it was the first public admission by the family that things were not at all as they should be at Mary's Place.

The Barretts were definitely, officially, in trouble.

21

When Mary got back home, she laid out all eight bulletins on "When Your Income Drops." Then she began working through the steps for determining their net worth. She rounded up all their insurance policies, including life, automobile, farm vehicles, accident, disability, health, and homeowners.

Iron was an insurance salesman's dream.

Listing all their assets and liabilities took up the rest of the morning. At first it felt good. It felt a thousand times better than just waiting for Iron to make a move. Then her optimism dropped to the bottom of the well when she focused on all the safety nets they should have had and didn't.

Why didn't they have substantial savings accounts and CDs? Why did they always put every blessed cent they could get their hands on into land? Or a new piece of equipment? Year after year. They had always done so.

The only things they had of value besides the farm and the house were their furnishings and a few scattered antiques, which she had refinished.

On the plus side, as she followed the outline on her computer, she was proud of the fact they had no outstanding debts other than to the bank. Of course most of their vehicles were tangled up in the farm loan. But still, there were no credit card debts, or taxes owed, or installment notes payable, or loans against any of their insurance policies.

She inserted the market value of the land, downgraded by a full one-third practically overnight. Her lips thinned into a stark white line. They had a negative net worth of $100,000.

Paralyzed with dread, she sat rigidly upright with her hands under her thighs, her elbows locked. She pressed against the seat of the hard wooden chair until her muscles rebelled and relaxed.

She rose, poured a cup of black coffee, stretched her aching back, then sat back down to predict their cash flow. Connie had told them there were too many people trying to make a living off one farm. *She's right,* thought Mary. *We're bleeding the place dry, and it's getting worse every year. There's just too many families living off this one piece of earth.*

She gave up trying to predict their income and expenses, let alone that precious cash flow projection bankers were seeking like it was the Holy Grail. Who knew? Who could tell?

If pests invaded, they would need to spend money on spraying. If one crop got hailed out, they would plant something to replace it. If it were dry, they would spend more money on fuel to keep the irrigation flowing to their corn. If the pasture burned up, they would have to buy hay for their cattle.

Finally she threw up her hands and settled down in her chair clutching all the publications on Ag Law. She read steadily for an hour, fighting a rising sense of panic.

I don't understand any of this, she thought wildly. *How can I be expected to understand all this stuff?*

She rose and went to the phone and started to call Elizabeth then replaced the receiver before she had dialed the last two numbers, worried that it would stir up more problems with Iron. He had been mortified when they had to borrow grocery money from his daughter to begin with, and that was when they had been certain they would pay it back within a month.

But after the cattle sale fell through and Iron sensed their troubles might be prolonged, he was sick with humiliation each time he accepted an additional dollar. He had asked Mary to put a good face on their finances when she talked to Elizabeth.

I can't work on this any longer, she thought. *It's making me crazy.* She saved her work and turned off the computer. She shoved the piles of paper aside and started out the back door, intending to put up a better barrier against the rabbits invading the rose garden.

But she suddenly recalled Elizabeth's words. Words that still haunted her. "You always march off and build something, Momma. Something you can see."

She trembled and covered her face with her hands.

"I will see this through," she whispered. "I'm the only one who can until Iron takes over again."

She went back inside, sat down at the desk, and rebooted her computer. The terminology and details were over her head. *In the old days,* she thought, *we would be turning to J.C. for advice.* Now there was no one.

Then she thought of a lawyer who had been one of her high school classmates. Dale Culp had the reputation for being honest, even if he wasn't a mover and a shaker. Suddenly honest sounded better than anything else in the world. Impulsively she dialed him, still staring at the spreadsheet.

Dale Culp, attorney-at-law, looked like an old basset hound with sad, aging eyes. In his late forties, he was still lean, with thinning brown hair and sagging jowls that matched his melancholy view of the human race.

He rose to greet Mary when she stepped inside the office.

"Pleasure, Mary. Have a seat."

She smiled warmly, suddenly glad she had come. "I know you're wondering what I'm doing here without Iron," she said. "I'm gathering some preliminary information about our farm and dealing with the FDIC, so we won't make the wrong moves. They've taken over our note. I can hardly make myself say the words," she mumbled, chagrined at her lack of courage.

She tracked his eyes, wanting to know what he thought of her. Was he judging them? Did he think they were fools?

"I'm glad you came to me first," he said. "Some folks are starting to show up in my office too late for me to do the job I could have done at the very beginning."

"Oh, I'm plenty late in doing this," she said. "You'll have your work cut out for you, all right. But I know you're wondering why Iron isn't here with me."

"You're not the first wife who has shown up on her own."

"He will come with me soon." She fingered a fold in her jacket and looked away. "He just needs a little more time."

"Mary, I've known you both all my life. I understand more than you think."

Suddenly she felt sheltered, at ease with this homely man. And wild, absolutely wild, to talk with someone outside the family. "Tell us what to do, Dale. That's what I came here for. I just don't know what to think of all this."

"It doesn't matter, Mary, what you think or what I think. What matters is what the FDIC thinks of your farm, and the very fact that the new bank owners didn't retain your notes says they think you're on shaky ground."

"But we're really not. This mess is of their own making, Dale. That's what's so frustrating. We've never missed a payment."

"It doesn't matter," he said sharply. "They think your note is under-secured. They don't think you have the chance of a snowball in hell of paying back this kind of money. What they're really saying is that there is no way for you to service your debt."

"We always have."

"Not at these interest rates. Not at these prices for grain."

"But we have, Dale! We're good managers. We've always, always paid our bills. Look at this net worth statement."

Her hands shook as she handed him the papers. "Do you see any debts there other than to the bank? Any credit card balances? Any installment payments? That's why we've always been able to pay what we owe. We organize our finances around paying bills first. I'm here to help my husband. Not argue."

The lawyer looked at her with compassion then cleared his throat. "Like I said, Mary, it doesn't matter how I see things. You're preaching to the converted."

He glanced at the printout.

"Is this a clear look at where you stand financially? What you own and what you owe?"

She nodded.

"Excellent. No long-term debts at all other than to the bank?"

"No, none."

"I'm going to stay in the background a while," he said, "and coach you a little on dealing with the FDIC. I want you to get your hands on security agreements. We need to know what you actually have listed as collateral and whose names are on all your notes. I want to see your universal commercial code statements."

"I wouldn't know them if I saw them," she said.

"That's the public notice the bank filed at the register of deeds or with the secretary of state. They're little slips of paper about 5 x 8, and they list what you agreed to give the bank for collateral for each loan."

"I've never even heard of these things." She jumped up from her chair as though she were taking flight then abruptly sat back down. "Oh, I could just wring Iron's neck for not coming with me."

"Did you give him a chance?"

"No. He's too upset right now, and we're giving each other a wide berth."

"I want him to get a copy of all the documents that are in the FDIC's possession," he said. "As soon as possible, and I want this done discreetly. We need to look at them. Perhaps there's a mistake. A signature missing, some other omission, a loophole."

"You're making it all sound so sleazy."

"You're playing with the big boys, Mary. If you don't know that now, you soon will."

"Anything else I need to know?"

"Don't, for God's sake, sign any blank papers," Culp said. "Don't sign anything without showing it to me first. Document every single word you say to those people, and everything you do. Think paper trail. You and Iron both. Like you're Hansel and Gretel and these little scraps of paper are your only way out of the forest. Which they are. Write letters to confirm everything and start keeping a daily diary."

She pulled a notebook out of her purse, and he looked on with approval as she started a list.

"Your motto needs to be the five w's. I want a written record of who, what, when, where, and why for every single word exchanged with the FDIC from here on out."

"You make it sound like we're dealing with the Mafia."

"No, Mary, they're just people with a job to do. They do it very well. Just keep one thing in mind. The FDIC is a liquidator, not a lending institution. Their job is to see that Uncle Sam gets back the most money possible."

"We've blown our best chance, haven't we? Getting our note picked up by the new owners of the bank."

"I'm afraid so."

"What's the next best thing to do?"

"Let's try to get you certified for a one-year guaranteed FmHA loan for money to operate on. Iron is going to have to sign a waiver giving the county committee access to your files."

"He won't do that. He's never liked the FmHA. He hates Clifton Hathaway. The feeling is mutual. We don't stand a chance of getting approval with Hathaway on that committee."

"Well, Iron had better start toadying up to someone fast. He needs to move before Clyde Peterson leaves town, because that man has the authority to write down loan amounts."

She swallowed hard. "Actually, our chances with Peterson aren't any good either."

"In a couple of months, the main FDIC force will move out, just leaving a skeletal staff behind who will go by the book. There won't be anyone left to talk to who can actually help you."

"I'm going straight home and try to reason with Iron."

"Keep your chin up and keep reminding yourself that you're not the only one in this position. And if it gets to the place where you want to work outside the home, I hope I'm the first to know. We always have extra clerical work around here. If I can't have the daughter, perhaps I can have the mother."

"The daughter?"

"Yes, I was real sorry when Elizabeth decided not to come into practice with me. I just supposed you knew."

Too stricken to speak, Mary just looked at him, the tears rolling silently down her cheeks. She fumbled in her purse for a Kleenex, blew her nose, and squared her shoulders. "We had a fight over making a will," she said. "A real humdinger. I think Elizabeth just decided that living in the same town with all of us wasn't going to be worth it. But I'm so sorry. So terribly sorry. It would have been wonderful, having all three of my children in the same county. So we managed to ruin things for her too."

"Put that thought out of your mind, Mary. Her job with FACT is a wonderful opportunity. She probably would have snapped it right up, anyway. This old practice is pretty small potatoes for someone with her abilities."

Mary smiled, but she didn't believe a word he was saying.

As soon as Mary left, Dale called the Farmers Agriculture Conservation and Technology office in Manhattan and asked to speak with Elizabeth Barrett. He told her about his slip and apologized.

"But that's not the main reason for this call, bad as I feel about it," he said. "I'm calling to tell you that if you have any influence over your father, you'd better tell him to get his act together before it's too late."

Mary saw Iron walking toward the machine shed. She sat slumped at the wheel of the car for a moment then started across the farmyard.

"Need something?" he called from behind the tractor.

"I need to talk," she said, too exhausted to try for the right tone, the right time. "I've been to see Dale Culp. I had to go, Iron. This is all driving me crazy."

"Christ."

"I'm sorry. But one of us had to take the bull by the horns. Don't be mad."

"I'm not mad at you," he said mechanically. "Elizabeth just called and got me all riled up again. Now you're telling me you've found someone else who wants to stick their oar in my water."

"I don't want us to fight again, Iron."

"Well, how did Dale Culp think I should be running my business?"

She told him everything Dale had said. Iron listened with quiet skepticism until she got to the part about applying for an FMHA loan.

"Absolutely not," he said. "That's out."

"That's what I told Dale, but he's says it would still be the best way."

"Hell, if you buy a package of chewing gum it has to be written down somewhere. A man can't get any work done dealing with them. Besides, Hathaway hates my guts. He would never give me a break."

"We don't have many choices," said Mary. "Believe me."

"There are a few," Iron said. He wiped his hands on a grease rag and stared at his boots. "Elizabeth read me the riot act for not staying on top of all this. She told me about ways of dealing with the FDIC that have worked for other people. I'm going to start looking into them this very afternoon. All that financial information you came up with is going to make my job easier. I'm going to talk to bankers outside this county."

She was weak with relief that Elizabeth had finally gotten through to him.

"Do you need me to get some clothes ready?"

He smiled broadly for the first time in two weeks. "If you think it will help. Won't hurt to try a step above jeans, I guess."

He was back by five o'clock, white-lipped and weary with defeat.

"What happened?"

"They're flooded, for one thing. Every single borrower the new owners turned down has come to see them. Seems as though everyone had the same bright idea I did about two weeks ago."

"What are you going to do?"

"I'm going out again tomorrow. Bright and early in the morning. As you pointed out, we don't have too many choices."

He was home at noon the next day, and she brightened at the hope on his face. "You got the money?"

"Not exactly, but I got the promise of money, if I can get the note down to just where it would have been if the cattle sale had gone through."

"So we're selling them after all?"

"Yes. And this time, I'm going to dot all my i's and cross my t's. I'll have all the processes approved by the FDIC first. The check will be made out to them and applied against my note."

Iron asked Mike to negotiate the sale with the FDIC.

"I think you sit a little better with the man," he said with a wry smile. "But don't let the sumbitch know we're switching to another bank just as soon as the sale goes through. Peterson is supposed to be acting in the best interests of the government, but personally, I think he would just love to see me lose this place."

Mary watched Iron move about the farmstead, putting things in order. He cracked jokes about his new banker. This was the old Iron she knew and loved. A stayer and a fighter.

Beyond her kitchen window lay the giant expanse of the fertile prairie. She abandoned herself to a surge of optimism. They had done their best and hadn't given up. The Good Lord had seen them through.

Her wide, wild heart needed a farm. She just knew it couldn't, wouldn't, be anywhere but on a wheat farm in Western Kansas.

22

Chief liquidation officer Clyde Peterson agreed to the new auction. "I assume your family is aware of all the procedures this time? Isn't going to try to pull another fast one?"

Mike took a deep breath to control his temper. "Dennis didn't know he couldn't sell the cattle without the FDIC's permission. Now we know, and we want to cooperate with any and all regulations."

Peterson nodded stiffly. "We'll notify you when all the paperwork has been processed."

Mike rose and shook Peterson's hand.

Peterson reached for the phone when Hewlett left. He was getting acquainted with a few people, and Clifton Hathaway had been the first to come forward and offer a little hospitality. He appreciated the information Hathaway had given him about some of the no-account farmers who would be out to screw the government. Iron Barrett was at the top of the list.

Just last week, Hathaway had pointed out some of the opportunities that existed for a man in Peterson's position. Opportunities that depended on timing and advance information.

"If you know of some property that might be doomed to the auction block no matter what people try to do, let me know," Hathaway said.

There was nothing really illegal in what the man was proposing. Nothing at all.

Then Hathaway added, "I admire your head for business, Peterson. If you need financing, for whatever, let me know. I'm always looking for good people to finance."

Peterson blinked at the subtly disguised bribe. "Property does come up, from time to time. Land you might be interested in."

"Just let me know."

Dennis laid down his wrench when Clifton Hathaway shouted a hello from the open doorway of his machine shop. He was glad for the interruption. Thoughts he didn't like much had been chasing around in his brain ever since Dad had shut him out. The most troublesome of all had to do with Grandma Alma.

He had managed to piss the old woman off. Since childhood he had always known the minute he crossed some line with her. She hadn't liked the mangled video sale one little bit and told Dennis she didn't believe for a second Iron would have made the same mistake. She was judgmental as hell when it came to managing money.

"Got a minute?" asked Hathaway.

"Sure."

His neighbor came inside and looked around with admiration.

"Quite a setup you've got here. I've got a tractor that needs a little work. I understand you're the man to see."

Dennis hesitated. Iron had made it clear years ago there were certain men he was not to do business with. Clifton was one of them. "Bring it by."

"Wednesday, okay?"

Dennis nodded.

"Hear you're having a few problems out your way."

Instantly alert, Dennis shrugged. "Just a little misunderstanding with the folks at the bank."

Hathaway eyed him with amusement. Details of all the Barretts' various encounters with the FDIC were all over town.

"Sorry to hear that. Guess they're putting the squeeze on a lot of people. I've known your dad for a long time. We were in the same class together." Hathaway talked on, keeping his expression bland but scrutinizing Dennis's, taking note of any minute twitching or tightening. "Course Iron always did have a stubborn streak."

When Dennis's eyes hardened at the last comment, Hathaway pressed his advantage. "Good thing he has a son to lean on. My Henry is about your age. I've practically turned my whole operation over to him."

Dennis flushed, and the cords tightened in his neck. It was all Hathaway could do to keep from smiling. "Course I reckon it would be a hard thing for a man like Iron to turn loose of the reins, if he's still as set in his ways as he used to be."

He broke through the final barrier. In twenty minutes, Clifton Hathaway pieced together enough information about the Barretts' finances to get a very clear picture of a family struggling to keep their heads above water.

"The hell of it is, Dennis, there's no need," Hathaway said carefully. "No need for any of you to go through all this."

Dennis looked at him hungrily.

"I realize that as behind times as Iron is, he probably can't see the forest for the trees, but it's the folks who are taking a write-down or declaring bankruptcy who are actually coming out ahead."

"Could you bring yourself to do that?" Dennis asked, shocked.

"Could if I had to, but I'm not in that situation. Your father is. Point is, there's more ways to get out of paying debts than there are to skin a cat."

"Not for my father."

"Well, times have changed. Everyone plays by different rules now. It takes you young folks to even things up. If you were *my* son, I sure wouldn't have any problem turning things over to you."

Dennis looked at him gratefully.

"I can just tell by looking around this place you've got a head for business. You make decisions based on good judgment instead of sentiment."

Dennis flushed. "I've done all right."

"You know what this county needs," Hathaway went on, "what the town of Gateway City needs is a home plate umpire for all these farmers. Someone with the guts to tell them they've struck out and even hurry them along a little when they've gone down for the count."

Dennis quirked his eyebrows and waited.

"We'd be doing them all a favor. Doesn't mean they couldn't get back in the game again. Just means they struck out in that particular inning and are being benched before they kill themselves swinging at foul balls."

"That's a different way of looking at it."

"It's the truth. It's the merciful thing to do. There's more uses for land than just crops."

"What uses?"

Clifton glanced at his watch.

"Haven't got time to go into them now. We'll talk more Wednesday when I bring my tractor by."

By then, Dennis had spent three days thinking. As he worked on the tractor, he again listened to everything Hathaway said.

"Despite what your dad thinks, Peterson isn't out to get anyone. He can't find anyone to talk within your family. You know how sentimental Mike's thinking is, and Iron's like talking to a stone wall. I've told Peterson you're the one he should be dealing with."

By the end of the week, Dennis could barely stand to think of the harm his father had caused the family by his mismanagement. It was a crying shame. By Monday morning, he knew that if the Barretts were to survive, it would be through his more up-to-date views, not Iron's clinging to the past. He gave Hathaway a ring.

"Good. Glad to hear you're with us. We need your cooperation on something that's coming up right away."

J.C. Espy brooded as he watched people come and go from the Agland State Bank. His living room window was across the street and diagonally down from the bank. The bank that should have belonged to an Espy for another hundred years. Obsessed with peoples' doings in that institution, he had ordered a set of binoculars from Sears and spent hours every day studying the faces of people who entered and left.

It didn't take more than a glance at Mike Hewlett's face one October morning to know that there were deep troubles brewing in that household. Deep indeed, for Iron to send his son-in-law to deal with the FDIC. But Iron deserved all the trouble the United States government could give him.

All the farmers did.

One week later, he smiled grimly when he saw Dennis Barrett and Clifton Hathaway come out of the bank together. Hard telling what those two were cooking up.

J.C.'s hands trembled with frustration. In the old days, their paperwork would have told him everything. He turned away from the thin lace curtain and went out to the backyard to rake leaves.

Iron stewed and fretted at the red tape that had delayed putting the cattle on the market while it was high. The district office had to approve the sale. Their precious supply of feed was steadily being depleted.

"Thank God in heaven," Mary said, the morning before the new video sale, as they heard the latest upbeat market reports broadcast over the radio. "It's going to work out. It'll be over by this time tomorrow." She grinned through a quick welling of tears as she squeezed Iron's arm. "We'll be fine, honey. Just fine."

This time, Iron and Mary and Mike and Connie watched the auction by themselves. It was the middle of the week, and there were no grand-children clustered at their feet, as they were all in school. Alma was home nursing a cold. Lisette was going over later to fix supper and check her blood sugar levels.

Alma had made it a point to inform Mary that Dennis was going to Hays to pick up a motor for a truck he was working on. "Don't suppose Iron would have invited Dennis over anyway." She didn't miss a chance to reproach Mary for Iron's shunning of his only son. "I never was one to carry a grudge. He doesn't get that from me."

"Let me see the catalog," Iron said. "With any luck at all, ours will be sold early, before buyers have a chance to get spooked."

"We didn't get one," Mary said, "but I'm sure they used the same information we gave them last time."

"I'd like to know where they are in the line-up anyway. Oh Jesus!" he erupted suddenly. Iron slammed one fist into the palm of his other hand as he watched the tail end of the preshow. "This isn't a special breeding sale. It's mixed between breeders and fats and feeders."

By midmorning, their expectations had given way to despair. All the cattle were selling low, and seller after seller passed out—rejecting chances to bid. The auction company had required a new video, but Iron had been too angry over the additional expense to watch the day of the taping. As a few preview shots of the herd flashed across the screen, he saw with relief that the video had been produced with the same expertise as last time.

"Lot number 119," said the announcer. "Offered by the Agland State Bank."

"They didn't give your name, Iron," Mike yelled. "What the hell? Half the buyers in the state know you've got a premium herd. They won't bring nearly as much without your name."

Grimly, they listened to the auctioneer.

"This nice set of feeder heifers are top quality and should bring top dollars when they're ready for the packing plant."

Iron exploded to his feet. "They can't do this. They're being sold as feeders instead of breeding heifers. We've got to get this stopped. How could this have happened?"

"They've split your herd." Mike's voice shook with outrage. "They're not even selling them as cow-calf pairs."

"I've got to get the sale stopped. Right now." Iron raced to the phone and dialed the auction company. He listened, then he slammed down the receiver, knocking the phone and half the items on the desk to the floor. "They won't take my call because I don't have an identification number and an authorization code."

"Phone the bank right now, Mary," Mike ordered, "and get a hold of Miss Winston and then put me on. I want to talk to her. We've got to stop this sale."

Mary's hands shook as she fumbled through the numbers. Mesmerized, she stared at the TV set while the receptionist put her through.

Their heifers had sold for two-thirds of the price they had brought during the original auction. Her stomach contracted in protest. The cows followed. They were described as good, usable cows, extremely gentle, with several good years left. Tears stung her eyes. The announcer made it sound like they were all ready to be put to sleep. Finally, she was put through to Miss Winston.

"Here." She handed the phone to Mike.

The family's attention was torn between the television and listening to the one-sided conversation.

"Miss Winston, there's been a terrible mistake made with our cattle. Stop that sale at once."

Mike's face flushed with rage. "You cancel out that sale right now or we're going to turn you anywhere but loose. I can promise you that you're about to bring so much grief down on your heads that the FDIC will wish they had never heard of the Barrett family."

"Too late." Iron's voice broke. "Too late. They just sold for a fraction of what they did last month. Too late." Then he sank to a level of cursing that made Mary put her hands over her ears.

"Any buyer with a lick of sense will know something's wrong," Mike said.

"So?" said Iron bitterly. "We didn't pass out. It's a done deal. Do you think the buyer's just going to give them back? Or do you think he's going to count his blessings at having been handed a gold mine."

"We've got to get to the bank right now and talk some sense into those people."

"I'm going with you," Mary said. Connie grabbed her jacket, and they ran out to the station wagon.

Miss Winston half rose when they stormed into her office.

"Call the video company right now," Iron ordered.

"Who the hell was responsible for that script? That's what I want to know." Mike slammed his fist on her desk.

"I . . . I wrote the copy," she stammered. "I thought I did a good job. Mr. Peterson gave me all the information."

"Pick up that phone and make things right, or everyone in the Agland State Bank will pay and pay and pay."

"Look here. I'm sorry." Her chin quivered. "It was a *natural* mistake. They can't expect someone from Boston to know all about cattle."

Then she got a grip on herself. Toughened up. Acted like a liquidation specialist. "And you can't come in here threatening me like this. Like I'm some ogre trying to do you in. All of you. This whole *town* is down on me." She stabbed at the buttons on the telephone. "Security please. I need security in my office at once."

"Miss Winston," Mary said, "call that video company right now. There's no need for you to ask for security. No one is going to hurt you."

But Miss Winston clung to the arms of her chair and refused to pick up the phone. The security officer rushed into her office.

"Show these people out, please."

"You can't do this," shouted Iron as the man took him by his arm. "We need to know who bought those cattle."

"Let's go," Mike said, with a warning shake of his head. "This isn't getting us anywhere."

All four of them filed silently out of the bank, ignoring the stares of curious customers.

"Come on," Iron said. "Hurry. We're going to see the sheriff."

Mike looked at him skeptically.

"I want to get a restraining order against that buyer. I don't want him near those cattle."

"Do we need to see a lawyer first?" Mike asked.

"How the hell would I know? We're going to start with the sheriff." He ran toward the station wagon.

Four livestock trucks pulling possum belly trailers were dispatched to Mary's Place. Since Iron had not herded and penned his cattle, one of the drivers phoned the buyer. The man had been involved with FDIC auctions before. In a short time, a pickup came rattling up the lane pulling a horse trailer. Two men stepped out, unloaded horses, and started rounding up cattle.

"That's all?" asked the driver when the pasture was empty.

"There's a calf in a barn out back."

"I'll back the truck around and we'll finish up."

In one hour's time, one of the finest herds of breeding cattle in Kansas—years building—was loaded and trucked off Mary's Place.

Sabrina's school bus passed the farm at 3:45 that afternoon, and when she saw the empty pasture, she begged the driver to let her off at her grandparents' house. She ran through the field, crying frantically.

She stumbled and dropped her books and the wind sent loose papers skittering, but she didn't try to retrieve them. Instead, she turned and ran toward the Old Barn.

"Molly." She went inside and looked everywhere. Her voice echoed through the empty barn. The pigeons fluttered wildly.

"Molly!" She flung herself into the far corner of Molly's stall.

When she began to scream, there was no one to hear her.

23

The Barretts spent an hour trying to convince the sheriff that the bank had so grossly misrepresented the cattle that they had a legal claim to the livestock. They wasted another half hour listening to him explain why the FDIC was legally entitled to conduct its business ineptly if it wanted to.

"Possession," Mike said as they returned to the car. "It's important to keep possession. Let's go."

They wheeled into the farm an hour after the last truck had left. Stunned, the four of them stared at the empty pasture.

"They're gone," cried Mary. "They took them all. We weren't even here."

"No chance of that new banker taking me now," Iron said bitterly. "I'm worth sixty percent less than I was two months ago."

"We'll get our money out of them," Mary said, dabbing at her eyes. "You know we will. With something this outrageous, lawyers will jump at the chance to take this case."

"Oh, right," Mike said sarcastically, "considering our unlimited funds for legal work." He stormed out of the car into the house. The rest followed slowly, their faces registering defeat. He dialed the phone and asked for Miss Winston. A few minutes later he called the Superior Livestock Company then slammed down the receiver.

"Neither one of them will give me the name of the buyer," he said, turning to face his in-laws. "They say it's against their policy when banks and the FDIC are involved, because folks have been known to get violent and try to stop the buyers from taking their cattle."

Iron did not speak. He stood clenching and unclenching his fists.

Lisette first assumed that Sabrina had stayed late after school and had just forgotten to tell the family. After a few phone calls to Sabrina's friends, she knew that was not the case.

The three women found her in Old Barn.

As they entered, they heard the child's atonal sobs and rushed to her side.

Gently, Mary pried her granddaughter's fingers off her calf's show halter. Other than making frightened little cooing sounds, like the pigeons inhabiting the cupola, the terrified women could not speak.

They led Sabrina away from Old Barn.

Mary started, hearing Iron's footsteps on the back porch. The night was eerie. She hated the short days of deep fall. It was a full two weeks after the second, ruinous, cattle sale. She felt there would always be more darkness than daylight now.

She was hypersensitive to noise. Even the tiniest sounds reverberated through her soul. She tracked her husband through her familiarity with his little movements. The soft thump of him hanging his jean jacket on a peg.

Now he was tossing his cap on the shelf.

Now the door would open and she would seize the moment to speak with him and he would help her think and they would hold and comfort each other.

But Iron's was the face of a stranger, gray and remote. He went upstairs without speaking. Mary choked back a sob then blew her nose and tried to pull herself together.

First things first, she thought bleakly. Only two things matter; the first is taking care of Iron, protecting him, until his old self kicks back in. The second is keeping things from getting worse.

Iron's despair was so deep she felt she didn't know her own husband. It was like falling off the edge of the world. She would go crazy if she couldn't figure out how to penetrate his silence.

Mary slipped over to Alma's daily and gave her an insulin shot, then she found any excuse to leave as quickly as possible. Her mother-in-law's pitiful little economies were infuriating. Alma poured water through old coffee grounds two days in a row and had removed the light bulbs from every other room in the house so the great-grandchildren wouldn't accidentally waste electricity.

Tomorrow morning, Mary thought, she and Iron would talk. She would make him talk. Then she would make a list of everything they absolutely, positively, had to do.

She confronted him again the next day. "Iron, let me call Elizabeth. Please." She knew her timing was terrible since they both had lain awake for most of the night. But she couldn't wait any longer.

"I've asked you not to do that, Mary. Don't make things any worse than they are."

"Honey, she deals with these kinds of problems every day. She's the expert."

"I said no." He shoved his plate of bacon and eggs to one side and pushed back his chair.

"It's been two weeks since the sale. All Elizabeth knows is that the cattle didn't bring as much money as we were expecting. It's not right. Besides, she might know what to do."

"I said no, Mary." He started toward the back porch.

"Why are you fixing fences when we haven't even got cattle anymore? Please. Talk to me about this."

He stopped and whirled around.

"No. There's nothing to talk about. Don't call Elizabeth. We're draining her dry as it is. She's already buying our groceries and paying our utility bills. What more do you want her to do? Finance a whole farm?"

"I just want her advice. She helps people like us for a living. Every day."

"In the first place, it would be like a doctor trying to treat his own family. She's too close to the situation. In the second place, I'd like to see a little consideration for her feelings. She's just been through a divorce. Her first long visit home in God only knows how long was a nightmare for her. We don't have the right to get her embroiled in all this."

Mary listened as her husband's heart spilled out. So his refusal to call Elizabeth wasn't all pride.

Iron stretched out his calloused hands and studied them. "I also don't want to rile up any more hard feelings in this family than we already have. You go asking people for advice, they usually get pissed off if you don't take it. What if we don't want to do anything she suggests? What then? Asking our own daughter is a little different from talking to a stranger."

Mary knew better than to interrupt. *Why didn't you tell me some of this before,* she thought. *I wouldn't have felt so lonely, so left out.*

"I'd kind of like to hang on to my two daughters. I've lost my son through all this bullshit. He might not have been any prize, but he was my boy. And I've lost my . . ."

He couldn't finish. Mary's heart lurched at the minute quavering of his jaw as he turned and grabbed his coat off the peg.

You've lost your grandson, she silently supplied the words. *And I've lost my granddaughter.*

There had been no contact with any of Dennis's family since the night they found Sabrina in the empty barn. Bitter over Iron's criticism of his cashing in Alma's CDs, Dennis had forbidden the children to set a foot on their place.

Mary had gotten a tearful phone call from Lisette apologizing. "He says you two are keeping the kids upset, and he blames Iron for all the problems to begin with. I just want you to know that none of this is my doing."

"I know it isn't," Mary said gently. "We'll work it all out somehow. I don't think Iron ever dreamed Dennis would use the grandchildren against him."

Now Mary heard about them secondhand through Connie. Heard about Sabrina's listlessness. Heard she never went near the piano. Heard about Benjy's white-faced despair at being forbidden to go near Iron.

Mary watched from the window as Iron walked to the fence bordering their pasture. She stared at the empty field and closed her eyes. When she opened them, for an instant, a splendid herd of mahogany white-faced Herefords appeared in the fog shrouding the pasture. They bawled and spooked like blood-red ghosts in the shifting vapor. She smelled the pungent odor of their urine. She blinked and they were gone, and her heart ached for her husband.

She rubbed the tense cords at the base of her skull and walked over to the desk. She switched on her computer and, while she waited for Lotus to load, she plunged back into worrying about Iron.

In the course of her work, she considered the advantages of living on a farm. They had a roof over their heads—and food.

There never had been a time when the Barretts didn't have a full freezer of beef and a cellar full of fruits and vegetables. Although they didn't milk any cows, the point was they could have if they'd wanted to. Now there were no cattle. Not a one. Not for income, not for slaughter, not for milking.

Frantically, she ran to the paper and checked the ads at their only remaining grocery store. The FDIC had been plumb happy to sell out Henry Green to a fast-growing regional chain when the new bankers decided they didn't want anything to do with the swearing, spitting little merchant.

Mary was stunned at the price of a pound of ground chuck. It was astronomical. But they had a whole freezer full of beef, and so did Connie and Mike and Dennis and Lisette. She started a grim list, ranking expenses. *What do we really need? Rock bottom?* she asked herself, over and over. *What can we do without?* They needed food. They had always had that in abundance. They needed water, and each of their families had a water well. Connie and Mike's had been dug just five years ago.

They needed to keep warm, and there was enough old timber to be had for the cutting, down by the creek bank. They needed clothes. She laughed, thinking of their closets bursting to overflowing, the stashes of material waiting to be sewn up.

If they lived in a city, housing, food, water, and fuel would be the major problems. In the country, the basics were taken for granted. Warmed, she went from an overwhelming panicky sensation to an inexplicable sense of thanksgiving.

Her sudden cheer lasted long enough to buoy her through the next tier of needs and even then, when she began to pinpoint those areas that required cash, she was deeply aware of the family's safety net.

Alma had to have insulin. That cost money, pure and simple. They should keep up their health insurance premiums, no matter what, she decided. The children would need shoes. They had to have electricity and a telephone. All of these things required money.

Then she moved up to the next level. She stared at the monitor, the piles of leaflets. They had to find money for the children's 4-H projects.

At the next level, they had to have money for legal expenses and their farm operation. The tendons in the back of her neck tightened and throbbed.

She stood and paced the room before she could bring herself to face the figures again. Operating money, too, was in the rock bottom category. If they couldn't pay for legal expenses and keep the farm going, they might as well kiss everything else goodbye. Where would they get that kind of money? She looked over their balance sheet and underlined all their possessions that were now tied up by the FDIC. For all practical purposes, they might as well be paupers.

She swallowed, realizing how well off they would have been if they had sold some of their land at the right time or if they hadn't expanded at the wrong time. Too late to be thinking of that now, she thought.

Farming was for gamblers and daredevils, not thinkers. It had never been easy. Farming was dangerous. Accidents happened—limbs were torn off in equipment; men were crushed by vehicles; belts slipped, putting out an eye; animals charged, breaking bones; lungs were seared with a whiff of anhydrous ammonia; chemicals and insecticides sprayed by crop dusters drifted in dangerous patterns.

Farming required a mindset that could live with high risk and thrilled to a life dependent on chance. Farming required carrying on after seeing a field of wheat flattened by hail the night before harvest. Carrying on after disease wiped out a pen of cattle. Carrying on after the bottom dropped out of the grain market. Farming meant coping with crazy-making government programs that shifted like sands in the desert with the wind of each administration.

Iron had always been a man who could take it all, usually with humor and always with courage. Until he got his old fighting spirit back—and she was sure he would—there had to be someone who could tell her what to do. Someone who understood the big picture.

In the past, Iron would have talked everything over with J.C.

That old man still would know, she thought, suddenly inspired. He still would know everything that needed to be done. No point in asking Iron to talk with him. He didn't trust any banker now. But she could see J.C. Ask him a few questions. No one understood the ins and outs of banking like that old man did.

Mary parked in front of J.C. Espy's house. No one answered the doorbell. She turned and began walking back to the car then stopped as he called from the backyard. "I'm out here."

She pushed through the gateway in the high fence and stood mutely in front of their former banker, shocked by his gauntness.

He looked at her in silence, not saying anything to dispel her discomfort.

"I'm here on business, Mr. Espy."

"I don't have a business anymore," he said. Putting one boot on his spade, he bent back to his digging.

"I'm so sorry," she said, "for everything that happened to you. We know how much you've always done for this community. We've appreciated it, J.C. Both of us."

"Get off my property."

"I came to ask for advice."

"Go away."

"Do you want me to beg?" Mary said furiously. "Okay, I'm begging."

He straightened for a moment and looked at the loosened soil. "The shoe was on the other foot a while back. I'm the one who begged and begged. Begged your husband and all the rest of the damn farmers to help me out just a little. Sell off a little land and pay down your notes so they would look better to examiners. Begged all of you to give me proper financial and cash flow statements. Begged all of you to stop assuming you were entitled to more loans for whatever struck your fancy. Begging didn't get me very far then, did it?"

"We're sorry, J.C. We're so terribly, terribly sorry."

"Too late. Now go."

"I need help. Help in dealing with Iron." Her voice quavered. "Tell me what to do. You're the only one I can ask, because Iron has always trusted you. I'm at my wit's end right now, and he simply refuses to face a single thing."

J.C. smiled bitterly. "Yes, I can well imagine. I've dealt with Iron for more years than I care to remember." He pulled the spade out of the dirt and sent it sailing into a morning glory vine. "And where was the help for me when I needed all of you?"

Ashamed, she looked down. Then tears streamed down her face. "We didn't understand. Believe me, we just didn't know."

"Where were the precious farmers when I tried to get a little cooperation? When the bank could have been saved?"

"We didn't understand."

"Well, now you know. Now get out and leave me alone. I'm an old man. I'm probably not going to live a hell of a lot longer, and I'd like to spend those few years in peace. I'm tired of all of you. Tired of your whining."

"We need help," she said stubbornly, digging a Kleenex from the pocket of her jeans. She dried her tears. "Where can we go? What can we do?"

"There's help all around you, Mary. Government organizations, church groups, farm advocacy meetings. But I'm willing to bet you can't get your husband to consider any of them. Not a damn one. Not in planning or coping."

"Iron doesn't like outsiders telling him what to do," she protested.

"What he wants," J.C. said furiously, a vein popping out in his temple, "what all you farmers have always wanted, is to have it both ways. You want the government and the bankers around in bad times, and you want us all to get the hell out and let you do as you please in good times."

"I just don't understand," Mary said, choking back tears, "I just don't understand how we could be worth a fortune one minute and dead broke the next."

His eyes glittered. "Well, join the club, lady. Do you think farmers are entitled? That you deserve to be bailed out and the rest of us don't? Who told you you're in a holy calling and should be protected from adversity?"

"Plenty of people besides farmers get bailed out," Mary protested.

"If you're Chrysler or Lockheed," J.C. said. "If you're big enough. But have you ever seen the government try to save a cafe or a small-town implement business from going under? Or an itty, bitty small-time bank?"

"We've never asked for a handout."

"Oh, but you have. All of you. Year after year. And now look where it's gotten you. You'd better change your thinking, Mary. If you don't, you're going under. Take it from someone who's been there. You should start thinking in terms of bankruptcy right now."

She stared at him. "No, never. Never. At least Iron and I are united on that."

"Oh you are, are you? Better think about it, Mary. You'd get to keep that wonderful house of yours and two cars."

Disgusted with her naivety, J.C. went to retrieve his spade, but he was stopped after a few steps by the sheer silent force of the woman willing him to turn around and face her.

"No bankruptcy, and they are not going to make liars and cheats out of us, either," Mary yelled. "That above all." Her hair, haloed in sunshine, flamed from underneath her scarf. She turned to leave.

Ashamed of his petty urge to hurt this woman, his face softened. He remembered himself as a young banker who had once pledged his life to the community. His brain protested against engaging his sense of justice. He could not afford to be put back together again.

He shouted after her, his voice shaking with anger. "If I knew what to do, I would have saved myself. And even if I knew, I don't owe anyone in this community a damn thing."

24

Mary's cheeks were blotched with tears. She turned into their lane, hurried into the house, and stared at the telephone. She wanted to talk to Elizabeth, but she hated to go against Iron. She wondered what advice her daughter would give to another family.

Maybe if Elizabeth didn't know it was her, she thought hopefully. She had seen a person in a movie change the pitch of their voice by muffling the receiver. She went into the kitchen and got a tea towel, and she wrapped it around the mouthpiece and fastened it with a rubber band. She called the FACTS office.

"This is Elizabeth Barrett," her daughter said pleasantly.

"The FDIC has taken over . . ." Mary choked on her tears.

"Mom? What's wrong? You sound like you have a cold. Mom? Has something happened to Dad?"

"Oh Elizabeth. No, no, honey. He didn't want me to call you. He didn't want to worry you. I feel like I'm letting him down."

"Mom, pull yourself together and tell me what's going on."

Mary stumbled through an account of the disastrous meeting with J.C. and Iron's despair over being cut off from his grandchildren. Then, feeling like she was betraying her husband, she told her about the wreckage evolving from the sale. About Sabrina's calf.

"The cattle sale ruined us, Elizabeth. Just ruined us. And Sabrina. I don't know if Sabrina will ever get over this. We don't know what to do."

"Mom, I need some time to think. There's something about the sale that doesn't make sense."

"Nothing makes sense anymore. I don't understand anything that's going on."

"There are a few people I want to check with. I'll call you back later today."

"Mr. Espy? Elizabeth Barrett. I understand my mother was there to see you earlier."

"Yes," he said curtly.

"And you all but threw her off the place."

"That's putting it a little strongly, Elizabeth. But I'm sure you understand why I wasn't thrilled at being asked for financial advice."

"I know it's hard, but I, too, am asking you to help. Dad won't listen to me directly. So I'm going to approach him through the back door. He's always put stock in what you say. I need some information. Did Mom tell you about the second sale of the cattle?"

"No. What do you mean, second sale?" He clutched the receiver tightly and lowered himself into a chair. "I didn't even hear about a first sale. Why would Iron want to sell his cattle at all? That herd is a good portion of his net worth."

"Not anymore," she said tersely.

"I've never heard of anything so outrageous," he said, after Elizabeth filled him in on the details. "It doesn't make sense. Peterson's job is to get the most money back for the government. I know the bastard doesn't give a damn about human beings, but he's supposed to be looking after the government's interests."

J.C. had known Iron's notes would be turned over to the FDIC, and he had taken perverse pleasure in Mary's visit—knowing that Iron Barrett was squirming. But it seemed the FDIC had a vendetta against one farmer in particular.

Chief liquidation officer Clyde Peterson was clearly out to get Iron Barrett.

He drew a sharp breath. The Barretts were in terrible shape. The five hundred acres of land he had personally financed for Connie and Mike Hewlett by selling his gold was now at risk too. When the bank had gone under, he had lost every cent he had other than that one investment.

At the time, he had been absolutely secure in his belief Iron would pay back the loan. The fool bank examiners might have thought the Barretts were marginal, but he knew better. Paper didn't tell half the story. But if the Barretts went under, he wouldn't even be able to afford a decent meal, let alone health care or a retirement center that didn't make him want to throw up. All the Espys were long-lived. He would spend his remaining years on welfare. Drooling. Cared for by imbecilic sadists with body odor.

"Will you talk to Dad?" Elizabeth asked. "I'll tell you what he should do. And believe me, I do know by now. Are you still there, Mr. Espy?"

"I'm listening."

"If you don't, I'll have to come home. I need access to records at the courthouse. I don't want to quit this job. But if I must, I will."

"No," he said quickly, "that won't be necessary."

His stomach lurched at the thought of Elizabeth Barrett snooping around, taking charge of her folks' affairs. Riling things up. Pawing around at the courthouse. Examining documents.

Signatures. Signatures.

"I'll help," he said. "I'll help."

He swallowed hard as Elizabeth thanked him over and over. She thought he had agreed to help out of the goodness of his heart. This girl, this woman, whom he thought of as a daughter, had no idea of the personal stake he had in Iron Barrett's well-being. Beyond the money, beyond the fact that if Iron went down, he, too, would be as penniless as a railroad bum, was his desire to protect his good name.

The bastards had stripped him of everything else. But he still had his reputation. If Elizabeth discovered the forged signature, his good name would go too. He could not bear to have Mary and Elizabeth Barrett look upon him as a common criminal.

"Advice will sit so much better with Dad if it comes from you."

"Maybe."

"Here's what they must do," Elizabeth said. Briskly she outlined the steps. "There are a few private investors out there who are willing to take a chance on troubled farms. I want my folks to have a shot at that kind of money."

"Be a cold day in hell before you can make Iron Barrett out as anything other than what he is," said J.C.

"What he is, is what these private investors are looking for. I just want that side of him to show. Please don't tell my folks I'm coaching you. Dad would resent it. But something about all this doesn't sound right. Maybe I'm paranoid since it's my own family—"

"You think something's fishy?" he asked, cutting her off. "I agree."

"It would be best if Mom thought everything was your idea until I find out what's going on."

"I want to do a little snooping myself," J.C. said. "And I don't want anyone in the community to know I'm helping Iron. Not even your brother and sister. Will Mary keep her mouth shut about my involvement?"

"As long as she's free to tell Dad, she can handle keeping a secret from the rest of the family."

"She'll wonder why I changed my mind about helping her."

"Just tell her I called and put a guilt trip on you."

"Which is the truth, or most of it," he said flatly.

"Tell my mother to keep quiet because you don't want to be pestered to death by everyone else who's having trouble with the bank."

"True. God knows that's the truth."

Mary parked the pickup in the alley behind J.C. Espy's house. He stuck the spade in the dirt beside a pile of tulip bulbs and waited for her to come through the gate.

He had scoffed at Mary's gullibility when he called, saying he had spoken with Elizabeth and she had persuaded him to help the family.

For old times' sake. Friendship. Any noble word would have worked. Any high-flung explanation. All he had to do was dangle an ideal in front of this family and they took the bait at once.

"Hello, J.C. Thought you might like a little home cooking," Mary said brightly. She showed him a loaf of homemade bread. "I'll run in and put it in the kitchen before we get started."

"Thanks," he said, wincing at the naked hope on her face. Elizabeth had insisted that he begin by getting a clear account of everything that had happened to her parents. "Tell me what has happened to you since the bank closed," he said when Mary returned.

She told him all the details of the bungled cattle sale. The loss of Sabrina's 4-H calf. Rage built over the ineptness of the people now running and ruining the community. The community his family's bank had spent one hundred years building.

"If I help you," he said glumly, "you've got to promise me that you and Iron won't tell a soul I'm advising you. I'm not up to people swarming at me."

"We won't."

"You need to figure out how much income you're all capable of generating."

"I have. Over and over."

He shook his head.

"Not just what the farm will produce. Not anymore. All of you must get jobs. The kids, everyone. I mean everyone. Sabrina can babysit. And that boy—"

"Benjy," said Mary, "his name is Benjamin."

"The boy can pick up aluminum cans."

His head snapped up at her smile.

"You think I'm being cute, woman? You think I'm kind of funny? You think a little money doesn't add up? A lot of little moneys? Let me tell you something. I've seen fortunes built from the nickels and dimes you all sneer at nowadays."

"We're trying to keep the kids out of this as much as possible.".

"Bullshit. A little work will be good for them. Put your wages in a bank in another county. That's the first step."

"Lisette asked right off if we could put wages in another bank," Mary said. "In fact, she's the one who told us not to sign anything until we talked to a lawyer."

"Jobs come first," J.C. said. "Then I want you to put on a unified front. Like you're the Brady Bunch."

"That's going to be touchy. Iron is mad at Dennis."

"Tell him to get over it."

"It's not that simple, believe me."

"I don't give a damn. It's essential. I know some people who might help you out, Mary. Private investors."

"Here? In this county?"

"Back East," he said. "But they won't touch your family with a ten-foot pole if they think you're quarreling. Working against each other."

She looked at him wearily.

"When Iron gets over his tantrum, send him over."

"All right," she said. "We'll all get jobs. But it still won't be enough. Not enough to operate a farm."

"Just do it," he said curtly. "The next time I talk to you, I want to hear that you're all gainfully employed and being considered for a Family of the Year award."

J.C. sat down stiffly on a dilapidated steel lawn chair. Although the day was chilly, its faded red fan back and rusty white tubular arms were warm from the rays of the noonday sun. He slathered more cheap sun protection lotion on his face so he could work longer outside. He rested his elbows on his knees.

He wanted, by God, to smell the last blossoms of late fall. He wanted to inhale the rich smoke of burning leaves. Instead, the scent of fear mixed with crazed hope had invaded his garden. An old, familiar odor that had permeated his bank. Fear and hope. The stench wouldn't go away.

His stomach contracted against the memory of ghost clients, hands like old yellow talons, clutching at him, tearing at his heart, pleading, their eyes hollow, wild with terror.

"Help us, J.C."

"You wouldn't turn an old friend down, would you?"

"Hell, you know I'm good for the money, J.C."

"You and me, we go way back, J.C."

You would think, he thought savagely, *you would think the bastards would have the courtesy to leave me alone here. Leave me be. I'm not a public man anymore.*

Some days, the memory of Black Thursday would assault him right there in his garden, like an attack of screaming birds diving at his mind—the black cars, that door closing. With the memory came a quick surge of bile.

Other days, he missed his bank, missed the structure it had once given to his days. Most of all, he missed the game. Keeping people solvent. Keeping his bank afloat. He missed the heat of the daily battle.

On the worst days, when he could not keep these thoughts at bay, he thought of Forrest, who was now serving a term in a fancy low-security prison as penalty for just a wee bit of fraud. Not much, mind you. Just enough to ruin a community.

He started at the crackling of a branch overhanging his fence. The tree spilled a skiff of oak leaves over his newly raked lawn, spoiling a morning's work. He looked up at the dark clouds boiling below a layer of silver, as though there were two separate skies vying for control.

He felt defeated. Edgy. Money wasn't a game now. When he learned that Mike and Connie's five hundred acres would be at risk, he knew he would be fighting for the quality of the remainder of his life. Not just the fortunes of the Barrett family.

His eyes were drawn to the clouds again.

Lord, I've lost my son. Lost my bank. If you're up there, keep me from spending my old age like a pauper. I've put up with enough bad smells for one lifetime. Keep me from the smell of piss and Lysol in the county old folks' home.

He slept fitfully that night. The way he used to when he was sleeping on a problem plaguing him at the bank. Especially during those times when his dreams were warning him something was wrong. Out of whack.

The next morning his bones ached, and even several cups of hot coffee could not dispel his apprehension. He smelled a rat. Something was wrong as hell.

Iron and Mary Barrett were more than vulnerable. They were the way all the starry-eyed idealists thought farmers should be. Stalwart, honest, pink-cheeked, healthy, good-humored. Wholesome as homemade bread. *And dumb*, thought J.C. *Dumb as rocks.*

Hell, the trust evident on their stupid, happy faces invited exploitation. They might as well be wearing signs. Grand Champion Sucker.

Lisette was the only one who had a lick of street sense.

He flushed with indignation and jumped to his feet. He had contributed plenty to their naivety by being their one and only banker. He didn't fleece people. Never had and never would. Sometimes he had capitalized on a man's recklessness. Sometimes he had indulged in teaching mean-spirited people a lesson because he didn't like them. Sometimes he had taken advantage of men's greed. He had never given a bit of slack to lazy bastards. None at all.

But he didn't steal.

Iron and Mary Barrett didn't know the first thing about dealing with crooks and the United States government. Not that they weren't one and the same.

Help us, J.C.

He heard those words over and over, and he knew he would help them for more reasons than he had given himself yesterday afternoon. The reasons went much deeper than protecting his personal finances or helping Iron out of nostalgia. The truth was, it was bred in his bones. He simply could not do anything else.

Besides, he did not believe the sale of Iron's cattle had turned disastrous by accident. The auction had to have been rigged. Someone had told Miss Winston to list those cattle as fats rather than breeders. She may not have known better, but he would bet she was acting on someone's instructions.

He knew where to start. He always knew where to start! Look for the money. Always look for the money. Who stood to gain? Identify the ones who would benefit, and the trail was usually clear.

Mary had said the cattle were gone by the time the family returned from the bank. What were the odds of any livestock truck line close to the Barrett farm having that many trucks on hand? Slim to none.

Still, he had to check it out. He made a few quick calls to local trucking companies. None of them had hauled the cattle. That meant a more distant truck line had been involved. For that to have worked, someone must have known in advance that they would be allowed to buy the cattle. Which meant the auction had been rigged.

J.C. brightened. He wondered if someone in the community had been involved in the sale. Although several of the ranchers had semis, none of them had enough equipment to haul four loads simultaneously. If the cattle were hauled a very short distance, the men might have the time to make a couple of trips, but that didn't make sense. No one would be dumb enough to pasture them within the county. If he could look at everyone's bank statements the way he used to, he could have said in three hours' time if someone in the community had bought the cattle. But that way was closed to him now.

Mary had asked for help. Well, she was going to get it. He smiled at the image that flickered in his mind. Of him. Sitting astride a horse. The old banker leading a surprise attack. Sitting Bull against Custer.

Once the decision was made, the juices started flowing again. His dry old body started coming back to life. Of course he would help them. The question was how.

This time around there would be no holds barred. No deferring to an outdated code of honor that had probably existed only in his head. He knew all the ropes by now. He would show the United States government just who they were messing with.

25

Iron Barrett sat like an old stone lion in his wing chair. He had an enemy. He knew it in his guts. He had been thinking, thinking about the cattle sale. There was only one man he knew who could possibly hate them enough to want to see him lose everything—Clifton Hathaway. But he couldn't see where Hathaway would benefit from ruining his sale.

His reverie was broken by the sound of Mary's pickup coming up the drive. They had quarreled over Dennis yesterday. Afterward he had vowed not to lose control again. A man owed it to his family to keep a level head. He should have been mindful Mary couldn't stand broken things and broken relationships. Not for a second. She had always moved heaven and earth to get people back together.

Besides, his willful redheaded wife was the only person he still trusted completely.

Iron's stomach turned to pure bile when he thought of Dennis cashing Alma's certificates of deposit. The money had undoubtedly gone for trips and cars, not supplies and equipment, as Alma assumed. How could he and Mary have produced such a son?

Now, as he heard her slam the door to the pickup, his eyes clouded with grief and his lips thinned into a grim line. As she came up the walk his stomach lurched at the thought of her mentioning Dennis again. She was like a little terrier, constantly shaking and worrying the subject of their son. Wanting him to call Dennis and say all was forgiven. Always wanting to fix things.

He braced himself for a new onslaught, but she joyfully burst through the door, her hair cracking with electricity. He saw at once that yesterday's quarrel had been magically erased from her mind. Her cheeks were rosy, her delicate coloring heightened by the cold air. "I've got some terrific, fabulous, out-of-sight news, honey."

He waited.

"J.C. Espy is going to help us save our farm."

All his intentions of avoiding a quarrel flew out the window.

"My god, Mary, you could have had the decency to leave that poor old bastard out of our troubles. What cockamamie scheme has someone dreamed up on my behalf this time?"

"Stop it!" Her eyes widened with bewilderment. "Stop putting down everything I try to say before I even say it."

"So now what?"

"So J.C. has promised to help us. He knows of investors back East. Money people. But there are stipulations. We've got to present a united front. He says his investors will have a whole bunch of families to choose from, and we can't afford to miss a trick."

"What does he mean by a united front?"

"They won't help us if we're quarreling or too lazy to work at off-farm jobs or if we seem unstable in any way."

"Is he asking me to make up with Dennis?"

"Yes. Yes, of course you'll have to do that."

"And you actually had the sheer hypocrisy to just—by God—stand there and let him think I would do it? Like Dennis hadn't robbed his own grandmother blind?"

"Dennis did not rob anyone. He simply asked his grandmother for some money, and she gave it to him."

"She thought it was going for a business, not expensive toys."

"I'm not the one who came up with these rules. Don't attack me. It's not fair. You call J.C. if you don't like it." She stabbed her finger toward the phone.

He lit a Camel, taking his time.

"Personally, I'm grateful to have J.C. on our side again," Mary said. "It's a good feeling, Iron. A wonderful feeling after we've been kicked in the teeth over and over again."

"Maybe the new people he's dug up would be on our side. Maybe not."

"We've got to present a united front. That's it! Take it or leave it. Your choice. And J.C.'s not doing this for anyone else, Iron. He made that clear."

"Well, I'm leaving it. No choice here a 'tall. Not for me and not for you. It's bad enough having people tell me how to run my farm. Telling me how to feel toward my own kids is going too far." He swung around, hot red furrows creasing his brow. "I'm turning down J.C.'s offer and you will too. You are not to have anything to do with Dennis."

She stood straight as a plumb line, her fists clenched at her sides. "Don't tell me what I can or can't do with my own kids. That's what you said J.C. was trying to do to you."

A muscle worked in his jaw.

"Husband or not, I'm a grown woman, and I'll see you in hell before I jump when you say frog. Now if you'll excuse me, I'll leave you to your perpetual brooding. I think you can fix your own supper. As for me, I've got a farm to save and not much time to do it in."

Iron slammed out the back door. The pictures rattled on the walls.

She pressed the palm of her hand against her forehead, then she weakened and raced out on the porch and called after him. "Oh don't, please don't leave me alone in all this."

It was starting to spit snow. She shivered on the back step, her arms folded across her chest. But he kept walking toward the barn and didn't look back.

"That's right. Just leave it all to me," she yelled. "All right, I'll go it alone. It's what I've been doing."

Winter came early, and it was nasty and erratic, preceded by stunning frosts. The next day, Mary pushed against the stinging sleet and pulled her hood over her head as she hurried toward Connie and Mike's front porch.

The family's precious winter wheat had already sprouted and lay waiting for the nurturing blankets of snow that sent deep, life-giving moisture. So far, all that the fields had received were these blitzes of ice that did more harm than good. She rapped quickly at the screen and stamped her feet.

"Well look what the storm's blown in," Mike said as he opened the door. "Phone line down?"

"No." Mary laughed as she reached for Andy and Andrea, who jumped up from the corner where they had been arguing over who colored pictures better.

"I want to talk to you face to face." She wished she could tell them J.C. was advising her. She pulled off her wool gloves and hung up her coat and hat on the wire hooks mounted in the hallway. Ridged panels of dark wainscoting set off the homey floral print of Connie's blue and mauve wallpaper. A pool of light, filtering through an etched glass oval in the old oak door, brightened a braided rag rug.

Connie had set bread to baking early that morning. Red and green bows for Christmas crafts were scattered on her round oak table.

Overwhelmed by the warmth emanating from this room, this couple, Mary's face softened, knowing the self-discipline it took to keep up all the systems in Connie's household. It was her legacy.

She walked over to the table, sat down, placed her palms on the polished surface, and braced herself for a difficult conversation.

"What's up?" asked Mike.

"I've come to ask you to look for work," Mary said. "Both of you. All of us need to get jobs in town."

"Mom! We can't! We all work full time now on this farm. Anything on top of what we already do would be like holding two full-time jobs."

"I know that!" Mary said. "But we've got to have some money. If we sell anything, the FDIC can take the money away from us. We have to finance everything through wages and put the money in an out-of-town bank. Every penny—until wheat harvest."

"Has Iron paid Newark and Piker for the seed yet?" Mike asked.

"No. He was counting on the profit from selling the cattle to do that. Which is another example of why we all must be earning wages. It won't be forever. Just for a year. We're all good workers. Very employable."

"That's nonsense, Mom. You know it is. I don't have a degree. What am I going to do? Stock shelves at Alco?"

"If you must. But surely with all your talents—"

"All my talents won't amount to a tinker's damn in the marketplace. Not in this town. I'll bet there's not two new jobs every six months around here."

"I know it's not going to be easy."

"Does Dad know you're doing this? He doesn't, does he?" Connie shot Mary a knowing look.

"We've discussed it in a general sort of way," Mary said, "and he's sort of left it up to me. I won't tell you we see eye to eye, because we don't. We'll fill him in on all the details after we've found jobs."

"You're right, Mary," Mike said. "If we try to argue this out with Iron, we'll end up doing nothing." He took a slow sip of his coffee and looked at Mary thoughtfully. "It just might work. If we all hold jobs, we might be able to swing our living expenses plus operating money."

"Right," Mary said, relieved that he saw the simplicity of what she had proposed. "Connie, I'm not trying to slip something over on your father. God knows I don't want to go behind his back, but he's in a terrible state over this thing with Dennis. I have to take charge right now."

"Iron will get in gear pretty soon," said Mike. "It always takes him a century to think things over."

Mary worried there was much more involved with Iron's state of mind than simply being slow to seize the reins, but she didn't say so, not wishing to burden them any more than she already had.

"Will you keep Andy and Andrea, Mom? And Susan needs someone here after school."

"No details yet, Connie," Mary said, with a small shake of her head. "The arrangements will all depend on who finds work first."

"I don't want Lisette keeping my kids. I want them with you."

"I have to find a job too," Mary said. "So will Lisette. I want prospective investors to be able to look at us and see a perfectly united family. Elizabeth has already done more than her share since she sends us money on a regular basis."

"You've thought of everything." Mike didn't disguise his bitterness. "But it will be hard. All of us need to find jobs? Does that include the kids? I suppose the twins can sell pencils on the street corners. Or apples."

Mary looked at him sharply and then looked down, ashamed. She dug a Kleenex from her coat pocket and blew her nose. "Or a lemonade stand," she quipped feebly, "we could put one up in front of my three-story house with a sign saying 'Fallen on hard times—help us make a lemon into lemonade.' What do you think our neighbors would say to that?"

"Don't joke about all this," Connie said, bursting into tears. "No wonder

Dad's about to go crazy with worry. How can you make fun of our troubles? Dennis would be enough to drive anyone to drink, let alone fighting the government day after day."

"I'm sorry, honey," Mary said. "I came here to ask you to find jobs. I didn't mean to make light of the demands this will place on all of us."

"The work doesn't bother me," Connie said, reaching for a tissue. "No one has ever accused me of backing off from work. But I hate the thought of leaving my kids. Isn't this a deal now? With all the women wild to get out of the house, I'm trying to figure out how to stay home. Oh, why did you talk me out of going to college?"

"Honey, that's not true." Shocked, Mary reached for her daughter's hand.

"You did," Connie cried. "All of you. You said getting an education wouldn't matter if being a farm wife was what I really wanted. You said it was just fine not to go. Just dandy. Well now look where I am. Good for nothing but wiping noses and doing dishes and needing to find work after all." She whirled around and ran out of the room and up the flight of stairs.

Aching with remorse, Mary looked at Mike. "I know how much she wants to be home, Mike. Don't you think I know that? But we have no choice. We must use our heads. If we fall to quarreling instead and lose the farm, we'll never forgive ourselves."

"Connie will come around," Mike said quietly, "just like Iron. You can count on me. I guess you know that by now. I can find work as a hired man several places. But it will be tough to figure out how to keep things up around here at the same time."

"Thanks. You know, Mike, I think you're the only peacemaker we've ever had in the family."

"Dubious honor," he mumbled.

She smiled wanly, rose, got her coat, and left. As she pulled out of the drive, she was haunted by a glimpse of him in the rearview mirror, head bowed, leaning against the doorjamb.

"I'll call Dennis," Lisette said. She crossed over to the telephone and dialed the extension to the machine shop, which rang six times before Dennis picked it up.

"Your mother is here. She wants you to come to the house. She needs to talk to us both." Lisette's cheeks flushed and she stared at a spot on the floor.

Mary recognized the signs of someone fielding an embarrassing conversation. She sighed, imagining Dennis's reaction. It had taken all her resolve to defy Iron and come here.

Her eyes lingered on a huge macramé wall hanging Lisette had made several years ago. It was interspersed with feathers and turquoise beads and natural stones and shells. In a corner was a huge pot holding eucalyptus leaves. Mary didn't understand this room, this look, but she knew it pleased her.

Lisette had installed skylights. It had struck Mary as foolish and unnecessary at the time, but now as she sat warming in a pool of natural sun, the light made her feel hopeful. Maybe it wasn't so foolish after all.

Her daughter-in-law hung up, mumbling, "He'll be here in a few minutes."

Dennis came through the door, scowling, his face proud and wary.

"I've come to beg you to make up with your father," Mary said.

"No."

"Hear me out, Dennis. That's not all. I want you both to get jobs."

He looked at her with bitter amusement.

"Anything else?"

"There's a few things about the farm I'm not free to discuss right now, but we've been promised help with financing under certain conditions."

Dennis's eyes fixed on her alertly when she mentioned new financing, and he became very still. Too still. Suddenly apprehensive, she wished she had kept her mouth shut about the new financing. But since she had brought it up, she felt she should say a little more. She bit her lip and drew a deep breath.

"The conditions are that we be willing to work. All of us. And that we all get along. The party who is interested isn't going to mess with a quarreling farm family on the verge of lawsuits."

"Is there any other kind?" Dennis asked.

Mary quietly studied his face and controlled her temper. Iron had given their son every chance in the world.

"Let Dad make up with me." Dennis's eyes darkened with hostility. "If he wants to save his farm so damn bad, let him be the one to make the first move."

"Oh, Dennis. You know that isn't going to happen. He just won't do it."

"Well now. Looks like he's between a rock and a hard place then, doesn't it, Mom?"

"Please?"

"No."

"All right then."

She jumped to her feet.

"Now just a damn minute here," Lisette said. "I want to get something straight." She swiped her long black hair away from her face and looked hard at Dennis. She leaned against the sink, her arms folded across her chest. "Count me in, Mary." Her eyes swung from her husband to her mother-in-law.

"You don't need to work, Lisette," Dennis snapped. "You've got plenty to do right here."

"I care if this family goes under, and I'm going to find work and, frankly, I'm not a bit particular about what kind."

Dennis's face tightened with fury. Lisette stared him down, despite knowing she would pay for the outburst. She was simply thrilled to have a chance to support Mary. Thrilled to be asked to make a contribution to the family.

Thrilled to have an excuse to get off the damned farm.

Mary drove home, furious with Dennis's mean-spirited refusal to cooperate. If only she had been able to persuade him to pitch in! He could bring in his fair share by just increasing his work in the machine shop.

With a sinking feeling in the pit of her stomach, she knew she would have to drop their health insurance. If Iron wouldn't get a job and Dennis wouldn't get a job, they wouldn't have enough money to cover the premiums.

Oh well, she tried to tell herself. It was just for peace of mind, nothing more.

In all honesty, they never used the policy. The only medical expenses for the last seven years, apart from Alma's insulin, were occasional antibiotics. She could keep Alma in serum for a year for the price of one month's Blue Cross payment. They weren't accident prone. The whole family was blessedly healthy. They simply did not need it.

Yet the idea of dropping it filled her with apprehension. *Beyond this point there be dragons*, she thought grimly.

Worried Iron would be angry with her for taking over, making all the decisions, she decided not to mention dropping health insurance. Also, she would wait and see what kind of work they could find—then tell Iron about each job as it came along. One by one.

It would seem less like a conspiracy.

26

Much to the family's amazement, it was Connie who found work at once—in a day care center. Mary dropped by after Connie had been on the job one week. She found her daughter happily buried in scissors, pastes, paints, crayons, and poster paper.

"I don't know how we ever did without her," the director said, as they watched her kneel to comfort a little girl. "I think she knows how to do every craft that ever was. And she's absolutely tireless. The kids just dote on her, and the other teachers know Connie is the one to ask. About everything."

"Yes." Mary beamed with quiet pride. "She always has been."

In a couple of weeks, the director said the twins would be welcome without charge and Susan could come to the center directly after school.

Mary leaped at the chance to tell Iron how well everything had worked out. Connie was drawing a salary and taking care of her own kids to boot. What could possibly be better?

But the most stunning coup came from Lisette.

She came racing into Mary's Place one evening and gave a little twirl as she broke the news. "You are looking at the newest employee of this county's department of agriculture. They're going to train me to be an aerial observer."

"You'll be a Sky Spy?" asked Mary.

"Yes, that's what some folks call them. And I'll be going to workshops to learn how to handle such rude questions."

"Sorry," Mary said, "but I can just see me telling Iron this."

Lisette was a born natural for the job, with her photography ability and her love of excitement. As a Sky Spy for the department of agriculture, she would be going up with a crew in a small plane, photographing all the land in an area to make sure farmers were complying with their stated crop management plans. Farmers growing grain they had promised not to grow, in areas they had promised not to plant, would be penalized at once.

Sky Spies didn't sit well with the farmers. It made them feel like they were being watched by the CIA or FBI, although most agreed someone should be keeping an eye on their neighbor.

Mike announced a couple of weeks later he had found a general handyman's job working thirty hours a week at the local feed store.

"Well good for you," said Mary brightly. But she thought her heart would break. It was a poor use of his fine, quick mind. Mike would be little better than an underpaid gofer, lifting sacks, scooping grains, putting up stock.

"It's just for a year. It's all right. I had to find something part time, or we wouldn't be able to get the farm work done here. It's going to take a bit more hustle, that's all."

Iron listened listlessly to Mary's cheery reports. When she said Benjy had volunteered to help with their neighbor's milking, he gave a slight nod then turned away and buried his head in the newspaper again. Curiously, the burst of optimism coming from the children had heightened her anxiety over her husband's depression.

One night Mary woke up with her heart pounding and her breath coming in tight little rushes. Her chest tightened. But the pain eased as suddenly as it had come. Fear abated, she lay there silently until dawn.

It happened again the following night. She awoke with a start—jarring bolt upright—and realized she had been swearing in her dreams. Using vile, unthinkable words. *It's not the farm that's driving me crazy*, she thought resentfully. *It's my husband who's making me a nervous wreck.*

The next morning she was drained from lack of sleep. But she had to get a job. It was part of the agreement with J.C. She wanted Iron's approval, but with or without it she had to find work and she resented having to factor in his reaction to her every move.

She abandoned her attempts to control her erratic thoughts, and she let them pummel her weary mind. Why couldn't she just do whatever needed to be done, up front? Why did she have to go through the back door all the time when she worked with her husband? Why did she have to coax and wheedle and flatter and beg everyone in this family to do what they were supposed to have enough common sense to do on their own?

Working around Iron and his precious ego was wearing her to a frazzle. She had to pet him and praise him and make over him like he was a little leaguer who had struck out.

Suddenly she rose and hurled her cup of coffee at the fireplace. The shards flew everywhere. Appalled at her loss of control, she started to cry. Then she flew to the sink and got paper towels from under the cabinet and began to pick up the pieces of glass.

Oh Iron, Iron, she thought bitterly. *We've never been this way with each other. I've never once had to pretend in any way. How could you do this to me?*

That evening she watched him stare at the fire. Smoking, smoking, his face cast in tragic Lincolnesque lines. Her stomach tightened. Was he the suicidal type the mental health folks were warning about? Was he? Should she be watching for something? Doing something?

That night, after he had come to bed and turned out the light in silence—always in silence now—she cupped herself against his broad back and lightly trailed her fingers down his thighs. Throbbing with desire, her breath was harsh and erratic against his body. He lay rigid and unmoving. She stifled a sob.

Always, always, they had made love. Before. Before God had turned on them. Now Iron wouldn't. Just wouldn't, pure and simple, and she didn't understand it. Pointedly, she turned away and scooted to the edge of the bed. They lay back to back listening to each other breathe.

She woke up in the middle of the night and pressed her palms against her cheeks. She had been crying in her dreams again. Even in their sleep before—they had always moved closer.

Toward each other, not away. Never, never away. *And he moves away from me in the daytime too,* she thought. *In a thousand different ways. It's not just physical.*

The next morning, she rose early and slapped his bacon and eggs and toast on the table with a note to warm them in the microwave if he wanted them hot. She quickly applied makeup, put on her rust corduroy suit and a bronze printed blouse, and drove into town.

She stopped at the Daylight Donut shop and lingered over a cinnamon roll and a cup of coffee as she waited for Dale Culp's office to open. The attorney had offered her part-time work, and she intended to take it, if the job was still available.

She tried to shut her husband from her mind. She felt like she was betraying him. She suspected Iron was angry because she could and would act and he simply could not. He was furious with her for not being depressed. Like him. Then, unbidden, all the words she had been struggling to keep at bay seared through her mind like lightning. They were far worse than the ones she had scolded Lisette for using.

She slid out of the booth and rushed into the bathroom. She splashed cold water onto her face and tried to compose herself. She stared at herself in the mirror. Her husband was offended by the very core of her being. Rejecting her strength. Her exuberant self-confidence. "Oh Iron, I need you," she whispered. "Please, please, please, come back to me."

To her relief, Dale Culp seemed delighted when she applied. Moreover, the word processing would involve only three afternoons a week.

That night she booted up the computer after she cleared away the dishes. Iron was asleep in front of the TV as he was night after night now. He awoke when he heard the whir of the hard disk and the metallic beep as the system booted up.

He snapped upright, buried his face in his hands, then suddenly stood, walked to the coat rack, and yanked a seed cap off the peg.

Mary watched anxiously. She had to tell him about her job. There was no point in prettying anything up. "I've found work, Iron. At Dale Culp's. Part time," she called after him.

He hesitated, then turned. "Well," he said, "well now." He looked at her and stood helplessly twisting his hat, his face a study of mixed emotions. Then he walked out the door.

Tears streamed down Mary's face. She knew he was too honest to lie and tell her he was proud of her. The truth was, his shame at not being able to support his family went so deep it was poisoning him.

"Please, please, please, dear God," she whispered, "tell me what I should do. I can't go on like this. Second guessing, double guessing." She switched off the computer, and when he came back into the room later, she tried not to aggravate him.

Her very guts protested this betrayal of that which made her Just Mary—her unrelenting energy, her compass. Her core. Her self.

Iron barely looked at her when he came through the door for the noon meal the next day. They sat down and he filled his plate in silence. The thought of tiptoeing through another meal made her stomach roil.

Her blood exploded with a surge of rage. The rage she tried to suppress day after day. Black spots swam before her eyes. She could not bear his closed, impassive look a moment longer. Infuriated, she jumped to her feet, fled from the kitchen, and started up the stairs.

She tripped. She sank onto the step and, with her elbows resting on her knees, she pressed her forehead into her cradled arms. Sobs tore from her throat.

"Mary?" Iron wiped his face on the towel Mary had dropped and came to her slowly, like someone waking from a dream. "What happened? Did you hurt yourself?"

But she wouldn't reply.

"Honey, what's going on?"

She couldn't stop crying and he sat by her and started to draw her head against his chest in the old familiar gesture.

"Leave me alone," she protested. "Leave me alone. That's what you want to do, isn't it?"

She shoved him away as though he were an enemy.

Stunned, he stared at her as though he were really seeing her for the first time in months.

"Mary?" He reached for her again. "Mary?"

She lifted her head then clambered to her feet. "You hate me for taking over," she sobbed. "I knew you would, but I had to. Someone had to think and plan."

"Mary, Mary. Honey, I'm sorry. Don't cry. Do you really think I want a birdbrain for a wife? We'll work together on this. I swear to God we will."

He reached for her, but she flung his arm aside and ran on up the stairs. Iron watched white-faced from the doorway as she rushed to the closet, dragged out a suitcase, and started hurling clothes into it.

"You want to be left alone," she yelled. "All right. I'm leaving you alone."

"Where are you going?" he asked hoarsely. "Where are you going?"

"I don't know. Away. Somewhere. Anywhere."

She slapped the lid shut, grabbed the luggage, and shoved Iron aside.

"Get. Out. Of. My. Way," she said between clenched teeth. "Get out of my way."

"Mary, goddamn, honey. Don't do this. Please don't do this."

Further enraged, she ran down the stairs and out the door. Iron rushed after her. She ran to the garage and got into the car and backed out onto the driveway.

Then he, too, lost his temper.

"Wait a minute. I know something else that belongs to you."

He wheeled around on the heel of his boot and stalked over to the old windmill and began to climb the wobbly wooden steps.

Mary shielded the sun from her eyes with the flat of her hand. Too fearful to cry out to him, she followed his shaky progress.

The wind was blowing softly. As Iron continued up the crisscrossed rungs, the rickety old windmill swayed. He was too angry to place his feet carefully as he covered the distance to the top, bypassing several of the rungs with his long legs. His foot slipped on a rung.

She gasped and got out of the car and ran to the foot of the windmill. She was sick with dread—imagining him falling, falling.

Iron steadied himself and then stopped for a moment. She buried her face in her hands, unable to watch any longer. Her anger spent, she began to weep.

When she could bring herself to look again, Iron had reached the top and was unwinding the blue light that had been there for twenty-seven years. Then he looped the long cord about his shoulder and started to climb back down.

A gust of wind came up. The windmill swayed and Mary's heart sank to her toes.

"It's all my fault," she whispered tearfully. "Please God, don't let anything happen to him. Please, please, please."

He was halfway to the bottom when one of the rotten boards broke. She looked up, white-faced, at the ominous crack. Iron stiffened and tightened his handhold on the rung above, then he felt with the toe of his boot for the step below.

That board, too, broke away from the nails when he applied his weight. He grabbed the plank bracing the side and awkwardly clung to the lumber.

Iron shuddered, too paralyzed with fear to move. Chilled by the brisk north wind, he looked down, down. He was a big man, and the rickety old windmill was very fragile. *Being crippled would be worse than dying. I've done this to myself*, he thought. *Put myself in jeopardy.* His heart pounded at the thought of lying below. Smashed. Disabled.

Stiffly, he clung to his precious handhold, frozen, unmoving, buffeted like a weathervane with every wintry gust. Suddenly, he was furious with himself.

Who did he expect to get him down? Just who did he expect to come after him?

He looked at the clouds, and his soul appealed to the God with whom he had only a nodding acquaintance at best.

"Help me," he prayed silently. "Then give me strength. If you help me get down from here, I'm going to do my best. For my wife, and my family. No one is going to climb up here after me. And no one is going to save my farm for me. All I'm asking you for is to give me back my strength."

Something firmed up inside him. "One step at a time," he told himself softly. "With intelligence. Think first." He felt with his foot. Tested the rung first. Eased his weight onto it slowly, slowly, before he risked shifting his bulk.

"With intelligence. Think first." He chanted the words under his breath like a mantra, determined to safely descend from the windmill.

Then he would go after the men who were trying to take his farm. With intelligence. With every ounce of brains he possessed.

But first, he wanted to make things right with his wife. He doubted there was any way she could understand the hell he had come back from.

She couldn't leave him. She had to understand what had happened to him up there.

Mary stood with her hands tightly clasped, her arms held stiffly in front of her, and anxiously watched his cautious descent. He jumped off the last couple of steps to the ground and walked over to her and held out the loop of wire with the single blue light on the end.

"Here. This belongs to you."

She pressed her hands against the sides of her face and swayed back and forth for a moment but refused to reach for the string of lights with the single working blue bulb.

"No," she said, "I don't want the light. Don't you understand what I've been trying to tell you. We can't go it alone anymore. It won't work. We have to be together. The days of one of us blue lighting anything are gone forever."

"Don't go, Mary. Don't go. Please. I can't live without you." His voice quavered. "You have to understand how much I need you. I'm back, Mary. All the way back."

Dumbfounded, she saw tears in his eyes. He never cried. Never. Shocked, she laid her hand on his arm and could not speak. They looked at each other wordlessly for a few seconds, and then she flew into his arms.

"I won't," she whispered fiercely. "I won't leave. I can't bear to go. I'll die without you." They were both crying shamelessly, and he smothered her face with kisses until she was weak with desire. The blue light lay at their feet, and she pulled away and started to crush it with her boot.

"No," he said sharply, reaching for the jumble of wire. "No. I'll hang it in the barn. It's a souvenir of a different time. A different couple."

"All right," said Mary. "But we have to work together on everything from now on."

Iron swallowed hard and nodded. Then he scooped her up and carried her into the house, up the stairs, and into their bedroom. He held her against his chest as he clumsily attempted to pull down the covers with his loose hand.

He laid her on the bed and fumbled at the buttons on her jeans, and she tugged at his belt buckle and he was inside her quickly, as though they had to be fused together before they each flew into a million pieces—needing the comfort of solid, linked flesh.

When they were spent, she wouldn't let him leave. She kept him locked against her, and when he moved away, she pulled him back.

"No, no, no. Stay. Oh please, don't go yet. Please. Keep me covered, so nothing will get me," she said.

"With nothing sticking out?" he laughed gently at her familiar words.

"Yes, with every single bit of me under you."

He chuckled softly.

She was warm again. Warm to the core.

"There you are," she said, burying her face against his shoulder. "I thought I'd lost you."

"I don't suppose anyone but you will ever know how close you came," he said slowly. She trembled, feeling a deep shudder ripple across his body.

27

Dennis stared at the check. It was nothing. Chicken feed. A mere $25,000. He looked at Hathaway, then at Peterson. The backstabbers had used him. Figured him for a simple country bumpkin.

His stomach plunged. By cooperating in the second sale—seeing to it that there was no one around when the trucks came to take the cattle—he had demolished his family's financial condition. "$25,000 isn't much," he said coldly. "I assumed you had more in mind."

Hathaway shot a quick warning look at Peterson, who clearly was about to tell Dennis off. "It's a lot of money," he said patronizingly. "It's enough to leverage financing for any business you want to go into."

Dennis's inherent shrewdness came into play. He listened, taking a few seconds to control the expression on his face although he fumed inwardly over being complicit in a rigged auction for a piddling $25,000. They thought he could be bought off that easily.

When Hathaway had referred to other uses for the land, Dennis had thought the man had meant something big time. A nuclear waste dump or a military base. Big money. Hathaway and Peterson said he would be amply rewarded. Said the money would be plenty to make his whole family get over losing the farm. Said, "They'll look on you as their savior."

And I believed them, Dennis thought. Instead, Hathaway wanted his father's land. Another greedy dirt farmer wanting to get his hands on more acreage.

He couldn't figure out Peterson's stake. Obviously, the man would receive some money under the table from Hathaway, but there was something else at work here. He couldn't see where breaking Iron would benefit Peterson. "If my father loses his farm—"

"Not if." Peterson smiled. "When. He's going to. And when he does, others will understand the futility of going against the government. His failure will be an example to other farmers. Keep them from getting ideas. I'm in line for a promotion, and it will depend on how well things go in this county."

Dennis sat with his hands casually linked behind his head to disguise their trembling. A promotion! Possibly another five thousand dollars a year for the man. He had thrown in with penny-ante chiselers.

Now Peterson and Hathaway were blurting out information better kept from him, as though he would not have the brains to act on it anyway.

"Your family won't be able to pay the interest payment due in December on last year's operating loan," Peterson said. "When they default no bank will touch them, and it will be the last nail in the coffin for private financing."

"My wife wants that house," Hathaway said. "No Barrett will ever live in that house again. I'm going to see to it."

Dennis stiffened and moved to the edge of his chair. There was no way in hell he would allow Hathaway to have Mary's Place. At once, he decided it was in his best interests that these men not know how much he coveted the house.

"You'd better take the money, son," Peterson urged. "If you don't, we'll point out that you knew the details of the sale all along. But we would rather be spared the trouble and the publicity."

Dennis forced an ashamed, confused look on his face to mask his rage. He had devastated his family's net worth through the rigged video sale. But Hathaway and Peterson would be sorry by the time he got through with them. He needed a chance to think. Getting up, he headed for the door.

"This offer won't be on the table forever," Peterson called after him. "Better not turn your back on it."

J.C. picked up his binoculars. He watched people come and go for a good half hour. Something tugged at the back of his mind. Something he was supposed to put together—something out of whack. But the connection wouldn't come. It was like trying to remember the name of a song.

Finally, he laid the binoculars aside and rubbed his eyes. He had never been one to postpone thinking about hard things. It was time to make a phone call to Elizabeth Barrett. Last week he had asked her to make one last attempt to persuade Iron to make up with Dennis.

"The answer is no," Elizabeth responded. "He won't."

"Did you tell Iron no private financer will go near a quarreling family?"

"Yes, he knows it's the smart thing to do. But Dad says he would be living a lie."

"Will he consider a write-down?" A write-down would lower the amount owed. The FDIC did it all the time.

"My father says even if he would—which he won't—Peterson wouldn't give him a break if he were the only farmer left in America."

"Your folks still won't consider bankruptcy? They would get to keep that wonderful house."

"No, and even Dennis won't hear of it."

"I'm surprised Dennis is dead set against bankruptcy. He would rather see you folks lose the place than keep a house and two cars?"

"It doesn't make sense to me either. Dennis knows that house is a show-place. He's always thought it would be his someday. When Mom said she would leave it to Connie, he exploded."

Wearily, J.C. rubbed the bridge of his nose. Fathers and sons. He knew all about fathers and sons. He couldn't stop his voice from rising. "Have you explained bundling to Iron? Have you told that man that if he doesn't get financing at the end of two years, his notes and a bunch of others turned over to the FDIC will be bundled? They'll be grouped with other notes and auctioned off to some hotshot back East who can afford to buy fifty farms at a time. Men who can buy casinos and oil wells."

"There's no need to yell, J.C. I probably know more about bundling than you do. On bad days when there's not many bidders, I've seen these notes go for a penny on the dollar. A quarter-of-a-million dollar note going for $2500, and that's all these new people are ever going to owe."

"Then why in the hell can't the little people, the farmers and their bankers, buy those farms at that price? The government would get more money back in the long run."

"Because my father, you, and nearly everyone else can't buy fifty farms at a time. I'm not saying it makes sense. I'm saying that's the way the government does things."

J.C. hung up the phone and walked over to the buffet and reached for the bottle of Jack Daniels. He was not a boozer. Nevertheless, he poured a double and carried his glass back over to the recliner. His loan from Charlie Accor to finance Iron's feeder cattle would soon be due. Iron was still unaware it had been a personal loan from him. Those cattle, of course, had been swept up and trucked off after the video sale.

He could take out a mortgage on his house to pay Charlie back. His house was his ace in the hole. His throat tightened. An Espy had lived in the two-story native limestone house since John Foster Espy built it in 1905. Surely he was entitled to keep something. It was enormous and expensive to heat, but he loved it. In all the years he had lived alone, he had never considered moving to a smaller place.

It would be a small mortgage, of course, for a fraction of the amount the house was worth. But he would not, by God, go through anyone local. It would be all over town by sundown. Folks would be abuzz over another financial crisis in the Espy family. Drunk or sober he knew selling the house would gut him. He simply couldn't do it. Then he decided he wasn't going to mortgage it either.

The next day, all coffeed up, J.C. put his pride aside, called Charlie Accor, and asked for an extension on his loan. "I'll mail the interest when the note is due, of course."

"No problem," Accor said. He didn't ask one question. Grateful for his friend's respect for his privacy, J.C. closed his eyes and heaved a sigh of thanksgiving.

"Are you sure you don't want to make it longer than nine months, J.C.?"

"No. That's plenty of time." Time enough for a wheat crop to come in. Time for reaping. Time for families to be broken or redeemed. Time as the farm world measured it.

However, next year's wheat crop wouldn't solve the immediate problem of Iron's upcoming December interest payment. J.C. grimaced at the familiar release of acid as his stomach protested. As usual his finances were tied to those of a crazy Western Kansas wheat farmer.

⁓⁓⁓⁓⁓⁓⁓⁓⁓⁓⁓⁓⁓

Mary moved restlessly in their bed. Missing her husband's body heat, she was chilled to the bone. After Iron had come back from whatever hell he had descended to, he had found a job driving a cattle truck and was often on the road for a week at a time. He was now the family's highest wage earner. With all their combined incomes, operating money was no longer a concern.

She hated being alone at night, but seeing the pride on Iron's face, the spring in his step, more than made up for it. After the cattle had been trucked off their farm, they had all agreed someone should always be on the farmstead. Luckily, Dale Culp had agreed to let her take her work home on the days when Iron was trucking.

Now the only totally miserable Barrett was Alma. Iron had finally told his mother that it would take a miracle for them to come up with the money for the December interest payment. The old woman had called him untrustworthy, a bad manager, a poor excuse for a son. Understanding her despair, Iron had endured her tongue-lashing. Rejoicing in the marvel of his regained strength, Mary had praised him for his ability to withstand the onslaught.

Mary moved closer to the center of the bed then clutched Iron's pillow. Then she couldn't remember if she had locked the back door. She got up, put on her robe and slippers, and went downstairs. Her eyes were drawn to the farmyard, which was bathed in silvery light. Clouds rolled across the face of the moon, dappling every piece of equipment, every building, with shifting patterns of ebony.

She saw a dark silhouette sway in the moonlight, and her blood chilled. Terrified, she waited, but whatever had caught her eye did not move again.

She dropped down and duck-walked away from the glass panel of the door. When she reached the far wall, she straightened and eased toward Iron's gun cabinet. She withdrew the key from a magnetic holder high on a special plate anchored to the back.

After opening the cabinet, she took out the 20-gauge Browning and pressed five shells into the chamber. Quietly she opened the back door and stepped out onto the porch. She opened the screen door and went outside. Her throat was as dry as straw. The sensible thing was to stay inside and phone the police, but she hated to stir up a fuss if there was no need.

I could call Mike, she thought. On the other hand, what would her son-in-law think if she rousted him because she was afraid of the dark? She walked toward where she thought she had seen the figure and called out, "Hey! Who's there? Is anyone there?".

Dennis peered at his mother from behind the tractor. He started to answer then stopped, mesmerized by the eerie pantomime. He had walked over in the dark to get some fan belts as he didn't want to risk encountering Iron in broad daylight.

I'm being forced to act like a thief, he thought, as he watched Mary. He was merely taking back what was rightfully his: an item from the inventory of small parts the families usually shared. Parts he had probably paid for in the first place.

He studied Mary's features, which were illuminated by the moonlight streaming from the cold winter sky. It was a face he had never seen before: lined with worry, gaunt from lost weight, clearly terrified.

A rabbit leaped from under the tractor, streaked in front of her feet, and darted under the hay bailer. She lowered her shotgun. Her hands shook as she clicked on the safety.

It was just one of her rabbits again. And she did have a thing about them.

She lowered her shotgun and propped it against the planting drill. Putting her head into her cupped hands, she began to weep. Still Dennis did not call out. In a few moments, she looked fearfully around the farmyard, retrieved the shotgun, and scurried back into the house.

Iron loved driving the truck. He was amazed at how much easier it was to think straight when there was some money coming in. When he finished a run, Mary fussed and clucked over him like he had returned from a war.

He enjoyed the blocks of time when he could think about the farm. Never before had he been isolated from great swarms of family, exhausting him with their demands and desires. Like a mantra, he chanted to himself the words God had put in his mind when he was up on the windmill. *Think. I can win by using my wits. Think.* He mulled over different scenarios.

He wondered what would happen if they didn't summer-fallow next year and planted on the same acreage he had planted in wheat this year. Long-term planning and conservation could surely be set aside for one season.

He wondered what would happen if he didn't fertilize for a whole year. It would save a bundle of money, and surely the soil would sustain a crop for one year without any additives.

He wondered what would happen if he didn't apply anhydrous ammonia or herbicides to the soil. Would it be possible to just cultivate all the weeds, like his father used to do, years ago?

He came up with all kinds of ways to make do with less cash next year, but he couldn't figure out how to get the money for the December interest payment.

He knew if he ran up and down the road till Doomsday, he wouldn't think of a way.

Alma Barrett sipped her watery coffee and smoldered with outrage. Iron didn't like to be reprimanded, but she didn't regret one single word she'd said to him. The man had allowed things to get into an awful state. She had been counting on him to tend to her affairs. And where had it gotten her? They were fools. All of them.

She started at the knock at the door, then opened it to find her grandson on the stoop.

"Dennis, come on in." She gestured toward a chair then went over to the tea kettle. She stood with her back toward him, in a snit that another disappointing Barrett male probably expected refreshments.

She plopped a cup of weak tea in front of Dennis and looked at him sorrowfully.

"Something on your mind?" she asked bluntly.

"I've figured out how to pay the money due for the interest on our loan, Grandma. I wanted you to be the first to know. I'm selling my Corvette. It's vintage. A collector's item. It won't make a dent in the principal, but it will pay the interest due right now and buy us some time."

Dennis smiled at the look of pure joy on the old woman's face. Things had not been quite the same between them since the Will Fight and had worsened after the ruined video sale. "I'll have to find the right buyer, but it's worth a lot of money. I've checked."

He grinned broadly at her look of pure devotion. The way to put the screws to Peterson and Hathaway had come to him just last week.

"You've always been such a good boy, Dennis." Alma's eyes moistened. Suddenly she was ashamed for having doubts about her wonderful grandson.

Having finished a series of runs, Iron was dozing in his chair, luxuriating in Mary's pampering. She gently shook him awake and stood before him with her hands on her cheeks, swaying from side to side.

"The most wonderful, heavenly, fabulous thing has happened." She plopped down on his lap and laid her head against his broad chest. "We're going to be able to make the interest payment."

His arms tightened around her.

"We won the lottery?"

"No," she said, laughing. "No, no, no. But it's just as unexpected. Dennis is doing it for us. Dennis is selling his Corvette and making the payment."

"He's selling his car? I don't believe it."

"It's true. It's a done deal. Oh Iron, you're always saying that the proof of the pudding is in the eating. Look what Dennis has done. Actually done. Never mind what's gone on in the past. He made this sacrifice. People change. You know they do."

Iron was stone silent. It was hard for him to take in their good fortune. "Well, I'll be damned. I didn't think the boy had it in him."

Mary's heart swelled with joy at the look of pure wonder and pride that came over Iron's face.

"Yes, yes, yes," she said tenderly, smothering him with little kisses. "The apple never falls very far from the tree. He's our son, honey. They're all coming over this evening. We'll get to see Benjy and Sabrina again."

He eased her off his lap then stood. "I'm going to check on the . . ." He halted before he said "cattle." It was the way he would have finished the sentence in the past. He smiled through his tears. "Guess I'll just step outside for a spell."

Sabrina and Benjy stood in the doorway behind their parents.

"Company," Mary called brightly to Iron as she hung their coats on pegs.

"Well, so there is," he said, rising from his chair. His face mirrored his contradictory feelings toward his difficult son.

"Come right on in," Mary said eagerly. "It's a good night for popcorn and apples."

Too stern for hugs, Iron and Benjy just beamed at one another.

"Dad," Dennis said. "Come with me into the living room. I have something I want to say to you in private."

Mary winced at the hope on Iron's face. Begging to be convinced of his son's integrity.

The two men left the kitchen. Then Dennis handed his father the check drawn on the out-of-county bank where the family deposited their wages.

"I want you to take it to the bank," Dennis said. "You should have the privilege of seeing the look on Peterson's face when you make the payment."

Iron studied the check then looked at his son with wonder.

28

Clyde Peterson looked at the check. He slowly raised his eyes to meet Iron's triumphant gaze.

"Like you to meet Linda Kipling," Iron said, nodding at the woman sitting next to him. "Mrs. Kipling, this here is the chief liquidation officer, Clyde Peterson."

Peterson nodded curtly, acknowledging the introduction. His eyes swept over the stern little birdlike woman, clad in a navy polyester pantsuit.

"Mrs. Kipling is a notary public," Iron said. "Just in case you plan to claim you never got that check, Peterson. Just in case it crosses your mind to lose this check or not cash it, I have two other little pieces of paper here. Mrs. Kipling is going to witness the signing of one of them. Your choice."

Peterson looked at him suspiciously.

"The first, we'll both sign. It's a receipt saying you got this check today. The second will have just my signature, saying that you refused to acknowledge the receipt of this check. She'll notarize one or the other. A refusal will be sent to your district manager."

Peterson's face blanched. "No need for this paranoia, Barrett. Our job is to work with people."

Iron grinned, knowing the man's remark was for the benefit of Mrs. Kipling.

"Hand me that first paper," Peterson snapped.

"Not so fast. We need two witnesses."

Peterson stabbed at the intercom and asked Miss Gladstone to send two tellers to his office.

The men signed the paper as the women watched, then Mrs. Kipling added her stamp and signature. Iron carefully placed the receipt in the briefcase he had borrowed from Dennis. He had never carried one before.

Iron rose to leave, but Peterson called him back.

"Oh, by the way, we have the obligation to complete an inventory. We'll let you know when. Couple of weeks or it could be a couple of months." He shrugged.

"Legally we must be notified forty-eight hours in advance."

"Don't worry, Barrett. It'll all be by the book."

"You bet it will," Iron said coldly.

———

One night, when she couldn't sleep and had gone downstairs to fix cocoa, Mary saw a movement in the farmyard again. Resolutely, she put on her coat and cap, got her shotgun, and stepped into the night air. It wouldn't hurt to check. When a search revealed nothing other than rabbits staring into her flashlight, she hurried back inside.

Something is always there, she decided, as she sipped the hot chocolate. *It's not that I'm seeing things. But it's never anything to worry about. What I'm seeing belongs there.* She would simply resist the impulse to go outside at night. She wouldn't look. If she didn't look, she wouldn't see.

She threw herself into preparing for Christmas, as she had done every year of her adult life. Although they were uneasy over the lack of rain that fall, there was enough subsoil moisture to sustain the wheat. Besides, good snowfalls in January and February would make up for everything. Her anxiety over losing the farm had vanished after they made the December payment.

Exhilarated by the restoration of her boundless energy, she strung decorative lights on the first-floor eaves and then began to make pine wreaths and weave long rows of greenery for the staircase. Soon the house looked just as it always did during the Christmas season.

"We're going to make it," she thought gratefully. Hope grew with each carol she sang and each card she received. Their long, dark night of the soul was over, and Elizabeth would be coming home for Christmas.

Her family was fixed again.

Iron called Mike and Dennis over to the house early one Saturday morning in February to tell them the FDIC would be there to take inventory the next Monday. Before the three men entered the machine sheds to look at the equipment, Iron searched the bleak morning sky for signs of snow or rain.

Tattered dry weather clouds skittered across the strata day after day, teasing the farmers with false promises. Inside and out, the air crackled with electricity. Kansans just naturally began and ended all conversations with comments about the weather, but a winter devoid of snow was so ominous that the Barretts avoided such talk.

"Peterson gave us forty-eight hours' notice just like he was supposed to. No more, no less," Iron said, as he switched on the lights in the shed.

"I'll take off work," Mike said. "In case they send the same thugs that scared Sabrina. No one is coming on this property again without a man around."

"I'll drop a trip," Iron said. "The three of us can surely keep an eye on them."

"Does it say what kind of shape that equipment has to be in?" Dennis asked.

Iron was now an authority on all the rules for dealing with the FDIC. He highlighted information, made notes of anything requiring action, then tucked all the paperwork into an elaborate system of files.

"No, it doesn't. As long as it's in plain sight. But don't bust your butt fixing anything before they get here. You can't switch equipment either. Keep it honest. I won't have anyone in this family hiding a good tractor on our neighbor's land and swearing some broken-down old Farmall is all we have."

"Wouldn't think of it. I have something different in mind. I just want to make sure I'm on solid ground." When Dennis explained, Mike and Iron stared at him then began to laugh.

"I'll see if the *Wichita Eagle* will send a reporter. If they won't come, the *Hays Daily News* will."

Having been promised a scoop, Monday morning a reporter and a photographer from the *Hays Daily* followed Clyde Peterson and his team of three men to the Barrett homestead. The photographer gazed out the window with some bewilderment as they turned up the lane to Mary's

Place. They climbed out of their car and clumped along after the chief liquidation officer.

"Holy smoke." The photographer let out a long whistle. Quickly he streaked ahead ten feet, squatted down, focused, and snapped Peterson's astonished face just as his mouth gaped open. There were no orderly rows of equipment. As far as their eyes could see were thousands of pieces of parts glinting in the sun. The photographer began to click away.

Angrily, Peterson strode over to the Barrett men, who watched with amusement. "You can't do this. It's illegal."

"Nope," Iron said. "It isn't. The law says all I own must be on my land, in plain sight and available for your inspection. Here it 'tis. Inspect away."

The reporter snorted and scribbled down every word.

"I want this kept out of the paper," Peterson yelled. Furious, he imagined this charade giving other farmers ideas. The district office would blow sky high. "I'll sue you."

"Are you threatening a member of the press?" the reporter asked gleefully.

"No, of course not. I'm crazy about the press."

His three employees stood helplessly like cub scouts cheated out of a field trip.

"Jim, Pete, you too, Nathan. Go back to the bank. We'll do this another day." Face dark with hostility, he whirled around and marched toward the car.

The Barrett men were overcome with laughter as they watched him speed away. The work ahead was formidable, but it was worth it. Dennis had kept a list of the placement of all the parts and had drawn a grid. The engine to the big tractor was in the right quadrant of the fourth quarter of Grandma Alma's furthermost section. The wheels to the drill bought in March of '83 were sitting in front of Old Barn. It was all there in black and white and had been neatly alphabetized on a database.

Back in his office, Peterson slammed the door shut and locked it. Now it was more crucial than ever to bring Barrett down. If this man was successful in saving his farm, his methods would serve as a blueprint for others in the area. His hands shook as he poured himself a double shot of bourbon.

The uppermost thing on his mind was damage control. Pacifying the bean counters in the district office. Then he would take care of Barrett.

J.C. Espy chortled with approval when he read about their shenanigans. Iron was his old fighting self again, no doubt about it. He called Elizabeth, expecting her to share his delight. Instead she was appalled.

"I'm sick, just sick. It's not like Dad to do something this stupid. I've been working my tail off, trying to make it look like he has a few brains. And believe me, anyone that would go out of their way to aggravate the FDIC doesn't have a lick of common sense. He's undone all my hard work. Now who will we get to finance him?"

After he hung up, J.C. thought about what Elizabeth had said. A shiver went up his spine when he realized Iron had made things worse.

Later that week, after the story ran in the Hays paper, a crew from the *Wichita Eagle-Beacon* came out to interview the Barretts. The family was also featured on the local TV station's evening news. In a very short time, the wire services got wind of the story.

When Dennis figured that Clyde Peterson had enough, he called him. "Now," he said softly. "Are you two ready to talk a little business?"

Clyde Peterson glanced at his watch. It was 9:00 at night, and his office was the only place where the three men could meet with any degree of privacy. It would be a very short meeting. He didn't bother taking off the nylon windbreaker he had worn under his parka.

Hathaway simply nodded when he arrived and headed for one of the chrome-armed chairs. He did not remove his Stetson and resented being summoned.

Peterson was extremely tired of the people in this county. He wanted to get the hell out while he still had a decent job and a chance for advancement. Stunned to learn that Dennis, not Iron, had been the originator of the scattered parts fiasco, he had been rehearsing the words he would use to dismiss the little worm—before he told him that he was withdrawing the offer of $25,000. Barrett would soon learn just what his crazy publicity stunt had cost him. He intended to tear up the check before his very eyes.

"Where in the hell is he? He should have been here half an hour ago."

Hathaway looked at him with surly contempt and continued to study a tile on the floor.

Dennis came down the hall, and Peterson pounced when he walked through the door. "Just what in the hell did you think you were doing, Barrett?"

"I came here to talk business. Right now business. Not to hash over something that happened last week. The thing last week was just for fun."

"You're not in a position to talk about anything at all."

"Oh yes I am, gentlemen, I'm in a position to talk about authorization numbers."

Peterson looked at him blankly.

"For video auction sales," Dennis explained. "Your number in particular, Hathaway. Registered with a very specific video auction company. Used recently."

Peterson's eyes narrowed and he listened intently, trying to figure out what Barrett meant since he, too, had been behind the rigged sale.

"Funny thing, all it took was a little money to get this number out of those people. But then I guess you two know about spreading a little money around. Damn little money."

"So you found my number," challenged Hathaway. "So what?"

"So it links you to the sale." Dennis smirked. "And Miss Winston—formerly employed by this institution—that same Miss Winston gave me a memo telling her how to write up the copy for the video company. In Peterson's handwriting. Seems as though she has a conscience, after all."

Dennis's arms were crossed in front of his chest, and he slouched against the wall, one foot cocked, the sole of his shoe blatantly smudging the polished oak wainscoting. Peterson looked at him hard. Barrett seemed taller, heavier, than he had a month ago.

And smarter. Much, much smarter. Not at all like the kid who had sulled up at being offered a $25,000 check. And there was something about those cold green eyes.

"Then a very cooperative young lady in another town printed a copy of a check from their slaughterhouse, made out to Clyde Peterson," Dennis continued. "Then his bank was happy to verify that another check, for half that amount, written to our good friend Clifton here, cleared a couple of months ago. In fact, that's where you each are going to get the $50,000 you'll need soon. Very soon. From the sale of those cattle."

"What $50,000? How did you find out where I banked, Barrett?" Peterson's voice shook.

"Why, Mr. Peterson, sir, the name of your bank was on the check you offered me. The one I didn't take," Dennis said blandly. "The one I wouldn't touch with a ten-foot pole. The truth of the matter is, there's not one piece of evidence linking me with that sale. Not one. I was in Hays that day. My name isn't on anything. Moreover, there's no way I would have profited by blowing that sale."

Peterson shot Hathaway a look of sheer despair.

"Look, if it's a matter of more money."

"Oh, it's a matter of a lot more money and a few other things besides. Money and my mother's house is just for openers."

"You won't get away with this," Peterson yelled. He ignored the angry look in Hathaway's eyes coupled with a slight shake of his head, warning him to shut up.

"Yeah, I will." Dennis grinned. "Everyone in my family will swear to how hard I've worked to save the farm. My own grandmother will testify that I sold my vintage Corvette to pay the money we owed for interest."

Peterson groaned softly and whacked his forehead with the palm of his hand. So that's where the money had come from.

"And I guess I don't have to tell you what the penalty is for fraud."

All the color drained from Peterson's face.

"What do you want, Barrett? If you want the FDIC to leave your parents alone, you've got it. A write-down, new financing, anything."

"That's not what I want at all. I need to own that land outright. It's no good, having my father call the shots. And while I'm at it, there's a few more farms I have my eye on."

"You would do this to your own parents?"

"I'm not doing it to anyone. I'm doing it for me. That's all. No malice intended. I want $100,000. I figure that $50,000 is exactly the amount you each can give me without attracting too much attention. That will be a down payment on the financing I'm going to get. Then I want you two to go with me to Abner Wise when I deposit that check in his bank. And you'd better swear that backing me will be the best investment since buying stock in IBM."

"What do you want to finance?" asked Hathaway.

"Farms," Dennis replied. "Land. When all the loans are bundled from this county, I'm going to bid on them. I want to get in on those penny-on-the-dollar deals. Including my father's farm. And you're going to see to it that my bid is tops."

"We can't do that," scoffed Peterson. "It's impossible. Other people will be bidding. From back East. Big money. It'll be run by the government. We can't control what people are willing to pay on any given day."

"Oh, but you can," Dennis said. "The description, the evaluation of the property comes from your office, Peterson. You have the power to make a place sound like a worn-out pile of dirt, or the All-American homestead. I should know. I've seen this technique used to describe my father's breeding herd. Words like 'gentle old cows.'"

"What if your father declares bankruptcy first, Barrett?"

"He won't. Doesn't believe in it."

"What if some of the other farmers you're hoping to catch in your snare do? Declare bankruptcy before their loan is bundled?"

"Naw. They'll wait until it's too late. Folks out here would rather hope than eat."

Peterson exploded when Dennis left. He swore steadily at Hathaway, blaming him for vouching for Dennis Barrett to begin with.

"If you'll shut up and calm down and keep your head and think for a change," Hathaway said, "we're going to come out of this all right, both of us. I still have the money from selling the cattle, do you?"

Peterson nodded.

"Okay. We'll write the damn checks. It was found money anyway. Besides, the minute Barrett cashes them, he's linked back to us. That guarantees his silence. Then we'll swear to the president of the Agland State Bank that he's the greatest thing since sliced bread."

"He's like dealing with the devil," Peterson said. "Abner Wise deserves to get tangled up with him."

"Recommending him to Wise won't cost us a penny, Clyde. We can't get in any trouble with the law for doing that. Then when the time comes for bundling those notes for auction, you're going to make all those farms sound like rejects from the Dust Bowl."

"Then we'll be shut of the slimy little bastard."

29

It was early March. It would soon be St. Patrick's Day, time to plant potatoes. There had been a high, steady wind for the previous two days. Taking advantage of a lull in trucking, Iron was readying tractors for the spring work.

Midmorning, Mary stopped cleaning and went to the kitchen for a cup of coffee. Suddenly, she gasped for air then struggled to draw a deep breath. Her favorite country-Western station sputtered into steady static then quit.

She gazed out the window and saw a wall of black moving across the prairie. A dense mass, bearing down. She ran outside. The air was saturated with stinging particles.

"Iron!" she called. "Iron."

He appeared in the doorway of the machine shed and looked at the dense billow swiftly rolling along the north edge of their wheat field.

"It's dust," he hollered. "Nothing's swirling. It's not a tornado. Just dust. Go back. Quick." He bolted the machine shed door and started toward Mary. "Go back. Don't worry about me."

A wall of wind carrying black, gritty dust slammed against her; the force nearly knocked her off her feet. Thousands of needles of Kansas black pepper prickled her face.

"Iron, go back to the shed," she hollered. Dust immediately coated her tongue and throat, muffling her words. She shielded her eyes with her hands.

"Iron," she called again weakly. Something hard and metallic whacked her shins, and she yelped with pain. Her fingers traced the outline of their tiller. Better oriented, she knew the equipment had been lined up perpendicular to the house.

She had to get inside the house and find some way to help Iron. She thrust her arms in front of her. There was no way to walk against the wind. It was nearly strong enough to lift her off the ground. She dropped onto her hands and knees and inched along through the dirt. It seemed like an eternity before her fingers came across the sidewalk. She crawled forward along it until she bumped against the storm panel on the back door of the porch.

Standing slowly, carefully—not taking her fingers off the glass for a second—she pulled the door wide enough to squeeze through. The wind was from the west, or it would have ripped the door right off its hinges. Opening the kitchen door, she plunged into the house. Exhausted, she leaned against the wall.

If only Iron hadn't left the machine shed. Neither the dinner bell she used to reach him in emergencies years ago nor the CB radio that had taken its place was a bit of use to her now. But she had to help Iron find the house. Noise. Only noise would work.

She ran to the desk drawer and pulled out the silver whistle the twins had given her for Christmas. She opened the kitchen door and stepped onto the porch. Bracing herself, she opened the aluminum storm door a fraction. Pushing desperately against the gigantic force of the wind, she blew the whistle as hard as she could.

"Yo," she heard Iron shout. Heartened, she kept blowing the whistle and listened for him to answer.

Crawling now, his voice edged closer. He was nearly at her feet before she saw him. She knelt and extended her arm through the doorway. He clutched her hand, then rose, not loosening his grip. She pressed against the door with all her strength, bracing her feet against the frame for leverage until there was an opening wide enough for Iron to squeeze through.

Once inside, his tense muscles quivered spasmodically. "Oh damn, damn, damn." His voice broke. "What in the hell's going on?"

Mary shook her head and could not speak. The air in the kitchen was brownish and smoggy. It tasted like old, spoiled rhubarb. There was no turning away from it. The air had become a heavy, brackish, soupy concoction—alive and evil.

The lethal fragments coated her lungs, and her throat constricted. Mary felt like she was being choked slowly and relentlessly by unseen hands. She edged toward the sink, wetted down tea towels, and handed one to Iron. They draped the cloths over their nostrils and breathed damp, filtered air.

Outside, dust blew into capped gas tanks and under glass window shields on their equipment. Dust blew through openings too tight for the devil to enter. It ruined tractors and trucks and blasted like sand against a lifetime accumulation of equipment.

Inside, dust seeped into their computer and CB base station, their CDS, and TVS, and VCRS and stereo speakers, and their satellite dish, and their answering machine, and their digital receivers, and their tape decks. Every little electronic gadget attracted dust.

Iron's eyes were sinkholes in his weathered face. He stared blankly out the window. The wind blew for six hours and died down about four o'clock. Then the wall of dust moved on.

"I want to see the wheat," Iron said.

"I'm coming with you."

They went out onto the back porch and stood there, straining to see against the blood-red sun. Mary gave a startled cry.

It was as though a mysterious force had drained the world of color. Dust lay over everything in the farmyard. It covered the leaves on the trees, their buildings, and their equipment. Dust fine as a woman's face powder.

Mary's heart pounded. They raced for the field that lay behind the barn. When they reached it, she turned abruptly and hid her face in Iron's chest.

Fine, silty fragments blanketed their wheat. The crop that would rescue the family was now buried under a layer of malevolent dust. Wherever they put their feet, dust puffed up from the ground and hovered. In the late afternoon light, a pearly pink hue prismed off the hazy tan particles that fogged the air. In the fields and all around, for as far as the Barretts could see, the land lay like an exotic cloth of crushed gray velvet, pocked and shimmering with a strange iridescent gleam.

"Our wheat, our wheat," cried Mary. "Oh, no, no, no, no."

She pushed away from Iron, ran to the edge of the field, and looked across the land that had been swept nearly bare. The shallowly rooted wheat had been blown right out of the ground. "It's gone," she moaned. "It's gone."

She sank to her knees, her hands clasped and extended in front of her in supplication. The wind whipped her hair across her face in snaky red tendrils, and tears streamed down her cheeks.

The field was as gray and barren as lava. The dry, water-starved roots had yielded at once to the dust-laden wind. Then blowing tumbleweeds and debris from other farmers' crops had sliced off any wheat left standing. What had not been blown away was smothered under deadly piles of dirt.

Iron lifted her to her feet. "Mary, honey. My God."

She ran sobbing toward the house, leaving Iron behind.

Iron's huge hands dangled helplessly at his sides as he stared at the unfamiliar earth that had been green as spring and sparkling with life hours before.

Mary curled into a tight, miserable ball of pure despair in the wing chair. Iron came into the room. His face was as devoid of color as the wheat field.

"I'm walking over to Dennis's, then Mike's. I want to make sure everyone's all right. No use trying to drive. If I try to start up something before I get all the dust out, it'll just ruin the motor."

"I'll pull myself together in a little bit," she whispered. "I'll check on Alma. See what everyone needs."

"Are you okay, honey? I can stay here for a while, if you want me to."

"Go ahead and do whatever needs to be done."

"Well, just rest a while," he said awkwardly. "Don't try to clean anything until I'm back and can help. If this isn't a hell of a deal."

From the window, she watched him slog through the dust.

Iron was going to see if everyone was all right! *We're not all right and we're not going to be all right*, she thought bitterly.

There was a good chance they would never be all right again.

A couple of weeks later, Iron and Mary both lay on their backs, staring with unseeing eyes into the dark. She couldn't sleep and could not bring herself to speak. What words could possibly comfort her husband? What was the point in asking questions he couldn't answer?

Finally, despite her resolve, toward morning, her mouth moved with a will of its own.

"What are we going to do?" she whispered. "Whatever are we going to do without our wheat?"

"I'm going to plant milo in its place."

Mary knew he had been mulling it over ever since the dust hit, or her question would have hung there unanswered. He waited for her response.

"Milo," she said carefully, trying to imagine the alien grain in the field where they had always grown wheat. "Milo! There is time, isn't there?"

"Yes. We won't have to plant it until May. But it's touchy to grow and won't mature until fall."

"I guess it's worth a try."

"It'd better be."

Neither spoke again for the rest of the night. At first, she breathed a prayer of thanksgiving, relieved that Iron was not defeated. But, heartsick, she wondered if she herself could endure building hope again.

Mike called the morning after they decided to gamble on a new crop.

"Just checking, Mary. How's Iron doing?"

"Fine. He's going to plant milo. He just left for town."

"Where's he going to get the money for seed?"

"I don't know. I don't know." Her mind blanked. "I was so glad he wasn't becoming depressed I didn't think of that."

"Better start penciling, Mary. If we have to come up with the money for seed out of our wages—and I think that's what we would have to do—we'll have to live even tighter than we're doing right now."

"We can't. Mike, we just can't!"

"I don't know what else Iron could have in mind."

Mary winked back tears at the weariness in his voice.

Iron called her around ten o'clock. "We've actually gotten a break around here," he said the moment she answered the phone.

"What?"

"Piker and Newark are going to give me the seed and let me pay for it and the wheat seed after I harvest the milo."

"Oh, that's wonderful. What a generous thing to do."

"Damn right it's generous," he said, his voice husky. "They said they don't know of a better farmer than me anywhere. They're just sorry I've fallen on hard times. I've been a real jerk and avoided them. Couldn't stand to look them in the eye. Figured their feelings had changed toward me so much that they couldn't stomach the sight of me."

"Oh, honey!"

"They're the best friends a man could ever have."

Several nights later, Mary shot up in bed, drenched with sweat. Iron was on the truck and she was alone. She had dreamed she was on a white-winged horse, rushing toward the sun with dazzling speed. Then the horse started to fall, fall, fall and she screamed—helpless, terrified dream screams—through the slow-motion descent.

But nothing, nothing she said or did could make the horse rise again. Sick with terror, she lay shaking in the cold, empty bed.

Finally she got up and went downstairs to fix a cup of hot chocolate. It was becoming a nightly ritual. She poured milk into a cup, dumped in a couple of spoonfuls of cocoa powder, and put it into the microwave. She waited for it to heat.

She shivered and pulled her robe around her. She had begun dreaming of falling horses after they planted the milo. She did not need a psychologist to tell her how much she was dreading another crop failure. During the day, she willed herself not to think of it.

But at a much deeper level, a piercing longing for a rich, bountiful, perfect crop of milo was inching upward as surely as the grain. She was becoming very good at selecting the thoughts she would or would not allow herself, but it seemed she could not prevent hope. Like spring, it swelled, throbbed, greened up in her soul.

She sipped her chocolate and resolutely averted her eyes from the back door.

Then against her will, her heart plummeting sickly, she slowly turned and let her eyes be drawn to the glass, after all, and saw at once the murky movement of a shadow in the barnyard. She was positive she saw it. It's *real*, she thought. *Someone is there.*

Quickly she went to the gun cabinet and got out her shotgun.

The phone rang, and Mike reached for it, absently keeping one eye on the TV set.

"I'll be right there." After hanging up he quickly kicked off his slippers and laced on his boots.

Connie came out of the bedroom at once, alarmed by the unexpectedness of a late call. "What's wrong? It's 11:30."

"That was Mary. She wants me to come over."

"Has something happened?"

He shook his head. "No. She thought she saw someone out in the farmyard and wants me to check."

"Shouldn't we call the sheriff?"

"Let's not, until I see what's going on. Might just be some tramp looking for a place to bed down for the night. All the buildings are locked up tight, so the place is slim pickings for a thief. I'll walk so I can come up through the back of the farmyard and call you as soon as I get to the house. But just in case, if you don't hear from me in twenty minutes, call the law."

Mike took his twelve-gauge shotgun from the rack on the porch and shoved a handful of shells into his pockets.

"Better take the keys to all the buildings," Connie said.

There was a full moon. Mike walked slowly around the buildings. Seeing nothing, he walked to the front porch. He unlocked the main door and pushed on inside. At once, Mary shoved a shotgun in his ribs.

"Don't shoot! Mary, it's me. Don't shoot."

"Oh, my God," cried Mary. "My God, my God, my God." The shotgun clattered to the floor. She backed away, covering her face with her hands.

Instinctively, Mike placed one foot on the shotgun to prevent her from picking it up again. Mary moved toward her son-in-law. She patted his face, his solid flesh, over and over.

"Thank God I didn't hurt you. Thank God."

"Mary. It's okay. I'm fine."

"Someone has been hanging around this farmyard. I swear they have."
Her knuckles were white, and her shoulders throbbed from tension.

"You mean it's happened before?"

"Yes. I just haven't called anyone. I was afraid it was all in my head."

Dumbfounded, he could not understand why Mary hadn't said something, done something. Suddenly he was aware of her weight loss, her dry, pale skin, her thin lips. Even her hair seemed to have lost its life. She was racked with a violent siege of coughing.

"Need some water," she said weakly. She went to the kitchen and drank deeply.

The quietness of the night was broken by the sound of a siren in the distance. They turned and saw a revolving red light. The sheriff's vehicle came up the lane.

"Good," he said glancing at his watch. More than twenty minutes had passed since he left the house. "Connie went ahead and called the cops."

He went to the driveway and greeted the undersheriff. "Hello, Dan."

Mike explained that Mary had seen a prowler. "He's probably slipped away by now, but I'm glad you're here."

"I'll take a look around."

"Can't hurt," Mike said. "I'll come with you as soon as I call my wife."

Connie answered on the first ring.

"Mary's fine," Mike said quickly. "I didn't see anyone. Odds are whoever it was hightailed it when he heard the siren. You can rest assured that he won't be back. Not after all this fuss. Gotta hang up. Dennis just came through the door."

"I want to talk to you about Mom," Dennis said after all three had thoroughly searched the grounds and Mary had gone to bed. They watched the undersheriff's taillights turn the corner. "I'm worried about her. I didn't want to say anything when she was around, but this isn't the first time it's happened."

"You knew someone has been hanging around here then?" Mike asked.

"I don't think there is," Dennis said reluctantly. "Mom's called me over three times to check for a prowler. She didn't want me to tell the family because she was embarrassed."

"Mary is hardly the kind of hysterical woman who goes around seeing things," Mike snapped.

"I'm not so sure," Dennis said. "She hasn't been acting like herself at all."

As he walked back to his house, Mike mulled over the contradictions between what Mary had said and what Dennis had said. One of them was lying. Or confused.

Was this the first time Mary had called anyone? Or had she asked Dennis to investigate three times before?

Normally he would take Mary's word over Dennis's in a heartbeat, but he remembered the terror on Mary's face when he came through the door.

The face of a woman struggling very hard to keep herself together.

30

It was April. 4-H Days again. Mary swung the station wagon into the parking lot and turned off the ignition. Connie and Lisette both had to work and had dropped off Susan, Benjy, and Sabrina at the high school.

She circled the steering wheel with her arms and rested her head against her hands. She had been totally, utterly exhausted for the past two weeks. She opened the car door, squared her shoulders, and began carrying in the first load of boxes.

She was still smarting from the phone call she had made to the extension office explaining that Iron would be on the road and therefore unable to participate in the model meeting.

"Will it count against the club," she'd asked, "if we don't have the male community leader?"

"Well yes, it will, Mary," the county agent had replied. "You really do need to find a substitute if you're sure Mr. Barrett can't make it. The young boys need role models, you know."

"No problem. Just checking. I'll run in a substitute."

Her substitute was to have been Dennis, but a major repair job had come in last night, and it would take him all morning to finish the work.

Sick with guilt, she knew she should have found someone else. Just last year, she wouldn't have dreamed of letting it go. But yesterday evening, after dealing with a series of petty problems with some of the younger club members, she could not force herself to pick up the phone and make one more arrangement.

She walked into the home room and placed the box on a table. Kids swarmed around her at once. There were three families whose posters were a mess. Wearily, she realized she had left the box of stencils, magic markers, and crayons on the kitchen table.

Years of habit kicked in and she started out the door to phone someone in the family to swing by the house to pick up the supplies. Then she remembered. There was no family to call. They were all working.

She turned back and looked around at the needy hands stretched toward her, clutching at her, pinching her clothes, surrounding her on all sides.

"Mrs. Barrett, Mrs. Barrett, I need, I need, I need . . ."

Panic-stricken, her throat started to close, choking off her air. She slowly backed away, trying to disentangle herself. "Just a minute," she said. "Just a minute, kids. I need to get a few things from the car."

She resisted the impulse to flee and willed herself to walk slowly toward the heavy glass exit doors. Then something in her soul lurched and wanted to keep away from the end of the hallway. The doors loomed up like shiny opaque heads of tombstones. These were the same doors she had stood beside, last year, when Iron had told her the bank was not going to lend them any operating capital.

She pulled herself together and, on the next trip inside, asked others to help her carry the remaining boxes.

"Do you want me and Susan to go pick up the chicken, Grandma?"

Startled, she turned and blinked at Sabrina. She had forgotten to order the food, and everyone was expecting it.

Humiliated to the roots of her hair, she knew that there was no way in the world she could have paid for it anyway. Last year, the Barretts could have fed every child in all the clubs without batting an eye.

This year, she couldn't have paid for enough peanut butter and jelly sandwiches to go around without thinking and planning for it a week ahead of time.

She turned to her granddaughter. "Honey, I forgot. I can't believe it."

"What are we going to do?" asked Sabrina. "A lot of these kids haven't brought any money or anything to eat. They've always counted on you."

"Let me think," she mumbled. She splayed her fingers across her face. *I can't believe I was so stupid.* Her mind was numb. What was it she always told the kids?

It's not the purple ribbons that make you a winner. It's the attitude you allow yourself to take toward the whites.

Well, she could not, could not, summon up any attitude right now but total despair.

"Grandma? Do you want me to run to Walmart to get some bread and lunch meat? How about some apples?"

No more little grocery store, Mary thought. Henry Green had gone under. *The new bank owners didn't like the looks of his loans either. Just last year the man who used to be a friend would have let us run up a bill for hundreds and hundreds of dollars if we wanted to charge food for any reason.*

"No," Mary said. "We can't put anything on a credit card. Besides, you only have a learner's permit. You're not supposed to be driving without an adult with you. I can't leave. I've got to stay here with these kids."

"But there isn't another parent here to go with me," Sabrina said. "Mrs. Linden and Mrs. Smith left to watch their kids' demonstrations."

"More parents should volunteer to help," Mary snapped. "We're too short-handed." Other husbands and wives, too, had started working part time or full time to supplement farm income.

A couple of kids stopped talking and looked reproachfully at Mary, who was hardly ever critical. Sabrina, their idol, looked miserable.

"I'm sorry," Mary mumbled. "I just don't feel well today and I'm . . . I'm not myself."

"Maybe you're coming down with something," suggested Susan kindly. "Anyway, it's nearly time for the model meeting. We'll all have to eat afterwards."

Dumbly, Mary filed into the room with the other members.

"Mrs. Barrett?"

Startled, she focused on the club president, who was calling the roll.

Her mind emptied. What was the roll call response? A Kansas bird? A flower? A fact about Kansas? No, that was last year.

Slowly her eyes trailed across the bewildered and embarrassed faces of the children, who turned in their seats to look at her. Their faces grew larger and larger then began to recede as though she were seeing them through the wrong end of a telescope. As she looked at Jimmy Brown, his glasses grew larger and larger—as large as the glass panels in her back door—and in one black instant, she saw a shadow shift and mock her beyond the thick, thick lenses. In a blink, a little boy was there again.

She tried to think, think of the roll call. Jolt her blank mind. Then, dropping her clipboard, she turned and ran from the room.

"I think my grandmother has the flu," Sabrina said, rising swiftly to the occasion. Flawlessly, doing Mary proud, the children closed ranks. "Recover." The word passed swiftly down the row.

"Recover."

Mary's word. They had all heard her say it countless times.

Mary's eyes fluttered open. Iron leaned over her and squeezed her hand. She blinked against the bright light radiating from snow-white sheets.

"Where am I?" she asked weakly, trying to sit up.

"You're in the hospital. And you're one sick woman. You have pneumonia. Doc Clayborn says it most likely started as a bad case of bronchitis after the dust storm. The infection finally settled in your lungs. It was a long time getting there."

"I've got to get out of here. Right now." She tried to sit up then winced as pain knifed through her chest. "Oh God." Tears filled her eyes as she sank back down on her pillow. "If I haven't made a mess of things. Iron, we don't have any health insurance. I had to drop it."

"So we discovered. Didn't take much for me to figure out that's why you didn't go to the doctor to begin with."

"What are we going to do? We can't afford to have me lying around in a hospital bed."

"You're staying right here until the doctor says you can go home."

She swallowed hard and bit her lip.

"I can't do that. Every penny counts."

"You're staying. I don't care if we have to strap you in. Besides, a few medical bills is just a drop in the bucket to what we owe. Practically nothing."

She laughed bitterly, which made her cough again. Then, totally resigned to the fact that every decision was out of her hands, she fell deeply asleep. She slept nearly constantly for three days.

"She's also suffering from physical exhaustion," the doctor told Iron. "Just totally run down. How much fieldwork has she been doing?"

"Too much. She helped plow under the wheat."

"Was the cab enclosed?"

"No, she was on our oldest tractor."

"Knowing Mary, I 'spect she raced right back into the house at day's end and cooked a hot meal for everyone."

Iron nodded, ashamed.

"Don't expect me to turn her loose too soon. She'll go back to working like a dockhand the minute I take my eyes off her."

After a week of bed rest, Mary's old energy began to return. As her body renewed, she realized her mental state had had a great deal to do with her physical condition. Her head was part of her body. It, too, had been worn out. No wonder she had jumped out of her skin every time she saw a shadow. Doc Clayborn said she had probably run a low-grade fever for weeks before it raged out of control. Her lungs couldn't cope with the invasion of dust. She suspected she had become obsessed with movements in the barnyard because she was fighting fever and infection.

That afternoon, she called Iron and asked if he would bring in her collection of seed catalogs when he came to the hospital.

He swore under his breath and called Elizabeth the moment Mary hung up. "Any way you could come home for a while? I need someone to keep her whacked back while I'm on the truck. If we don't, she's going to wear herself to a frazzle again, making up for the time she's been down."

Elizabeth jumped at the chance. "Super. I have vacation time coming, and I really don't have the bucks to go somewhere glamorous."

"Try to think of an excuse to come home. You know Mom. If you imply she needs help, she'll run you off. Doc wants her to take it easy for a while."

Elizabeth hung up the phone and drummed her pencil impatiently on her desk. She wished she could leave before the end of the week. She rose and walked over to the window. For all her expertise, she couldn't think of a way to keep her parents from losing the farm. Sick with worry, she watched a groundskeeper spearing pieces of paper.

Since the scattered parts episode, the Barretts appeared to be too radical or crazy to acquire financing from a commercial lending institution. In one more year, the FDIC would bundle their notes along with those of other failed farms, and the highest bidder would take possession of all of them. She winked back tears.

Although she had investigated every legal possibility, she was plagued by a feeling she had overlooked something.

A university student stopped to take a picture of a squirrel, and as suddenly as the camera flashed, she knew. She knew. The picture!

She could prove beyond a shadow of a doubt that Sabrina's calf had been picked up after the video auction. The Polaroid picture of Molly. It was proof in living color that calf had been in a show recently. It belonged to Sabrina Barrett. The men had been little better than rustlers. Bringing criminal charges for theft against the FDIC would force out all kinds of information: who had bought the cattle, who had trucked them off the property and, best of all, who had arranged the sale to begin with.

She smiled, imagining herself pointing out to a jury that this was clearly a calf belonging to a 4-Her. Its switch had been teased into a ball; its hooves were polished to a military shine; its hair was trimmed into varying lengths.

4-H calves were legally owned by the youngsters, not the parents. The FDIC couldn't sell the children's assets. And when she put Sabrina on the stand! No jury could resist the appeal of that fragile, heartbroken little girl.

~~~~~~~~~~~~~~~~

"Welcome home, sweetie."

Elizabeth groaned when she saw her mother waving wildly from the front porch. Mary hurried toward the car and insisted on helping carry in her luggage. "I'm just tickled to death you have time to come home for a visit."

"Mom!" she protested, as she walked inside and saw a large angel food cake—her favorite—sitting on the island.

"Now don't scold. You know it's bad for me to just sit around."

Elizabeth looked at her helplessly.

"You can help me with the barbecue."

"Surely you aren't still having the barbecue this year!"

"Of course we are, Elizabeth."

"All that meat. All that work. I'm supposed to be taking care of you."

Uh oh, she thought, seeing the astonished look on Mary's face.

"Oh you are, are you? And whose bright idea was that?"

"Dad's of course," Elizabeth said, chagrined at her slip of the tongue. "He really has been beside himself, Mom."

"I'm fine. The best I've been in a year. We're going to have the usual celebration we have after wheat harvest. Even though there's no harvest this year."

"Won't buying all that food be a problem?"

"People will just have to pitch in a little. I'll ask them to contribute. Folks know we've been going through some hard times. They won't mind. Having the barbecue as usual will just show them that we're not down and out."

The next morning Elizabeth asked for the picture of Sabrina's calf.

Mary slid open the middle drawer to her desk and took out an envelope and handed it to her daughter. Elizabeth took out the picture of Molly. She smiled as she studied the elaborate grooming.

"I want you to put it in your safety deposit box today," said Elizabeth.

"We don't have one. Just our home safe. Thank goodness we didn't have that to worry about when Abner Wise took over the bank. You think we could actually trust that den of thieves to keep their paws off our things?"

"No one could get in without having your key. It takes two to open the boxes. Yours and the master key from the bank."

"I don't care how it's supposed to work. We don't trust them."

"Never mind. I'll take it back to Manhattan with me and put it in my own box. It's a crucial piece of evidence."

Mary brightened. Elizabeth had told her and Iron last night that, although she didn't want to give them false hope, she was putting together a lawsuit against the FDIC.

"Okay. Take it back with you," Mary said, putting the envelope back in the drawer. "I'll be glad to have it out of the house. I still can hardly stand to look at it. Those men nearly ruined Sabrina."

"How's she doing?"

"Not well since the dust storm," Mary said. "We had to drop her piano lessons when the medical bills came in for my hospital stay. So now she doesn't play at all. But I think she'll be better after we bring in the milo crop and she can see that we're going to make it."

"Maybe I can help her while I'm here," Elizabeth said hesitantly. But much as she wanted to fly to Sabrina's side, she avoided any contact with Dennis. They couldn't even discuss the weather without getting into a fight, and their last confrontation had been a real humdinger.

Dennis had been stunned when Iron decided to plant milo. He had even swallowed his pride and called her, asking her to try to talk their father out of it. "He's just too dumb to know when to quit," Dennis said. "All Dad's going to do is rack up more debt."

"Where'd he get the money for seed?"

"Believe it or not, Newark and Piker are staking him."

"You don't say."

"Those two men are a couple of damn fools, and our father is grasping at straws," Dennis said angrily. "There's no way in hell you can save a farm with a single crop of milo."

But they might clear enough to keep going until I can take Sabrina's case to court, thought Elizabeth.

"Look, Dennis. Just whose side are you on, anyway?"

"My parents'," he said frostily. "Someone has to keep these two in touch with reality. The truth is all this flailing around in quicksand is killing them and the kids too. We'll all be crazy if Mom and Dad keep this up. Not that Mom isn't halfway there already."

She'd hung up on Dennis when he slammed Mary, then she'd called her parents and praised them for their efforts.

Now, as she listened to Mary talk about Sabrina's state of mind, she was sobered by the stakes involved for the poor little girl.

31

Two days before the barbecue, Elizabeth walked over to Connie's to return a cake pan. She stopped at the north field, now planted with milo. This crop was all her parents had talked about since she came home.

Iron had planted it the first week in June. Much later and the crop wouldn't reach the cutting stage before frost. If he had planted it much earlier, emergence would have been delayed, leaving the plants vulnerable to diseases.

The development of the intricate root system was critical right now. If something happened at this stage—such as drought or disease—the head might not fully emerge or the plant might not be fully pollinated, or the roots and the stalk would not be sturdy enough to bear the weight of the mature head of rusty-brown pellets.

Even if there was plenty of rain, so much could go wrong. Although there were herbicides to control annual and perennial weeds, Iron hadn't known last fall that he would be planting milo in this field, so he hadn't used any pre-emergence mixtures.

A multitude of diseases could ruin this crop. Even more lethal was an invasion of insects. Some of the sprays used to control them could cause more trouble than the bugs if they weren't applied properly.

If the milo survived everything else, too heavy plants could bend on fragile stalks. If the header reel on the combine turned too quickly, the grain could shatter—too slowly and the heads might drop. If the cylinder speed were too fast, the grain could crack, or the stalks would be crushed.

Mindful of all that depended on chance for a farmer, Elizabeth had always scoffed at the predictions that large corporations would take over the land someday. No CEO in his right mind would want to oversee an undertaking so dependent on the whims of the gods.

The twins tugged Elizabeth inside when she came up the walk and wouldn't loosen their grip until Connie shooed them back outside with a fresh supply of graham crackers and Kool-Aid. Connie put away the cake pan, kicked off her moccasins, poured them each a glass of iced tea, and settled down at the table for a good visit.

"Mom seems to be real worried about Sabrina," Elizabeth said, reaching for an oatmeal cookie.

"We all are. Sometimes I wonder what all goes on at that house," Connie said.

"What bothers you the most about Sabrina?"

"She's obsessed, that's what. All that child can think about is getting her calf back. She's turned religious on us, and not in a good way either. She seems to think Jesus is a kind of rabbit's foot, that if she carries him around long enough, she'll have good luck and Molly will be back in the barn someday. Just like that."

Elizabeth groaned.

"And as for the rest of the kids, Benjy's like an old horse grinding grain, the kind that used to go 'round and 'round in circles till they dropped. He plods from one chore to another. It's no life for a little boy. He seems to think if he works hard enough, everything will turn out all right."

"Why wouldn't he think that?" Elizabeth said. "It's all he's heard all his life. It's all we've ever been taught."

"And my Susan! Sometimes I think she wants us to lose the farm. She's delirious at the thought of moving to town and running the streets with her friends. It's even affecting the twins. Andy has started wetting the bed, and Andrea has gone back to sucking her thumb."

Just then, Andrea slammed the back door. Her face was hot with indignation as she marched over to her mother.

"Didn't," protested Andy, who came charging in right on her heels. "I didn't do it. She's a liar."

"Andy, she hasn't even accused you of doing anything yet. Go to your room and cool off. And Andrea, don't even think about tattling, if that's what you have in mind. You go into the living room and sit there. Without the TV," Connie added, seeing the outraged look on Andy's face. "And you're to stay away from each other."

They obeyed their mother, but Andrea's lower lip quivered and Andy's shoulders tensed with defiance as they left the room.

"See what I mean?" said Connie unhappily. "They've always been inseparable. Now they can't play together five minutes without getting into a fight. And keeping track. They watch each other like hawks to make sure the other one isn't getting a little more."

"There's been too many changes," Elizabeth said. "Too many for all of us."

"If I had to name the one main thing that's throwing us all off whack," Connie said as she refilled their glasses, "I think it's losing the wheat. It's just plain creepy not to be cutting wheat. Mike acts like the sun doesn't come up in the East anymore."

"I feel like I've personally planted the milo," Elizabeth said. "Between Mom's and Dad's phone calls, I've had a blow-by-blow account of everything from picking the right variety to deciding whether to plant it at one or one-and-a-half inches."

"Mike even argued for two inches because it's so dry," Connie said earnestly, "but Dad said he didn't want to take a chance on having a reduced stand or slow emergence."

Elizabeth smiled. She had forgotten how literally and seriously Connie would debate farming techniques.

"If something happens to the milo, we're done," Connie said.

"No. We can't lose hope. We've got to keep fighting. I know it's hard because even though I work with people like our folks every day I still don't believe this can be happening to us."

"Well, it is. We're one crop away from being on the street."

"At least that can't happen. They can't take Mom's house. They can't take Mary's Place, if the folks file for bankruptcy," Elizabeth argued.

"Dad says there's no way he would ever do that, and Dennis is backing him."

Every nerve in Elizabeth's body was suddenly alert. "I know that, Connie. I've heard Dennis say it myself, but why?"

"Dad says he's a chip off the old block," Connie said sarcastically. "Bullshit."

"Dennis is saying all the right things to get into Dad's good graces again. Iron took him back with open arms. Our dear brother doesn't need to do anything to get on Dad's good side. He's already there."

"There's hope, Connie. Hope for us all. I didn't want to say anything until I had all my ducks in a row." Elizabeth leaned forward, intending to tell Connie that she was going to court with a case based on the picture of Sabrina's calf.

"Hey, now. Speak of the devil!" Connie said abruptly, warning her to be still.

Dennis came up the walk. "Mike around?" he asked.

"No, he's working in town today."

"I came by to slap a coat of paint on some extra horseshoes for the barbecue. Makes them easier to see. We might add more stakes too."

"Okay, and Mike said we need to paint the rake we use in the pit this year. Last year, the coals burned down so low no one could tell where to hook it onto the chain."

"Will do. 'Lo there, Elizabeth. Hear you're home for a little R and R."

"The rake," she said. "You've got to be kidding. Are you screwy men still throwing the chain into the pit?"

"You betcha. It's what makes the meat turn out right."

She rolled her eyes. The barbecue rake was used to snare the mammoth iron chains wrapped around a six-by-four-foot sealed iron box. It contained seasoned, foil-wrapped meat: hams, turkeys, roasts of venison, roasts of beef, pheasants, and quail. It would be lowered onto a white-hot fire.

Dennis went to the shed, and Elizabeth finished her tea. Andy slipped in the back door.

"Andrew, you were supposed to be in your room." Connie slammed down her glass of tea and jumped up from the table. "What in the world have you gotten into this time?"

"I didn't mean to," he whined. "Honest, Mom."

His hands were smeared with the phosphorous paint Dennis used to make the horseshoes glow in the dark.

"Time for me to leave," Elizabeth said with a smile.

"Oh no you don't. Go get the turpentine."

Cars started pulling into the deeply shaded clearing by the creek where the barbecue was held. There were never any invitations sent. Everyone in the county knew they were invited.

The older children immediately started playing hide-and-seek, ducking in and out of shrubbery. The youngest snatched at fireflies. Several junior high girls in shorts and halter tops, their hair identically permed and frizzed, strolled along the creek bank. It was a warm, mild summer evening. The rich, succulent odor of roasting meat wafted through the night air.

"This is the first time we've ever asked people to donate food," Mary said, "but they've been wonderful about it. All of them."

Startled, Elizabeth turned to her mother. She hadn't heard her approach.

"That doesn't surprise me," she said. "There's a lot of good people around here."

The night before, Elizabeth and Mary had washed off the picnic tables with hot Clorox water and picked up tossed tin cans and loose papers. They tested the lights and electrical outlets that would be powered by a generator. Then they watched the men prepare the pit.

Mary coached them every step of the way as they backed a truck with a winch close to the six-foot-deep concrete-lined pit. They carefully centered the meat-laden iron box then slowly lowered it onto the fire.

Working together, four men maneuvered a slab of corrugated iron over the opening, then layers of dirt were shoveled onto it. Lack of oxygen would soon smother the fire, but the enormous heat remaining in the coals would slowly cook the meat overnight and throughout the day of the gathering.

Now a group of men were playing horseshoes, and the two women walked over to watch as the gleaming phosphorous-painted ovals were lobbed toward iron stakes. There were intermittent clangings of metal on metal and shouts of approval when someone scored a ringer.

Mary went back to the picnic tables to check on the rest of the food, and Elizabeth joined her.

In a huge black cauldron, lighted by a wood fire, dozens of ears of corn bubbled in boiling water. A small group pulled up lawn chairs to listen to a shy guitar player who had been coaxed into singing old country songs.

Elizabeth was suddenly pierced with a fierce longing to preserve the goodness of it all: the gathering of grandparents, parents, and children playing together, loving together. A young mother cuddled her little boy against her shoulder. A father warned his son to be careful around the fire.

Mary had taught that young woman to make cookies when she was the 4-H food projects leader. Iron had taught that young man to make a seat for a swing when he was in charge of woodworking. They, their parents, their grandparents and their great-grandparents had lived in the same county since homesteading times, the same as the Barretts.

"Elizabeth!"

She turned and waved at Lisette.

"Shades of Amelia Earhart. I heard flying agrees with you."

"You'd better believe it," said Lisette. Her dark eyes glistened with enthusiasm.

Elizabeth smiled. Her sister-in-law's carriage bespoke her new self-confidence. She had lost the cynical expression that had added years to her age. She no longer looked like an old hippie with one foot in the past, fighting for identity.

Benjy and Sabrina trailed along after her, and Elizabeth winced at the changes in her niece. She looked like a sick cat. But Benjy was going to be all right, she decided, noting the stubborn set of his jaw and the firm strength in his handshake.

"It's ready!" someone shouted. People gathered around to watch the men who would be bringing up the meat. They shoveled off the dirt covering the iron slab and heaved it to one side.

Sonny Newark backed his truck up to the edge of the pit. Much to Elizabeth's relief, a very young man volunteered for the privilege of raking up the chain and hooking it to the suspended cable. A cheer went up when the tines connected and he manipulated enough links onto the hook. The box was raised, swung away from the pit, and lowered to the ground.

Elizabeth headed toward a classmate, then a group of men caught her attention.

"The cheating, lying, thieving son-of-a-bitch. He took a write-down and then bought himself a brand-new pickup."

"That's not the half of it. I hear the missus is adding a room onto the house."

"There's a funny taste in my mouth, let me tell you. My note wasn't turned over to the FDIC. I have to pay back every cent I owe. And I sure ain't driving no new pickup. And at the price wheat is right now, it's going to be a cold day in hell before my wife gets a new piece of furniture, let alone a brand-new room."

"You're not going to believe this, my wife saw the missus at McCook, buying groceries with food stamps."

"No."

"God's truth. I swear it."

"I could have sworn they were as honest as the day is long before all this came up."

Elizabeth exploded into the conversation. "I couldn't help overhearing you," she said. "You all know where I work and what I do. Sometimes the people who are buying an extra car and doing something to their house are getting ready to declare bankruptcy. It's the only way to hang onto a little money. They get to keep two vehicles and their home."

"Adding a room onto the house is your idea of hanging on to money?"

"It's legal. If a family knows they are going the bankruptcy route, they can buy a better car and keep it or put any cash they can get their hands on into improving their home beforehand."

"Still ain't right. And you know what kind of people use food stamps."

"Yes, poor people who need to eat," she said hotly. "Some of these families are so ashamed that they'd rather starve than use them in their own town."

"Well, they ought to be ashamed. Most of their troubles is sheer mismanagement."

"There are circumstances that you wouldn't understand unless you've been there."

"I'm not in trouble, by God. I didn't go out and buy every piece of equipment in sight."

"Oh go to hell, Nick," she said crossly. "No wonder my office has to deal with folks who've let everything slide until they're about to go under. I've never seen such a lack of simple Christian charity for your own kind."

Nick shrugged. "They bring it on themselves, Elizabeth. I'm telling you, you're butting your head against a stone wall. The same ones you manage to rescue will be broke again. Flat on their ass in three years' time. I don't care how much of a write-down they wangle."

"That's not true, some of them need me to get the government off their backs for a little while."

She turned and saw her father, stricken, his face sober and impassive, listening to every word. Iron Barrett's shame hung in the air like sulfur. *My parents are dying inside,* she thought. *Made sick by the need to keep up a brave front. Some of the rest of you are too. Why don't any of you talk about it?*

Then inspired, she walked over to Mary, who was sitting on a bench next to Dennis.

"Mom, I have the best idea. Why don't you start a group to share some of the experiences you all are having on the farm? It would help with stress, and you could trade information."

There was an immediate leap of interest in Mary's eyes.

Dennis broke in at once. "Organizing a group is the last thing Mom should do right now. The responsibility would be too much for her."

"Your brother thinks our big old house is too much for me too. He thinks it's wearing me down." Mary smiled sadly. "Guess you know what I thought of that idea."

"Mom," Dennis said sharply. "You're taking what I said the wrong way. I said you need some help taking care of it. The kind of help other women your age have."

"Sorry, Dennis. Guess I misunderstood what you meant. You did mention me and Iron being better off in a smaller place."

The hair prickled on the back of Elizabeth's neck. Her age indeed! Her mother was just forty-eight. How dare he undermine Mary's confidence in any way? "Well, talking with other women would be a good idea," Elizabeth said carefully, determined not to make a scene. "Support groups are big in cities. But some things that work in cities won't work out here."

"There's lots of smart-assed city ideas that don't work out here," Dennis snapped.

Elizabeth knew he had no awareness of the depth of her anger. He thought she would just stand back and let him badger Mary, who was still recovering from a long illness. She was furious at the sly, knowing expression on his face as he eyed their mother. He was like a cat batting at a mouse.

"Can I talk to you a minute in private, Dennis?"

He followed her to a grove of trees about twenty feet away.

"Just what in the hell is going on here?" Her words sprayed in her fury. "How dare you imply Mom can't keep up her home? She needs lots of love and support right now."

"She's acting dingy half the time," said Dennis. "Like she's not playing with a full deck."

"That's a cheap shot. She's been under a lot of stress. How do you expect her to act?"

"Sane," Dennis said flatly.

"She needs this family's help. Physically, emotionally, and morally."

"Oh yeah?" said Dennis. "You really think spurring our parents on in a lost cause is the right thing to do? You're the one who's not doing them any favors, Elizabeth. Dad should wake up and smell the coffee before he kills Mom off."

"What are you saying? That they should throw in the towel? And do what? Sell out?"

"They are going to be sold out in time. It's inevitable. But there's no need for them to keep butting their heads against a stone wall. Like planting milo. The milo was a dumb-ass thing to do. It won't clear enough money to make a real difference. It just increased their indebtedness."

"We've got far more than one milo crop going for us, Dennis. One of the reasons I came home was to get that picture of Sabrina's calf."

"What picture?" he asked, standing very still.

"You saw it. That photo will prove that the FDIC picked up a calf belonging to Sabrina. A good old-fashioned 4-H calf sprayed and polished and back-combed. And we're going to sue, sue, sue. I can hardly wait. The

Supreme Livestock Company will wish it hadn't been so tight-mouthed with information when I get through with them."

Dennis sullenly waited for Elizabeth to finish.

"By the time I collect punitive damages on behalf of your little girl, the Barrett family will be on Easy Street. We'll save the farm with one hand tied behind our back."

Dennis shifted his eyes toward his pickup. "If you're through carrying on, it's time for me to go," he said. "I told Lisette we wouldn't stay too late tonight. She's got to work tomorrow."

Elizabeth yelled at his departing back. "And those bastards are going to have to name names and tell us who stood to make some money out of this deal. Someone did! And best of all, I'm going to bomb the FDIC back to the Stone Age."

"Yeah? Well, I'm beginning to think that all the women in this family belong in an institution."

He walked away quickly, not giving her a chance to reply.

"I've got to stop by the folks' for a minute and pick up some papers," he said to Lisette.

Once there, he opened the middle drawer of Mary's desk, where she kept papers and files that needed her immediate attention. He took out the envelope labeled "Molly's Picture." Then he went to the bookcase next to the fireplace and removed one of his mother's 4-H photo albums. He located a picture of an ordinary Hereford calf, removed it from the album, and switched it with the one inside the envelope.

He glanced at the original Polaroid of the fussily groomed calf and smiled.

Hathaway and Peterson would pay big bucks to get it back.

32

Elizabeth walked briskly through the lobby of the Manhattan State Bank. Putting the picture of Sabrina's calf in her safety deposit box was at the top of her list of errands today. She signed the record the teller shoved across the desk and retrieved her key from her briefcase. A woman holding the master key preceded her into the vault, and they followed the double key ritual for accessing the box.

When Elizabeth was alone, she withdrew the envelope on which Mary had written "Molly—Sabrina's calf" and put it inside the steel drawer. She made a note of the time and date in her DayRunner then pulled a voice-activated cassette recorder from her briefcase.

"A picture of Molly, Sabrina Barrett's calf, was placed in my safety deposit box at 12:45 p.m., July 15th," she chanted. She put the tape recorder back in her purse.

The milo looked perfect. The deep green plants were broadly rooted with sturdy stems. Mary checked on it several times a day. Each time the leaves dipped and swayed, the field seemed to beckon her to believe again. With each passing day Mary's heart stretched skyward. At night, she was blessed with deep, satisfying sleep. Hope increased with each sunrise.

Cattle shipping was unusually busy that summer, and Iron was on the truck most of the time. He kept his truck parked at the house, and when she heard the playful "skunk-in-a-rat-trap, pe-yew" blast of his horn as he came up the lane, she ran out of the house, as gleeful as a teenager. He joyfully pulled her into his waiting arms. .

Day after day, explosions of energy surged through Mary's veins. Buoyed by an onset of joy, after Iron left for Omaha one day, she put on a Credence Clearwater record and began a marathon cleaning session. "Proud Mary" pulsed through her mind even when she was out of speaker range.

Down came the curtains and drapes in every room. Soon the washer was churning out load after load. She added a bit of ammonia to the sudsy water in her scrub bucket, gathered a pile of newspapers, and hauled a twelve-foot ladder out of the shed.

She sprayed a homemade vinegar-water concoction onto the windows. Her mind raced as she worked. She would vacuum, dust, polish, and wax every surface, go through every drawer, and throw out old junk.

Doing all the windows and washing drapes took three solid days. Then she began to vacuum and clear out cabinets. After harvest, she would repaint. Every week she drove to town with another offering for the thrift shop. Each night she added items to purchase to her list.

When the crop came in.

For the first time in a year, she permitted herself the luxury of daydreaming. She would order new clothes that wouldn't be easy to make. A snazzy, extravagant dress perhaps.

Then she would make Iron take her to Denver to a concert, where they would spend a wickedly self-indulgent weekend. They would make love and lie around watching TV, ordering from room service. She would come home with a stack of coordinated fabrics and craft supplies. She would start her Christmas shopping early and buy each child and grandchild their heart's desire.

She vowed she would sniff out every family in the county who was going through hard times and help them. Never again could she just stand by and watch her friends and neighbors grapple with government harassment. She would advise them, take them in hand, show them how to fill out forms and develop paper trails.

Giddy with virtue, she wondered if they could manage to set 20 percent of their income aside to help others. Finally, all of her work was caught up and her house was spotless. When she looked at her face in the mirror in the mornings, she no longer saw a gaunt, haunted woman.

Sabrina came over one afternoon, clutching the tailoring project booklet. "Mom says we're going to have enough money to buy my wool this year, Grandma. Do you think I should choose navy or brown for my basic color?"

Mary jumped up at once and happily spent the next two hours holding swatches of material up to Sabrina's face and poring over sketches.

Sabrina was hoping, planning, caring. Her entire outlook had changed. Elizabeth had had a long talk with her niece about their chances of winning the lawsuit. In the process, Sabrina now saw herself as a key person in saving, not losing, the farm. Sabrina understood the picture was crucial.

"Uh-oh, I'd better start picking up," said Sabrina, glancing at the clock. "I'm going to see Grandma Alma before I go home. She's pieced together old dresses for a quilt, and I promised her I would help her stretch it onto the frame."

Mary grinned. Alma never missed a chance to point out how much her thriftiness had helped in saving the farm—and her strength of character, her self-discipline, her magnificent will. Ironically, each person in the Barrett family was beginning to feel that they, personally, had been responsible for saving the farm. *Rightfully so*, thought Mary. *They all had done their fair share.*

"Your suit will be just wonderful," Mary said, "in every way." She hugged Sabrina and tenderly smoothed a stray wisp of hair back from her forehead. She helped collect her booklets and watched fondly as her granddaughter straddled her bicycle and headed up the lane.

Mary lingered outside for a few minutes. The sun slipped down in a rosy arc through blazing gold and orange layers. "We're going to make it," she whispered gratefully. "In every way."

A week later, Mary walked between the rows far into the field. The milo would soon be heading out. Her fingers trailed along the tops of the plants. Suddenly, she stopped dead still. Her heart pounded. She reached down the stem of one of the plants and slowly drew back her fingers. There was a heavy, sticky substance on it. She gave a little cry and bent to examine the lower leaves. Her hands shook as she turned one over.

On the underside of the leaf were light-green, soft-bodied insects. Frantically, she reached for a lower leaf on the plant next to it. All the leaves were unnaturally shiny and gummy. To her left was a cluster of plants where there were already reddish areas on the leaves.

Greenbugs, she thought. Just beginning, but they would wipe out the whole crop if something wasn't done.

Heartsick, she gazed at the milo. It still looked healthy. Still looked as though it were thriving. It was still green, still lush. It was only when she examined the undersides that the damage was visible. Her pulse raced. She looked around the field then ran down the row toward her house.

"When do you expect Iron to call in?" Mary breathlessly asked the dispatcher.

"In about an hour."

"Please have him call home."

"Is this an emergency? I can get the highway patrol to run him down."

"No. No one's been hurt. Don't scare him. But I've got to talk to him right away."

She sank into a chair and waited. They had to act at once, but they couldn't afford to do anything. Having the milo sprayed would cost four dollars an acre. A spray pilot would charge them four thousand dollars to rid a thousand acres of greenbugs.

She jumped up and began pacing around the kitchen. Then she picked up the phone and called Connie and Mike.

"We've got to spray," Iron said grimly. The family had gathered in the kitchen the day after Mary's discovery. "I had lots of time to think on the way home. We can't afford a crop duster, but if we field spray and do it ourselves, it will only cost five hundred dollars."

"Your sprayer is old," Dennis protested. "You haven't used it in several years. Hard telling what it will take to get it into shape."

"I'm counting on you to do that, Dennis," Iron said.

"Looks like Piker and Newark pulled a quicky on you." Dennis scowled. "No wonder they were so willing to stake you. They had a chance to shove seed off onto you that isn't a good hybrid. Some strains stand up just fine to greenbugs."

"Those two men are the last ones who would take advantage of anyone," Iron snapped. "I don't want to hear any more of that kind of talk."

"Yes, sir." Dennis's face darkened.

"We have to spray in the daytime." Mike pointedly ignored the tension between Iron and Dennis. "You know it's not smart to spray at night. Too much can go wrong that we wouldn't be able to see. So we have to take lost wages into consideration. My boss isn't going to be too thrilled, either, if I miss more work. Dennis is right. As old as your sprayer is, the chances of something falling off or plugging up is sky high."

"We have no choice," Iron said. "We can't do nothing."

"It'll take too much time." Mike rose and walked over to the window. "It'll take one man four days working his butt off, and that's not going to sit well with any of our employers. Besides, field spraying doesn't work as well as crop-dusting."

"I know it's not as good." The lines in Iron's face deepened. "But we have no choice. As to time, we three men can work at once."

"How?" Mary asked.

"I'm going to borrow. I've thought of a couple of neighbors who have high-boom sprayers they would lend out in return for a favor or two. Same goes for tractors."

"Thank God." Mary clasped her hands. "I couldn't see any way out of this at all."

"It's a go." Mike looked at Iron with a nod of approval.

"If we do it this Sunday," Iron said, "no one will have to miss work. It'll be a good fourteen-hour day for all three of us, but if we start at sunrise, we'll be done a little after nine. We'll even have a little daylight to spare."

"I wish I could be out there with you," Mary said. "How I wish."

"Over my dead body," Iron said. "No more fieldwork. You're following the doctor's orders if I have to tie you to the bedpost."

"All right. But I want to help. I'll mix the insecticide and get everything ready."

Connie picked up the coffeepot and began refilling cups. Then she glanced at Dennis, who had not spoken since being rebuked by his father. His face was impassive. He stood with his arms folded against his chest. But in his eyes was a strange mixture of triumph and malice. She stared at him for a moment, trying to guess what he was thinking.

Sensing Connie's silent scrutiny, Dennis turned and looked directly into her eyes.

She flushed. "More coffee, anyone?" she asked crossly.

Saturday evening Mary carefully rinsed the five-gallon bucket she had used to dilute the Parathion and placed it against the wall of the shed. Wearily, she placed her hands on the small of her aching back and stretched her sore muscles. Iron would get home later that night.

He'd be dead tired. She was, too, but at least she had the satisfaction of knowing everything was ready for the men. Dennis had checked all the moving parts of the sprayers, and she had made a little test run with pure water just to make sure all the nozzles were clear and the flow was right before she filled the tanks. The pumps worked, and the filters were clean.

She gave the cap on the drum of Parathion another firm twist, making sure it was tightly secured, then she took off her safety mask and laid it on a shelf. She carefully stripped off her rubber gloves and laid them on top of the mask. She stepped over to the doorway and looked around one last time, double-checking she had put the chemicals away properly.

Satisfied that all was in order, she switched off the light, stepped out the door, and snapped the padlock into place. She gave an extra precautionary tug on the lock. No matter how often the grandchildren were cautioned to leave herbicides and pesticides alone, she had a horror of the children's curiosity getting the better of them.

It was a half hour before sunrise. A rosy glow was beginning in the East. Iron walked toward the shed. He frowned at the open clasp of the Yale lock. It wasn't like Mary to forget to lock up. He decided not to say anything to her. She would take it as scolding, and Mary had been under enough strain. He stepped inside and checked the sprayers and the tanks.

He would work from the north side of the field toward the middle third, where Dennis was beginning. Mike would spray the last third, working over to the south edge.

As Iron started his tractor, he thought of how easily he would have handled this infestation just two years ago. He would have picked up the phone and called a crop duster. But, as the day wore on, he decided it felt good to work the old-fashioned way even though he was on the oldest tractor. It did not have an enclosed cab. The hot sun burned his face and his arms below the rolled-up sleeves of his chambray shirt.

He twisted around in his seat to monitor the sprayer as it dampened the rows of milo. He swung wide arcs at the end of the row and saw that Dennis and Mike, who had newer equipment, were gaining on him.

One of his biggest satisfactions with farming was that every job had a distinct beginning and end, and the work couldn't be undone. A plowed field couldn't be unplowed. A harvested crop was a done deal. The work was totally opposite from dealing with the idiotic paperwork the government kept sending in a perpetual circle.

About 9:30 that evening, the three men wearily climbed down from their tractors. The day had gone without a hitch. They flushed out the sprayers and tanks then walked toward Mary's Place to eat their fill.

For the next three days, when Mary checked the milo, she cautiously walked along the edges of the field. Iron called nightly for a report on the crop. She would wait ten days for the Parathion to dissipate before she walked out among the rows.

On the morning of the fourth day, she glanced down the field and stopped short. The plants were bleaching to a light whitish-green and yellow. Incredulously, she stared at the leaves. Her heart pounded as she knelt to examine the plants closest to her.

"No," she cried, "this can't be possible." She ran to the next row and peered down the line. Some of the stalks of milo were turning a dull straw gray. Her heart caught in her throat, and blood pounded in her ears. The whole field was dying.

The next day Iron stood with his hands on his hips and stared at the field. His milo was shriveling up into lifeless stalks; the life was draining out of them. Mary hung back, unwilling to speak. Every word she could think to utter sounded hollow in her mind.

When he turned, the lines in his sorrowful face were like tunnels.

"There's no natural cause for a field to do this," he said. "I want to know what the hell is going on."

"I don't know what could have happened," Mary said.

"Are you sure you mixed everything right?"

"Of course," she said, shocked it would even occur to him that she had been negligent. "Of course. I know the right water ratio to Parathion, Iron."

He nodded, knowing she was not a careless woman. Then he slammed his fist into his hand. He yanked a lifeless stalk out of the ground and stared at it. He studied each leaf, hoping one would reveal the cause of death.

"Maybe they accidentally gave me methyl Parathion instead of the ethyl formula," she said. "Some milo burns real bad if it's the wrong kind."

Iron shook his head. "This isn't simple burning. These plants are dying. The crop will be dead by the end of the week. I'm going to take a sample from that drum to Dick and have him test it."

Dick Manchester had been the county agent for the past five years. He was tall and lanky, with a thick thatch of wheat-bright hair. He knew Iron and Mary well through 4-H work. "It's the right kind of Parathion, all right. Tests came in this morning. Are you sure there wasn't something else in the sprayer tank itself? Something that got mixed in?"

"I'm positive," Mary said. "I checked everything myself, Dick. The tanks were bone dry."

"And even if there was something," Iron added, "we flushed the tanks afterwards, and drained everything. Any moisture would have evaporated."

"How much of a sample do you need?" asked Mary suddenly. "We've got to know, Dick. Will a bit of residue be enough? Our water is very alkaline. There's bound to be some deposits around the nozzles."

"Just a pinpoint will do."

Manchester called them back into his office two days later. "I heard from the lab at K-State this morning. You're not going to like this, and I don't know what to make of it."

"So there was something," Mary said, sitting on the edge of her chair.

"Yes," He cleared his throat. "The second sample you gave me contained Roundup."

"Roundup!" Iron's head swiveled toward Mary.

"No way," she blurted. "There's no possible way I could have gotten Roundup mixed up with Parathion. My God, Iron, the smell, everything about Roundup is different."

"It's something we have around. And you use plenty of it on weeds."

"What are you saying? Are you blaming me?"

Furiously, she forgot that there was another person in the room to witness their fight. She could not believe Iron would think it possible that she would pour such a deadly herbicide in with the Parathion. Roundup killed. Used in a strong enough dose, it would sterilize the soil, and nothing would grow in the earth for five years.

Iron's eyes were sinkholes in his gaunt face. "Oh, there's plenty of blame to share in this, Mary. Most of it's mine for shoving a man's work off on you all the time. I'm just saying you could have been so tired that you made a mistake. It wasn't the only one you made that day."

"What are you talking about?"

"The shed door was unlocked the morning we sprayed. And I know for a fact that normally you never forget to lock up. I wondered about it at the time. It's proof positive that you were dead tired. Not thinking."

In the space of a few seconds, she vividly recalled pushing shut the clasp on the lock. She knew she had. "I did not forget," she said fiercely. She turned to the county agent. "As God is my witness, I did not forget to lock that shed."

Iron rose abruptly. "Dick, thanks for the information, unwelcome though it may be. 'ppreciate it. Sorry to drag you into our troubles."

Manchester nodded unhappily.

In the pickup on the way home Mary tried to convince her silent, stoic husband that she had locked the shed, that she had been herself that day. "I did," she said again. "I remember."

"I said it's okay," he said gently. He reached for her hand and squeezed it. She recoiled with despair. He didn't believe a word she said. She could hear the resignation in his voice. "At least now I know what happened. Even if I don't know how it happened. I should have known right off that the field had been treated with an herbicide."

"What are we going to do?" She dug in her purse for tissues. "Oh Iron, we're back to trying to decide what we should do again."

33

Still outraged that Iron thought she was an absent-minded bimbo, Mary controlled her anger and managed a dutiful response to his goodbye kiss before he left on his run. "Have a safe trip," she said mechanically.

"Will do."

She went outside and watched the truck move slowly down their lane. Suddenly her heart began to beat faster and faster, and she raced after the rig.

"Wait," she called. "Wait. What are we going to do? You haven't told me what you want us to do." Her steps slowed, knowing she was too late. There was only the wind to hear. He had already pulled onto the main road.

Wanting to sit in the sun, she dragged a lawn chair over to the edge of the yard and stared out over the dying milo.

Something happened, she thought. *Something went terribly wrong.* That was an indisputable fact. She rose and ran into the house for a legal pad and came outside again. Then she began to write down some of her thoughts.

If Iron says the shed was unlocked, it was unlocked. That's a fact. I did lock it. That's a fact too. Someone had to have deliberately put Roundup in the tank. There was no reason for someone to do that. But it was no trick at all to jimmy a Yale lock.

Immediately, the shifting shadows she had seen in the farmyard acquired a new and more sinister meaning. Someone had been out there. She was positive now. She had doubted her own senses. She had decided it was her imagination, or a feverish delusion, when she was sick and exhausted. But someone had been in the farmyard. That was a fact.

She felt oddly exhilarated. She could deal with that which was real and tangible. She shuddered, knowing someone had easy access to the shed, her house. Someone had sabotaged the milo. Slowly she let the pencil slide through her fingers onto the grass.

Writing it down wasn't going to help. No one was going to believe her yet. She stared at the paper. None of the facts made sense. The only fact that mattered was that their crop was dead. No amount of wishing would bring it back to life.

She was sick of thinking, reasoning, planning. Elizabeth was wrong, she thought fiercely. There was nothing wrong in marching off and building something she could see. All the thinking was making her crazy.

She looked around at the array of white resin lawn furniture. Plastic. Manufactured. She yearned for real wood. Something natural and real. She jumped up and ran inside the house and got her carpentry apron. After strapping it on, she went to the shed and rummaged through her collection of boards. She gathered up a stack of thin cedar and set up her sawhorses. She went back into the house, opened her file cabinet, and extracted the folder of woodworking projects.

By day's end, she still could not make sense of how Roundup had gotten mixed in with Parathion. She could not reconcile a number of facts; she had locked the shed—but if Iron said the shed was unlocked, it was unlocked. No one had any reason to contaminate the spray. That made the least sense of all.

Now she was positive that on a couple of nights she had seen someone out in the yard. That was the truth. She didn't care if she was the only person in the whole known universe who believed it.

She had no answers, but she had a new Adirondack chair for the lawn. It was sturdy and solid and real, and she had accomplished something.

The telephone rang. She ran across the yard and answered on the third ring.

"Hi, Mom."

"Let me catch my breath, honey. I was out in the yard."

Elizabeth was startled by the upbeat tone in Mary's voice. "Dennis called me about losing the milo." She chose a neutral statement, not wanting her mother to know how much the call had infuriated her. "Told you the stress is getting to her," he'd taunted. "Now do you see what I'm talking about?"

"I still can't believe it," Elizabeth said.

"I can't either."

"Well, don't be too hard on yourself. You've been under a world of stress."

"And why would I blame myself?" Mary's voice was cold, her words clipped. "What did Dennis tell you? That I'm a crazy old woman who doesn't have enough sense to keep chemicals straight? If he told you I mixed up Parathion and Roundup, it's a lie. I don't know what happened, but it was none of my doing."

"You think someone did it on purpose? Why would they?"

"I don't know. But it wasn't me. I'll talk to you later. I have work to do." Abruptly, she hung up the phone, went outside, and sat motionless in her brand-new lawn chair.

The next day she rounded up a group of 4-Hers. Jack and Eunice Cummings were being sold out. The Gateway Go-Getters were going to sell pies and ham sandwiches during the day-long auction.

Seeing the despair on Eunice's face, as she helped set up tables and carry boxes out to the yard, Mary tried to think of something to say. What comfort could she offer these poor people?

"We're losing the farm," Eunice said softly to Mary. "I still can't believe it."

"Losing the farm." The words throbbed through Mary's mind like the tired rhythm of an overburdened heart: beating, beating, beating, despite its weariness.

One 4-H member after another came up to tell Eunice how sorry they were. Mary was overcome with grief for the poor woman.

"It's all right," Eunice said, over and over. "We'll be just fine, honey. It just might take us a while to get our bearings again."

When little Janie Rendell asked Mary what the Cummingses were going to do—and she explained that Jack was going to work for a seed dealer, and Eunice had been promised a job at Alco—she could see in Janie's eyes she hadn't answered the question at all. She was unwilling to lie to these children, unable to tell them the stark truth. She didn't know. She honest to God didn't know what people did who had lost a farm. That question filled her with wild despair.

What did people do who didn't live on a farm? How did they fill their days? It could be her standing there.

If she and Iron lost the farm, she would never again have a two-acre garden. Never see her shining jars arranged in her cellar. Never smell the overturned earth, never feel the heat on the back of her head as she hoed with an eye on the sun so she wouldn't be late with a meal. She would have a garden the size of a postage stamp.

"Eunice, I'm so sorry," she said suddenly. "We're going through some hard times ourselves. Don't blame yourself. None of this is your doing."

She was tempted to turn the day over to the junior leaders and flee the wrenching reminders that she and Iron could be going through the same thing in less than a year. She swallowed hard and patted Eunice on the back.

On the drive home, the 4-H boys' song pounded in her ears.

> A growing sun and a waking field
> And a furrow straight and long.
> A summer's sun and a summer's rain
> And we'll follow with a song.

She braked sharply in the driveway. Her stomach tightened as she walked across the farmyard. The hot late-afternoon sun poured down on her head as she looked across the pasture far into the distance.

There was a profusion of green: the lush emeralds of bluestem, the greenish gold of wild oats, the deep forest green of their cedar windbreak, the pale lacy thrusting of wild asparagus, the chartreuse of wild onions, and the blue green of rusty buffalo grass when it turned in spring. She needed this color to live.

Seasons wouldn't matter if they lost the farm. Her life would no longer be ordered by springtime and harvest and plantings—time to drill wheat, to plant corn, to gather, to put food by. At this thought she drew in a sharp breath and bit her lip. She had worked, lived, breathed according to the seasons for so long she couldn't imagine doing otherwise.

Then, in the space of a heartbeat, a rabbit scurried out from the cedar windbreak, stopped dead in its tracks, and looked right at her. Paralyzed, Mary stared back. The rabbit's eyes seemed to mock her: you're losing the farm. Then she could not stay the surge of anger that jolted her whole body like a bolt of lightning. She trembled with rage. "I'm not going to let it happen," she called after the rabbit as it bounded back into the cedars. "You hear me? It's not going to happen. I won't let it."

Heart afire, she ran to the Hewletts'. Mike was just getting off work.

"Mike, we've got to have a crop. We've got to plant wheat. Even if Elizabeth wins that lawsuit and stops them from selling the farm, we have to have a crop. Hard telling how long it will take to drag this through the courts. The FDIC won't give in without a fight. It won't do us any good to stop them if we haven't got money coming in."

Warily, Mike hung his hat on a peg and looked at his mother-in-law. "No way we can, Mary," he said gently.

"We've got to plant." Her voice was urgent. "I figured out a way."

"We can't borrow, Mary. The FDIC will stop any move we try to make. There's no money for seed wheat or anything else. Stop tormenting yourself."

"There's a way," she said. "I've checked. The Interfaith Rural Life Committee is giving out seed wheat to farmers. We have to go through our pastor. He'll do a needs analysis."

"You're going to ask Iron to take charity? Are you out of your mind?"

"It's not charity if you pay it back. Come summer, after harvest, we can pay them back."

"My God, Mary. Have you lost your mind? We can pay them back if we have a crop that actually materializes. If Elizabeth succeeds in winning a lawsuit. If something else doesn't go wrong."

"I don't care. I don't care if you think it's a good idea, Mike. I'm asking for your help. But whether I get it or not, I'm going to do it. I'll start the ball rolling tomorrow and fill out papers. A number of seed dealers have donated to this program, and the grain goes to those who can't get seed from any other source. That's us! If you won't help me, I'll do it myself."

"What do you plan to tell Iron?"

"I don't plan to tell him anything in advance. I just plan to surprise him after it's a done deal. When it's too late to do anything about it."

Mike groaned. "God, he's going to be pissed off."

"Oh, I know how he'll carry on. I can just hear him. That's why I'm going to do it myself. Then after it's all done and he can't do a damn thing about it, I'm going to pray to God he doesn't hate me for it."

"He will, you know."

"I'll patch things up later. Nothing matters now but planting wheat. We have a little over a month to make all the arrangements, so we can plant the first week in September. I want to get my name in the hat before too many others have the same idea."

"Are you sure the seed is free? No strings attached?"

"None," she said happily.

"Okay. I'll have Dennis check out the equipment."

"No." Mary's mouth tightened. "Absolutely not. I don't want him involved at all. He's been telling Elizabeth that I'm a doddering old woman who can't think straight. He won't listen to anything I say. If I say 'down' he says 'up' just for spite. And right now, I don't want to hear his thousand and two reasons why this is a bad idea."

Mike grinned.

"Get the ground ready for me. That's all I ask."

"What are you going to do for fertilizer?"

"I'm going to see my banker. Ask him to loan me the money."

"Since when have you had a banker?"

"Since practically forever. I mean J.C."

Jay Clinton Espy's stomach tightened as he stared at the sacks of seed wheat in the bed of Mary Barrett's pickup.

He knew about the milo. Everyone in Gateway City had heard about the milo.

"What in the hell are you up to now, woman?"

"I'm fixing to plant wheat. I got the seed through the Seeds of Hope project. Now I want you to loan me money for fertilizer so I can do this right. Please, J.C."

I don't have any damn money, he thought. *Why in the goddamn hell don't these stupid sons-a-bitching farmers leave me in peace.* "I'll have it for you tomorrow. Late afternoon," he said gruffly.

Mary whooped with delight.

"I knew I could count on you," she said. "Just knew you would come through. You always do."

He wheeled around and walked back into his house. He sat in his wing chair and sipped Jack Daniels while he gazed out the window. When he was all whiskeyed up, he walked over to his desk, pulled open the middle drawer, and pulled out his utility knife. He tested the blade with his thumb. It was plenty sharp enough.

Then he slowly walked over to the north wall in his living room. On it were the pictures of John Foster Espy, Frank Leander Espy, and Porter Cleveland Espy. He took them from the wall and laid them on the rug. He knelt down and carefully braced the tip of the knife along the upper edge of his great-grandfather's portrait. His hand trembled. For a second he could feel John Foster Espy's eyes on him. Accusing. Blaming. For the trust he had broken. For the legacy he had destroyed.

He shook his head then bent back to his work. When he was finished, he propped the three magnificent antique frames against the wall, walked over to the telephone, and called Rachel Wise.

"J.C. Espy here," he said when she answered. "If you're still in the market for my antique frames, I would like to give you the first shot at them."

The sun beamed pink and crimson rays across a clear sky. Mary watched the delicate hues of dawn color her farm. The air was pure, exhilarating. She inhaled deeply. Nervously, she started the tractor and watched the console automatically complete the self-test. She adjusted the air conditioning in the enclosed cab and peered out the back at the enormous Case air drill, which was their most high-tech piece of equipment. The drill delivered seed and fertilizer in a precise stream. A function monitor warned when seed was blocked or when the fan speed was incorrect. It automatically gave an acreage read-out.

A sensation of raw power surged through Mary's body as she pulled out into the field. She was giddy with relief. She had fretted that it would rain, or blow, or do something to delay the planting.

But the weather had held and, like a miracle, Iron had a load of cattle going to California. He wouldn't be back for a week. It had been hard to get Dennis out of town. She was not a natural-born liar. Deception did not come easily to her. But she didn't regret for a second calling J.C. and having him ask Dennis to drive him to a Triple I show.

"Having trouble with night vision," J.C. told Dennis. "I'm willing to pay you a little dab. Though you might like to see the newest equipment."

Dennis had jumped at the chance.

Mike had cut down and raked up the milo several weeks ago. Then he had the soil tested. Manchester assured them that all traces of Roundup had vanished, since it was just a surface application. Mike plowed under what was left of the stalks. It was easy to get the ground worked for planting under the guise of proper soil management for a failed crop.

It went perfectly. Yet as she headed across the field, she suddenly felt like a willful child defying her parent. There was a little catch in her throat as she worried about Iron's reaction. She knew she was doing the right thing. They had to have a crop. And what she could bring herself to do—accept a little help—Iron simply could not do. He could not accept charity. He was too crippled by honor to bring himself to do the things it would take to save the farm.

But will he still love me? She shivered and turned down the air conditioning in the cab. *Iron, my darling, will you still love me if I work and act—and be—as smart and fast and clever as I possibly can?*

Then peering behind her at the huge territory the drill was covering, she gave an exuberant little bounce on the seat. *When it's over, Iron will surely thank me for this.*

First things first. After she planted wheat, she would smooth things over with her husband. She would make him understand.

Then she would track down the bastard who had ruined their milo.

34

Too stunned to speak, Iron Barrett stared at the tilled field for a long time. Time enough for the blood to start pounding in Mary's ears.

"Where in the name of God did you get the seed?"

"It was given to us." Her speech was steady. "By people who care. And it was in the name of God. You've got that right."

He turned and walked toward his pickup with long, angry strides. The gravel spun from under his tires as he tore out of the driveway. Mary stood firm, her arms folded across her chest. Although there was a lump in her throat, she suppressed the gorge rising in her stomach. She had prepared herself for this.

There's nothing he can do about it, she thought fiercely. *Nothing. He can't unplant a field of wheat.*

Iron returned at sundown.

She followed his movements across the farmyard as he came toward the house. She continued to stand at the sink, slowly drying dishes, when he walked into the kitchen. Feeling his eyes on her back, she turned.

"We need to talk," he said heavily. "Sit down a minute."

Sensing one of his rare speeches coming on, she braced herself.

"Mary, we've been through some terrible times. I know we don't always see things the same way, but we had an agreement that we would stop just marching off and doing things on our own. It was you who said it had to stop. 'No more blue lighting anything,' you said. 'We have to work together,' you said. And I want to know how you could have done such a thing to me. Without so much as a by-your-leave."

"If I had told you, you would have tried to stop me."

"Didn't you trust me to take care of you? Didn't you think I was going to provide for you? Do you think I'm just half a man? Without the brains God gave a green goose?"

She reached for his hand.

"Iron, there's something you must understand. What I did had nothing to do with you or me or being a husband or a wife. I did it because there was a very simple fact staring me in the face: we had to have a crop. Swallowing a little pride and accepting a little help was hard enough for me. I knew it would be impossible for you."

She saw the shift in his eyes, the acceptance, the reluctant acknowledgment that she was right. Then the pain on his face was replaced by an obdurate look.

"What you did was wrong."

"What I did was smart."

They stared at each other. Then she rose, wanting to get away from him.

"Sit back down. I'm not finished talking to you," he said. "There's something I need to tell you."

Iron crossed over to the stove and poured a cup of coffee. He set it down to cool then stood with his hands stuffed in the back pockets of his jeans.

"There's something I did I should have told you about." He glanced at her quickly. "Should have told you months ago. I thought about it all afternoon while I was trying to sort this out."

"What?" she pressed.

"I sold our five hundred acres to Mike and Connie."

"You couldn't have," she stammered. "You couldn't possibly have done that. Why didn't you tell me? Why?"

He looked at her sharply. His lips quirked up into a slow crooked smile and she blushed, remembering the wheat.

"I was afraid you would try to stop me," he said.

She looked away and drew a deep breath.

"At the time I sold our land, I had my doubts about Dennis. I don't anymore, but I did back then."

"How did you swing it?" she asked. "Shouldn't I have signed something?"

"Your name wasn't on the note J.C. had at the bank," he said. "The bank always keeps a copy of what I sign, makes a copy for us, and then files the original at the courthouse."

She put her hands against her cheeks and swayed from side to side. "I never signed the main note, did I? That's why J.C. let you make a deal all by yourself without your having to tell me. My name has never been on any of the main papers for the land."

"J.C. said it didn't matter, but it didn't seem right at the time, and it doesn't seem right now." Thoughtfully, Iron stroked his jaw. "It was wrong to leave you in the dark. It was no better than the stunt you pulled with the wheat."

Ignoring his reference to the wheat, her mind raced. "Iron, something smells to high heaven here. No banker in his right mind would let you pull such a deal. It puts the bank too much at risk for the loan. If I'm not liable for the debt, I could file for divorce, take half the assets, and leave you holding the bag."

"J.C. had to know that," Iron said. "That old man always knew everything."

"I want to talk to Elizabeth," Mary said. "We need to get to the bottom of this."

"Reckon you've heard things are going our way for a change, Sonny," crowed Alma Barrett.

Dennis smiled and cradled the receiver between his chin and his shoulder as he wiped his hands on a grease rag and picked up a pencil. Everyone thought things were going their way. He received daily updates from Alma on one little victory after another, but the family was sailing along on false hope.

At first he had been stunned when he'd learned his mother had planted wheat. Then he relaxed, knowing the wheat would allow them to carry on only if Elizabeth won their lawsuit. He had to give his mother credit, though. She had been smart enough to see that even if they won they had to have a crop.

"Good news is always welcome around here, Grandma. What is it today?"

"Your father pulled off quite a little deal behind our backs. Seems as though he sold Connie and Mike five hundred acres on the sly last year." She told him that Mary had not signed the main note on the land either. "That means she's not actually liable for the family's debts. No matter what happens, she won't have to sell her house." She waited for him to respond. "Dennis? Did you hear what I said?"

"He couldn't have." Dennis snapped the pencil he was holding in two and threw the pieces across the shed.

"Could and did."

"You're sure Mike's name is on the deed for the five hundred acres too? Not just Connie's?"

"Dead sure," said Alma. "And with your bright lawyer sister raising all kinds of hell over that picture the FDIC people took, there's going to be a world of trouble over who owns what around that place."

Dennis hung up the phone as soon as he could without offending his grandmother. Mike Hewlett's face, in shades of red and burnt umber, drifted before his eyes. His lying, conniving brother-in-law. How could he have ignored all the signs he was weaseling in?

It was Mike his parents had asked to go to the bank to talk with the loan officer. It was Mike they discussed farming with on a level that never included him.

He walked out into the bright September sunlight. He had to calm himself. It was getting harder and harder to control what he said and what he did. He slapped his hand hard against his thigh.

Sabrina was peddling down the lane. He scowled. That photo. This kid he had given a name to, clothed, and fed had tried to rob him of his heritage. His hands trembled and dark spots swam before his eyes. She had too much freedom anyway. She should be kept home. She was of an age that bore watching.

He took a deep breath to calm himself. He did not dare get into a fight with Lisette over Sabrina. So far, no one sensed the depths of his tension, although last week Lisette had commented he seemed "a bit jumpy" and asked if he was anxious about the lawsuit.

There would be time enough after everything was over to straighten out his wife and family. Time enough to pound some respect into Lisette. Time to let her know he had seen the wildness in her eyes after she started flying around. Time to teach Sabrina a little obedience.

All I have to do is stay calm and wait. Just wait.

Elizabeth took the envelope from her safety deposit box. After she had copies made of Molly's picture, she would put it right back. She waved at her favorite teller as she walked through the lobby, then she drove back to the FACTS office.

"It's all coming together like clockwork," she said triumphantly to Bill Spiegel, another attorney who worked killing hours to help farmers.

"The Old Man is sure counting on this, Elizabeth. We'll open a huge door against the government if we can prove the FDIC sold off a calf belonging to your niece."

"Don't I know!"

Harold Scott, the regional administrator, had made that clear from the beginning.

Spiegel grinned. "Let's see the infamous Molly."

She handed him the envelope.

He pulled out the picture and studied it. Bewildered, he said, "Looks like an ordinary calf to me."

"What?" She hurried to his side and looked over his shoulder. Her chest tightened. "That's not the right picture!" Shocked, Elizabeth stared at the photo.

"Did you look at it first?" Bill asked. "Before you put it into the safety deposit box?"

"No. I was in a hurry that day. The envelope was labeled in Mom's handwriting. It said 'Molly—Sabrina's Calf.' I personally had watched her put the photo inside. When I put it in the bank, I made a note documenting the time. I even made a little tape memo, stating that I was doing it. But no, I did not actually look at the picture that day." Her voice broke.

Bill reached for her hand and gave it a little squeeze.

"Bill, I can absolutely and positively swear this picture is not the one that was taken of Molly when the men came to take inventory. This is not the one I looked at in my mother's house. This is not the picture on which we based our hopes and the hopes of God only knows how many other farm families."

Iron paused in the kitchen doorway. Mary was slicing Jonathan apples for a pie and flashed a happy smile. It faded when he didn't respond. She laid down the knife and pressed her fingers against the hollow of her throat.

"Some bad news, honey. The very worst, in fact." Quickly, he told Mary about the photo, braced for her panicky questions.

"That can't be! I put that picture in the envelope myself and put it in the middle drawer of my desk." Her voice shook with agitation.

"You didn't take it out again? Before Elizabeth picked it up?"

"No, no, no," she said firmly. "I knew how important it was. You've got to believe me! I certainly did not misplace a picture that would save our farm. I didn't! Don't you see, Iron? I didn't mess with that picture, and I didn't leave that shed door open either. I didn't mix Roundup with Parathion. Someone did that to us. Someone is doing things to us. Elizabeth stood right there and watched me put that picture in the envelope."

"I believe you, Mary," Iron said. "I believe you." He made a fist, opened it, and stared at his wide-splayed fingers. "If someone took that picture, then someone is trying to do us in. If that's the case, I'll bet you mixed the Parathion right. You've been right about everything all along."

"Thank God," she said. "Thank God you finally understand. You don't know how alone I've been in all this."

Ashamed, he pulled his cigarettes from his shirt pocket and flicked his lighter. His eyes narrowed against the smoke as he inhaled deeply.

" I wish my runs were closer to home. No matter how much we need the money, I can't have you here by yourself with this kind of stuff going on."

"Oh, I'm plenty safe enough now," Mary said bitterly. "No point in locking the barn door after the horse has been stolen. Someone just wants us to lose this place, that's all. It's a clear pattern, Iron. And they've just about got the job done. It's all over but the shouting, isn't it? I don't see how we can possibly hang on to things now. I don't think we'll have to worry about anything else happening."

His face sagged. "There's only two people I can think of who would be capable of this. Clifton Hathaway always hated my guts and wanted my land, and I wouldn't put anything past Clyde Peterson. I've known from the start he would do anything to put me under."

"No one else would even have a motive," she agreed.

"I'll call the sheriff and tell him someone has been trespassing. He'll pay more attention when he knows someone has been in the house," Iron said. "He would need a pretty good reason to start investigating either Hathaway or Peterson. We might as well prepare ourselves for the possibility that Sheriff Watson won't turn up a thing. Neither one of those two just fell off the turnip truck. They'll have their tracks well covered. Then I'm going to have decent locks installed on this place."

"All right," Mary said. "I hate to see us act like city folks, but it's the smart thing to do."

"We're keeping this house, no matter what, Mary. I've decided that no one, including me, should get to take a profit on your labor. Your sweat and your imagination. It wouldn't be so bad if you were forced to sell the shack you started with, but I can't stand to see the bastards get the increase. No one is getting your house. I can promise you that."

Mary searched in vain for the missing Polaroid. As she predicted, there were no more incidents. After Iron was convinced she wasn't in any danger, he began making longer runs that paid better money.

One night Mary watched sadly as he pulled out of the drive. He was going to New Mexico, then California and wouldn't be back for two weeks. She stood with her face pressed wistfully against the window until the lights on his bull rack disappeared from view. She might as well be living her life as a widow.

She realized it would be like this from now on unless Elizabeth found the picture or thought of another way to win her case. To keep from selling Mary's Place, Iron would work night and day, set aside every penny, and take every load. Then, too, there was the money they owed Newark and Piker.

Despite her resolve to be realistic about their chances in court, from time to time she was ambushed by hope. Because of the land sale to Connie and Mike, Elizabeth was now concentrating on the muddled ownership of the Barrett property. However, Elizabeth had made it clear that since they no longer had the picture of Molly, they couldn't expect a lot of money. The best she could do now was to keep the FDIC from selling them out.

"There's still a chance," whispered Mary. "Still a chance." Then she firmly beat back the siren call of rising expectations, knowing something at her core could not survive one more catastrophe.

"Well, Hallelujah," said Lisette. "That's wonderful, Mary."

"Good news," she said to Dennis as she hung up the phone. "That was your mother. Elizabeth just called and said she is now positive no one can force her to sell Mary's Place, since her name wasn't on the main land note and the house was deeded to her separately. At least something is working out around here."

"Good," Dennis said, faking sincerity. If he destroyed his mother's desire to live in that house, everything else would fall into place. It would require a little patience. If he directly opposed Elizabeth's efforts to save the farm, it would make people suspicious. Suddenly rage welled up in him like black bile. Why didn't they all just give up? Why didn't they know when they were whipped?

Then he calmed down. His mother would change her mind about keeping Mary's Place. He was going to see to it. He smiled.

It wouldn't take much to push her over the edge.

35

Several nights later, Mary awoke, chilled to the bone. The wind had come up during the night, and she didn't have enough covers on the bed. She heard something banging, listened closely, and sighed. She suspected Benjy hadn't fastened the door to the Quonset hut when he finished choring. She pulled on her jeans and a sweatshirt then went downstairs. She took her flashlight out of the desk drawer, put on her parka, and walked toward the shed.

It was early fall and there was a cold, whistling gale. Moonlight glinting on pieces of machinery threw a wavering pattern of shadows. Sure enough, the door was not secured. Mary flipped the tin slab over the projecting half-moon and clicked the padlock into position. She put her ring of keys back into her jacket pocket, turned, and hurried toward the house. She stopped. Blood pounded at her temples. Her heart raced erratically, as though it were trying to leap from her body.

At the edge of the row of machinery, her beam picked up an eerie flash of light. Dizzy with disbelief, she trembled and swallowed hard. Gasping, she touched the side of the tractor to steady herself.

A blue-white gleam bobbed and jerked. Terrified, she watched as it gave a little twitch—like a rabbit—and darted under the plow.

Fear-crazed, she took off for the house at a dead run. She slammed the door shut behind her and stood with her back against it, her arms braced. If she was seeing gleams of light—spots and shadows, shiny rabbit phantoms—instead of a real person, then clearly her mind was playing tricks on her. She was going crazy. Horrified, she realized she couldn't tell what was real. She couldn't tell the difference anymore.

Dear God, she thought suddenly. Dear God in heaven, what if I did get the chemicals mixed up? What if I did do something to that picture? No, she had done no such thing. She had not. Trembling, she bolted the locks and pressed her palms against the solid wood. She leaned her forehead against the door.

She went up to bed and for the next two nights would not allow herself to be lured outside the house for any sound or sight. Nevertheless, despite her attempts to exert control, she lurched awake over and over again. She switched her soggy, tear-stained pillow with Iron's, which was fresh and dry. Trying to read herself back to sleep, she stupidly mouthed the words on the same page, over and over.

Once again, her dreams were filled with ruined or broken things: haunting images of ships sailing away, stalks of hollow-headed wheat blighted with grainy, putrid mold and crawling with bugs, winged horses suddenly plummeting. Dreams of falling, falling, falling.

Then three nights later, there was a sound. One she had never heard before. It was dull and atonal, like the wind blowing hollowly across the mouth of a pipe. She pulled on her clothes and went downstairs. She got her shotgun and walked out into the cold night air.

At the edge of the farmyard, bunnies were leaping and cavorting in the moonlight. When she shone her flashlight on them, only a few were paralyzed by the light.

"Take that! And that, and that!" she yelled, firing blindly at their furry bodies. She pushed shell after shell after shell into the chamber. As soon as one round was finished, she shoved in another. Then, exhausted, she began to cry. She needed her husband. Needed him home beside her in their huge bed. But if they lost their land, from now on he would always have to drive long trips to bring in enough money to maintain the house.

She was finished. There was no way she could continue living in Mary's Place.

Iron called Elizabeth three nights later.

"We're selling out," he said wearily. "Lock, stock, and barrel. The house too."

"You can't," she said, shocked to the core. "What can you possibly be thinking?"

"I'm thinking about your mother. We've talked and talked. She's terrified to be alone at night. She says it's driving her crazy and it isn't worth it."

"Send her to a psychologist then. But don't sell out."

"Face it, Elizabeth. I would be a slave to the place for the rest of my life, trying to keep it going out of a truck driver's wages. We fought the good fight, but we're done. In some ways it's a relief. We can pay back Newark and Piker. Connie and Mike can keep their acreage. And we'll be shut of all these mean-spirited bastards who are out to get us."

"Listen to me," she yelled. "Don't do anything that stupid. You'll finish out your lives in penny-ante hell. You're going to owe a staggering amount to the IRS for capital gains when you sell that house. Have you thought about that? If you don't declare bankruptcy, the FDIC can attach your wages for the next thirteen years for the amount you still owe on the farm after the sale."

"We want shut of this place, Elizabeth."

"Daddy, please give me some time to sort this out. It's absolutely unthinkable."

"Your Mom and I are going to tell Connie and Mike and Dennis and Lisette tomorrow." He twisted the cord on the phone, knowing Elizabeth was crying but he could not offer her any comfort.

"Give me a little longer to find out who took that picture. Please wait."

"I'm not putting your mom through any more turmoil," said Iron. "Now Mary even thinks she might have misplaced it."

"That's ridiculous! I saw her put it in the envelope."

"The fact that she would entertain such a thought shows how much the stress is getting to her. She's started blaming herself for anything that goes wrong."

"Dad, who do you think is behind all this?"

"Someone connected with the FDIC, or Hathaway, maybe, but by the time we track the bastard down, I'll be under."

"And spend the rest of your life trying to pay back what you owe?"

"Yes," Iron said heavily. "The rest of my life if that's what it takes. Every cent."

He stabbed his cigarette at the ashtray next to the phone. He had spent the afternoon thinking, listening to Mary cry.

"It's not the end of the world, Elizabeth."

"Yes it is, Daddy. The end of our world as we know it."

"Well, like the song says, you've got to know when to fold 'em."

"There are other angles I haven't tried."

"Elizabeth, please understand me on all this. I know how hard you've worked, but I'm just too damn worn out to care. We've both reached the end of our rope. Your mother has had all she can take."

"She's not getting sick again, is she?"

"No, but her nerves are shot. Mine are too." He took a deep drag on his cigarette. He was reluctant to tell her how upsetting Mary's crying jags were to him. "If anything comes up, talk it over with me first, not your mom. She's plumb worn out."

<hr>

Together, they went to Mike and Connie's to tell them they were selling out.

"The house too, Momma?"

"The house too, sweetie. I just couldn't stand back and see your father work himself into an early grave. Besides, we're probably doing you a favor in the long run. It really is a white elephant."

Connie gave her a look and ran out of the room.

Iron was outside talking to Mike. When the two men came in, Mike looked sick. Older. It had not been an easy conversation. "Sabrina has been doing so well," Mary said as they drove toward their son's house. "I just hope she doesn't slip back."

Iron reached for her hand and squeezed it, steeling himself for the task ahead.

"How'd it go with Mike?"

"It was hell. Pure D hell. He wants us to keep trying. Had all kinds of ideas to make things work."

"We can't," said Mary, "why don't they see we just can't."

Dennis Barrett stared at his parents. "Don't do it. Why in the hell would you even consider doing such a thing?" It had never occurred to him—not once—that they would want to sell out ahead of the FDIC deadline. Before their farm would be bundled. "Don't do it. It's not fair to any of us."

Mary shrank into her seat and looked at Iron. He looked like a cur with its tail tucked between its legs. She winked back tears.

"It's the right thing to do, Dennis," she said quickly. "We'll clear more money by selling now. We'll be able to pay back more to the people we owe. We'll still owe the bank a fortune, Elizabeth made that clear. But we will have less to work off. Waiting until our note is bundled is too risky. We can't take a chance of our land going for a penny on the dollar and spending the rest of our lives paying off the remainder of the loan."

Dennis cleared his throat. He had to find a way to prevent them from selling out before the deadline. "This family is your first obligation. You owe it to us to keep trying."

"Please try to understand," Iron pleaded. "We can't do it anymore."

Benjy and Sabrina came through the door, their arms loaded with homework.

"Kids, your grandparents have something important to tell you." Dennis's eyes glittered with malice.

Stricken, Mary looked at her son. How could he? How could he possibly put all the burden of the failure onto them? The children obviously didn't suspect a thing. They were simply too young to understand the implications of losing the milo crop and had pinned all their hopes on the picture. Now missing.

Sabrina beamed at Mary. "Let me put up my books first, Grandma, and I want you to check the basting on my collar before you leave."

"Grandpa, have you heard?" Benjy said. "Mom scraped together enough money for me to buy a calf. She says I can pay her back after the fair. There's going to be a critter in Old Barn again." His chest puffed out with pride, and he grinned mischievously as he thumped it with his thumb. "Mine."

Just then Lisette came running up the sidewalk. Bringing the crisp, woodsy scent of early fall with her, she entered the room just in time to hear her son brag. She took off her coat and gloves and squeezed Benjy's shoulder.

"How about that, Iron? We're back in the cattle business! And your grandson has talked of nothing else!"

"Can you go with me next weekend to pick out my calf, Grandpa?"

A vein throbbed in Iron's temple. Mary closed her eyes. Her face was chalk white. Dennis smirked, cupping his hand over his lips to hide his amusement. He wouldn't have to come up with a way to keep Iron and Mary from selling out. The kids would do all the work for him.

He could keep his parents hoping, praying, trying until the very last minute. If he played his cards right, the old man wouldn't give up until his very soul was on the auction block.

And his mother! By the time he finished with her, she wouldn't be able to remember her own name, let alone sign it. "The folks have something to tell you, Lisette," he said with a bland smile. "You and the kids."

Mary looked at Benjy and Sabrina, who waited expectantly, their faces bright with hope. Then she turned to her husband and saw the despair on his face—a good man, a decent man, asked to choose between salvaging his wife's mental health and fighting for his grandchildren's heritage.

She interceded before he could speak. "We just want you all to know that there's a problem with the picture. A big problem. But we're not throwing in the towel. We're going to be just fine. All of us." She looked deeply into her husband's startled eyes. "Just fine."

"I'll call Mike and Connie," Mary said as they drove back to the house, "and tell them we've changed our minds. We're going to see it through till the end."

"I can't let you do that."

"Yes, you can," she said fiercely. "If we sell out just because I have the jitters, it will haunt me the rest of my life. It won't kill me to be a little bit crazy. A little bit scared. If it's a person, maybe they'll come out of the woodwork again. But either way, if worst comes to worst, and we lose the place, at least I'll be able to look Benjy in the eye and say we didn't quit. We're just talking six months."

Iron did not reply. She patted his thigh and watched the fence posts pass in a blur. She couldn't deny Iron the right to fight just so she would not have to experience her own descent into hell.

Something soured in men who spent their lives catering to high-strung, weepy wives.

She did not believe that anything they could do would stave off the FDIC. *But I will not hope*, she decided. *I'm not ever falling into that trap again.* When they lost the farm, she would help Iron pick up the pieces, hold his hand, love him, and bring him back to life.

"Elizabeth, Mr. Scott would like to talk with you, when you have a moment."

"It'll be a while," she said, smiling apologetically at Millie Galli, the communal secretary who kept the office together. "I need to finish this brief, before my brains get jumbled again."

Millie shook her head. "Better make it now," she whispered. "He has that look."

Elizabeth sighed, set aside her stack of papers, and walked to Scotty's office.

Harold Scott was a slight man, made crazy by lawyers and legislators. He had weak, myopic eyes from poring over fine print and a permanent furrow between his brows. He knew more than any man living about losing farms in Kansas. He organized his life and his work around one fact: the worst that can happen will. He was uncannily skilled at predicting the abrupt turns of the state and national congressional herd as they careened from one cliff to another. He adjusted his goals for the FACTS office accordingly.

"I won't mince words, Elizabeth. There's a chance they're cutting our funding again and there's going to be a review of all the employees. You're not going to like this, but there's talk around this office that you spend entirely too much time trying to save one farm in particular."

"I what?" She flushed to the roots of her hair. "What a mean-spirited, petty thing to say." Then the full impact of what he was saying hit. "Are you trying to tell me that I'm about to lose my job?" she asked incredulously.

"I'm trying to tell you to mind your p's and q's. Certainly your home county is as important as any in the state, but no more important. There are other counties that need help, Elizabeth."

"And other farmers, besides my father. That's what you really want me to know, isn't it?" She stood and braced her arms on his desk. "You'll have my resignation on your desk Monday."

"Don't be silly." Harold Scott looked at her sternly. "You're one of our best lawyers. That's not what we want. Why don't you take some time off? Go home. Without pay, of course. See if you can get things straightened out, then we'll talk about resignations if that's what you really want. I don't think it is."

She studied his kindly, harried face and knew he was trying to help. She suddenly felt tired, drained of all anger. "Thanks, Scotty. The remote-control thing with my folks really isn't working."

36

Elizabeth went back to her apartment and packed. She tried to call Mary several times to let her know she was coming but couldn't get an answer.

She had a lot of time to think on the long drive home. Wearily, she reached for a cup of coffee wedged in the console.

She laughed suddenly at the irony of nearly losing the worst job she had ever had. It was worse than rotten. She was overworked and underpaid and lied to and yelled at and threatened and cussed out, and she was dying to tell them all just what they could do with her stupid position. But Scotty was dead right. Her folks were on her mind day and night. Getting to the bottom of the missing picture had become an obsession with her.

She reached Mary's Place around midnight, pulled up the driveway, and found her mother on the porch, sitting in a lawn chair, a shotgun resting in her lap.

"Mom?" she said, standing stock still on the walk when she saw the gleam of metal, "what in the world is going on?"

Mary had remained seated when she saw her daughter's Subaru coming up the lane. Just a year ago, she would have scurried inside, put up the gun, done anything and everything to present herself as cheery and composed.

"Mom, are you all right?"

Mary looked at her and nodded. When she came downstairs at night, she didn't go farther than the edge of the front yard. She knew there were limits to what her mind could handle.

"I thought I saw something, heard something," she said, pleased with the accuracy of her quiet words. She was finding an unexpected strength nowadays in holding herself to a standard of absolute truth. "Lights. Sounds. But I've been told it's all in my head."

If she saw something or heard that flute-like tone, she was better off sitting here on the porch. Willing her fears to go away didn't work. Stepping outside for a moment, making friends with her demons, did.

Sometimes, she even felt peaceful, feeling the presence of women who had gone before her. Women who had lost everything. It was as though they joined in her prayers, comforted her, soothed her. Then if the night were not too cold, she would sit on the porch a while, just as she was doing right now, and invite memories so poignant at first her heart had rebelled.

She saw Iron coming across the field on their first tractor, yodeling the chorus to "The Lovesick Blues," his deep bass voice carrying on the soft evening air.

She saw herself, running, running toward her young husband and him spinning her around before they sank to the rich black earth.

She heard herself calling, calling home her own. "Suppertime, kids." Her voice echoed joyfully across the seasons and the years. "It's suppertime."

She looked at her daughter and laughed gently at the worried look on her face. "I'm doing okay, Elizabeth. Not terrific, but okay. What are you doing here?"

"I'm going to find out who took that picture," she said. "And don't try to tell me you misplaced it. I don't believe it for a minute." She went back to the car to get her luggage.

"Before we go inside, there's something I want to show you." Mary switched on a flashlight and led Elizabeth to the edge of the field that lay behind Old Barn. She beamed the light down the land. Dark emerald clumps dotted the acreage.

"Have you ever seen such wheat, honey? Isn't that fine wheat? Just look at what I planted. Seeing that wheat is the only part of this I really can't take. We would have a field of wheat to harvest next June. If we weren't losing the farm."

They went back to the house. Inside, when Elizabeth switched on the kitchen light, Mary's lined face shocked her. She stared at the deadbolts.

"Do you want some cocoa or something? Something to eat?"

Elizabeth looked around at her mother's wonderful kitchen. Seeing her quivering lips, Mary came over and enfolded her. "Hush now," she whispered, stroking her hair.

"Oh God, Mom. I came home to see if I could help you. Now I'm going to be one more person for you to take care of."

Mary looked at her with infinite tenderness and resigned herself to a difficult task in convincing her stubborn, intelligent daughter to quit. "Let's go to bed now," she said gently. "We'll talk tomorrow morning when our heads are clear."

Elizabeth awoke before dawn. She had gotten up several times during the night. Sadly, she peered out her bedroom window. How many times had she stood in this same spot while she was growing up, dreaming about leaving the farm someday? And how many times since had she wished she were back home?

Suddenly a flash of light caught her eye. Lights bobbed and winked again and again from different places in the farmyard. Her whole body chilled, and she stood there paralyzed trying to make sense of what she saw. Mary's lights! They were real. She could see them herself. But there had to be a logical explanation.

Determined to get to the bottom of this phenomenon that was ruining her mother's mental health, Elizabeth quietly pulled on her jeans and a shirt and slipped downstairs. Daybreak increased in soft increments of mellow light. She let herself out the front door. Then she crept along the side of the house and peered at the shadows cast by the row of machinery. When she got to the back side, she pressed against the siding and peeked cautiously around the corner.

There was no movement. She stepped out into the gathering light and walked confidently over to the row of equipment.

Then again, she saw a flicker. She hurried toward it. When she reached the disk, she stopped in bewilderment. There were several balloons tied to the rows of machinery at various spots. All of them were gray or brown and had large ovals of vivid fluorescent paint. She instantly recalled horseshoes whirling crazily toward gleaming stakes.

"Dennis!" she cried, as she knelt to look closely at the balloons. "It's the kind of paint he used to paint the horseshoes." The sun warmed the air, and one balloon popped and then another.

The bastard. The absolute bastard. How could she have been so blind? How many times had Dennis said Mary should give up her house?

Tears stung her eyes. The balloons moved and shifted in the slight breeze then bounced up again. Elizabeth was stunned by the simplicity of it all. The balloon would pop or deflate when the sun got hot. Undoubtedly her brother came over and gathered them up during the day.

As the light became stronger, more balloons sank to the ground. The fluorescent paint wasn't visible in the daytime. Even if Mary had come across one, she would have thought it was one of her grandchildren's toys. *And when Dad is home,* Elizabeth thought bitterly, *Dennis simply doesn't set them out. These are all rigged for Mom.*

It's their own son who is doing this. My brother!

Blind with pain, she rose and ran sobbing toward the house. Daddy. I want Daddy to know what Dennis has been doing to his mother. His very own mother. .

Inside, she scanned the list of numbers Mary kept by the phone. Quickly she found the one for the trucking company where her father worked. Too agitated to dial accurately the first time, it took her three tries.

"I need to reach Iron Barrett," she said, when the dispatcher answered. "Right away."

"He should be clearing the Nebraska port any time now," the man said. "I'll call ahead. Is this an emergency? Do you want the highway patrol to run him down?"

"No. Just have him call home. This is his daughter. I need to talk to him."

Shivering, she hung up and waited. Startled by the harsh jangle fifteen minutes later, she jumped up and answered on the first ring, hoping Mary hadn't heard the phone.

"Elizabeth? What's wrong?" Iron asked.

She became a little girl again in a flash, needing her father.

"Dennis has been doing terrible, terrible things to Mom." She blurted out the details between fits of sobbing.

"I hate him," she said when she was finished. "Just hate him. Why would he do a thing like this to Mom?" Then her heart skipped a beat as she realized Iron hadn't spoken more than a few words. She heard his harsh breaths. "Dad? Daddy?"

"Don't do anything. Don't say anything to Mary or anyone else," Iron said. "I'll be home in about an hour."

Softly, she replaced the receiver and sat down at the table, hoping Mary would stay asleep until Iron got there. She rose and walked over to the window and stood with her hands clasped tightly behind her back, staring directly at the blood-red sun.

She checked her watch a dozen times before she heard his truck in the driveway. He arrived fifteen minutes sooner than she would have thought possible.

"Daddy!" She rushed to his side as he slammed the door of the cab.. "How could he do this? Why?"

"Show me." His low voice was filled with cold anger. Suddenly terrified, Elizabeth led him to the row of machinery. Iron knelt down and stared at the deflated balloons. "He wants us to lose everything." Iron shuddered and drew a deep breath. He picked up one of the balloons.

"But why?"

"He's always coveted this house, this farm."

Elizabeth remembered the look on Dennis's face the night Mary announced she was leaving the house to Connie and knew Iron was right. "He doesn't want you to keep the house." Stunned, she tried to take it all in. "Why? That doesn't make sense. If you and Mom lose the place, it doesn't mean he will get it."

Iron rose abruptly, his fists clenched into hard balls. "It all fits somehow, someway we don't know about yet. Dennis has always worked things toward his own ends. How could he do this to his own mother?"

Her heart sank at the devastation on his face. It was a look she had known and feared on the faces of men she had been obliged to defend. He turned and headed for the house.

Mary came down the stairs as Iron came through the back door. Still in her robe, she flew into his arms. "You're home early," she said. "I haven't even put on coffee yet. And Elizabeth is here for a surprise visit."

Iron pressed her against his chest. "Yes. I know. I've already talked to her."

Then he turned and said to Elizabeth, who had followed him into the house, "Stay here with your mother. Tell her all the ways our son has been trying to drive her crazy."

Wide-eyed, Mary stared at him as if he had lost his mind.

"And now I'm going to deal with Dennis." He rushed back outside and the women heard his pickup tear out of the driveway. .

Elizabeth's heart plummeted.

Quiet, deliberate men, slow to react in anger, could become white-hot and deadly.

37

Sabrina Barrett flew inside the house and began rummaging through her father's desk, looking for a spare key to the pickup. She jumped at every chance to get behind the wheel, as did most fourteen-year-olds with learner's permits. Her mother had called from the airport a couple of minutes ago asking her to bring the portfolio with all the maps and diagrams.

Although her father probably had the main keys in his jacket pocket, Sabrina decided not to risk asking him for them. He had been touchy, unpredictable lately. Just for spite he might say she had no business driving and take the aerial maps to her mother himself. Or worse, call and bawl her out for leaving anything behind to begin with.

The drawer was stuck. Sabrina eased her hand under the lip of the desk and tried to wiggle her fingers under a wedge of paper. Bending down, she saw that the removable wooden slat covering an inner compartment had come off the track. She and Benjy had always known about this supposedly secret place. She picked up a letter opener and slid it under the wood.

An envelope slid out into the main drawer. She picked it up and slowly opened it. With a cry, she looked at the Polaroid of Molly.

A shadow loomed in the doorway. She turned and saw Dennis watching her, his face as still as a death mask. Her mouth opened, forming a silent scream. She shoved the envelope into her jacket and ran wildly from the room, bolted out the back door, and streaked across the farmyard.

Dennis ran after her.

Benjy answered the phone on the tenth ring.

"Sorry to get you up so early on a Saturday, honey, but I want to know what's keeping Sabrina. We're ready to take off, and she should have been here twenty minutes ago. Would you please check and see if she's left yet?"

Benjy laid down the receiver, went to the door, peered out. The pickup was still there. He turned to go back, then a flash of red caught his eye. Sabrina raced out the back door of the machine shed and headed for the silo. Their father ran after her, gaining ground.

Wide awake now, Benjy dashed back to the phone. "Mom, something's wrong. Dad's chasing Sabrina."

"I'll be home in a flash," Lisette said.

"Hurry," Benjy pleaded. "He looks mad, Mom. Crazy mad."

Lisette's heart plunged to her toes when she heard the fear in Benjy's voice. She knew at once this was more than one of Dennis's moods. Sabrina was in danger. "Stay put and call 911," she ordered. "I'll be right there."

"Something's wrong at home," Lisette yelled at the crew. "Call the sheriff for me and send him to my place." She jumped into the jeep. Dennis had been impossible lately. He would be depressed one minute, higher than a kite the next. Her having to put up with his erratic ways was one thing, but damned if she was going to have the kids go through it too.

She gripped the wheel tightly and sped toward her house.

Mary ran down the stairs and into the kitchen, fully dressed in jeans and a sweatshirt. Again and again, Elizabeth called Dennis's house, but there was no answer.

"It's Saturday. The kids should be home. But doesn't it ring in my brother's shop too?"

Mary nodded.

"Then someone should answer the phone."

"Would someone please tell me what's going on?" Mary's eyes were dark, enormous. "What did Iron mean when he said he was going to 'deal with Dennis'?"

Elizabeth put her arm around her shoulders and led her to a chair. "I wish I didn't have to tell you this!"

Mary folded her hands on her lap and looked at her mutely, waiting.

"It was Dennis all along, Mom."

Mary listened to Elizabeth's stark account of her son's treachery. "I'm his mother," she said blankly, trying to understand. "I'm his mother."

"I know, I know."

"We've got to stop Iron," Mary said. "If he hurts Dennis he'll regret it for the rest of his life. We can't just stand by." She sprang to her feet, grabbed her car keys, and ran toward the door. Elizabeth followed.

Dennis shaded his eyes and looked up at the top of the silo. Sabrina's head appeared for an instant over the rim of the concrete half moon bolted to the side of the structure. She looked around then ducked back in like a prairie dog.

Dennis darted toward the silo. The entrance to the narrow concrete channel was slightly above his head. He looked straight up the tunnel and saw his daughter clinging to the slim iron rungs. "Throw down that picture, Sabrina," he said softly.

"No." She screamed with terror and started toward the top again.

Dennis swore, knowing that she was beyond coaxing. He cursed the perverse streak that had made him hang onto the picture of Molly to begin with. He should have settled for derailing the lawsuit. But he had been reluctant to destroy tangible proof that he had a superior mind to all of them: Elizabeth, Iron, Hathaway, Clyde Peterson. All of them. Plus there was a chance that Peterson would pay to get the photo that was clear proof of his ineptness in handling a bank closure. Now he would give anything if he had burned it at once.

"Drop the picture, Sabrina."

"No," she screamed. "I hate you! I hate you."

"Then I'll have to come and get it," he said.

Benjy flew out of the house and ran to Iron's pickup when he drove up the lane. He jumped on the running board and sobbed through the open window.

"Grandpa! Something's wrong. Dad's trying to hurt Sabrina. She climbed up the silo. Mom knows. She's coming. We've called the law."

Iron gave a low cry when he saw Sabrina's head emerge from the top of the silo. She hoisted herself up on her elbows, finished scrambling through the opening, and shakily wobbled to her feet.

His head reeled with shock. *I've got to think,* he told himself. *Think.*

Next to him, his grandson gasped. Iron glanced at him and swore softly. If Sabrina fell, it would ruin the boy as surely as it killed the girl. Benjy would never recover from the tragedy. Then he heard a car coming up the road.

His heart pounded. *I've got to stall them. One sound, one voice, and Sabrina will lose her concentration. That's all it will take.*

"Benjy, someone's coming. Tell them to stop before Sabrina sees or hears any commotion. Be very quiet, son. Very careful. Run." His grandson took off at full speed, and Iron reached for the rifle on the gun rack mounted on the back window of his pickup.

Seeing that the vehicle was his mother's jeep, Benjy began to wave wildly. Lisette slammed on the brakes, slid to a stop, and leaped out. He stumbled breathlessly into her arms. His words came out in staccato jerks. He pointed hysterically to the top of the silo. High in the sky Sabrina slowly edged around the foot-wide rim. Away from the tunnel.

Terrified, Lisette hugged Benjy's face against her chest. She saw Sabrina sway for an instant and then recover her footing. "Don't fall. Don't fall," she chanted softly. "Don't fall, Sabrina. Dear God don't let my daughter fall."

Sunlight flashed off a windshield, and she turned to see Mary and Elizabeth driving toward them.

"Run, honey. Run like the wind and stop them from coming on in. We can't take a chance on their startling Sabrina." Benjy looked toward the silo for a moment, as though he could keep his sister up there by sheer force of will. "Go," Lisette hissed, giving him a little shove in the small of the back. "Go, go, go."

Dennis's head bobbed over the rim of the enclosure. Iron saw the movement and edged closer then sprinted toward the side of the silo opposite Sabrina and Dennis.

He crept around until he was directly under the concrete passage to the top.

The silo was empty—hollow, with a ghostly drumming vibration. The attached channel on the exterior acted as a natural conduit for their voices. Dennis was directly above him.

"Sabrina," Dennis called. "Give me the picture, Sabrina."

"No," she screamed. "It's mine. Molly was mine."

"I'm your father, Sabrina. You have to obey me."

"Daddy, don't. Please don't." She began to cry as though her heart would break. "Don't Daddy, please!"

"Just throw it down to me."

"No. Aunt Elizabeth needs it."

"I'm going to get it, whatever you do. Don't make me come after it."

Dennis eased his foot onto the next rung and then the next. He didn't like heights. She shouldn't be putting him in this position. She should mind. He had to get the picture. "Damn it Sabrina, do as I say."

Dizzy now, he drew a deep breath, stopping to think about the mess Sabrina had created. She was putting herself in danger. Both of them, in fact. Even if he got the picture away from her, she would tell. Of course she would. And he knew who the family would believe. Even Grandma Alma had turned against him.

Then he tried to tamp down an alien thought that came unbidden. No, he was trying to save Sabrina, he reasoned. Save her from a dark impulse.

Going after the picture was secondary. Other people, too, were very worried about Sabrina. Teachers, her mother. Her grades were down. She had dropped a lot of activities. It was only natural that he would go after her when she started up the silo. She hadn't been herself that morning. If she slipped . . .

"Dennis," Iron called. "Dennis, come down. Start backing down. Don't go any farther."

His son froze. Only the wind broke the silence. Wind that distorted their words like a ghostly echo from the bottom of a well.

"Back down, Dennis. That's your daughter up there. My granddaughter."

"Not my daughter. Not really. Not your granddaughter. Not really."

But Iron knew his son was rallying his thoughts. Concocting a way out with the lightning quickness that had always been his son's finest gift. A gift he distorted and abused. Put to ill use.

"Dad, Sabrina is cracking up. Having a nervous breakdown. I'm trying to save her before she slips and falls."

Iron took another step upward. Revulsion for his son welled up. Iron trained the rifle on Dennis. Anger rolled like hot lava through his veins. It was an easy shot. Straight up the channel. He agonized. If the sound startled Sabrina she might slip and hurtle to her death. On the other hand, if he let Dennis make it to the top he would push her off the platform.

"Not another step, Dennis, or I'll shoot."

He could not, did not pull the trigger.

He told himself that the noise might cause Sabrina to fall. He told himself that Dennis was already in an impossible situation. Benjy had said the sheriff was on the way. All he had to do was wait. But in his heart he knew there was another reason.

My son, my son.

"No, Iron, no." Even before he heard her voice, he felt Mary's fingers lightly touch his arm. "No," she whispered softly, "don't do it. Don't do it. For God's sake, no."

His muscles quivered. He hadn't heard her approach.

"I can't, anyway," he said, his words jerking from his throat. "I can't. I know everything he's done but I can't."

"Pray to God Sheriff Johnson gets here in time. When that poor little girl hears a siren, she'll know help is on the way."

No sooner had Mary gotten the words out of her mouth than they heard the familiar rising and falling whirr—whirr—whirr moving toward the farm.

Dennis swore savagely. His curses vibrated eerily down the length of the structure. Mary darted out toward the base of the channel and cupped her hands and hollered up at her granddaughter. "Sabrina, lie down. We're here. We're all here. Lie down flat. Hold on to the sides with your arms and press your knees against the silo like you're riding a horse. Stay there. Don't move."

"Dennis, it's all over," shouted Iron. "Come down."

Two cars rolled up and they were followed by men in a fire truck.

The sheriff quickly sized up the situation and ran over to Mary and Lisette. He huddled his two deputies and the men from the fire department.

He picked up a bullhorn. "Sabrina, don't move. Don't try to come down yourself." Then he yelled up at Dennis. "It's over. You're finished. Start climbing down. Slowly. Just back down."

"You, Iron. Get the hell away and put that rifle down."

The men all had guns trained on Dennis when he emerged from the opening.

"Thank God you're here," he said. "My daughter hasn't been in her right mind. I tried to stop her."

The sheriff turned him around, yanked his arms behind his back, and handcuffed him. "Shut up, Barrett. You can't lie your way out of this one. We're arresting you for attempted murder. Read him his rights, Leroy."

"Count me in as a witness for the prosecution," Iron said. "There's plenty of evidence."

Infuriated, Dennis turned to his father before he was shoved into the car. "You've got no right. No right. You bumbled away what was *mine*. You had no right to piss away everything that belonged to me just because you didn't have the guts to make any smart moves."

Iron said nothing.

"I wasn't the only one," Dennis blurted.

Triumphantly, Elizabeth looked at Iron, then Mary. "I always thought there were others involved."

"They suckered me in," Dennis hollered as the sheriff protected his head and shoved him into the caged back seat.

Elizabeth smiled grimly. There it was: her brother's same old habit of trying to shift the blame off himself. The details would come out.

"Sabrina, it's over," Lisette called. "Don't move, honey. Someone is coming to get you. Someone who will keep you safe."

A young man from the fire department swiftly unhooked safety equipment. "It's an Injured Personnel Carrier," he assured her. "An Israeli product, actually. A backpack for humans."

He went up the tunnel and ten minutes later brought the trembling child safely back into her mother's arms. Sabrina shook and sobbed, and when she could finally talk she pushed away from Lisette and pulled an envelope from inside her jacket.

"Here's what you need to save our farm, Aunt Elizabeth."

The women stared in disbelief.

"Molly," she said. "Daddy wanted to tear up my picture of Molly."

38

Mary watched Lisette and Benjy and Sabrina come up the lane. There was a curious dignity surrounding this little band of three. When they had taken Dennis away, Lisette had fallen on Mary's shoulder weeping as though the world had come to an end.

"I kept thinking he would change."

Mary comforted her. "No one is to blame. No one or everyone. We all just saw what we wanted to see in him. We're his parents. If anyone's to blame, it should be us."

"Maybe we should go away. Maybe I should find work somewhere else."

"Don't even think about it," Mary had said, shocked. "You're family, sweetie. You belong here on the farm. With us. You are us."

Now, as Mary waved at Benjy and Sabrina, she lifted her face to the sun, basking in its warmth. Just then her kitchen timer went off.

"I've got to take cookies out of the oven," she called to them. She hurried back inside.

"I know Grandma Alma is here," Lisette said as they came through the door. "We came to see how she's doing."

Mary smiled into her daughter-in-law's gorgeous dark eyes, now welling with tears. Alma had lost her starch when her favorite grandson was locked away. "I guess she's doing as well as can be expected."

A quick, stubborn look came over Lisette's face.

Mary flushed with shame remembering that she had once thought this tough little woman wasn't good enough for her son. She certainly wasn't what she'd had in mind as the mother of her grandchildren. But Lisette had outshone them all when it came to courage.

They filed into the living room. Lisette glanced at Alma then leaned down and whispered in Benjy's ear. Immediately he turned and went into the kitchen and cut up an apple.

He returned and handed his grandmother the plate. "Mom said to ask you about the time when Grandpa was a little boy and got lost in a blizzard and you found him dug into the creek bank."

Mary watched the old woman's face brighten. It was as though she were seeing this boy for the first time.

"It was the worst blizzard I'd ever seen," Alma said slowly, her cracked voice warming to the recitation. "You'll never see one like it in your lifetime, Sonny. They don't make blizzards like that anymore."

Mary rolled her eyes and winked at Lisette. "Thank you." She mouthed the words silently. Lisette nodded.

Iron came into the room. He smiled broadly when he saw his grandchildren. There was a hole in this family now. The ghost of the son that might have been. Dennis had received a stiff sentence, but doubtless he would knock off a few years through exemplary behavior.

Through Dennis's testimony, Peterson had been convicted of fraud. Hathaway had charges pending and was now a pariah in the community.

Iron knew Mary would dutifully visit Dennis in jail and he would not. Neither would Lisette or Sabrina or Benjy. They would rarely speak of this man. But the hole would be there. The empty chair, the yearning for his redheaded son's presence.

Iron smiled at Mary as he listened to Alma tell the old stories. Their family was coming back together.

Two days later, Elizabeth called Mary from the courthouse.

"Mom, I thought you hadn't signed anything. Your name is on the universal commercial code statement for the main loan. After we finally find a bank to take over your loan, that can throw a kink into everything."

"I didn't sign our main note, Elizabeth. I didn't."

"It's plain as day."

"I didn't, I tell you."

"Come see for yourself. I'll wait for you here."

Mary's heart beat furiously as she drove toward the courthouse. She had thought they were finished with scrutinizing papers.

She quickly crossed the marble lobby and ran up the stairs. Elizabeth waited for her in the county clerk's office. Gravely, she pointed toward the signature.

Too stunned to speak, Mary looked at her daughter. She pressed both palms against the counter and stared out the window. When she could find her voice, she turned to her Elizabeth. "Go home. Don't say anything about this. Don't think about this. Forget you ever saw it. There's something I must do. Someone I must see. I'll tell you about it later."

Her blood raced as she drove toward J.C. Espy's house. She had known when Iron told her about the sale to Connie and Mike that something was wrong with their paperwork. Her first instincts had been right, after all. J.C. never would have participated in such a sloppy arrangement if he weren't trying to hide something.

Her jaw tightened. She couldn't bear it if that old man, too, were involved in some underhanded scheme. *There has to be someone on God's green earth who can be trusted*, she thought. *There has to be someone who's honest and decent.*

She knocked once and then shoved open the door and called inside. "J.C."

Startled, he half rose from his chair, where he had been dozing.

"J.C., I just saw my name put to a document that I know I never signed. It was you, wasn't it? How could you? How could you?"

His face betrayed him before he could find the words and, even if they had come quickly, he was soul-sick of lying and hiding. Shame blanched his yellow skin to the color of old bones.

"I swear to God, Mary, I didn't do it to hurt you or to take anything from you. I was trying to save my bank."

She recoiled from his naked pain. Her voice quivered. "How could you? How could you? It's forgery, no matter what reason you gave yourself!"

His soul returned to his body, and he looked at her fiercely. "I did it for all of you. I did it for the community. I was trying to save my frigging bank. Do you understand that now? How important that was? Can't you see it was the right thing to do?"

A vein in her temple throbbed. "It was wrong," she whispered, drawing out each word. "Dead wrong."

"Your family has drained me of every cent," he said. "You don't think that's wrong, woman? It was my own money in back of your notes that last year. You cost me my bank, you cost me my gold. Hell, you've even managed to get my antique frames."

His hand swept toward the wall of his living room. His portraits of John Foster Espy, Frank Leander Espy, and Porter Cleveland Espy now hung there mounted on black matte poster board.

Slowly, with a dollop of malice, he told Mary in excruciating detail of each sacrifice he had made for the Barretts, each indignity he had borne on their behalf.

"Stop," she said finally, pressing her hands over her ears. "Oh stop, J.C. We didn't know. We would never have asked that of you."

"Oh yes you would, Mary. Your husband wouldn't, but you would. We're very much alike, you and I. Don't you know that about yourself yet, Mary? How different you and I are from people like Iron? They'll live and die for honor. And we're the kind of people who make it possible for them to do that."

"Iron belongs to a different century," Mary said slowly. "Times change, and he can't make himself do the simplest thing to get along in this day and age."

"You're the one who saved the farm, Mary. Think about it. It was you every step of the way. It was you who thought and saw and planned and schemed."

"I had to," she said. "I had to! Iron just couldn't."

"You were right to do the things you did, Mary. You were gutsy and bright and tough, and I'm proud of you. Even conning me out of my last dime to buy your goddamn fertilizer was the right thing to do. You showed the kind of spit and vinegar I used to look for when I decided to loan money in my bank. Well done, lady."

"I'm still ashamed. I wish I could have stayed like Iron."

"Pure and holy and unchanging?" mocked J.C. "He could stay that way because of you."

A lump rose in her throat and she swallowed hard. Gratitude for his left-handed praise, his flawed approval, washed over her parched soul. She had needed someone to understand.

"I didn't choose any of this," she said. "I was forced into it."

"Weren't we all," he said abruptly. His voice quivered, and he smiled at her crookedly. "Looks like I've got a little visit to make to the sheriff."

"No," she cried. "Do you think I want you to turn yourself in?"

He looked at her sharply, then gathering courage he turned to look once more at the stern faces of his ancestors. "At best, I'm only going to live ten more years. The last five probably won't be pleasant. Jail will be as good as a nursing home. Maybe better." His voice wavered for an instant. "It will take this one thing to make things right. Let me do it for Iron."

"I'm not going to let you do that. You were trying to help us in the first place. What kind of person do you think I am?"

"The kind who will do whatever it takes to save the farm," J.C. said.

"Not if it means betraying a friend. I had the bank make a copy of everything Iron signed, remember? A blank copy of that note is right there in our home safe. Under a pile of other papers, but it's there."

Later that afternoon, Mary went back to the courthouse. When the clerk's back was turned, she took out the universal commercial code statement with her signature and substituted the blank copy. She took the forged document back to J.C.'s house, and they burned it together.

"What will you tell Elizabeth?" he asked.

"That the one she saw was obsolete—very old. It was merely an oversight that the bank hadn't removed this one, and that it's all taken care of. And it is, J.C. The one that's there now is the right one."

J.C. brightened as the paper curled, then crumbled into ashes.

His nightmare was over.

One spring morning, Mary dressed, with a familiar sense of ritual, in her button-front Levis and a light blue chambray shirt worn over a white knit tank top. She tied a red bandanna around her hair.

She saw Iron walk behind Old Barn. Her eyes were drawn to the emerald field of wheat. Her wheat. Prices were up. It would be enough—this wheat—to pay back Newark and Piker. Enough to provide them with operating money for the coming year.

There were early rosebuds, and lilacs and late tulips. Reds and purples and yellows and blues and greens. Every shade of green was to be seen somewhere. The damp, promising, heady scent of the earth emerging from winter filled the air. There was a thicket of mock orange blossoms up the lane. A monarch butterfly headed toward the cloying odor. A cry from a cock pheasant came from the line of cedars surrounding their house. Suddenly there was the sweet clear trill of a meadowlark, and Mary's heart exploded in a wild surge of joy.

It was the farm, the farm—always the farm. Her blood flowed from this source. She ran toward her husband, ran toward her rock, her anchor, her first and only love.

"Iron," she called, across the farmyard, across the years, called to his soul.

Surprised, he swung around and braced himself as she came hurtling into his arms.

He held her at arm's length and smiled at her flushed cheeks as he smoothed back her hair. As they looked steadily at one another's faces, the years melted away.

There stood a young woman, alive and eager on the threshold of life, blazing with energy.

There stood a man, sure and strong, anchored in the world by his convictions, bound to centuries of farmers.

He pulled Mary against his broad chest and held her gently. "Lady, I found the funniest thing hanging in the barn. It's an old blue Christmas light. Just one. I think it would look right pretty on top of that old windmill. If you've a mind to climb that high." Then his voice was very low, vibrant with emotion. "Some of us ain't never going to climb that high. We don't want to. But we surely do admire those who do."

Her heart soared, understanding that everything she had dared hope for was there. He loved her at her highest, chanciest, best, and finest. The same as she loved him—rooted by honor, pledged to a code no one even understood any more. "Of course, I want to put that light back on the windmill. Oh, Iron, you're crazy."

"I'm not the crazy one around here."

"No, you're a stubborn, wrongheaded man, with his feet planted firmly on the ground."

"That's where feet belong."

They heard a car and turned as J.C. Espy pulled into the drive and climbed out of his ancient Mercury Marquis. He and Iron had not spoken directly since the bank closing. All communication had taken place through Mary and Elizabeth.

"Came to see your wheat," J.C. said gruffly. "Reckon I've got a right to, considering what I've got invested."

The sun went behind the clouds and came out again, shining brighter than ever. It shone across the field of wheat, and for a moment Mary was blinded by the light.

Iron solemnly looked over her head at the silvery green stalks. Hard telling what all he would go through with this crop. But wheat had nine lives. Everyone knew that. He turned and looked at his friend. A lonely old cuss.

It was spring. It was Kansas.

J.C. Espy was a banker. And Iron Barrett was a farmer.

Then, as naturally as the swallows came to the back porch to build their nest every year, Iron found himself walking over to the mangy old lion of a man. He offered his hand.

Cautiously.

In the manner with which Western Kansas wheat farmers had always approached money lenders, friend or not.

It seemed natural. The most natural thing that had gone on around there in a long, long time.

"Don't suppose you would know where I could get some operating money, do you?"

J.C. smiled crookedly and wiped his unsteady hand across a few tears that escaped his eyes.

"I'll see what I can do for you. Would you mind doing business with a banker in New York?" he asked wistfully. "I have connections."

Mary looked at them both and laughed, grabbed the light, and headed for the windmill.

THE END

ACKNOWLEDGMENTS

This book was painful to write because I was personally involved in so many aspects of a bank failure in my own town. I represented the Episcopal Diocese of Western Kansas on the Interfaith Rural Life Committee. I attended a dramatic community meeting after the bank closed in a neighboring county. The fury of those who had never missed a payment on their loans was so intense that some meetings in the state ended in violence. Whole communities were changed after "the bank closed." The experience was a shared tragedy.

The bitterness of African American landowners from Nicodemus, Kansas, was heart-wrenching. Land Black families had homesteaded and held onto since the 1880s, through World Wars, the Depression, and the dust storms, was suddenly seized by the government. An interview with Gil Alexander, whose ancestors migrated to Kansas from Kentucky, made me cry.

There's also a personal slant to this book. My husband, Don Hinger, owned a livestock truckline. He had a large loan at a failed bank and, because it was rejected by the new owners, it fell under the supervision of the FDIC. We were fortunate because our loan was picked up immediately by another bank. We had Joseph Corder, a loan officer there, to thank for this and the late bank president, Myron Dietz, for approving Joe's judgment.

I interviewed several bankers for this book. It was hard because it was done at a time when emotions were still raw. I was and still am passionate about the honorable role bankers play in supporting communities. Sam Smith, Don Mense, and Carol Cooper allowed me to tape sessions.

Keith Caldwell, retired now, but formerly president of the First State Bank of Hoxie, Kansas, generously vetted the material in *Mary's Place*. He drew on his vast financial background and knowledge of farming issues to coach me on loan issues and help me slog through complex farm programs. I can't thank him enough for his patience with my infernal questions.

The Interfaith Rural Life Community struggled valiantly to help farmers. My fellow committee members were Char Henton, Al Bruenger, Elaine Hassler, George Weber, Raymond Regier, Del Jacobsen, Alden Hickman, Dale Fooshee, Don Close, Lina Hessman, Merrill Boach, Jim Godbey, Dave Stewart, Dorothy Berry, Loren Janzen, George Sanneman, Larry Ahles, Charles Ayers, Jerry Zanker, and Minnie Finger. We were involved in everything from affecting legislation to tackling suicide prevention.

Comments about banking made by my dear friend Bette James found their way into this manuscript. Award-winning novelist Kathleen O'Neal Gear took the time out of her own writing career to read an earlier draft of this book and provided invaluable suggestions.

First and foremost, my dear friend Margaret (Peggy) Neves read this manuscript. She identified muddled passages and pinpointed several plot hitches. Thank you, Peggy.

I especially appreciated the editorial sensitivity of Stephanie Marshall Ward, who pin-pointed sections needing revisions.

My agent, Claudia Cross (Folio Literary Management), asked all the right questions and gave valuable input from a nonfarming perspective. Thank you, Claudia.

Of course, my acknowledgments would not be complete without expressing my delight that Clark Whitehorn, senior editor at University of Nebraska Press, wanted to publish *Mary's Place*.

Thank you, Clark. I'm thrilled!

Printed in the USA
CPSIA information can be obtained
at www.ICGtesting.com
CBHW020225210524
8864CB00002B/41